Tiffany Blues

Center Point
Large Print

Also by M. J. Rose and available from
Center Point Large Print:

The Book of Lost Fragrances
Seduction
The Collector of Dying Breaths
The Witch of Painted Sorrows
The Secret Language of Stones
The Library of Light and Shadow

**This Large Print Book carries the
Seal of Approval of N.A.V.H.**

Tiffany Blues

A Novel

M. J. ROSE

CENTER POINT LARGE PRINT
THORNDIKE, MAINE

This Center Point Large Print edition
is published in the year 2018 by arrangement with
Atria Books, a division of Simon & Schuster, Inc.

This book is a work of fiction.
Any references to historical events, real people, or real
places are used fictitiously. Other names, characters, places,
and events are products of the author's imagination, and
any resemblance to actual events or places or persons,
living or dead, is entirely coincidental.

The text of this Large Print edition is unabridged.
In other aspects, this book may vary
from the original edition.
Printed in the United States of America
on permanent paper.
Set in 16-point Times New Roman type.

ISBN: 978-1-64358-008-1

Library of Congress Cataloging-in-Publication Data

Names: Rose, M. J., 1953- author.
Title: Tiffany blues / M.J. Rose.
Description: Center Point Large Print edition. | Thorndike, Maine :
    Center Point Large Print, 2018.
Identifiers: LCCN 2018041776 | ISBN 9781643580081
    (hardcover : alk. paper)
Subjects: LCSH: Large type books.
Classification: LCC PS3568.O76386 T54 2018b | DDC 813/.54—dc23
LC record available at https://lccn.loc.gov/2018041776

To Carolyn Reidy:

*You always say how honored and proud you are
that we authors entrust our books to you.
Truly, the honor is all mine.*

*Your enthusiasm and unwavering support have
given me the freedom to dream on paper
and for that I am so very thankful.*

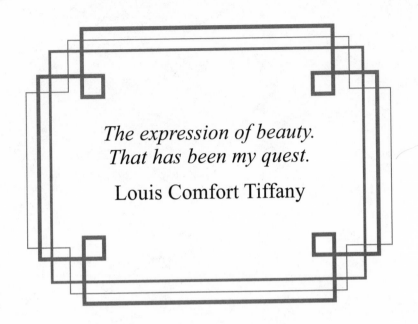

The expression of beauty.
That has been my quest.

Louis Comfort Tiffany

Author's Note

In 1902, Louis Comfort Tiffany began building Laurelton Hall on Long Island's Gold Coast, not far from where, years later, F. Scott Fitzgerald would place Gatsby's fictional mansion.

Housed on 580 acres in Laurel Hollow, the eighty-four-room estate would take three years to finish and would cost Tiffany $2 million—$54 million by today's standards. Laurelton Hall was Tiffany's personal effort to create a vision incorporating every aspect of his love of beauty, from the stained-glass windows and mosaics he designed himself, to the rooms of antique Japanese, Native American, and Indian objects he had collected during his lifetime, to the more than sixty acres of impeccably landscaped gardens complete with imported peacocks that roamed the grounds.

In 1918, Tiffany created the Louis Comfort Tiffany Foundation at Laurelton in order to aid artists, endowing it with his own funds as well as the estate and its contents.

Two years later, eight students attended the first summer session. They included two silversmiths, one sculptor, one designer, and four painters.

During the remainder of Tiffany's life, until his death in 1933, artists lived at Laurelton and attended one of two eight-week summer sessions during which they were afforded the time to imagine and create while surrounded and inspired by nature and the beauty that Tiffany had cultivated and brought into the world.

After Tiffany died, the Foundation struggled, and the mansion fell into disrepair. By 1949, parcels of the estate had been sold off, and the main house and a surrounding three acres were purchased by Thomas H. Hilton for what today would be $100,000. Over the next eight years, Hilton did nothing to restore the house, and it was virtually abandoned.

On March 6, 1957, at five p.m., a neighbor spotted flames coming from Laurelton Hall. The fire lasted until two a.m., with out-breaks continuing for days. The grand house, along with what was left of its gardens, was destroyed.

To this day, the cause of the fire has never been discovered.

I have been fascinated with Louis Comfort Tiffany since childhood. My great-grandparents' house in Brooklyn contained a Tiffany window of lush red roses with a border of verdant green leaves. I loved to watch its colorful reflections move across the oak floors as the afternoon slipped into dusk.

My mother, who always encouraged and nurtured my interest in the arts, sought out other

Tiffany windows in New York, and we visited them all.

In 1978, when the Metropolitan Museum installed the Laurelton Hall Loggia from pieces salvaged from the Long Island mansion, my mother and I were among its first visitors, and it was in the pages of the catalog accompanying the exhibition that I first read about Tiffany's magnificent estate and its fate.

I don't think I've ever gone longer than a month without visiting the Metropolitan Museum, and I always stop in the American Wing to sit in front of the wisteria windows from Laurelton Hall and rest for a moment—surrounded by all that beauty.

It's easy to look at artifacts from the estate and wonder what it must have been like to study under Tiffany's tutelage. Who were the students? What did they go on to create? How did the setting and the master influence them?

But most of all, why did the estate burn down in the first place?

In response, my creativity-prone brain began: *What if one summer there was a student who . . .*

I've written *Tiffany Blues* through the eyes of Jenny Bell, a young artist who, in the summer of 1924, studied at the renowned Louis Comfort Tiffany Foundation.

While Jenny and her story are fictional, Mr. Tiffany, the history of his family and namesake store, his windows, his aesthetic and personality,

11

the estate, and the Foundation are fact. If I've included a famous name, he or she was indeed involved in some way. For instance, Thomas Edison *was* a friend of Mr. Tiffany's and *was* working on a Spirit Phone. The amazing artist Paul Cadmus *was* a student at Laurelton in the summer of 1924. Stanley Lothrop *did* manage the Foundation, Sarah Eileen Hanley *was* Mr. Tiffany's companion (in every sense of the word, many said). The Art Students League, the Institute of Psychic Research, and Gertrude Vanderbilt Whitney and her studio are all real.

As often as possible, Mr. Tiffany's dialogue about art, architecture, and his own philosophy and quest are, if not verbatim, then influenced by his actual words recorded in letters, books, or articles. The same is true for Mr. Edison's espousing on his ideology.

Other parts of the novel are a combination of fact and fiction. While Tiffany did have many grandchildren, Oliver Comfort Tiffany is my creation. The history of Ouija boards is as described, but the Garland family and the Reverend are my invention, as are Minx and her family, Edward Wren, and Ben Montgomery.

All cities and towns mentioned are real, but the Reverend's specific church, the Weber Falls Cemetery, and the Fond du Lac Mausoleum are fictional.

And so I present *Tiffany Blues* as my way—

as a novelist fascinated with art and history and where they overlap—of imagining an answer to the lingering question of who set the Laurelton Hall fire in 1957 that destroyed so much beauty, and why. It is my hope that through my heroine, Jenny, readers may experience what guests and students at Laurelton were able to during its 1920s heyday, what Tiffany himself wanted them to experience, what he wanted everything he created to express: beauty. And while this book is a tribute to that opulence and beauty that were Tiffany's legacy, it is also a tribute to the power of art to overcome the worst of traumas.

Prologue

March 13, 1957
Laurelton Hall, Laurel Hollow
Oyster Bay, New York

I lost my heart long before this fire darkened its edges. I was twenty-four years old that once-upon-a-time summer when I fell in love. A love that opened a door into a new world. A profusion of greens, shades of purples, spectrums of yellows, oranges, reds, and blues—oh, so many variations of blues.

I never dreamed I'd come back to Laurelton Hall, but I always trusted it would be there if I ever could visit. Now that will be impossible. For all that is left of that arcadia is this smoldering, stinking mess.

Somewhere in this rubble of charred trees, smashed tiles, and broken glass is my bracelet with its heart-shaped diamond and benitoite charm. Did my heart burn along with the magical house, the primeval forest, the lush bushes, and the glorious flowers? I'm not sure. Platinum is a hard metal. Diamonds are harder still. Or did just the engraving melt? And what of the man whose hand had grabbed at the bracelet? His muscle and flesh would have rotted by now. But what

15

of the bones? Do bones burn? Back when it all happened, no report about a missing artist was ever made.

I take a few tentative steps closer to the rubble of the house. Bits of glass glint in the sun. A shard of ruby flashes, another of deep amethyst. I bend and pick up a fragment the size of my hand and wipe the soot off its surface. With a start, I recognize this pattern.

Patterns, Mr. Tiffany once said, be they found in events, in nature, even in the stars in the firmament, are proof of history repeating itself. If we see randomness, it is only because we don't yet recognize the pattern.

So it shouldn't surprise me that of all the possible patterns, this is the one I've found. This remnant of the stained-glass clematis windows from Oliver's room. I remember how the light filtered through those windows, radiating color like the gems Mr. Tiffany used in his jewelry. How we stood in that living light and kissed, and the world opened up for me like an oyster, offering one perfect, luminous pearl. How that kiss became one more, then a hundred more. How we discovered each other's tastes and scents. How we shared that alchemical reaction when our passions ignited, combusted, and exploded, changing both of us forever.

Clutching the precious memory, I continue walking through the hulking mass of wreckage, treading carefully on the broken treasures. I listen for the familiar sounds—birds chirping, water splashing in the many fountains, and the endless rushing of the man-made waterfall that I always went out of my way to avoid.

But everything here is silent. Not even the birds have returned yet.

I learned about the fire seven days ago. I was at home in Paris, having breakfast, eating a croissant, drinking a café crème, and reading the *International Herald Tribune*. The headline popped out at me like the obituary of an old friend with whom I had long been out of touch.

Old Tiffany Mansion Burns

> An eight-level structure with twenty-five baths, the house was owned originally by the late Louis Comfort Tiffany of the jewelry firm that bears his name. At one time the estate covered 1,500 acres of woodland and waterfront.

I didn't realize my hand was shaking until I saw a splotch of coffee soak into my white tablecloth.

> The structure later housed the Tiffany Art Foundation, which operated a summer school for artists.

17

The reporter wrote that a neighbor out walking his dog noticed flames coming from the clock tower of Laurelton's main house. Within hours, the mansion was ablaze. Fire companies came from as far as Hicksville and Glen Cove. Firemen drained all the neighboring swimming pools using the water to try to contain the conflagration. They carried hoses a half mile down to the Long Island Sound to siphon off that water, too. At one point, 435 firemen worked on the blaze, but the fire raged on and on for five days, defeating them. Those who lived nearby said the skies blackened as metal and wood, foliage, ephemera, and fabric burned.

The sky here is no longer black. But the smell of the fire persists. And no wonder, considering it burned for so long.

Once the present turns to past, all we have left are memories. Yes, sometimes we can stand where we stood, see our ghost selves, and relive moments of our life. See the shadow of the man we loved. Of the friend we cherished. Of the mentor who made all the difference. Our memories turn specific. The terrier that played by the shoreline, joyously running in the sand. We can remember the smell of the roses. Look at the azure water and see the glimmer of the sun on the opposite shore and hear a fleeting few bars of jazz still lingering in the air.

If you were the only girl in the world . . . Staring

into the remains of what is left, I see ghosts of the gardens and woods, the gazebo, terraces, rooms ablaze with stained glass—everywhere we walked and talked and kissed and cried. With my eyes closed, I see it all in my mind, but when I open them, all of it is gone, up in flames.

Mr. Tiffany once told me that there is beauty even in broken things. Looking back, there is no question I would not be the artist I am if not for that lesson. But would he be able to salvage any beauty out of this destruction?

No, I never dreamed I'd come back to Laurelton Hall. The Xanadu where I came of age as both a woman and a painter. Where I found my heart's desire and my palette's power. Where depravity bloomed alongside beds and fields of flowers, where creativity and evil flowed with the water in the many fountains. Where the sun shone on the tranquil sea and the pool's treacherous rock crystals reflected rainbows onto the stone patio. Where the glorious light streaming from Mr. Tiffany's majestic stained glass illuminated the very deep darkness that had permeated my soul and lifted me out of despair. And where I found the love that sustained me and remained in my heart even after Oliver and I parted.

Standing here, smelling the acrid stench, looking at the felled trees with their charcoal bark, the carbon-coated stones and bent metal frames that once held the master's windows, at the smoky, melting mess that was one of the greatest mansions on Long Island's Gold Coast, I know I never will see it again, not how it was that magical and awful summer of 1924.

The fire is still hot in spots, and a tree branch snaps. My reverie is broken. Leaves rustle. Rubble falls. Glass crushes. Twigs crack. Then comes a whisper.

Jenny.

But it can't be. The wind howling through a hollow tree trunk is playing a trick. Fooling me into thinking I am hearing his sapphire voice, its deep velvet tone.

As I listen to the repeated whisper—*Jenny*—I raise my hand to wipe at my tears and tell myself that it is the smoldering ash making my eyes water. The charms on my bracelet jingle as I lower my arm. And again the whisper . . . and again my name—*Jenny.*

1

March 20, 1924
New York, New York

I hadn't expected to find a waterfall in the middle of Central Park. Even there, so far away from home and the scene of the tragedy, the rushing water that pounded on the rocks made me shudder. The waterfalls in Ithaca and in Hamilton had been powerful, beautiful forces of nature, but I'd grown to hate them.

"Jenny, certainly this early-spring scenery is going to inspire you to use some color," Minx said, as we set up our easels.

A dozen of us from Professor Robert Pannell's class at the Art Students League of New York had scattered around the pond, preparing to spend the afternoon painting en plein air in the tradition of the impressionists. We'd walked from the school on West Fifty-seventh Street north into the park and then continued along manicured pathways into this untamed, romantic area.

"Your assignment is not to paint what you see but what you feel. Paint the atmosphere," Professor Pannell instructed. He always pushed us to go beyond convention.

After a half hour, I was still struggling to get

21

something worthwhile down on my canvas. The ceaseless noise of the water falling distracted me and made me anxious.

"So you're not going to use even a little bit of color?" Minx coaxed me. Christened "Millicent," she'd come by her nickname honestly. She had been a hellion growing up—bold, flirtatious, and cunning, much to her parents' chagrin—but she was just beguiling enough to get away with it.

I forced a small smile but didn't proffer an actual answer. I didn't need to. She hadn't really been asking for one but was rather expressing her never-ending surprise at how uninspired I was by the things that moved her so much.

"I know you are fascinated by the shapes of the trees and the negative spaces and patterns they create, but there are colors out there, Jenny. Look at the colors. Winter evergreens and spring's very first buds."

Minx had been questioning my reluctance to use color for months and knew that nothing— not spring or fall or flowers or fabrics—would inspire me. Despite my unchanging black, white, and gray palette, she believed she could help and refused to give up trying. I loved her for that and for her generosity.

She was the daughter of the Deerings, a wealthy shipping scion and a socialite whose fabled family had helped found the Bank of New York. Her parents, Eli and Emily, had spoiled her, and in return, Minx spoiled her friends. All her life, she'd witnessed her father showing his love and his remorse with gifts; for her, then, expressing love meant showering people with her largesse. And as her best friend and flatmate, I was often on the receiving end of her generosity.

Minx's family was wealthy and worldly. She'd grown up in a mansion on Sixty-second Street and Madison Avenue in New York City. The first time she took me home with her for dinner, I'd been awed. Yes, I'd seen opulence in museums, theaters, and government buildings but never in a home where people lived.

The Deerings were also serious art collectors with eclectic tastes. The walls of their mansion were crowded with Renoirs, Manets, Monets, Rembrandts, Titians, and Renaissance drawings. There was even a Leonardo da Vinci sketch done in sepia chalk. Marble stands showcased seventeenth- and eighteenth-century bronzes. Mantels were crowded with bejeweled bibelots from Fabergé, Cartier, and Tiffany. Plants were potted only in majolica. Sofas and chairs upholstered only in silk and damask. There was not a corner that didn't hold a treasure, not a wall that didn't showcase a masterpiece.

"Miss Deering, are you painting your canvas or Miss Bell's?" Professor Pannell called out.

Minx rolled her eyes at me, and as she returned to her own canvas, she picked a sprig of holly and tucked it behind her ear. In the sun, the leaves gleamed like jade.

Even there in the park in painting clothes, Minx was distracting. She never walked into a room without eyes turning. Everything about her gleamed, from her bobbed helmet of blond hair to her couture clothes in the palest shades of beige, pink, champagne, topaz, and citrine.

Like Minx, my hair was bobbed. But unlike hers, mine never agreed to lie flat and exploded in a profusion of curls that fell over my forehead. It made me look bohemian and mussed, whereas her smooth helmet of gold made her look chic and coiffed.

When Minx moved, the silks and satins glowed like liquid candlelight. Her deep brown-red lipstick blazed. Even her perfume shimmered: Ombré Rose from the House of L'Etoile in France. It contained minuscule flecks of gold, and sometimes you'd catch a glimmer where she'd applied the spicy, rich scent.

Despite all her dressing up and embellishments, I always saw the frantic light behind Minx's electric green eyes, her longing for something she couldn't name and didn't know how to satisfy. Gifted as both painter and sculptor, she was trying to find that something in art. And when she wasn't in the studio, she was trying to find it in too many glasses of champagne or in bed with men she never knew well enough. Like so many of our generation, even if we hadn't been at the front, we were shell-shocked in the aftermath of the war, and someone like Minx tried to chase away the sadness and loss with whatever it took—drink, drugs, frivolous theater, literature, music, forced gaiety, or a lot of sex.

After another half hour, I glanced over at Minx's canvas. She'd captured the charm and romance of the glen perfectly. We were in a section of the park called the Rambles, a particularly lush area that Frederick Law Olmsted had created to resemble natural woods. After the waterfall rushed over the rocks, it spilled into a pond surrounded by bushes and trees in configurations that didn't look man-made but indeed were.

During the three-hour period we were in the park, Professor Pannell strolled among us, examining our work, critiquing in his notoriously staccato sentences, and gesturing ferociously with his arms. He always carried his own paintbrush, which he often dipped into our palettes—without apology—to correct mistakes on our canvases.

He approached Minx and studied her work in progress.

"Lazy, lazy. You *can* do better. You *are* better. But this—" He broke off and threw up his arms.

He was tougher on her than the rest of us because—as he often repeated—she had more promise than most. And he made sure he said it loudly so we could all hear him. He believed in playing us against one another, a habit that didn't endear him to many students. Yet he was one of the most popular teachers at the League, because once you got over the shock of his methods, you could learn so much from the brushstrokes he applied to your canvas.

"More *depth,* Miss Deering," he said, as he dabbed his brush into the white oil paint and, with just two or three strokes, created the illusion of deeper space on the two-dimensional surface of her painting.

Leaving Minx, he stopped beside Edward Wren. Though not tall, Edward vibrated with energy. He had chestnut hair, a high forehead, and hooded hazel eyes. He had been at the League longer than Minx or I had. And while he'd taken several classes with Minx before, this was the first time the three of us were in a class together. As of late, I'd noticed Edward and Minx exchanging glances, and at home she mentioned him often. This surprised me. With his working-class aspect, Edward had neither the grace of the high-society gentlemen Minx had grown up with nor the aesthetic of the bohemian artists we spent time with. Yes, many were rebels devoted to their art, but few had scars on their cheeks or knuckles. Yet Edward did. At thirty-one, he was older and gruffer and not as polite as the other men in our set. At times, he could seem aloof or distant, as if something were preying on his mind. I knew virtually nothing about him except what I saw in his paintings—a powerful and raw talent often ruined by his impatience to invest the necessary time in finishing them. Even so, his canvases always exuded an exciting crudeness that made everyone take notice. Perhaps that rawness was why he reminded me of boys I had grown up with in Hamilton, Ontario. The sons of steel-factory workers and railroad men. The boys my mother had taught, hoping she might discover a budding artist in their midst.

Having finished critiquing Edward, Professor Pannell came to stand behind me. He hadn't yet been satisfied with anything I'd done in his class, and judging from his groan as he examined my interpretation of the pond, nothing had changed.

"Miss Bell, is that how you *feel* looking at the scenery?"

"It is."

"Then, Miss Bell, look *harder*. Examine Miss Deering's work. Note the colors she's used. Even with the lack of dimension in her rocks, pay attention to the *feelings* she's expressed. Don't you realize that your determination to stick to your colorless palette restricts you? Why are you handicapping your efforts?"

I looked from my best friend's canvas back to my own. We'd both painted the same scene, but where she saw spring greening the copse to life, I saw a forest out of a Grimms' fairy tale. Woods no little girl would want to enter willingly, a foreboding waterfall from which to flee.

"Miss Bell," Professor Pannell instructed, "look at *this* scene, *this* day, *this* sunshine and spring. Paint how *this* makes you feel." He then proceeded to inspect the next student's work.

I glanced from my painting to the waterfall, pond, trees, and grass. Back to the painting. Back to the rushing water. Back to the painting. Back to the rushing water. Of course, I could see the colors, but they weren't my focus. They were a distraction from my subject. I used a monochromatic palette because I wanted to capture light, to show how it illuminated the water and shadowed the trees. I wanted to master *chiaroscuro*. DaVinci, Rembrandt, and Caravaggio all knew that what we see is a result of light falling against it. It's the light that matters. Without it, there would be no subject. But light was so elusive. If I could just capture that simple bit of—

Suddenly, I saw a flash of blue tumbling over the edge of the waterfall. It was clothing. Child-size.

Then a woman's high-pitched voice called out: "Jeffrey!"

"It's a child in the falls!" I cried, as I dropped my brush and my palette and ran. The water was so powerful. A child who fell in would be caught in the current of the rushing cascade. His little

28

body would be thrown against the rocks. Unless someone reached him quickly, he might drown.

I reached the edge of the pond. I didn't know how deep the water was, but that didn't matter. If a child was in danger, if there was a life to save, I had to attempt it.

"Jeffrey, you bad boy. Look at that, your jacket is all wet!"

The voice expressed exasperation, but no panic. A jacket?

I circled around to see a woman tugging a well-groomed Maltese on a light green leather leash. She approached the edge of the pond and looked down at the errant piece of clothing.

"Jeffrey!" she called. "Come out here and see what you did!"

With that, a little boy, about seven or eight, emerged from the woods. He stood beside her, scuffing his shoe in the dirt and looking sheepishly from the floating jacket to his mother. And then he leaned over and started to reach toward the jacket.

"No, Jeffrey! Don't. You could fall, and then you'd be all wet, too. Let's find a stick and drag it in." Before she moved away, she looked at me. "Thank you," she said.

I nodded at her and took a deep breath. Although the boy was clearly fine, my heart continued racing as I returned to my easel. I'd seen the jacket and jumped to the conclusion that a child was drowning. My vision was warped, you see. Damaged by what I had endured as a girl. By now, at age twenty-four, I had long viewed the world through one particular lens, taking in what was there and pulling out the color so I could focus on the light and how it fell and created highlights. How shadows created depth. And in the process, I never failed to notice the potential for catastrophe and heartache.

I couldn't help it any more than Minx, who looked at the world through her own starry eyes—and saw only beauty.

2

Though filled with its own combination of colors and light and a variety of textures, my childhood was modest. It began in Upstate New York. Both of my parents were students. My mother, Faith Garland, studied painting at Ithaca College, and my father, Robert Fairburn, studied architecture at Cornell. To pay for tuition, both worked at night in the same coffee shop, Westoff's on State Street, which was where they met. They married less than four months later, and she became pregnant within weeks of the ceremony—or had it been a few weeks before?

Tragically, my father never finished school. He was killed in a bicycle accident on a snowy night a month before I was born, when he skidded on a patch of ice and broke his neck in the spill. Mother, nineteen years old, widowed, and pregnant, moved in with her sister, my aunt Grace, who at age twenty-five was an unmarried suffragette and spiritualist.

A few years before, Aunt Grace had taken over her father's job with the Kennard Novelty Company, selling Ouija boards. It was almost unheard of for a woman to be a salesperson, but my aunt was nothing if not a firebrand about women's opportunities. And then, once we moved in, Aunt Grace had the idea to have my mother paint customized boards, which made them even more desirable, and to have her sell them at a premium.

My family's history with the boards went back to my grandfather, Harold Garland, who'd worked in Kennard's factory from 1891 until he passed away. He revered the Ouija boards but not for their rumored psychic powers. It was simply the livelihood they afforded by giving us a healthy business.

Grace and Faith grew up with several incarnations of the "talking boards" and relished tales of others communicating with the dead. They both told me stories of trying to get their boards to work. My mother never succeeded. But eventually, Aunt Grace did, after being schooled by Helen Peters, a women's rights activist and supposed "medium," whose brother-in-law, a patent lawyer, helped bring the boards to the marketplace. Some people thought *Ouija* meant "good luck," but the mysterious word was nothing but a name engraved on a gold locket that Helen had found in an antiques store and thought sounded curious.

As the boards grew in popularity, so did the public's reactions to them. Many spiritualists believed in them and were against their commercialization. They insisted they needed to be used in the right way, or else they could harm the user. Some devout Christians viewed them as tools of the devil, while scientists considered them baseless pseudoscience that shouldn't be taken seriously by anyone.

Aunt Grace wasn't deterred by anyone's opinion. She liked working with the boards. Drawn to helping friends who were in mourning connect to their loved ones, she selectively did readings.

And every bit of extra money came in handy, since, in addition to taking care of me, my mother was trying to finish her art studies at Ithaca College so she could get a teaching job. But when she did, it was at a high school in Hamilton, Ontario.

My aunt didn't want us to leave. And I didn't want to go, either. We were a decidedly eccentric trio, and I had a happy childhood in the Queen Anne house on Eddy Street, with its towers and turret and warren of rooms filled with eclectic furniture and antiques.

The house was right on the electric trolley line that came up State Street before continuing on to the Cornell campus. In the winter, when Beebe Lake was sufficiently frozen, we'd grab our skates and join the crowds. There was sledding, too, and both my mother and my aunt would join in.

I can remember my mother's hair escaping from under her hat as her sled flew down the hill.

Like my mother, I had auburn curls and artistic ability. She'd begun teaching me how to paint as soon as I could hold a brush, and she praised every splash and squiggle and promised I had talent whenever my desire outpaced my ability and I grew frustrated.

Also like my mother, I was shy, yet I had romantic ideals and could be stubborn. Like Aunt Grace, I had strange purple-blue, peacock-colored eyes, long limbs, and a love of music and theater.

Like both women, I had a strong work ethic from the start and a willingness to make my own way in the world. I only wish my mother had been just a bit less anxious to strike out on her own and live away from her older sister.

However, despite protestations from both me and Aunt Grace, Mother felt that she and I needed to find our own way in the world, at least for a while. She would still paint the Ouija boards, and she and Grace could write letters and visit anytime. And after all, it was just half a day's journey.

Oh, the power of that single decision. Had my mother and I not made that journey north and west across the border past raging Niagara Falls, our lives would have been very different.

I wasn't the only one to experience trouble and trauma while growing up. Minx had upheavals in her life, too. But hers were the result of parents who believed indulgence could make up for lack of attention while they traveled and partied and doubled the wealth they'd inherited. The apartment I shared with her on West Ninth Street in Greenwich Village was just one example of their bounty.

I had arrived in Manhattan a year before, directly from Ithaca, where I had returned to live with Aunt Grace when I was eighteen and, like my mother, study art at Ithaca College. Five years later, when Grace passed away from pneumonia, I discovered she'd borrowed against the house for both her suffragette causes and my education, leaving me with only a small inheritance— just enough to get me to New York City, rent a room, and pay for three months of classes at the League. Just enough to get me started on a new life with a new name: Jenny Bell, in memory of the nickname my mother had given me because of the bells she heard ringing the Sunday morning I was born.

I attended the Art Students League five mornings a week and worked the rest of the day, and often evenings, at Mrs. Bullard's Tea Shop in Greenwich Village. I'd found a boardinghouse in Hell's Kitchen. The room was drafty and smelled of grease, and the cracked windows leaked cold air. Damp spots stained the ceiling. Most challenging of all, I shared a bathroom in the hallway with six other girls. But none of that really mattered; I was finally in New York City, studying at one of the most prestigious art schools in the country.

I met Minx in a figure-drawing class when we found ourselves sitting next to each other and realized we were the only two women in the class not nervously twittering about drawing a nude male. He wasn't even totally nude, with a cloth covering his privates. Minx drew him so easily that I found myself staring. I was so caught up in her swift strokes and assuredness.

"That's beautiful," I whispered, nodding at her work.

"Thanks," she said, as if she was used to compliments, and leaned over to inspect my sketch.

"And your *idea* is perfect," she whispered back.

"My idea?"

"To leave him unfinished. So clever of you. It's quite a statement when everyone else is trying to cram in every single aspect of him. You've made him into a bit of a hero the way you've done it."

I looked at the drawing I had abandoned, searching for the meaning that Minx saw, but it eluded me.

After class that day, as we were packing up, she invited me for a drink at a speakeasy not far from the League.

"Their sidecars are to die for. And despite the

swanky uptown address, they won't give our costumes a second glance." She gestured to our trousers. Working women had started wearing pants during the war, but once that ended and the men came home to reclaim their jobs, many women had gone back to dresses. But pants remained an option, and almost all the female art students wore them.

"And if they do have a problem with Coco Chanel's pants outfits, they can stuff it," Minx said, pointing to her outfit and then batting the air dismissively.

I knew who the French designer was, of course. You couldn't read a fashion magazine without seeing a sketch of something new she'd created or scan the society columns in the newspapers without reading about this socialite or that one wearing one of Chanel's creations. Until that moment, I'd guessed Minx was well-off from the way she spoke, the cut and fabric of her jackets, because her shoes were never worn out. But if she was wearing an actual Chanel outfit, she was more upper-crust than I'd guessed.

We walked north a block and then went east. Dusk in New York can be either romantic or disturbing depending on how you filter the world. I, for one, always peered into the shadows. We passed a row of walk-ups on Fifty-eighth Street between Seventh and Eighth Avenues. At that time of day, you couldn't clearly see the recesses under the stoops of the massive brownstones that rose up around us. But the man who leaped out from one of them had no trouble seeing us.

Caught by surprise, Minx wasn't ready for him, but I, always on guard, sensed him and saw him pounce. Just as he reached out to grab Minx's purse, I jerked her back and away from him. Before he could try again, I kicked his shin hard. He tripped on the curb and fell to his knees.

"Thief!" I yelled. "Police—thief!"

The scoundrel rose.

"Thief!" I yelled even louder.

From the opposite direction, a voice called out, "You in trouble?"

The crook decided Minx's purse wasn't worth getting caught and took off, running west, his footsteps a fast staccato on the pavement.

We both watched as his retreating form disappeared into the twilight, just as the gentleman who'd called out reached us from the opposite direction. "Are you two all right?" he asked, trying to catch his breath.

"We are. Thank you for coming to our rescue," I said.

"You're not hurt? Neither of you?"

Minx rubbed her arm, looked at me, and smiled. "Just a little where my friend here pulled me away."

"I'd be happy to escort you both to the police station or the hospital," he offered.

Minx told him he didn't have to do that, that nothing had been taken and we really were fine, but he insisted on at least walking us to our destination.

Two blocks south, he waited with us at the door of the speakeasy until the proprietor let us in.

"Are you sure you're all right?" I asked Minx.

"I'm fine," she said, but I could tell she was shaken.

Inside, we ordered sidecars and took a long sip when they arrived.

The incident had a different impact on each of us. I was angry, while Minx was scared. But I'd been attacked before. Circumstances had forced me to learn how to protect myself.

"Better?" I asked.

"Right as rain, thanks to you. It's my favorite purse, too. I owe you one." She pulled the pocketbook into her lap and petted it like a dog.

"As long as he didn't hurt you," I said.

"No, he never touched me. I'm still rattled— but nothing this drink isn't fixing. What about you?"

"He was all muscle. My foot feels like it hit a brick wall."

Minx looked down under the table at my right foot.

"You did kick him hard, didn't you? I couldn't believe you had the nerve." She leaned back and gave me a long once-over. "You're just a little thing, too, but you took him on. How'd you get to be such a brave bunny?"

There was so much about us that was different. I was suspicious of everyone from the start. People usually needed to work to earn my trust. But for all her worldliness, Minx was endearingly innocent. She believed her money and her privilege would keep her from harm. Someone had always come to her rescue. No one, not even my father's ghost, had ever come to mine.

Following the "purse incident," as Minx forever after called it, we sat next to each other in class and spent a lot of our free time together. We went to museums or out for meals, and sometimes, if I wasn't too tired from Mrs. Bullard's Tea Shop, I went with Minx to a club or revue or speakeasy.

Sometimes when we stayed out late, I slept over at her apartment in Greenwich Village. The location was perfect for Minx. In addition to studying painting and drawing at the League, she also apprenticed with the renowned sculptor Gertrude Vanderbilt Whitney in her Eighth Street studio. Mrs. Whitney was certainly high society—the highest in New York—but to those of us who worked and lived in the Village, we knew her as an artist first, a benefactress second, and a social scion last.

I waited tables in the tea shop every afternoon and took on second shifts to make enough for my art supplies, while Minx went out on the town to parties, jazz clubs, and Broadway musicals.

I harbored no resentment. Minx and I came from separate circles. That our lives had even overlapped in the first place proved that I had some luck after all.

We'd been friends for about six weeks when Minx finally saw where I lived. A few days later, we were sitting in her Greenwich Village living room, drinking her favorite cocktail: champagne poured over one sugar cube. I'd never even tasted champagne before I met her.

"This place is too big for me alone," she said, gesturing to the divans, sleek tables, and fireplace. Everything in copper hues that set off her coloring. Even the walls and ceiling glinted with metal filaments mixed in with the paint. Elaborate rust-colored silk curtains draped the west-facing windows and pooled on the carpeted floor.

Mrs. Deering's designer had furnished number 5B without skimping on any inch of the decor. The bathroom overflowed with piles of fluffy towels and trays of fancy soaps, lotions, and perfumes. The finest-quality pots and pans hung from hooks over the stove in the diminutive kitchen, which was more than adequate for Minx, who never cooked and kept the refrigerator filled with more champagne than food. In the foyer, a lacquered table and chairs for four accommodated meals. There was even a small guest room with an elaborate window treatment to distract from the air shaft it faced.

"You should move in with me. We would have such fun. And my parents not only approve, they insist you aren't to pay any rent. They hate that I'm living alone so much that they'd probably pay you to move in."

"I can't let them pay my rent, Minx."

"Yes, you can. They have more money than Croesus. And your job is arduous. Just think, you could leave Mrs. Bullard's."

"But my job isn't that bad. Mrs. Bullard loves her artists, whether they frequent the shop or work there. When there aren't any customers, she is happy to have me sit in the corner and draw. And the people who come in make it almost an adventure. Edna St. Vincent Millay was there just last week."

"Your hours are too long. If you didn't have to work as much, you could come out with us at night. You're missing so much fun, Jenny. So many jazz clubs. Have you been in a single speakeasy raid?" Her vibrant laughter sounded like the coppery glitter of her dwelling.

When I was a little girl, my mother and I played a game in which we would assign colors to sounds. A neighbor's voice, a robin's chirp, a duck's quack, a dog's bark, the sound of rain, thunder, chimes, a child's cry, wood being chopped, glass breaking—each one was a color. By rote, I still designated colors to sounds that I found interesting or appealing, curious or disturbing. Sometimes it brought back memories of my mother. Good memories of the times before the trouble started.

Minx continued to tempt me. "And if you came out with me to more parties and plays, who knows who you might meet? Not just starving artists who can't even afford to buy you a drink. But men who have well-paying jobs and can buy you bracelets and hats and bring you orchids and take you to Broadway plays in chauffeured cars."

"You do all that *except* give me orchids and bracelets," I said. "And I can live without those."

"I'm talking about romance, Jenny. Meeting men who will seduce you."

I shook my head while running my fingers up and down the rust-colored velvet arm of the chaise, feeling the soft nap against my skin.

"I can't accept charity," I said.

"It's not charity. You'd be keeping me company. My parents would be so thankful someone is watching out for me. They'd have my old nanny move in if I'd let them."

But to me it *was* charity. And I didn't want to be in that position again. When my mother was married to the Reverend, we partially lived off the largesse of his congregation. I saw what it did to her pride and honor. I saw how people—

even when they willingly gave—came to resent you and how in the end it made it even easier for them to turn on you.

"You are too stubborn, Jenny," Minx went on, having become quite expert at reading my silences. "How about this? The second bedroom is the size of a postage stamp. You can pay a postage-stamp fraction of the rent. The same amount you are paying for the room in the boardinghouse."

And so I moved in. But I continued working at Mrs. Bullard's, and in the next eight months, Minx became even more of an expert at reading my expressions and moods.

That spring afternoon, as I made my way back to my easel at the edge of the pond in Central Park, Minx ran up beside me and watched as the little boy's mother retrieved his jacket and wrung it out.

"Jenny, what's wrong?" Minx's forehead furrowed, worry clouding her green eyes.

"I'm fine," I said.

She put her arm around my shoulders. "No, you aren't. You are as white as a sheet. Maybe you should sit down."

"No, I'm all right. I just thought . . ." I started to explain.

"I know, you blurted it out. You thought a child was drowning. And you were going to jump into the pond and save him, weren't you?"

"Well, someone had to do something."

"You really are something else, aren't you?"

I was, but not the way she meant it. I shrugged and was about to answer when Edward Wren came over.

"Are you OK?" he asked.

"Of course," I lied.

"The way you ran out there, it looked like you believed someone was drowning." He frowned, clearly worried.

I shrugged again. "Well, for a second, I did."

"Drowning." He shook his head. "That must be a terrible way to die. Your lungs filling with water . . . not being able to breathe . . ."

"Edward, don't be so morbid! Jenny's just had a scare. Don't make it worse."

"Of course. I'm sorry," he said to me. His voice wasn't a deep rich color but a watered-down ash, and something about its tenor gave me pause. He was about to say something else when Professor Pannell came over and told us to return to our paintings.

Edward walked back to his easel, and Minx and I headed to ours.

"One day," Minx said, "you're going to tell me what happened in your past that has caused you to be so nervous all the time."

"I'm not nervous, Minx."

"You are not seeing yourself accurately. I am. What just happened spooked you."

I tried to make my voice light. My mother once told me I had a silver voice that tarnished when I wasn't giving her the whole truth.

"I grew up near waterfalls. I know how dangerous they can be." But despite my efforts to sound nonchalant, Minx's face told me that I had inadvertently responded more mysteriously than I had intended.

3

New York was alive, each new day bringing with it a colorful explosion of buds bursting on the trees and tulips blooming in the tiny sidewalk gardens I passed on my way to the League. Minx considered two miles too far to walk in the morning when there were trains and plentiful taxis, but I liked to watch as New York woke itself up.

A few days after our Central Park excursion, I was reaching Fifty-seventh Street and Fifth Avenue when the wind picked up and blew through the canyon created by the buildings around me. Always sensitive to the cold, I shivered as I crossed the street and hurried on. As I approached 40 West Fifty-seventh Street, I noticed that a commotion was occurring in front of it. I passed that building at least five times a week on my way to the League and knew that the Institute for Psychic Research was housed there.

Minx's mother donated to the institute, and often, when I dined with the Deerings, she talked about its newest findings. Once she even insisted that Minx and I accompany her to be tested. A scholar at the institute believed there was a connection between artistic talent and one's connections to other psychic planes. Little did

47

Mrs. Deering know that I didn't need a test to tell me I had a link to the spiritual realm. Or at least a doorway to it through my aunt Grace.

Outside the institute was a man dressed all in brown who stood talking to a group of reporters, each of them scribbling down every word he said. I managed to maneuver myself to the edge of the crowd to get a better look. It wasn't often I stumbled onto news in the making.

"I was able to read the note that Marjorie had written," the speaker declared with a thick accent. German, I thought, though I wasn't a very good judge. He was thin and balding, with a mustache.

I pulled out a sketch pad and pencil from my satchel and quickly—so as not to lose his precise expression—committed my impression of him to paper.

"Yes, the police have given me permission to tell you my findings. I believe that the person who signed the note, Marjorie, was not, in fact, a woman at all but a man."

A gasp came from someone behind me.

"How do you know it was a man?" a reporter shouted.

Cameras clicked, flashbulbs exploded. Meanwhile, I kept sketching. The drawings weren't bad, but I didn't feel I was truly capturing what I wanted on the page.

"Yes, Marjorie was certainly a man masquerading as a woman—and an inebriated man, at that. Of this I am sure." The man said this with a theatrical manner that I tried to catch in my sketch.

"May I see?" A man's voice came from behind me. In its timbre, I saw a flash of forest green. The color of holly in the summer when its leaves are at their glossy best.

He looked to be about my age, not striking except for the excitement in his warm brown eyes as he glanced from me back to my drawing.

And then he tipped my pad toward himself.

"Hey," I said, pulling the pad back.

"No, no, don't. Let me look. These are so good. You've captured so much more of him in one drawing than I can with this," the man said, pointing to the camera slung around his neck.

Before I could stop him again, he took the sketch pad from my hand and was riffling through my series of drawings.

"You have absolutely no right—" I tried to grab the sketch pad back, but he held tight.

"Please say you'll come to the office with me. I want to show these to my boss. I'm sure he'd want to buy at least one from you."

"The office? Your boss?"

"I work at the *New York Herald Tribune*."

My heartbeat quickened. "No, no," I said. "I have to go. I have class. And you are being amazingly rude!" I held out my hand for the sketch pad.

He returned it with a sheepish grin. "I'm sorry," he said.

I slipped the pad into my satchel and prepared to go.

"But I'm certain the paper would—"

I shook my head. "I'm really late and not at all interested." I walked away, not waiting to hear the rest of what he had to say.

My last run-in with newspapers and reporters had been almost nine years earlier. Enough time to give me perspective but not enough to take away the sting or to erase the memories. No matter how kind this man's eyes looked, he was obviously a reporter, and I knew from experience that reporters could not be trusted. The press was out for one thing only: the story that would give them a headline to sell copies.

I hurried westward, half walking, half running, crossing Sixth and then Seventh Avenue, and finally coming to a stop at 215 West Fifty-seventh Street. I took the steps two at a time, pulled open the door, and took a deep breath.

I was safe in the hallowed halls of the art school that had been training men and women for the last fifty years. The combined scent of oil paints, turpentine, primer, clay, wood chips, marble dust, and cigarettes was an aroma like no other. It could not be reproduced in even the finest perfumery.

I walked up two flights to the classroom, laid

out my supplies, and banished all thoughts of the scene on the street and the rude reporter. Instead, I threw myself into trying to capture the pose of the current female model on the dais.

Minx and I took different classes on Wednesdays, and then I worked a shift at Mrs. Bullard's, so I didn't see her until I got back to our apartment at seven thirty that evening.

As I twisted the key in the door, I heard voices, which wasn't at all unusual. Minx often had friends over. It amazed me she could be so industrious when it came to her work and still have such a busy social life. If it weren't for her, I'd have spent every one of my nights off at home with the radio and a book and never met anyone. But she loved having people around. She even preferred painting and sculpting in studios with other artists around. She said she wilted if she was alone too much.

I put my satchel and keys on the table in the foyer and walked inside.

"Well, hullo, I didn't think you were ever going to come home," Minx called out as I stepped into the living room.

She stood at the far end, by the windows, in the area we'd made our workspaces. Hers was to the left, where she painted and sculpted small pieces—she did her larger work at Mrs. Whitney's—and mine was to the right, where I drew and painted. The two spaces were a study in contrasts. Hers was cluttered and bright, with her brazenly colored paintings and dozens of clay figures all reaching, stretching, dancing, jumping—none of them in repose. Mine, meanwhile, was a bunch of monochromatic blacks, whites, and grays. My somber pencil studies of empty tree branches, rocks, leaves, and acorns, along with my partial figure studies focusing on one hand, one foot, or half a face, were all careful examinations of how light revealed its various dimensions.

There were paintings, too, all of them depicting the white marble crypt that I discovered in Hamilton's Weber Falls Cemetery when I was a girl. I continued to paint it over and over again, trying so hard to capture the elusive light filtering in through the stained glass, falling on the stone bench and on the floor. Holy light falling on my hands. In my mind, the light was cobalt and ruby and amethyst, but my canvas was still monochromatic. I hadn't tried to paint the window and its extravagance of color since I was sixteen. I wasn't ready to do so. Not yet.

"I'm just showing Ben our studio," Minx said, as she gestured to a man who was mostly hidden behind her easel.

"Ben Montgomery," he said, extending his hand as he stepped forward and I saw his face.

It was the rude reporter from in front of the Institute for Psychic Research.

"How did you find me?" I asked, as I reluctantly took his hand.

"Well, I did a little sleuthing. I saw your name on the sketch pad, so I did some research in the morgue—"

I blanched at the word. He saw it, hesitated, and then proceeded, clarifying what he meant.

"In the morgue at the newspaper, I mean, and I found your name mentioned in a group show at Mrs. Whitney's gallery. Minx and I are old friends, and I know she works with Mrs. Whitney, so I gave her a ring and asked about you. I never dreamed you two would be sharing a flat. That was just damn good luck, don't you think?"

"N-no," I stammered. Not good luck. Not for me.

"Well, I think it was. I couldn't stop thinking how much life your drawings would bring to my story. I really do want to show them to my editor. I'm certain he'd buy them." Ben smiled encouragingly, and the skin around his eyes crinkled.

"Isn't it exciting, Jenny?" Minx asked, without letting me get a word in edgewise as she took up the narration. "When Ben told me about your sketches, I insisted he come down and meet you properly and talk to you. Jenny, if the *Herald Tribune* wants to buy your drawings, you have to sell them. The money is amazing—five dollars per—that's more than you make in a week waiting tables at Mrs. Bullard's. You could save enough for Paris in just a couple of months."

Minx wasn't wrong, I had to admit. Studying at the League had been my dream since I was thirteen years old and my mother told me about it. And I'd achieved it. Now I was working toward my next goal: studying in Paris with the masters. Once Minx had discovered we shared the same dream, she'd started planning our year abroad. She wanted to leave sooner rather than later and had offered to pay my way. But just like the rent, I wouldn't accept charity. I was putting something away every week, but my savings were growing slowly. Living in the city was expensive; I didn't make a lot at Mrs. Bullard's, and art supplies cost a fortune.

Minx stopped to pour me a glass of the ever-present champagne. I sank into a chair and took a long sip of the delicate liquid, trying to concentrate on the bubbles bursting on my tongue instead of my sudden attack of nerves.

There is no reason to be nervous, I told myself, as I took a second sip and tried to control my breathing, the way Aunt Grace had taught me when I felt panicky. *Calm, breathe in, calm, breathe out, calm, breathe in.*

As Minx carried on with her chatter, I took another sip of champagne. But I *was* nervous.

I didn't want Ben or anyone searching for information about me. And despite my every effort, I recalled the third major event of my childhood, the one that would change my life most profoundly—the first being my father's death, the second our move away from Aunt Grace and Ithaca, and the third my mother's remarriage.

Just before I turned fourteen, in what must have been my mother's weakest moment, she married the Reverend William Haddon, who was associated with St. Theresa's, the school where she taught.

At first, it was easy to see how he seduced her. He was a well-educated man of forty-four, tall and broad-shouldered, with wavy light brown hair and intense brown-black eyes. His scarlet voice could cajole and calm when he sat and talked about a spiritual crisis, or it could rouse you and make you rejoice when he was at his pulpit. Mother was still so young then, only thirty-two, and she'd been on her own for twelve years. I could see how flattered she was to receive attention from such a highly esteemed man and how much she enjoyed being courted.

He made both of us feel special and wanted, not just bringing my mother flowers or candy when he came to take her out but always having a nosegay or a book for me as well. Mother marveled at how well loved he was by his flock of congregants. They called him the "paragon of soulfulness."

But once we moved out of our sweet cottage and into the damp, ancient parsonage, things began to change. With her salary, the Reverend's stipend, and the free housing, Mother assumed there would be more money, not less. That life would become easier. But it didn't. I didn't discover it for years, but the Reverend had been embezzling church funds to buy rare books for a collection he kept locked in the library and expensive wines and brandies that he enjoyed far too much.

Mother and I had never had a man in our lives, nor had we lived with one, and it was quite a change. The Reverend was a stickler for orderliness and punctuality. He wanted food at the same time every morning and evening. My mother and I, however, had never adhered to schedules. Not when we lived with Aunt Grace or when we lived on our own. Mother and Aunt Grace were too creative. Didn't a bunch of flowers look better if a few petals fell on the table? A book left open was more inviting than one with closed covers. And we all loved to talk and play piano and chatter away. But the Reverend needed long hours of quiet to work on his sermons in the evenings, which meant Mother and I often had to tiptoe around.

Every day, the free and colorful life that Mother and I had experienced together before grew more distant. Mother seemed a bit in shock in those early days. And then the shock grew to horror as the Reverend fell back into his old ways. Mother had told me he believed she'd be the reason he would stop drinking to excess. He'd put his faith in her. But my mother wasn't a magician. She didn't know how to quiet his demons and stop him from whatever drove him to the bottle night after night. He blamed her for his debauchery and made her suffer for her failure. And I, who had always done everything with my mother, also suffered.

In the Ninth Street apartment, the past was far away. I knew that. I'd put years and miles and a new name between me and that other Jenny. Ben Montgomery had no idea I was anyone other than just another artist trying to make it. I needn't give him any reason to wonder about me. I needed to play this game and act like anyone else would when offered five whole dollars for a mediocre sketch done in as many minutes.

I forced a smile to my lips and swallowed my trepidation along with the pale golden bubbles.

"You caught me by surprise on the street. I'm not used to strangers grabbing my sketchbook."

"I'm sorry about that. Truly I am. But I was so excited to see the life in your drawings. Please say yes."

I shook my head. "I need some time to think about it."

Minx and Ben both looked surprised.

"Not too much time, please. I want one of the drawings to run with my story."

"What story are you talking about? Who was that man?" I asked, trying to sound nonchalant.

"The man you were sketching is Rafael Scherman, a Polish psychic and handwriting expert. His claim—that a man masqueraded as a woman—is a brand-new clue in the stalled Ewell case. If Scherman is right, this could very well be the clue needed to solve a murder mystery that has eluded detectives for four years. That's my beat. Murder, high crimes, and serious misdemeanors."

And with that, I looked down into my glass, studied the long strings of bubbles in it, and took another very deep sip.

4

When I came out for breakfast the next morning, Minx was already at the table reading the newspaper. In front of her was last night's bottle of champagne in a silver bucket—or perhaps this was a new bottle.

"Minx, it's only half past seven. Did you just open that?"

"Yes. My mother always says that it's a sin not to celebrate every victory."

"What victory could you have possibly found out about while still in your pajamas?"

"Ben's story in the paper," she said. "Come look."

"But why would Ben's story—"

"Come look."

I peered over her shoulder at the front page of the *New York Herald Tribune*. In the middle of the top story on the front page was a drawing of mine—one that I had not sold to Ben Montgomery the evening before.

"Now, isn't this worthy of a celebration?" she said, lifting the bottle and pouring out two coupes of champagne.

"But how . . ."

Minx handed me a glass. "We have to toast your first paycheck as a bona fide artist," she said. "And to our being five dollars closer to Paris."

The realization that it was indeed my first paycheck as an artist distracted me from all my questions. I'd only had one painting in a group show—at Mrs. Whitney's—and that hadn't sold, and unlike many of our friends who put their work on display in the art fairs in the Village, I'd never tried to snare a tourist with my efforts.

Minx held out her glass. "Bottoms up, Jenny. You're official now!"

I did as instructed, but I couldn't help but try to clarify things. "Minx, I didn't sell Ben that drawing. I didn't agree to meet his editor. How did this happen?"

"When you excused yourself to powder your nose last night, I took the liberty of swiping one of the sketches so Ben could show it to his editor and run it if he liked it enough. I couldn't let you lose a chance like this."

"You went behind my back?"

"Don't be such a bunny. They're sketches, Jenny. You do ten in a minute. What's the harm? Why not sell them? Sometimes you confound me."

Since becoming my friend, Minx had done more for me than anyone I'd ever known besides my aunt. She'd shown me kindnesses that I didn't know how to accept or thank her for. Now she was asking a question that deserved an answer. A truthful answer. But I was incapable of giving her one.

I'd managed to scrape together a life in New York that was completely separate from what had happened in Hamilton almost nine years before, and I was determined to protect it. And so I did what I hated doing more than anything in the world, using a skill I had become far more adept at than painting or drawing.

I lied.

"When I was growing up, my best friend's father, Mr. Oates, got involved in a bad business deal. Even before the case went to trial, the press tried him with endless salacious stories, some exaggerations, some outright lies." I could hear my voice tremble. Did I sound too emotional? Or not emotional enough?

"I know what Mr. Oates did was wrong," I continued less theatrically, "but what the press did to him was far worse. They crucified him and destroyed his reputation. Mr. Oates killed himself, Minx. He lost hope, and he killed himself. My friend and her mother's lives were ruined."

Realizing how tightly my hands were clenched in my lap, I loosened my fingers and forced myself to breathe deeply and evenly.

"The press exploits our lives to sell more papers. It ignores our humanity. It acts as if there are no ramifications to its exaggerations and exposés. And there aren't. Even if they lie, the most that happens is they print a retraction on an inside page in small type. The banner headline's damage is done. We need the news, of course. But people's lives are not entertainment. Or shouldn't be. But trying to convince reporters and editors of that is not easy."

Minx poured more champagne and took a sip before offering her response. "They aren't always as bad as that, Jenny. Certainly not as bad as the people who've committed the crimes they report. I'm sure it was terrible for the Oates family"—she took my hand—"and I'm so sorry for your friend. But criminals should be exposed."

I took a sip, concentrating on the bubbles in my glass again. "It's blood sport, though. Don't you see that? The more salacious the story, the more the press milks it."

"One could argue the guilty deserve it."

"Except the 'guilty' aren't always guilty. Even when charged. Innocent people are destroyed, too."

"Jenny, you're crying!" Indeed, I was. "I'm sorry I sold your drawing if you didn't want me to. I thought you were annoyed that Ben had tracked you down, and I didn't want you to miss out on this chance."

I put down the glass and walked to my room, where I retrieved a handkerchief and wiped at my eyes. The action gave me time to calm myself. I didn't want to cause suspicion by overreacting.

Yet Minx followed and stood in my doorway. "I really am sorry," she said, and now she was crying, too. "Please don't be mad at me."

I handed her a handkerchief. "Let's go have breakfast. I'm not mad at you. Not really. You couldn't have known how I felt. But I do have mixed feelings about being part of something I have so many ethical problems with."

Arm in arm, we walked to the kitchen, Minx to make coffee, me to make toast.

"Well, you're going to have even more problems, because Ben's editor wants more drawings from you. Ben called late last night. His editor wants to hire you to cover trials. They can't take photographs in court, and—"

"No. I couldn't."

"*Five* dollars for every drawing they publish, Jenny."

I shook my head.

She poured the coffee. I waited for the toast, and then we sat at the table.

"Just think about it, please." She took a slice of bread, smeared blueberry jam on it, handed it to me, and made one for herself using twice the amount of jam to satisfy her sweet tooth.

"Your mother would shudder to see all that jam," I said, trying to change the subject.

"My mother shudders at everything in my life,

doesn't she?" Minx took a bite. "Jenny, seriously. Think about it. You work so hard at the tea shop. If you take the newspaper's offer, you will be able to devote more time to painting and save the money you need for our trip in no time. Lickety-split."

I'd told Minx I wasn't still angry at her for interfering, but in truth, I was. After spending the afternoon at the League, I went home to change, glad she wasn't there. I left at five for Mrs. Bullard's. As the city slipped into twilight, the streetlamps came on outside, illuminating the evening in pools of warm yellow light. Some people found this time of day depressing, but the encroaching darkness freed me. You could hide in the shadows. See but not be seen.

So many evenings like this in Hamilton, I'd sneak out of the parsonage, steal into the bordering Weber Falls Cemetery, and hide in the Fond du Lac Mausoleum, sitting and watching as the evening drained all the jewel-toned reflections out of the tomb. I'd stay there until I thought the Reverend would be drunk enough to pass out, and only then would I go back home.

The mausoleum didn't belong to me, yet during those years, the only footsteps in the dust were mine. Each time I visited, I worried that the door would finally be locked. But it never was. It wasn't the largest of the crypts, and there were others nearby decorated with stained-glass windows and ornate designs. But the Fond du Lac Mausoleum was the only one with an open door that summer afternoon when I was fourteen and my mother mouthed that I should leave the house quickly.

We'd been living in the parsonage for nearly a year. I knew by then that the Reverend drank too much and that it made him mean. At first, he only imbibed behind closed doors, and both he and my mother tried to hide the truth from me. But I could hear their arguments. She accused him of being on good behavior when he courted her, tricking her to get a warm body into his bed, his kitchen, and his parlor to serve parishioners tea. He'd turn on her, spouting crude insults and threats. Their arguments usually ended in him drinking even more before passing out in his library.

On Saturdays, the Reverend taught Bible study all afternoon and didn't come home until five in the evening. As he didn't approve of spiritualism or married women working, my mother used the time when he was away teaching art as a volunteer to some of the factory workers' children or catching up on Ouija board commissions for Aunt Grace's clients. The Reverend probably believed she'd stopped doing the boards when he'd ordered her to, but she'd told me he was being unreasonable. She had quit teaching when they married, but that was enough. She wasn't going to let Aunt Grace down or give up the extra income because of his demands.

Yet one Saturday afternoon at two o'clock, the kitchen door opened unexpectedly, and the Reverend walked in. He leaned at a strange angle against the counter and took in the scene—the paints and brushes and the Ouija board.

"I told you I didn't want those witch's tools in this house, didn't I?" he bellowed, slurring his words.

"I can't disappoint Grace, and—"

"So you sneak around doing it behind my back? What else do you do behind my back? You were a trollop before you met me, and I should have known a trollop you'd remain." He took two unbalanced steps and with a single swipe pushed half the paints and other supplies onto the floor. Standing in the mess of paints and turpentine and linseed oil, he raised his fist to the heavens. "Not in my house. Not in a house of God. You are fornicating with the devil, woman. I have forbidden this!" He picked up the board and smashed it down on the corner of the table. It splintered. Half fell on the floor. The other half he gripped tightly like a weapon and pointed at my mother.

"Didn't I tell you? Don't I provide for you?"

I rushed forward, arms out, grabbing for the board, wanting to protect her. She was out of her seat in an instant, pushing me out of the way.

"Go to your room," she said to me.

The Reverend wasn't paying me any attention. With his free hand, he reached out and grabbed my mother by her sleeve and pulled her toward him.

"Jenny, I told you to go to your room!" she shouted.

I didn't want to leave her alone with him. I didn't move.

"Jenny, I said go."

In my bedroom, I stood with my ear to the door, shivering with fear. I was too young and too innocent to understand the meaning of the sounds that emanated from the kitchen. But something was wrong. Cautiously, I opened my door, crept out into the hall, and stared.

My mother was bent over the table, her dress up around her hips, fear and disgust etched on her face. The Reverend, his eyes shut tight, head thrown back, was behind her, moving in a jerky rhythm over her.

I took a step forward, ready to do what I had to in order to protect her. I'd never seen my mother cry before. Never seen her in pain or scared. Before I could do anything, she shook her head at me and mouthed the words, *Go. Now.*

I wanted to stay and help her. But something in her expression was forceful, and I was afraid to do anything but obey. So I went back into the hall and through the parlor and out of the parsonage. I ran down the front steps. Across the backyard. Through the gates and into the cemetery. I ran past rows and rows of graves, deeper and deeper, until I tripped on a rock and went sprawling to the ground. After a moment of shock, I stood up and looked behind me. I was all alone. No one was chasing me. I brushed myself off. I hadn't explored the cemetery before that summer afternoon, but I occupied myself for the next half hour wandering up and down the rows of tombstones reading names, dates, and inscriptions, trying to forget what I'd seen in our kitchen. There were a few mausoleums, and I peered into each one. When I reached the Fond du Lac crypt, I noticed a sliver of cobalt-blue light coming from under the doorjamb. Drawn to the color, I got down on my knees and touched its reflection. The blue glazed my skin. Mesmerized, I stood up and tried the door. I didn't expect it to open, but if there was any chance that I could see more of that color, I had to make the effort.

When the door gave way, I was so surprised that I merely stood still on the steps for a moment. As soon as I walked inside, my trembling stopped. The late-afternoon sun streaming through a stained-glass window cast the entire vault into a chimera of light that spilled over me, and for the first time in my life, I really *saw* light. *Understood* it.

The design of the stained-glass window was

unlike anything I'd ever beheld. Ruby roses climbed on an iron gate in the foreground and opened onto a pond surrounded by irises and yellow lilies. In the background, pearly pink clouds floated in a deep orange sky over a water view and distant hills.

I remember holding my breath as I absorbed the magic. How I wanted to walk into that scene, visit that land, sit by the shore of that pond, listen to the water rushing over those rocks, and hear the birdsong.

The metal label at the corner of the window read *Tiffany Glass Co.* At the time, I didn't know the name of the artist who had conceived of this miracle. But in his hands, what might have been a saccharine depiction of heaven became a glorious message from beyond.

In an instant, gone were the shouting, the crying, and my mother's face frozen in fear. Here, quiet and majesty surrounded me. The window's creator had understood exactly how the sun would splash reflections on the walls and floors and bench and how healing the colored light would be for the viewer, even if she was a young girl hiding away from the world. Elated and exalted by my discovery, I twisted my hands this way and that, watching the colors shift and change. All I wanted to do was absorb the light. To become those shafts of blues and reds and purples and yellows and pinks. And then I wanted more than to become them. I wanted to be the creator myself, to arouse awe in someone else the way the window maker had aroused it in me. To be the one to enchant and seduce, to create work that made someone feel like this.

The Fond du Lac tomb became more than my escape. More than a perfect hiding place. It became my studio. With my watercolors, paper, and brushes, I used the mausoleum as a chamber of inspiration where I disappeared into making art.

Months after that, I saw an article in the newspaper about a church restoration in a neighboring town. The reporter wrote that the new stained-glass windows were being created by the New York firm of Tiffany Glass Co. I asked my mother if we could go see them once they were installed, and she promised we would. When she lived in Ithaca, she said, she'd been to a church with Tiffany windows, and her friend Martha Samuels had a dragonfly lamp made by them. Her face aglow, Mother described the beautiful glassworks and told me about the artist, Mr. Louis Comfort Tiffany, who had started out as a painter. One day, she said, we'd go to New York and visit his studio and the shop his father had opened in New York in 1837. It started as a stationery store, but now it sold his son's glassworks, china, and silver and some of the most beautiful jewelry in the world.

Years later, after Mother was gone and I moved to New York City, I made it my mission to visit all the nearby churches with Tiffany windows: St. Michael's on the Upper West Side, Middle Collegiate Church downtown on Seventh Street, and several more. I never visited during a service but at off hours, when there was no chance I would be subjected to a member of the clergy or choir. I had no interest in visiting God, only in worshiping at the altar of art.

I, of course, made a pilgrimage to Tiffany's store on Thirty-seventh Street, hoping to see a full display of his stained-glass windows. Though I was dazzled by the cases of jewelry, iridescent pottery, gleaming silverware, and jewel-toned lamps, I was disappointed to learn that the windows themselves were made to order in the studio and not available for viewing without an appointment.

However, I did discover something precious about Mr. Tiffany while dining at the Deerings' home one night. In their impressive library, nestled among hundreds of rare first editions, was none other than the artist's memoirs. Mr. Tiffany had them written by the former art critic for the *New York Times*, Charles De Kay. There were only 502 copies of *The Art Work of Louis C. Tiffany*, privately printed in 1914 at the request of his children and friends. The book, with its intricate cover—gold foil over a red-ground papier-mâché binding—had been designed by Tiffany himself and contained twenty-one tipped-in color plates and forty-two photogravures. Without hesitation, Minx lent it to me, and I pored over copy number 368 for months. Mr. Deering, either having forgotten he'd loaned it to his daughter or happy to let her have it, never asked for it back. It was still sitting on my nightstand, in fact.

As I walked the last block to Mrs. Bullard's, I thought about how Minx had borrowed that book just to please me, and I tried to let go of my anger toward her. She did mean well. She always did. But sometimes her enthusiasm got the better of her.

I spent the next two hours at the tea shop, waiting on tables. There was a lull at seven, and I took a break, sketching at a table in the back. When my pencil ripped through the paper, I realized my thoughts were back on Minx. She really was only trying to help. Share what she had. Bring someone up a step. But she *had* taken my sketch without asking. Even if she'd gotten me five dollars for it, she'd interfered.

"Jenny?" Mrs. Bullard called out from the front of the shop.

I looked up and took in her tall form—her shock of white hair, warm black eyes, and signature eclectic attire. Even though the colors and styles of individual pieces never quite matched, she always made the combinations work. That afternoon, she had on a pale peach and green Japanese silk kimono, accessorized with turquoise and silver earrings and a necklace from Mexico. Her parrot, Rudolf, perched on her shoulder, his resplendent plumage of reds and purples clashing with all the colors of her costume. Compared with her, my black skirt and white blouse looked drab, but my job wasn't to stand out.

"Jenny?" Rudolf squawked.

The bird often repeated the last few words Mrs. Bullard said. It had taken me a while when I first started working there not to fill some orders twice, once from Mrs. Bullard and once from her bird.

Mrs. Bullard was as well known to local artists as her shop was to tourists hungry for authentic Village atmosphere. She often fed us when we couldn't afford the full price of a sandwich, asking only for a sketch in exchange. Over time, her walls became filled with those payments. Sometimes, when we weren't busy, I'd study layer after layer of sketches from artists like George Bellows, Edward Hopper, Max Weber, and Georgia O'Keeffe, all of whom had once been unknowns but whose works were now— ten to twenty years later—selling for fortunes in galleries uptown.

"There's someone asking for you, dear," Mrs.

Bullard said, pointing to the door. "He wouldn't let me seat him. Said he'd only take a table if you'd sit with him. Do you know him, or is he a masher?"

I looked over and saw Ben Montgomery, fedora in hand.

"You don't seem happy to see him. Should I send him away?"

"Should I send him away?" the bird echoed.

"No, that's all right," I said, as I put down my sketchbook. "I might as well get this over with, if you don't mind."

"Sure, you can sit with him at a table, dear. Bring him a cuppa. It's always slow right about now, before closing time."

"Thank you, Mrs. Bullard."

I'm not sure who was more tentative, me walking over to Ben or him waiting for me.

"Mrs. Bullard said I should invite you to sit"—I gestured to an empty table—"and ask if you'd like something to drink."

"I'd love some coffee. Black, please."

I retreated to the kitchen. None of the china or utensils matched; like Mrs. Bullard, the eclectic look charmed the customers. I picked out a heavy white mug for me, the kind Aunt Grace always used. For Ben, I chose a forest-green one with a pale silver rim. I poured the coffee and put the mugs on a tray with sugar and cream.

Back in the main room, I put the tray on the

table, pulled out a mission-style chair, and perched opposite Ben, who was on a ladder-back with a woven seat. Each chair and table was as different as the china and silverware and linens. It was all part of the creative atmosphere that made artists frequent Mrs. Bullard's over other establishments.

"I wanted to apologize." Ben held the mug between both hands as if drawing succor from its warmth. "I think I've upset you."

I laughed sardonically. "You and Minx, yes."

"And I don't want to start off on the wrong foot."

"We're not starting off on any foot, Mr. Montgomery."

"Well, I've known Minx for ages, and now that I'm back in New York, we're bound to be seeing each other more, and I'd prefer you not scowl like that every time you see me."

"All right, I won't scowl."

"In a normal conversation, you'd ask where I'd been since I mentioned just coming back to New York, and you'd want to know how I know Minx."

"Mr. Montgomery, this isn't a normal conversation. I didn't give you any indication when you peered over my shoulder on that street corner that I wanted to continue speaking with you. I didn't give you my address or one of my sketches. And I didn't invite you here. You keep intruding."

He laughed. "You're awfully direct, aren't you?"

I didn't laugh. "Yes, very unfashionable, I know. But anything else is a waste of time."

"And you don't like wasting time?"

"Or answering questions."

"See—I did get off on the wrong foot," he said.

After he'd left the apartment, Minx had asked me if I'd noticed how handsome he was. I hadn't. She had a knack for surrounding herself with captivating men and beautiful, interesting women, but that didn't mean they did the right things or deserved to be let off the hook for their deceptions.

I played with my mug and remained silent.

"Why do I make you uncomfortable?" he asked.

"What makes you think I'm uncomfortable?"

"You're playing with your cup, you keep tapping your left foot on the floor, and you refuse to look me in the eye for more than a millisecond. What have I really done but admire your drawing?"

My reactions had exacerbated the situation, and the very last thing I wanted was to make him curious about me and have him think I was hiding anything.

"I'm just anxious about socializing while at work."

"The tea shop is empty."

"That doesn't mean I don't have things I should be doing."

"You were sketching when I came in," he said.

"And just about to wash some dishes."

"And that's the other thing I came to talk to you about."

"Washing dishes?"

He grinned. His eyes crinkling again. "You're a mysterious girl, aren't you?"

"I'm anything but mysterious."

"But you are. I'm something of an expert."

"You are something of a smooth talker. So what did you come to talk to me about?"

"A job. If you accepted a few assignments at the paper, you wouldn't have to wash dishes anymore. Or wait on tables. Your drawing got quite a lot of attention. There's a big murder trial going on, and we need a sketch artist at court. You know photographers aren't allowed in. My editor, Mr. Portside, will pay you a daily stipend plus five dollars for every drawing that runs and—"

"I couldn't."

"Whyever not? It's what you do anyway—draw."

I stood and picked up my mug. "I'm sorry, Mr. Montgomery. I couldn't sit in a courtroom. I couldn't cover a murder trial."

He put his hands on the table on top of my sketchbook. "Think of the money. At least two drawings a day for two or three weeks. And then on to the next trial. Would you at least think about it? It doesn't make any sense that you would turn down such a great opportunity. Minx said this is what you need—a faster way to save money for the Paris trip the two of you are planning. And you wouldn't have to quit the League. All your professors offer evening sessions."

"So the two of you planned it all out?" I stared down at him. Fuming.

"Minx cares about you. She said you are like a sister to her. Why does that upset you?" He cocked his head and looked at me intently.

I took a breath. I couldn't allow the conversation to end this way. It didn't make sense, and it would make Ben too curious.

I resumed my seat and reminded myself that I wasn't in Canada. I wasn't sixteen. No one suspected me of anything. I was a twenty-four-year-old artist in New York City, and this man was offering me a very good opportunity.

"I am overreacting," I told Mr. Montgomery. I took a sip of the now-lukewarm liquid, stalling as I tried to come up with a reasonable explanation for my attitude.

"Is it that you can't accept Minx trying to help?" Ben asked. "She said you were far too proud for your own good."

And there it was, my excuse. Ben was handing it to me as easily as I'd handed him the coffee.

"I suppose I am. She's always so generous. and there's no way I can ever pay her back."

"I've known her for quite a long time. She doesn't expect being paid back with anything other than your friendship. It's her nature to help. Sometimes too much. Sometimes for too long."

Now I was intrigued.

"Too much? Too long?"

"We first met when Minx was attending Radcliffe. I was at Harvard, and she dated a schoolmate of mine. They had it bad for each other, but he was a real rogue, the black sheep of a good family. Minx was convinced she could help him reform. We all warned her he was a lost cause, but she was determined to save him from himself before he got kicked out. Nothing changed her mind about him. She'd lend him money when he ran up his gambling debts. Even pawned some ring her grandmother had given her when he smashed up his car so he could have it repaired before his father found out and pulled him out of school."

I was surprised I hadn't heard this story from Minx. She loved talking about the scrapes she'd gotten into.

"What happened?"

"He got drunk one night and drove off the road. Minx wasn't in the car. A local girl was with him. Not anyone we knew; she worked in a tavern

79

nearby. The girl got thrown and amazingly wasn't hurt. But Timothy didn't fare as well."

"He died?"

Ben nodded. "It was a lot for Minx to take in. Not just that Timothy was dead but that he'd been with that girl."

Despite my shock at hearing this story about Minx, I found myself confessing more: "My mother was like that. Too trusting." As soon as I said it, I realized I'd divulged too much.

"And how did she fare?"

"Oh, you know. Just as well as any woman." I put a light tone on my words and went back to thinking about Minx. She had told me recently that, like many men of his class, her father had indulged in affairs. His current mistress was a twenty-eight-year-old Broadway dancer.

Ben scrutinized my face. I didn't like to be studied. I was the one who did the studying. Who watched other people move and talk and hold back and give forth. I watched them when I sketched them and tried to understand them as forms, shapes, and expressions, devoid of their humanity so I didn't have to be affected by it.

"You have a dark view of life, Miss Bell."

"Do you think? You barely know me."

"I'm a very good reader of people."

I took another sip from my mug.

"Most girls would have asked me right then how I read people so well."

"But I'm—"

He interrupted me. "No, you certainly aren't most girls. Neither is Minx. Must be part of what makes the two of you such good friends. You're ambitious, aren't you?"

"Wildly so," I replied. Relieved, perhaps, to move on to a subject that I could be honest and open about.

"And what is it you want to achieve most of all?"

"Beauty, Mr. Montgomery. I want to create beauty."

"But you have. I saw your painting in the living room on Ninth Street."

"Minx's painting, you mean."

"No, yours. The dark one, almost colorless, of the light."

For the first time, I wasn't sorry that we were chatting.

"You think it's beautiful?"

"I do," he said, with a little hitch in his voice, not taking his eyes off me. "Do you know why you have such a burning desire to create beauty, Miss Bell?"

"Of course. I've read as much Dr. Freud as anyone else. I want to block out everything that is ugly. And you don't need to be much of a psychic to see how very much ugliness there is all around us."

"Indeed, you don't. Do you agree with the

81

poem, Miss Bell? 'Beauty is truth, truth beauty,— that is all ye know on earth, and all ye need to know.' "

"No, I don't agree with Mr. Keats. I think beauty can be a great lie. Sometimes the greatest lie."

"But that doesn't lessen its pull for you?"

"No, in fact, the other way around. It might make me that much more interested in it."

He lifted his cup to toast. "Well, either way, then, to beauty. Its truth and its lies."

5

As I walked home that night after a long day at the League, followed by an even longer evening at the tea shop, I couldn't help but think about the job Ben had offered me. Could I manage to go to a courtroom and look at the defendant and his or her accusers and steel myself against reacting? The money *was* much more than I could ever make at Mrs. Bullard's, probably more than she made in a day.

Minx wasn't home but had left me a note to meet her at the Blue on Blue on Bleecker Street. But the idea of going out to a jazz club and making small talk didn't hold any appeal.

With the apartment to myself, I opened the windows. We were high enough on the fifth floor that the stench of the city streets didn't blow in with the breeze.

I made myself a cup of tea, mixed in a teaspoon of honey, and retreated to my half of the studio, where the melancholy canvas on my easel awaited me. Ben had said he found my painting beautiful. I wished it was, but I didn't think I'd managed beauty quite yet. I was still struggling to capture the allure and mystique of light through transparent oil-paint glazes.

I pictured light sieved through leaves on the oak

and maple trees in Central Park. Or splashing on the East River at sunrise. Or heavy with smoke in the nightclub. Or filtering through the stained glass in the Fond du Lac Mausoleum.

Painting light wasn't the same as painting a portrait or a still life. People and objects occupied space, had dimension and weight. I could only paint my light against something. Show it by how it altered what was around it.

Minx often questioned my reason for painting the same scene over and over again. I never had a good answer. I knew I'd become obsessed with capturing the light in the mausoleum, in my secret place, my private sanctuary. And that returning to it in canvas after canvas both challenged and nourished me.

My work had become more abstract since I'd been studying at the League. Partly, I believed, because of Professor Pannell's teaching that we should paint not only what we saw but how we *felt* about what we saw. For my classmates, even when their work became more nuanced, it was still recognizable. For me, I was getting so close to my subject, focusing so tightly on the illumination, that my representations were morphing into puzzling, monochromatic studies. My pencil sketches were another story. Light wasn't my goal there. Just capturing movement. And I received as much praise for those as I received criticism for my paintings.

I continued examining my unfinished painting on the easel. There was something about it that made me think of an earlier version, and I wanted to compare the two.

I sorted through my stack of paintings lined against the wall. The one I was searching for wasn't there. But that was impossible. One by one, I pulled out each painting and examined it to make sure I wasn't confused and misremembering.

But no, the painting I wanted to look at just wasn't there.

It occurred to me that I'd never examined all my canvases at one time. The more carefully I studied them, the more I became convinced of my mediocrity. I just wasn't good enough and probably never would be. I'd studied art history and knew that by the time most true artists were my age, their work was much further along. Maybe I was chasing the wrong dream, I thought glumly. Maybe I shouldn't be chasing a dream at all. Perhaps fine art was too lofty a goal. I should just take the job Ben's editor was offering. Minx was right. Only a fool would turn down an offer of five dollars a drawing.

I could hear my mother's voice in my head, telling me that I had talent that would save me no matter what. That I could withstand anything as long as, at my core, I stayed true to my quest to capture beauty with oil and brushes. But she hadn't been able to withstand everything. Her love of colors hadn't saved her after all.

Aunt Grace always told me that whenever I became overwhelmed by grief or anger, I should simply "get up and paint it out." So I took a long sip of my honeyed tea and picked up my brush.

Much later that evening, I heard a key in the door and looked up. Minx walked in, took off her hat and shawl, laid her bag on the table in the foyer, and, leaning against the entryway to the living room, took in the scene.

"Is this why you didn't come and meet us?" Minx asked.

She looked lovely, but the mauve circles under her eyes belied the midnight hour. Her lipstick was all worn off, and her sleeveless dress had slipped half off her shoulders. She flopped down on the sofa, her champagne-colored silk shift shimmering as she moved. There was a long string of creamy pearls wrapped around her neck four times, and the teardrop pearls hanging from her perfect earlobes swung back and forth.

Kicking off her satin shoes and stretching her legs out on the sofa, she lay back, as if the evening had taken everything out of her. She opened her bag and pulled out her gold cigarette case and lighter.

"Care for a gasper?"

I shook my head. I didn't smoke much. "How

was your night?" I asked, as I joined her on the divan.

"Crazy. Too many drinks. Suzanna got zozzled and got sick before she could get to the john. William showed up, and that led to even more drama."

William, the youngest teacher at the League, preferred fraternizing with the students rather than the faculty, much to the consternation of the school's board. For the next fifteen minutes, Minx entertained me with gossip and caught me up.

"Edward was there," she said, beaming.

"And from the expression on your face, that made your night."

"He's so much more mature than most of the boys we study with. I'm sure it has a lot to do with him growing up poor and then being in the war. I've tried to get him to talk about the terrible things he saw, but he just won't. He says being with me helps him forget all that darkness, and the very last thing he wants to do is relive it. I think that must be part of why he can't be bothered with a lot of the silliness that goes on with our group. He's endured so much more."

"And it sounds like you're liking him so much more, too."

"I think I might really be falling for him." She gave a little sigh.

"Well, it sounds like quite a night."

"And I'm not finished. Last but not least, Ben Montgomery stopped by." Minx looked at me from under her full dark lashes the way she did when she had a point to make.

"Until I ran into him, I never heard you mention him before, and now you're talking about him all the time," I said, trying to sound calm.

"Ben was away, Jenny, in California, writing a novel, and now he's home working at his uncle's newspaper."

"It's his uncle's paper?"

"It is now. His grandfather started it. Then his father took over. But Mr. Montgomery Senior isn't around anymore. Speaking of scandals, his was one of the biggest in the newspaper biz. Ben's father supposedly took a bribe and published false reports about a bigwig politician. His lawyers claimed he was set up, but the damage was done. During the trial, the paper failed and almost went under. Ben's uncle brought it back from the brink. But the paper's reputation was tarnished."

"What happened to Ben's father?"

"Two days after the judge called a mistrial, Mr. Montgomery Senior took a walk out of the window of his twentieth-floor office."

I shuddered. "How long ago?"

"About a year and a half."

"I'll take that cigarette now," I said.

She opened her gold case, offered one to me,

and, after I took it, took a cigarette for herself. Flicking her lighter, she held it out for me before touching it to the end of her smoke. Minx leaned back, inhaled, then exhaled. Then she daintily picked a piece of tobacco off her lower lip.

"Ben's helping with his uncle's mission to restore the paper's reputation."

I thought about my mother. So Ben and I had something in common: both of us were attempting to be the saviors of lost causes.

"I think Ben has a thing for you. That's why he dropped by tonight. Hoping you'd be there. He told me he stopped by the tea shop earlier in the evening to try to persuade you to take the job. I'm sure his editor does want your drawings, but let's face it, kiddo, sketch artists aren't exactly rare in this city."

I hadn't wanted the job, and now, for the first time, I felt anxious at the thought of losing it.

"Do you like him at all?" Minx asked.

"Way too fast. We just met." I shrugged. "Besides, I don't want to like anyone. I just want to work hard, save money, and get to Paris."

"That's why you should take the job, you silly bunny."

"It's good money, I know, but I don't want to spend time in a courtroom."

"Good money? It is *change-your-life* money."

She got up and poured herself an inch of brandy in one of her mother's castoff Baccarat glasses.

As she walked back toward me, she focused on my half of the studio again.

"What were you doing with all these?"

"Looking for one particular painting. I wanted to compare it to a new one . . . and it's the strangest thing, Minx. I can't find it anywhere. I've even wondered if I imagined painting it."

I stood and began restacking the canvases. Looking carefully at each for one last time, making sure I hadn't somehow missed it, as impossible as that seemed.

I glanced over at Minx, who was staring at me.

"What is it?" I asked. "You have the most peculiar expression on your face."

"Peculiar?"

"Yes, like you just tasted something gone bad."

"Too much brandy too fast." She stretched and then stood up. "I'm bushed. So breakfast tomorrow before we go to class?"

We usually ate together on days we went to the League. And we both had painting classes the next day.

"Sure. Like we always do. Why would you even ask?"

"Oh, no reason. Just checking."

She left her coat and her shoes and bag in the living room and went off to her bedroom, leaving me to continue putting my paintings away, wondering how on earth I could have lost one.

There were two possibilities I'd need to

investigate. Mrs. Whitney and the League had both held group exhibitions in the last few months. I'd submitted paintings to each. I knew exactly which ones. After all, they'd both been shown and were both back in my studio. But was it possible I'd submitted two paintings and then left one behind? I couldn't imagine being so lax or forgetful, but there had to be an answer.

I suddenly remembered the closet in the hallway. I certainly didn't remember putting the painting there, but it was worth checking. Standing on a pile of books, I inspected the top shelf. No, my canvas wasn't there, but one of my mother's illustrated Ouija boards was. I shuddered at even touching the box. I hated the thing for the memories it aroused.

When my aunt came to visit Hamilton for my fourteenth birthday, she decided it was time for me to experience the power of the talking boards. I'd never paid much attention to them. They weren't exotic to me; I'd seen Mother decorate them with her paints all my life.

If anything, they scared me. Since we'd moved in with the Reverend, I'd heard what he said about them. Devil's tools to tempt weak people desperate to speak to their lost loved ones. Evil instruments of heresy.

Aunt Grace waited for an afternoon when my mother was volunteering and the Reverend was at the rectory. We sat in the kitchen, and she opened a board that had a moon-and-stars theme with a cobalt sky, white clouds, and silver celestial bodies across its surface.

"We don't understand the realm beyond this one. But I believe that mysteries like this are what gives our lives magic. What gives us hope and solace." She pushed the wooden, equally decorated planchette toward me.

"Ready?" she asked.

I was nervous. We were doing something the Reverend had forbidden. And when I spoke, my voice shook a bit. "Yes, Aunt Grace."

"First, place your fingers lightly on your side of the planchette, and I'll put mine on my side. I'll also write down the letters the pin points to— sometimes they go too fast to make sense of them until after we're done."

I did as she said but noticed my side of the planchette was leaning toward me.

"Don't press down so hard," Aunt Grace said.

I lightened my touch.

"Now, ask the spirits a question."

"What should I ask?"

"I usually start by asking who has come to visit."

I whispered the question into the ether, unsure if I felt silly or scared.

The planchette didn't move.

"Sometimes it takes more than one try. There

are spirits who need coaxing and reassurance that your heart is in your quest."

"Is anyone here?" I tried again.

Suddenly, the planchette took off and moved swiftly to the word *YES*.

I looked at Aunt Grace.

"Ask them who they are," she urged.

I did. The planchette moved again, quickly through the letters on the board, stopping for only a second before moving on. Aunt Grace wrote down the letters as they were chosen.

W-A-T-C-H-I-N-G-O-U-T-F-O-R-Y-O-U

I looked at my aunt for guidance once again.

"Ask the spirit who he or she is," she said.

I did.

Y-O-U-R-F-A-T-H-E-R

Frightened, I took my fingers off the planchette and slammed the board closed, nearly smashing my aunt's fingers in the process.

"No, no, Jenny. I don't want you to be afraid of this." She opened the board again. "Put your fingers back. We have to finish what we started, and then at the end, always remember to thank the spirit for coming and close the portal."

Despite my misgivings, I did as she said. Without my asking a new question, the planchette began to move again, and with one hand, Aunt Grace rushed to commit each letter to paper.

I still have it, a scrap, inscribed with long

strings of letters. In order to make sense of them, Aunt Grace separated each word with a slash.

COMFORT/WILL/COME/BUT/NOT/YET/ THERE/ARE/TRIALS/TO/ENDURE/BE/ STRONG

I kept the paper. Not because I thought my father's spirit had spoken to me—I didn't—but because I believed my aunt wanted me to have a talisman so much that she'd lied to give me one. A promise to hold on to. A remembrance of that afternoon, before the trouble started, the first and last time I ever touched a planchette.

6

My missing painting was not at the League. After class, Minx and I went to Mrs. Whitney's impressive Eighth Street studio, and the doyenne of New York's thriving art scene let me look through the storeroom, where paintings from recent shows were held until the artists or buyers came to pick them up. But my canvas wasn't there, either.

Minx and I left together. When we reached the corner of Sixth Avenue, she looked around for a taxi.

"Aren't you coming home to bathe and change?" I asked. We would be returning to Mrs. Whitney's in just a few hours for a party.

"Not yet. I'm just going to run uptown and pick something up."

Minx hadn't asked if I wanted to accompany her for shopping, which was unusual. Even though I couldn't afford the stores she frequented, I never got my fill of looking at all the beautiful objects and clothes. That was one of the best things about New York; not all the artwork in the city was showcased on gallery and museum walls.

"Suit yourself," I said.

I arrived home minutes later, grateful for the quiet but still troubled by my missing painting.

Perhaps I *had* simply imagined creating it. I hung up my jacket, put my satchel on the whatnot in the hallway, and went to the kitchen. I'd just made myself a cup of coffee and sat down at the table when the doorbell rang.

I looked through the peephole to see Minx's mother, arms laden with packages.

After opening the door, I helped her with her parcels and her coat, a luxurious chocolate mink that I brushed my fingers over as I hung it up.

Mrs. Deering smoothed her silk dress, which was the same deep hue as the coat, and readjusted a strand of glowing topaz stones that wrapped twice around her neck before hanging down to her belt. With expert fingers, she smoothed her chignon, the same golden color as her daughter's hair.

She sniffed the air. "I'd kill for a cup of that coffee. I've been shopping all day."

Minx made fun of her mother's shopping habit, referring to it as her vocation. "My mother was called to be a shopper the way some women are called to the nunnery," she once said.

I poured coffee into one of the fine Limoges cups and placed it on a saucer. Then I put a matching creamer and sugar bowl on the table along with a silver spoon. The French china and English silver were originally from Mrs. Deering's own collection. Seeing them, she looked at them as if they were old friends.

As she prepared her coffee, making it light and sweet, much like her own personality, she chatted about her day's excursions.

"I found these delightful bookends that I imagined would look perfect on that bookshelf and linen cocktail napkins with the cutest embroidered sayings on them for the bar. I can't wait to show you both. When will Minx be home?"

"In a little while, I expect. We're due for a fete tonight at Mrs. Whitney's studio."

"Well, we can just chat while we wait for her. Do you have any of those butter cookies I sent over on Saturday?"

"Actually, no, they're gone."

"All of them?" She looked at me askance.

Mrs. Deering was a tall, slim woman who spared no expense on her own face and figure. She bought the most luxurious creams and hired the most expensive masseurs, manicurists, hairdressers, and couturiers. She had a fine French chef at home and made sure she exercised enough by playing tennis and horseback riding and taking ballet classes to keep the weight off. The idea that we had devoured all the cookies she'd had delivered horrified her.

"Not just the two of us, Mrs. Deering. We had some friends over."

"I'm relieved. You're both quite attractive . . . but then you're still in your twenties. The battle hasn't really begun." Touching the fingers of her right hand to the top of her left, she pulled at her skin, which looked smooth to me. I thought once again of her husband's dalliances. It wasn't easy, Minx had said, even for someone as lovely as her mother, to be nearing fifty and know her husband was amusing himself with a much younger woman.

Picking up her cup, Mrs. Deering took a second dainty sip, being careful to drink from the same spot where she'd already left a lipstick print.

"You said you had friends over?" She fidgeted with the spoon, running her finger around and around its oval edge.

I wasn't sure if it was just small talk or if she was getting at something more. Nodding, I said we had.

"Minx's friends from Radcliffe?" More fiddling with the spoon.

"No, some students from the League and other artists."

"Have you met her old beau, Gerald? Has he come around?" Another sip.

"Not while I've been here. I haven't met anyone named Gerald."

As Mrs. Deering got up and walked into the living room, I remembered what Ben had told me just the evening before about Minx's beau from Harvard.

She stopped at the fireplace and rearranged all

the silver picture frames on the mantel. "That's better; they were off-center," she said.

She stood with one hand still on the mantel but now facing me. Not quite far enough away for me to miss that her hand was shaking just a little.

"If Gerald ever does reappear in Minx's life . . ." Mrs. Deering's voice trailed off.

"Yes?"

She walked back into the foyer and then into the kitchen. From where I sat, I watched her over by the window. First, she moved a china cachepot that held a jade tree two inches to the left. Then she moved it back.

"I don't want you to turn into a spy for me," she said.

"That's good, because I wouldn't feel right talking to you about Minx's boyfriends behind her back, Mrs. Deering, if that's what you're asking. If you have questions, you need to talk to Minx." I knew I could come off as too direct—a trait that had gotten me into trouble in the past—and worried I'd just crossed a line.

Judging from the annoyed expression on Mrs. Deering's face, I had.

"I'm sorry, but—"

She interrupted my apology. "This isn't quite that simple, Jenny."

"Then I don't understand."

"Gerald borrowed money from Minx and

never paid it back. He stole more than half of her jewelry and then sold it."

"Did he go to jail?"

Mrs. Deering shook her head. "No, Minx wouldn't admit he'd done it."

"Then why—"

"Has Minx ever mentioned spending time in Greenwich, Connecticut, last year?"

"No, she hasn't."

"Have you ever heard of Blythewood?"

I shook my head. Mrs. Deering, still standing by the window, played with her diamond and gold watch, clasping and unclasping it.

"I don't want to break any confidences, but it's important to her father and me that you know what occurred so that if you hear anything about Gerald or see any signs with Minx, you can contact us."

My stomach clenched with nerves. Signs? Was something wrong with Minx?

"Is she ill?"

"Not in the way you think, no." She looked at the stove. "Is there more coffee? No. Is there any Lillet?"

We always had a full liquor cabinet. Mr. Deering's ships smuggled in the best wines, aperitifs, and brandies. While the ships were docked in New York's harbor, as passengers disembarked and collected their luggage, men dressed as porters made sure certain trunks were

100

hustled away. While most of the hooch—as Minx jokingly called the fine French wine—went to speakeasies around the city, she always got a generous delivery.

"Yes, of course, let me get you some."

I took a Baccarat crystal wineglass off the second shelf of the bar cart, opened the bottle of the French aperitif, and poured. After I handed it to her, she took a long sip, paused, and then took another.

"Sit down," she said, patting the seat kitty-corner to the sofa.

I did as she suggested.

Once again, she lifted the glass to her lips and took another sip of the aperitif. Putting the glass down, she took what looked like a bracing breath, as if she needed courage to tell me about her daughter's "little problem."

"Minx got in with the wrong crowd in college, Jenny. She fell in with one young man who was killed in a car crash. Vulnerable from mourning him, she quickly fell in with another. Gerald Tanner, among other nefarious things, was, or still is, an opium addict." Mrs. Deering stopped, closed her eyes for a moment, shuddered from head to toe, then took another sip of her drink and continued.

"He got Minx addicted as well. It went on for more than a year before we found out. We had no choice in what we did. She was so young, so talented. And she was wasting away." Mrs. Deering leaned forward and whispered the last part. "We had to commit her to a sanitarium. Blythewood in Greenwich, Connecticut. She was there for half a year and has been out now for sixteen months. She's fine, but I worry all the time about how susceptible she is. I am well aware how many artists indulge in these filthy drugs. And Madame Zakine," Mrs. Deering said, mentioning the psychic she and her friends visited regularly, "says that someone in Minx's life is involved with drugs. I—we—Minx's father and I can't bear to see her hurt again. That's why I was hoping I'd find you here alone today."

I'd believed she stopped by simply to visit Minx. But now I realized that had been a ruse. She wanted to talk to me without Minx present. I felt used and at the same time sorry for Mrs. Deering. But I was even more sorry for Minx. This was the second tragic story I'd heard about her in as many days.

"Her father and I will do anything for her and for you, if you'll keep an eye out. You seem like such a good girl and a wonderful friend to our daughter. Please, if you see the slightest sign that suggests she is once again involved in anything that we should be worried about, tell us. We worry all the time, and Madame Zakine says—"

The sound of the key in the lock startled both of us, and we turned in unison to the door and watched Minx step inside. She took another step. Noticed the wineglass and the bottle of Lillet.

"What do you worry about all the time, Mumsy?" Minx asked.

Mrs. Deering lied and told her she was worried because Madame Zakine had given her a warning about Minx being alone at night. Then she gave Minx the cocktail napkins and the bookends and left in a flurry of kisses.

Once Minx closed the door, she waited until she heard the elevator arrive and depart and then asked me, "OK, Jenny, spill. What was my mother really talking to you about?"

"She really *was* talking to me about how worried she and your father are about you being alone. Especially because of Madame Zakine's reading."

"I know she hates that sometimes we walk home at night from the clubs unescorted, but I've told her about you and the purse incident." Minx shook her head. "Besides, every criminal knows all us artists and writers and musicians down here are broke! They're after the tourists who are gawking at the rest of us like we're animals in some zoo. I've assured her a dozen times that I don't wear a sign on my forehead that says my parents are immensely wealthy and my pearls are real."

I giggled in spite of myself.

"It's good they only had one child," Minx

continued. "They'd drive themselves to drink if they had three or four of us to worry about. Now, come into my bedroom so we can go through my closet and find something for you to wear tonight."

I was relieved she hadn't second-guessed my response about her parents' concerns. But then again, I lied expertly. I'd learned at my mother's feet, along with how to paint.

My lie to Minx wasn't dangerous. Just a little "white lie," as my mother would have called it. Like the kind she told the Reverend when he complained that she spent too much money on my clothes or books or art supplies. Or when she said that no, there were no Ouija boards in the house, that she'd given up painting them.

Besides, my lie to Minx was justified. I hadn't asked to know her secret, but now that I did, I would keep watch over her. Opium was far too dangerous a drug to be shrugged off. Champagne and highballs were one thing, but this was serious. And Minx was my closest friend. My only friend. Her parents wanted to keep her safe, and so did I.

We stood in front of her closet as she sifted through the satin hangers searching for just the right outfit for me.

"Where did you run off to this afternoon?" I asked her.

"I stopped by Tiffany's for a quick second to

pick up the sterling-silver card holder I had engraved for my mother's birthday."

Before I could ask why she hadn't suggested I come—she knew how much I enjoyed visiting the store and looking at all the beautiful things on display—she pulled out a sleeveless scarlet silk frock.

"I think this one," Minx said, as she held it up to my face and we both looked at my reflection in the mirror. "It's the perfect complement to your hair." She pulled out a scarlet beaded purse. "Now for a bag . . . And shoes . . ." She picked up a pair of satin ones to match. Laying it all out on her bed, she inspected the outfit and deemed it perfect.

When I'd first moved in, I'd refused to borrow Minx's clothes, but she soon wore me down. I wished I could buy lovely things, but my salary didn't afford me any luxuries. My wardrobe was meager; whatever extra money I had went to art supplies. I owned only serviceable garments in blacks and browns—trousers and smocks for school, a few skirts and sweaters and blouses for day, and one good black dress and a pair of satin shoes for evening.

After I'd trotted out that black outfit for the fifth time, Minx refused to take me with her.

"You've worn that dress so many times the fabric is starting to get shiny, and it's not satin, it's crepe," she said with mock outrage, sounding just like her mother. "And really, Jenny, it's so old-fashioned it makes you look like someone's maiden aunt, not a Greenwich Village artiste. Where did you even buy it?"

"I didn't. It was my aunt's."

Minx gave me a meaningful look, as if to say, *There's your proof that this isn't age-appropriate.*

Now I slipped Minx's shift over my head and felt the cool silk caress my skin, wishing Aunt Grace could see me. She loved beautiful things and always took care to tell me how pretty I was. The sensation of the fabric made me think of many of the men I had encountered while living here and the looks they gave me, even though I'd vowed to focus on my studies and not be distracted. For now, nothing mattered more than my career. Certainly not a man. A man who, for all his kindness and sweet talk, could turn on you, cheat on you, and change you.

Minx never believed in being early to an event or even on time. So after we finished dressing, she opened a bottle of champagne, and we had cocktails.

At seven thirty, we left the apartment and walked, for the second time that day, the two short blocks to Mrs. Whitney's studio. The Village was crowded with cars and pedestrians on their way to restaurants, clubs, and vaudeville revues. Tourists came from all over the city and out of town to experience the counterculture where art, sex, and a disdain for the wealthy reigned. Since the end of the war, prices had been driven up, and it was getting harder for artists to live in the neighborhood, but it was still the center of our world.

We arrived to a party well under way. Mrs. Whitney's opening receptions were elaborate celebrations. Ben Montgomery waved when he saw us come in and made his way over to us.

"Are you here reporting on the opening?" Minx asked.

He shook his head. "I never cover the society news." He pointed to someone in the crowd. "Alan Green does. He's here with a photographer. I'm off for the night."

A waiter passed by with a tray of champagne, and Ben took two glasses, handing one to Minx and one to me, then taking a third for himself.

Having already had a glass at home, my second went straight to my head. But that was all right, because it would have been difficult looking at the artwork while sober. The artist, Jock Alexander, a tall Texan with a slow drawl and a wild spirit whose work often pushed boundaries, had painted a series of highly eroticized nudes of women pleasuring themselves. I'd seen both Klimt's and Rodin's erotic drawings, but I didn't know those artists or their models personally. Able to examine them dispassionately, I hadn't

107

been deeply affected by them. But I knew Jock. He was a friend of Minx's, often at the apartment and part of the crowd she went with to clubs and dinners. To look at these deeply personal, intimate portraits of naked women with their hands between their legs, heads back, eyes closed, lost in their own fantasies, made me shiver. In order to paint these, Jock must have used models. I moved from one to the next, wondering if I was blushing, afraid I might recognize one of them.

And then I did. I was certain I was looking at a painting of Minx. I didn't even know she had dated Jock, but she and I had been friends for less than a year. There were probably quite a few men in her past I wasn't aware of.

The nudes we painted and drew in class were objectified and desexualized. The act of them posing, their stances, all of us sitting or standing in a utilitarian studio studying them, neutered their nudity. But this private glimpse into a woman I knew shocked me.

"Isn't it too much?" Minx asked, as she came up beside me.

"So it is you?"

She winked. "Who else do we know who is a natural blonde?"

Leave it to Minx to be so blasé about it. We'd talked quite a bit about sex. Her experience far surpassed mine. I'd had a few brief romances back in Ithaca with college men who'd imagined a working girl would be easy to seduce with fancy dinners and sweet talk. My one serious relationship, with Lawrence Rice, a teacher at Cornell's art school, only lasted a little more than two months. Lawrence offered classes during the summer outside the university purview, and I'd signed up. Our ardor for each other burned brightly during those eight weeks. I even wondered if I might be in love with him, until I realized he wanted me to admire his talent and cater to him but never took my career seriously.

Of course, I couldn't stay with him. I'd known ever since that fateful afternoon when I watched the Reverend destroy one of my mother's Ouija boards and threaten her with it, then watched him rape her, that no man would ever denigrate what I did. I would never be under any man's thumb, even if it meant being alone. I took my cues from Aunt Grace, who advocated for bachelorhood over servitude. "Always have lovers, Jenny, never masters," she told me. "I've lived by that rule, and I've never regretted it."

Now Minx tipped her glass toward the canvas. "So what do you think?"

"How did you ever have the nerve to let him paint you like that?" I asked.

"How long have you known me, and you don't know the answer? For the shock value, Jenny. For the look on your face. For this moment."

"What if Edward sees it?"

She grinned wickedly. "I want him to—he should be here soon."

"You're a very bad girl," I said. "What if your *parents* see it?"

She stuck her nose up in the air. "If it's not in a Fifth Avenue gallery, they won't see it. Besides, it doesn't look that much like me."

"I recognized you."

"No, you wondered. And that's just because you have a painter's sensibility."

"Was Jock your lover?"

"For a few minutes last year. But other than his paintings, he's really quite boring." She drained what was left of her champagne, linked her arm in mine, and pulled me away. "Let's go get you tipsy. It's a party, Jenny. You don't have to stand so straight. The whole point of me making you wear that dress was so that when you relaxed, it would slip off your shoulder, and all the boys would see how fetching you can be."

At the bar, Minx blanched when a debonair older gentleman with a French accent made a big fuss over seeing her. "I'm here because I'm considering representing Jock," he said. "What do you think of that? But first, please introduce me to your friend."

Minx grabbed my hand and squeezed it hard.

"Monsieur Vallain has a wonderful gallery on the rue La Boetie in Paris," she said. "He handles Matisse and Vlaminck and Juan Gris. And my parents"—she squeezed harder—"buy quite a bit from his gallery." She swallowed her laughter. She'd been so sure her parents would never see Jock's portrait of her. I knew she was thinking of what would happen if Monsieur Vallain did indeed take him on.

Monsieur Vallain was gracious and, with what seemed like sincerity, inquired about my work.

Minx didn't even give me a chance to reply.

"She's too shy to tell you anything. But Jenny does the most dramatic monochromatic studies. Stark and utterly realistic. Quite shocking, really. She is on a quest to capture light."

The dealer asked me a few questions about my influences, and I answered the best I could, citing many of the greats. He listened intently to my answers, then asked my opinion of Rembrandt's use of light versus Caravaggio's, why I was following a Renaissance approach to light rather than the more modern masters, and what I thought the impressionists' work with light would look like drained of color. More than once during the erudite conversation, I feared I was out of my depth, but from the way he leaned in and listened to me, he seemed to be taking me seriously enough.

Minx hung back, sipped her champers, and looked delighted. She often complained that I was my own worst salesman and that until I learned to be bold and talk about my own work and ambitions, I'd never get anywhere as an artist. While I didn't disagree with Minx, I was reluctant to talk too much about my past. When it came time to tell Monsieur Vallain what had inspired me first on my quest to study light, I had to be careful, especially since my greatest inspiration was back in Hamilton, the site of my tragedy.

Minx had disappeared during the last part of my conversation with the dealer, but she approached now, arm in arm with Edward, whom she enthusiastically presented to Monsieur Vallain.

"And here's another artist you should know about: Edward Wren. His canvases are so real, so raw, so very much a response to our times."

Edward shook the dealer's proffered hand in his typical aloof style. I never knew if he really was uninterested in most people or acting that way to hide some other emotion. Like his paintings, there was a lot going on, much of it beneath the surface.

As Monsieur Vallain was now engaged with Edward, I took the opportunity to go and say hello to some of the other students from the League whom I hadn't yet greeted.

I'd been at the party for about an hour when I happened to be facing the foyer and noticed a new arrival. Mrs. Whitney approached the man, linked her arm in his, and waltzed him over to the bar, chatting with him the whole time.

He looked familiar. After watching him for a few moments, I was sure we'd never met, yet I felt I knew him. Then I realized, as impossible as it seemed, that I'd drawn him. He was so like a classic marble statue that I'd seen and drawn. There'd been a copy at the art school in Ithaca and the original in the Metropolitan Museum. And now, here he was, Antonio Canova's Perseus, come to life. Long and slim, he walked with a fluid grace and the hint of a limp. His jet hair fell in waves around his face, framing strong bones, icy blue eyes, and a mouth that struck me as tender. I wanted to go up to him and touch him, to see if he was real, if his skin was warm. There was nothing I wanted more in that moment than simply to be near him.

The experience was strange and made me think of Aunt Grace reminding me that when something unusual or special happened, even if we didn't understand it completely, we should embrace it and be grateful for it.

"You're staring, Jenny. Let me introduce you." Minx started to walk me toward the stranger, who watched our approach, a smile playing around his mouth. "He's the grandson of—"

Minx was about to tell me his name when there was a loud crash, a shout, and a scream.

In the main gallery, one of Mrs. Whitney's sculptures—a three-foot statue of a winsome young child—had fallen off its pedestal and shattered. The pedestal had toppled over as well and lay on Jock's foot. From his screams and the pained expression on his face, the stone column must have been crushing his bones. Celia Beacon, one of our classmates, stood by the wall, screaming. Her beau, Sam Framingham, another classmate, stood above Jock, jacket and tie askew, nose bleeding, in shock as he assessed all the damage.

Suddenly, camera flashbulbs went off, and I heard the click of a shutter. The reporter Ben had pointed out to us in the crowd when we first arrived took a second photo and then pulled out a pad and started scribbling.

From behind me, Ben whispered, "Too bad you aren't recording the scene with a sketch, Jenny. You'd do a much better job than that grainy photo."

The guests in the gallery became deathly silent as Mrs. Whitney approached the scene, taking in the tall Texan doing his best not to howl and the dozens of pieces of plaster scattered on the highly polished wood floor.

For a moment, Mrs. Whitney's face broke, and she grimaced in pain as if the pedestal had fallen on top of her. I didn't think her pain was sympathy for Jock but rather her horror over her ruined sculpture. I would have felt the same anguish. Months of work, an achievement, a piece of her soul, destroyed in what had devolved into a drunken fight between two jealous lovers.

For a few brief seconds, Mrs. Whitney remained in shock over the destruction. Then reason replaced emotion, and she flew into action, expressing worry and concern over her visiting artist and tending to his foot.

As we found out later, Jock and Celia had once been an item, and during that period, he'd used her as a model. The nude of her hung on the wall not far from Minx's. Sam had recognized Celia immediately and lost his temper over the lascivious painting. Enraged, he told Jock to take it down, and when Jock refused, Sam threw the first punch.

Mrs. Whitney determined that Jock had to be taken to the hospital and mobilized two men to help him get up and half-carry, half-walk him out. The sculpture pieces had to be collected, which Minx and I began to do. Celia had to be calmed, and Sam was escorted out.

As we cleaned up the mess, I looked around for the stranger to whom Minx had never managed to introduce me, but I didn't spot him anywhere. I felt a wave of disappointment and then surprise at my reaction. Aunt Grace had once told me that we can romanticize the unknown far too easily. It is much harder but more satisfying to assign wonder to what we were familiar with.

While we gathered up plaster chips and

chunks, Minx confided that the piece was a very important commission to Mrs. Whitney. She broke off and glanced over at Ben. "You are off for the night, right?" she asked him.

"Anything you say is off the record," he said.

"It's just so sad, and I wouldn't want to talk out of school. Mrs. Whitney planned on sending this to the foundry tomorrow. The eight-year-old little girl portrayed was a cousin of hers who died six months ago. The piece was for her gravesite."

With the cleanup completed, Minx organized her group, and we walked en masse to a speakeasy on Fourth Street that always had an excellent jazz band and liquor that wasn't too watered down.

Minx's parents' dealer tagged along, and there were ten of us crowded around a table, including Ben and Edward. Usually, we were a more boisterous group, but we were subdued that night. Listening to the blues, sipping bourbon, the air smoky with cigarettes and sweet with marijuana, we talked about the fight and Jock's work and the power of art to incite feelings. Ben mentioned the novel he was working on and how one of his themes was how dangerous and exhilarating it could be when feelings overtook logic.

Edward downed his drink and signaled the waiter for another. He took Minx's hand, held it, and then, after a moment, began stroking it hypnotically. I didn't remember having seen him do that before, yet something about the action was not only familiar but disturbing. The memory tickled my subconscious, but I couldn't pull up when or if I'd ever seen anyone do it before.

Ben must have sensed my agitation, because he slipped his arm around my shoulder. I found myself surprised at what a relief it was to feel it there.

"I can't stop picturing Mrs. Whitney's face when she saw that sculpture shattered," Minx said, unable to move past the scene at the gallery.

"We are a strange lot," I said, as I played with the cocktail napkin under my drink. "No matter where we come from or how much money we have or don't have, our need to create eclipses all else."

"Why are some people so committed to recreating the world around them, to synthesizing their surroundings and remaking them in their own vision? And others take the world at face value and are satisfied?" the French dealer asked.

It was a good question, and no one had an answer. I examined the faces of the three musicians on the slightly elevated platform at the front of the room. They'd taken in the world and were synthesizing it through horns and strings. The blues that emerged, filling the club with sad magic, were a reflection of our times as much as the paintings, the sculptures, the novels, the poems, and the plays were.

New York City in 1924, like so many other cities in America and Europe, was jam-packed with people doing everything they could to push the war and its horrors deeper into the background. We all knew someone who had died or who'd had a loved one die. Those of us who'd survived, either at home or at the front, had nightmares still. And I knew all too well how nightmares lingered. How they haunted your days. I had gone through my own battles, while the boys were overseas fighting the Huns. I had witnessed death at home, while they saw it on the battlefields in France and Germany. The music that summoned up their sorrows conjured mine as well. This place, this city, this life, was so different from where I had been just one year before. But as the band played on, I began to wonder how far I would need to go to truly escape my past.

7

I didn't have weekend classes, so the next day, Saturday, I worked at Mrs. Bullard's from noon through supper. Weekends were always the most hectic because of all the tourists coming to Greenwich Village to glimpse us bohemians—to visit jazz clubs and speakeasies, see revues, or experience an afternoon of titillating radicalism.

I served refreshments, sandwiches, and desserts, wrote checks, took money, made change, answered questions, and gave directions. As busy as I was, every so often, I'd think about my missing painting. I didn't know why I was letting it bother me. It wasn't as if any of my canvases was worth anything, as I'd never sold a single one.

As I served a middle-aged couple tea followed by egg sandwiches, I couldn't help overhearing their conversation.

"That house is my home, Billy. I was born there. It's where I have always gone when I need to feel safe. It's where my memories live."

The man took his wife's hand. "But moving in with your mother means giving up our own home."

Walking away, I realized that was why the missing painting disturbed me so much. My paintings were my home. My security. Other people returned to their families when things went wrong or to satiate loneliness or celebrate wonderful occasions. They visited parents and siblings and aunts and uncles and grandparents to remind them of their roots.

I had no home. And no family, since Aunt Grace's death. My father had been an only child, and there were some distant cousins on my mother's side, but I'd never met them and wouldn't know how to find them. My memories lived only in my paintings.

It was just me, on my own. Minx was as close as a friend could be, but it wasn't the same.

By six that evening, the crowd had thinned and I'd started to clean up for the day. A half hour later, Mrs. Bullard switched the *Open* sign to *Closed,* gave me a bag of doughnuts that wouldn't stay fresh till Monday, and said good night.

I walked out and into the cool evening.

"Hello there." Ben Montgomery was leaning against the lamppost.

I was surprised to see him and a bit wary. "Well, hello to you, too. I suppose you were just passing by?"

"No, just waiting for you," he answered. "That was some night last night, right? I was hoping you'd let me take you out for dinner. In what will be a quieter setting."

"Why?"

Ben let out a chuckle. "There you go again with your straightforwardness." He paused when he saw me bristle. "I was hoping you'd let me take you out to dinner because you worked all day and so did I, and I thought us breaking bread and having some spaghetti would be a nice way to spend the evening."

He was a bit nervy, not even apologizing about him and Minx tricking me by publishing my drawing without my consent.

"Mr. Montgomery, I usually go home and paint when I get off work. I don't have a lot of time to spare, and what time I do have I need to manage carefully."

"There's a little Italian speakeasy not far from here on Minetta Lane that I know. The best spaghetti in town. Dinner won't take more than an hour. Surely you have to eat. Surely you can spare an hour."

"Why would I want to? You're just going to badger me about that job. I can't figure out why it matters to you, anyway."

I started walking west, and he kept pace. The truth was that he was beginning to tempt me.

"I won't mention the job—which, by the way, matters to me because I want our paper to sell better than the competition, and my editor agrees your drawings would give us some real excitement. C'mon, Jenny, let's just have dinner.

Get to know each other better." He cocked his head bemusedly. "You know, you're a very curious girl."

"Which doesn't always work in my favor," I said.

We reached Seventh Avenue and waited for the light to turn. Yes, Minx was right about Ben. He was interesting and appealing. But I wasn't in the market for a boyfriend. Unlike my roommate, who couldn't live without two or three at any given moment, I didn't want the distraction. I'd promised myself not to get involved until I'd established myself as an artist.

The light changed. Ben took my arm, and we crossed the avenue. I didn't want him to touch me, but I knew that pushing back would make far more of a statement than simply walking along. We reached Greenwich Avenue. From here, I'd head east and north to go home.

"So what do you say?" he asked. "Doesn't a girl have to eat?"

What made me say yes? The gentle pressure on my arm? The way his skin crinkled around his eyes? Minx's insistence that I was too much of a loner and it wasn't good for me?

"It's not that complicated, Jenny. Just a plate of spaghetti. I promise not to be rude or spill food on my shirt."

"Or grill me?"

He cocked his head and gave me an inquisitive

look. "Do you think I grill people? Yes, I suppose I do. Nature of the job. But I promise not to do that to you."

"OK," I said. "Sure, a girl's got to eat."

So we began to head south.

"Minx told me you're from Ithaca," he said.

"I am."

"Small world. A buddy of mine who works for the *Times* grew up there in Cayuga Heights. I went home with him once for Thanksgiving."

"Oh, that's the rich part of town. Far, far away from us." I realized how bitter I sounded. "Where did you grow up?"

"Here, in the city."

"And then off to Harvard?" I knew this already but wanted to keep the conversation from drifting back to Ithaca.

"We went over that terrain the other day."

"So we did. What did you study at Harvard? We didn't go over that terrain."

"Literature. I wanted to go into the family business and be a writer."

We reached MacDougal Street and went east.

We walked half a block and then stopped at a brownstone with a wrought-iron gate. Ben rang the bell. We waited a moment, and then a buzzer sounded. Ben opened the gate and held it for me. We walked down three steps to a door. Ben knocked. A light shone in a peephole, and then the door opened.

"Mr. Montgomery, it's so good to see you," the proprietor said. "Welcome, welcome." His apron was stained with red sauce, and he smelled of garlic and oregano. My mouth began to water.

Ben introduced me to the proprietor, whose name was Sal. He took my hand, said he was pleased to meet me, and ushered us to a corner table in the back. A waiter immediately brought over glasses of water and a basket of bread, breadsticks, and butter. Ben ordered a bottle of red wine.

"Now, why is it you're worried about me grilling you?" Ben asked, once we'd been served the wine. "Though I can't imagine there's anything I could ask that you wouldn't want to tell me," he continued. "I'm not one of those guys who are curious about the secrets of women's love lives. I hope you have one. Or at least want one. But that's as far as that goes."

I laughed in spite of myself. "Well, that's a relief, because my string of suitors is so long I'm afraid I wouldn't be able to remember them all for the telling."

Ben chuckled, a deep caramel-colored sound that was warm and inviting.

The waiter arrived with menus. As I read the offerings, I reexamined what I was doing at the restaurant. Shouldn't I be home painting?

But I heard Minx's voice in my head: *It's not healthy for you to stay home so many nights just painting . . . you're already more conscientious than any other student at the League . . . you deserve to have some fun, too.*

Ben looked up from the menu. "Did you decide what you want?"

I said I did, and he motioned for the waiter to come over. I ordered the veal parmesan. Ben ordered the same plus an order of spaghetti and meatballs. The waiter topped off our glasses and walked away.

"So tell me about your painting. Where did you study before you came to New York?" he asked.

I took a sip of the sharp and fruity homemade wine. Ben offered me the bread basket, and I took a slice of soft semolina. He took one, too, and slathered his with butter.

"I thought no grilling." I knew he couldn't help it, but I really didn't want to be interviewed.

"Even about your artwork?"

I shook my head.

"OK, then, how about you ask me the questions?"

"Now, that's an idea." I was thankful for the reprieve and appreciated his offer. It was pleasant to be having dinner with someone other than Minx. "Let's start where you did. Tell me about when you were a student. What was the best thing about your time at Harvard?"

Ben looked wistful. "I loved college. I was one of the lucky students. I didn't have to work for tuition. My father paid my way and encouraged me to study what I was interested in. There were a lot of chaps who wished they could indulge in literature and the classics but were studying the law or medicine or business because it was expected of them. But Dad said if I was going to be a writer, nothing would be wasted."

"You *were* lucky. Did you write while you were at Harvard?"

"Yes, I got a job as a reporter for the *Crimson* and worked my way up to editor."

"Which, of course, made your father proud."

"Very proud." Ben raised his sleeve a little and showed me a fine gold watch on a black leather band. "His gift to me."

He unstrapped it, flipped it over, and handed it to me.

To Ben, my son, my pride. I ran my fingers over the letters, thinking about my own father and wondering how different my life would have been if he'd lived.

"I've worn it every day," Ben said. "Even when I didn't make him proud. And when he didn't make me proud, either."

"What did you do that he wasn't proud of?"

"He didn't like it when I returned to California to work on a novel after only a year at the paper with him."

"Why did you leave?"

"Have you ever lived through something that

126

you just couldn't process? That was just too big to make sense of?"

I nodded, not trusting myself to say anything for fear there would be too much emotion in my voice.

"My father was involved in a scandal. I couldn't accept he'd done what he'd been accused of. I needed to get some distance from him and the paper and our life."

"What brought you back?"

Ben looked away. "After he died, I needed to be at the paper. He loved it so much, and it was where I felt closest to him. I suppose I wanted him to forgive me for leaving. But he's the one who left."

Ben's grief was so swift yet palpable that I reached across the table and took his hand.

"I'm sorry. I lost both my parents. I know how much it can hurt."

For a few moments, neither of us said anything.

"I think I'm over it," he said. "But . . ."

"I don't think that you ever really get past losing a parent." I took a long sip of my wine.

"Tell me about your parents," he said.

I chose to tell him the easy part that I'd told Minx and her family, that I told anyone who asked.

"My father was an architect, and my mother was a painter. In addition to fine watercolors of flowers and birds, she decorated Ouija boards for the Kennard Novelty Company. Which is by far the most interesting thing about my childhood," I lied.

"Ouija boards? That *must* have been interesting. Did you get to talk to many ghosts?" Ben followed up the question with a ghostlike *WOOOO* sound.

I ignored this. "My family saw them as novelties for the most part," I said, not mentioning Aunt Grace's ability.

The waiter brought our food. Ben was right about how good it was. The veal was succulent, and the sauce was the perfect blend of garlic and oregano, with creamy melted cheese covering everything.

"This is delicious. The kind of food you dream about," I said.

"What else do you dream about?" He leaned across the table with an earnest expression on his kind face.

I was silent for a moment, wondering whether his question had been an earnest one. "Going to Paris to study art."

"Well, that's exactly why you should come work for the *Herald Tribune*. Minx said you both have a place to stay with her family and only need to save enough for the ship and living expenses. If the paper prints five or six drawings a week you could earn enough in a few months to do that."

I considered my meager savings and allowed myself to contemplate growing them that quickly.

"Paris is a damn beautiful city. Have you ever been?" he asked.

"No, but my mother had a book about Paris, and when I was little, we'd talk about going there. We'd pore over the pictures, picking out all the museums we'd see and all the artists' studios we'd visit." I hadn't been reminded of those conversations in so long. My words caught in my throat.

Now it was Ben's turn to take my hand. "It's so hard to lose the people we care about."

"It is," I whispered.

"When did your mother die?" he asked, in a kind voice.

"In 1916."

"How?"

"Giving birth to a baby who would have been my brother. But he was stillborn."

"And your father? When did you lose him?"

"He died a month before I was born."

Ben frowned. "So you have a stepfather?"

Ben was a reporter. I had to be careful with what I said.

"My stepfather was just another old so-and-so. I lived with my aunt after my mother died. I'd much rather hear about what you saw in Paris, if you don't mind. Minx and I are going to live in an apartment in Montmartre. Did you go there?

Where did you stay? Did you see any artists?"

Ben chortled, and before he could tell me what he found so funny, the waiter approached the table to refill our glasses. Ben thanked him, and then I asked, "Are you going to let me in on the joke?"

"You ask as many questions as I do. You should be a reporter."

I took another sip of wine. "Details fascinate me. When I paint, I'm looking for those infinitesimal differences in light that can entirely change a painting. Have you ever seen Monet's haystacks or his water lilies or his paintings of the Seine? He painted some of the same exact views twenty or thirty times, each at a different hour of the day in different weather conditions. And every one of them is completely unique, with its own mood and sensibility. All because of the property of the light."

"My, you're a very serious girl about your art, aren't you?"

"You say that as if you think it's unusual."

"I suppose I do. Since the war, so many men and women have stopped taking things seriously. A lot of girls I've met who claim to be painters or writers or reporters are just biding time, waiting to get married."

"That's what drew me to Minx," I told him. "Why we are such good friends. We're not looking to get married and have babies. We're dedicated to our art."

Ben raised his glass to me. "To artists."

I felt a new suffusion of warmth from the wine and then realized I hadn't actually taken another sip.

We finished our food, and a couple of times, I found Ben's eyes on me, studying me the way I sometimes looked at something I was painting.

Finally, I asked him, "Do I have sauce on my nose or on my blouse?"

"No, no. I'm sorry. I was just thinking about how I'd describe you if I was going to write about you."

All the warmth from the conversation and the wine was replaced with a chilly frisson of apprehension.

"Write about me? Why would you?"

He sensed my change of mood immediately. "Not in an article. Not like that. I was thinking of my novel. I started it three years ago. Nowhere near done. There's a young artist in it, surprisingly like you, and I was just thinking that I should give her your coloring. That exact shade of russet hair. And your eyes. You're the painter—what color blue are your eyes?"

"My mother said they are peacock blue," I said, thinking of the feather she painted once to show me the color. I had the sketch still, in a box along with a very few other keepsakes that my aunt had managed to save for me when she went to Hamilton to clean out the parsonage.

"Peacock blue," he mused. "I'm always searching for different words to use to say the same thing. I have to remember that." He pulled out a notebook and a pencil and jotted down the information.

I examined my glass and finished the last sip of the remaining wine.

"What is it that you are afraid of me seeing?" Ben whispered, as he pocketed the notebook.

"Absolutely nothing. I was just raised to believe being nosy is rude."

"If I remember that, can I see you again?" He caught my eye.

"Can you really *not* ask questions? It's in your nature, isn't it? It's your job."

"It is, but I think it might be enough just to know you now."

I didn't know what to say, and Ben looked as if he didn't, either.

His mouth moved as if he were going to ask me something else, but instead, he leaned forward and kissed me.

I tasted the wine and a little of the garlicky sauce. Rather than excitement—which I expected from a first kiss with someone—the move reassured me. I didn't pull back.

"I'm not sorry I did that," he said, sitting back in his chair with an expression full of mischief. "And I don't think you are, either—but note, I'm not asking you if you are."

I grinned nervously yet felt a release of tension. "Jenny Bell, you're quite an enigma. But that's true of every artist. And I'd rather be with a woman who can't be fully known than one who is all surface and no soul."

8

In the end, I accepted the job at the newspaper because of Paris. Because of the dream of going to study at the feet of the masters. I switched my painting classes to Saturday and my figure-drawing class to a night class. I even managed to keep my same teachers.

And so it was that on a brisk Monday morning in April, I took a very deep breath and climbed up the steps of the New York County Courthouse. I walked down its hallowed halls under richly painted ceilings into a courtroom to bear witness to a murder trial and to sketch the men and women who were taking the stand.

I expected my first time in court would be an ordeal and tried to steel myself to remain a removed observer. But as soon as the judge, in his stark black robes, took his seat, I panicked. All too familiar, the scene brought back a barrage of memories. Sweat dripped down my back. My hands shook. I struggled to draw a line that didn't waver.

All the while, my mind kept returning to the events that had brought me into another courtroom eight years before in Hamilton, Ontario.

At night, I would hear Mother crying and want to protect her, but the Reverend took to locking my door, and all I could do was escape out of my window and run, far away from the parsonage, into the cemetery and down the paths to my sanctuary, the mausoleum and the Tiffany window.

Mother made every effort to shield me from her misery, and in so many ways, we continued to make the most of our lives, despite the dark presence of the Reverend. I had friends at school whom I liked. Aunt Grace visited occasionally and wrote us many letters. Mother became more and more involved in community service and teaching art classes to factory families on the other side of town.

The next eighteen months passed, and by the time I was sixteen, I was winning awards for my artwork at school. Mother continued encouraging me, and I painted regularly, both in the crypt and in the lush areas and waterfalls near the parsonage. The world outside was full of beauty despite what went on inside our home. Mother finally had given up decorating Ouija boards, much to Aunt Grace's shock and concern. And I kept the only one remaining hidden underneath a loose floorboard in my closet. But the Reverend's abuse worsened.

When my mother became pregnant, the Reverend found the idea of soiling his unborn child with sex repulsive.

And so he decided that he wanted me.

He never got his wish. The one time he tried, my mother came into my room and found him hovering over my bed. Her shout woke me up. I looked up into his bloodshot eyes and smelled his stinking breath. My mother somehow dragged him from my room and locked him out.

While the Reverend slept it off in the yard, Mother sat with me in my darkened room and told me her plan. She'd sold as many of the Reverend's gifts as she dared and hidden away enough money for us to leave. And it was time. We'd do it the very next day. She wanted me to go to school as if nothing had happened, as if nothing were different. Except I was not to come home. She told me to set up my paints where I always did—below the waterfall—and wait till I saw her on the bridge. That would be my signal. We'd leave from there. The only thing I'd be taking with me were the clothes I was wearing and the paints I had with me. But we'd be fine, she promised. We'd be going back to Ithaca to live with Aunt Grace, who by that time knew about the Reverend's abuse. My mother's pride had held out for as long as it could, but eventually, she had confessed our sad situation to her dear, strong sister.

So the next day, I went to school. And afterward I went to paint at the foot of the falls. As she'd told me to do, I set up my easel in my favorite spot. I'd been there for almost an hour when I finally saw her on the bridge. I packed my paints and started to walk up the path to meet her. But before I got there, the Reverend did. He must have been suspicious and followed her. I watched as he grabbed her. They fought. I could see their mouths moving, but the waterfall's roar muffled the sound of their words. Then the Reverend slapped her. For a moment, she cowered, but then something rose up in her and she pushed him away. After that, it happened so fast. One moment there were two people on the bridge, and the next there was just one.

I ran up as fast as I could and then out onto the bridge. My mother and I stood there, holding each other, watching the water toss his body against the rocks.

The court system in Canada was not all that different from that in the United States, and during my first two days on the job for the *Herald Tribune*, I kept remembering the courtroom battle following the Reverend's death. The *Hamilton Spectator* had called it the "Trial of the Century," though it had happened as early as 1916.

Now I cursed myself for taking this job. I should have listened when my instincts told me that returning to a courtroom, any courtroom, would take me back to the darkest days of my life.

But I'd pressed on, my pride and the promise

of Paris pushing me. After my initial attack of nerves, I discovered that the act of sketching distracted me from my past. With my pencil moving over the paper, I didn't think about myself at all but only about capturing the expressions of the people involved in the trial.

That day's proceedings made the front page of the following morning's *Herald Tribune*, and the article featured two of my drawings. By the time the jury delivered its verdict on Friday, I'd had five drawings in the paper and made a nice bundle of cash.

The following week, the next "Trial of the Century" started—*The City of New York vs. Alfred Halstead*. The sordid murder involved a prominent New York banker, his wife, his daughter, his mistress, and his daughter's lover. The public defender called witnesses to the stand who laid out a tale of greed and passion. According to the lawyer, Halstead's mistress and his daughter's lover, a tennis player named Adam Allen, conspired together to steal more than a million dollars in artwork and jewelry from the Halstead home.

After Halstead discovered the robbery, he guessed who was behind it. He hadn't trusted Allen from the start and wasted no time in hiring a private detective to tail his daughter's boyfriend and confirm his worst fears.

But Halstead hadn't considered Allen's accomplice. That discovery was made when the PI gave Halstead his first report. The tennis player's address was listed as 112 East Sixty-first Street, apartment 10E. A very familiar address to Halstead, for it belonged to his mistress.

Halstead doted on his daughter, Dorothea, and didn't want her hurt. He planned on going to see Allen and threatening to go public—which would ruin the tennis player's reputation—if Allen didn't return the jewelry and then break it off with Dorothea.

Allen wasn't at the apartment, but Halstead's mistress, Mildred Conners, was. They fought, which culminated in her pulling a gun on him. But he had brought his own gun, anticipating trouble with Allen, and he was by far the quicker shot.

Mildred died. And now Halstead was on trial. Meanwhile, no one knew where Allen was.

Halstead's wife had stood by him. Dorothea had not. Refusing to believe Allen was implicated, she took her lover's side. And all of New York had become fascinated by the sensational trial. The descriptions of the jewelry that had been stolen had the entire courtroom salivating. Pieces from Cartier, Van Cleef & Arpels, and Tiffany & Co. were shown as evidence, and from my seat in the front row of the gallery, I could see their details.

I think I enjoyed drawing the jewelry as much

as the people. I'd never focused on jewels before, and I became fascinated with capturing the shine of gold and the sparkle of stones all with various shading and highlight techniques.

"Can you identify this as one of the pieces that was stolen, Mr. Halstead?" The lawyer held up a Cartier platinum, ruby, and pink sapphire bracelet.

I'd learned the first day that the best way to obtain the most interesting drawings was to get down the main action as fast as I could to capture the essence of the subjects' expressions and fill in the rest during a recess or after the day's session. I tried not to waste any effort drawing extraneous detail, so I chose not to look away from the front of the courtroom or the jury box for more than seconds at a time.

"Yes," Mr. Halstead said now without hesitation.

"Can you tell us how you can be sure?"

"I asked Mr. Cartier to make that bracelet for my wife on our anniversary. To match a pin I'd previously bought her with the same colored stones and—"

A door busted open at the back of the courtroom, quickly followed by a shout of "Wait!" and then "Stop!"

Along with the spectators, court officials, jury, and lawyers, I twisted around and saw a man brandishing a gun and running up the aisle. Two officers ran after him, trying to grab hold of him, but he had both a head start and surprise on his side. With the police at his heels, the man pointed his gun at Mr. Halstead and shot him in the chest. Once. Twice. Then a third time.

After the shattering sounds of the gunfire filled the room, an eerie silence followed for two or three seconds. Then the courtroom erupted in pandemonium. People behind me began screaming, ducking for cover, falling to the floor, running for the door.

I knew enough, somehow, to keep drawing, sensing the value of capturing these moments. I didn't think that I was in danger; after all, I'd seen Adam Allen drop the gun after taking the last shot. So I kept drawing as two guards grabbed him. I drew as they grappled with and eventually subdued him. I drew as the judge helplessly banged his gavel, in shock, it looked to me. I drew as Mrs. Halstead rushed to her husband and as Miss Halstead tried to get to her lover. I drew as guards tried to keep everyone from the front of the room, as they instructed the spectators to leave, assuring them there was no longer any danger.

Knowing I had a job to do, I kept sketching through all the tragedy and melee—flipping over sheet after sheet—filling each one with the action playing out before my eyes.

Minutes later, a group of medics entered with a stretcher. Mrs. Halstead held her husband's hand as they lifted him onto the gurney. Then they carried him out.

Allen was dragged out in handcuffs. Dorothea Halstead stood by herself, leaning against the wall, her clothes and hands stained with her father's blood, as she stared at the door through which the policemen had taken her lover.

In the aftermath of the drama, the police took statements from Miss Halstead, the judge, and members of the jury. I'd remained behind, sketching the activity, but finally it was time for me to go. As I started to pack up, I noticed that although she'd finished answering their questions, Miss Halstead hadn't left. She sat at the counsel's table, facing the empty space where minutes before she'd watched her father get shot by the man she loved.

I only had two hours to finish my illustrations and get to the paper to submit them, but how could I leave this distraught woman after what she had just endured?

As I got up to go over to her, the doors burst open again, and a gaggle of reporters rushed in, lobbing questions, pencils poised over their pads, waiting for her to answer.

Overwhelmed by their presence yet instinctively called to document the moment, I drew this scene, too, catching the expression on the frightened woman's face as the reporters descended on her.

I couldn't tell if she wouldn't or simply couldn't answer. Instead, she just sat, a martyr to their curiosity, examining the smears of blood on her hands. Clearly not understanding anything going on around her. She needed help. And none of the reporters was going to give it to her.

I searched through the crowd, found someone from the *Herald Tribune*, shoved my sketchbook at him, and asked him to turn my drawings in with his story. Then I elbowed my way through the crowd till I reached Miss Halstead's side. Putting my arm around her back, I whispered that I was going to take her home.

She looked at me. In her eyes, I read fear, and I tried to soothe her as I helped her stand up.

Holding on to me, she took a few steps and slipped in some of her father's blood. I kept her from falling, but I couldn't stop her from looking down at it.

I kept a grip on Miss Halstead's arm, and together we pushed our way through the reporters, out of the courtroom, down the hallway, and through the crowd. All the while, reporters followed, hollering questions that we both ignored.

We left the building, but at the top of the steps, before we descended, Dorothea looked at me again, as if she was seeing me for the first time.

"I don't know who you are, do I?"

"No."

"Then who are you?"

"I work for the *New York Herald Tribune* as a sketch artist. My name is Jenny Bell. I'm going to help get you home. Do you have a car and driver here?"

She had to think. "Yes, we did. Mother and I came together." She scanned the street below, as if expecting her mother and their car to be there.

"I don't see it. Not anywhere," she said.

"Let's get a cab, then."

"But where is the car?"

"Perhaps your mother took it?"

Another look of surprise came over her face. "My mother? Yes, where is she?"

"She went out with the medics. Maybe she took the car to the hospital."

Miss Halstead nodded as if that made sense. "Yes, the hospital," she repeated.

"If you give me your address, I can see you home."

"You don't need to . . ." she said, in a soft, small voice.

"I think it would be better. You've had a shock."

With that, she burst out with a hysterical cackle as loud as her words had been soft. "Everything has been a shock. This is just one more shock in a series of shocks."

Holding her arm tightly, I escorted her down the granite steps and, once we reached the sidewalk, signaled to one of the loitering cabs.

144

After following her inside, I asked her to give the driver her address, and he proceeded uptown.

Dorothea Halstead wept quietly during the entire ride from City Hall through the canyons of skyscrapers and uptown into the West Side residential area bordering Central Park.

The driver pulled into the driveway in front of the Dakota apartment building on Seventy-second Street, and I paid him. While he made change, a liveried doorman arrived and assisted Miss Halstead out of the cab.

Upstairs on the fourth floor, a butler opened the door as an older woman came rushing out. Based on her chignon, long dark skirt, dark cardigan sweater over a crisp white blouse, and the simple gold cross on a thin chain around her neck, I surmised she worked for the family. And from the way Miss Halstead collapsed into the woman's arms, I guessed she'd known her for most of her life.

The woman held Miss Halstead with one arm and with the other pushed her hair back off her forehead.

"You're home now, Miss Dorothea, home now. Let's get you some hot tea and a bath and then to bed."

The woman escorted her charge across the black-and-white marble floor.

The butler started after them, then seemed to remember I was there. "We heard what happened.

145

It's all so terrible." He was distraught. "We're lucky you were there. Thank you, Miss—"

"Bell. I'm Jenny Bell. I was in the courtroom. I'm an artist . . ." I started to explain, then realized there was no reason. "The police might have more questions for Miss Halstead but not today."

He thanked me for telling him and then asked how much the taxi fare was so he could reimburse me.

"I don't actually remember how much it cost," I told him. And I didn't. I had reached into my purse and given the driver some bills and gotten change, but I'd been so concerned for Miss Halstead that the amount hadn't registered.

"Let me call down and ask the doorman if he saw the fare."

"No, that's all right," I said. Though it seemed a crass thought to have, I was going to be making money from my drawings when they appeared in the paper. I could spare the carfare.

Despite my willingness not to be reimbursed, the butler went off to phone the doorman. Meanwhile, I watched as the housekeeper helped Miss Halstead through a door at the far end of the hallway. How lucky she was that she had someone to help, I thought, as I remembered another day and another courtroom, how very lonely I had been afterward. Even in the midst of such immediate tragedy, the past had a way of calling out to me as ferociously as it always had.

9

The newspaper used four of my drawings in the evening edition. Mr. Halstead passed away during that night, and four more of my sketches appeared in the next day's issue, set off with a black border around them in a front-page story. For my efforts, I received the enormous sum of forty dollars. I was back in the courtroom the following week, when Adam Allen was indicted for murder, remanded without bail, and thrown into the Tombs, New York City's prison for those awaiting a court date. On Thursday of the next week, my editor assigned me to yet another trial, a tame case of insurance fraud involving a high-profile society matron and a parure of rubies and diamonds from Cartier.

That Friday, Ben was waiting for me outside the courtroom when the day's session ended and asked me if I'd have a drink with him. I assented.

He took me to a speakeasy near the courthouse, a favorite haunt of prosecutors and off-duty detectives. He ordered us each a Gin Rickey, which had become my favorite drink lately because of its tart lime taste.

"My editor's asked me to move up to Albany for the rest of the spring and summer. Covering the political beat is the plum assignment I've been vying for. But now . . . I'm just getting to know you. I hate that I'm going to be away."

My first reaction was disappointment. In just a few weeks, we'd gone from just meeting to the feeling that we'd known each other forever. But I was also relieved. Ben's interest in forging a romance exceeded mine, and there was none of the fireworks or thrills, the swooning or daydreaming I'd read about in novels and that Minx recounted when describing her amours. His departure would give me an opportunity to see if I missed him and, even more important, let me focus one hundred percent on my painting. I had goals and a timeline, yet Ben's frequent invitations to dinners, cocktails, and shows often conflicted with my time in the studio.

I reached out and took his hand. "I'm so busy now, between the courthouse and classes and working on my own paintings, anyway. It will be good for us both to concentrate on our dreams. Besides, this way you can write me love letters. And I've never gotten one!"

"Not a single one?"

I shook my head.

He lifted his glass. "To four months of love letters," he toasted.

When I arrived home an hour later, Minx was in the living room with a bottle of champagne in an ice bucket and two crystal glasses waiting on the coffee table.

"Who are you expecting tonight?" I asked, as I dropped my bag and jacket by the door.

"You. Come over, sit down."

As I approached the divan, I saw it, propped up against the far wall—the painting of the mausoleum I had been searching for, the painting whose disappearance had disturbed me for an entire month.

"You found it! I'm so relieved. Where was it?"

"Well . . ." She grinned as she popped open the bottle. "Here you go." She handed me one of the fine Lalique coupes. "First the toast, then I'll explain about the painting," she said.

"All right. What are we drinking to?"

"Our summer excursion. We are going to take eight weeks off from work and classes—" She shook her head as she saw me begin to object. "Nope. Just hear me out. We are going to have an experience second only to going to Paris. You and I are going to spend eight weeks starting in mid-May on Long Island at Louis Comfort Tiffany's artists colony to paint and draw and sculpt and be inspired by nature."

I had heard about the Tiffany Foundation. Edward Wren had told us all about it over drinks one night at a club. Fascinated as I was with Mr. Tiffany, I'd never dreamed of applying, because I couldn't afford to take eight weeks off, and even if I could, I couldn't expect Mrs. Bullard to take me back on when I returned.

Louis Comfort Tiffany had opened the Foundation in 1918 on the grounds of his Laurelton Hall estate overlooking the Long Island Sound. The mansion and grounds were rumored to have cost more than $2 million dollars and were known as a paradise of light and color, art, and nature. Each season, a dozen or so fellows—Tiffany didn't call them students—were invited to live there and devote themselves to their art.

"But I didn't apply . . . I'd never be chosen . . ."

"You didn't have to apply; I did that for you. And you *were* chosen. You don't even have to pay the nominal stipend, because Mr. Tiffany always accepts two students per session whose fees are waived."

"How could you apply for me?" I looked from my friend to my painting. "You took my painting without asking me and submitted it?"

"Edward was accepted and encouraged me to apply, and I didn't want to go without you. If I deserve an infusion of nature, so do you. You work even harder than me, and you earned a chance. And apparently, Mr. Tiffany and the rest of the acceptance committee thought so, too. Our session starts in just a couple of weeks, right before your birthday. My parents are taking care of your share of the rent here as an early gift to you."

I had stopped hearing all the specifics. Minx

150

had taken my painting without asking and shown it to Mr. Tiffany and the group of strangers on the acceptance committee.

"How could you just take my painting without asking? And then lie to me about where it was?"

"But everything has worked out so well. You already have half the money saved that you need for our trip to Paris. When we come back from Laurelton Hall, it will only take another two or three months for you to earn the rest. We should be in Paris by January."

"How well it's gone with the paper isn't the point, Minx. You can't just decide things like this. You can't make up my mind for me. I'm sorry, but I can't go there with you."

I took the painting and carried it into my bedroom, where I leaned the monochromatic study of the crypt and its Tiffany window against the wall and proceeded to pace back and forth. It wasn't that I didn't want my work seen. It was the lack of respect for my property that had upset me. I knew Minx hadn't stolen it, had only borrowed it. But by doing that, she'd made me feel like I was something she was trying to fix. I didn't need Minx Deering to save me. I wasn't one of her troubled beaus, nor was I a sculpture fallen off its pedestal. I hated being pitied.

I'd stared out at a sea of pitiful faces in the courtroom years ago. As everyone looked on

151

and watched the barrister argue my defense—which was sounding weaker and weaker by the second—I hoped and prayed someone would rise up and save me. Then again, it had all been a part of the plan. A plan of my making.

As we'd watched the Reverend's body disappear down into the falls, my mother's right hand moved to cover her fast-beating heart, her left to cover her stomach, over the pregnancy. And in that moment, I became an adult.

The bridge was out in the open, and it was a clear, beautiful day. While painting, I'd seen several people pass by and stop to admire the cascade. My mind was racing. The Reverend's fall was accidental, but what if it hadn't looked like that from the gorge?

What if someone had been watching? What if no one believed my mother when she said it was an accident and she was convicted and sent to jail? A few years before, Lucy Moore, a local pregnant woman, had been caught stealing. She'd had her baby in jail, only to have the state put the child in an orphanage.

We stood on the bridge, both of us scared, and discussed the options. Should my mother confess? Would that be safer than waiting to find out if there was a witness to the incident? She didn't want to go to the police. She thought we should proceed with the plan. Leave Hamilton. Go to Ithaca.

Ever since I'd discovered the Reverend abusing my mother, I'd wanted to protect her. And now, finally, I could. Only months before, I'd read about a girl my age who'd been accused and convicted of manslaughter and released two years later. I knew how to protect my mother and my unborn sibling.

My mother and I were both five feet, five inches tall. We both had auburn hair that we wore in similar styles. We were both wearing dark clothing. We were both slim, as my mother was just barely showing her pregnancy. To anyone passing by who had witnessed the accident, we might have been the same person. The same person who might have wished the Reverend would fall to his death that day. Or the same person who might have ducked his assault in self-defense or pushed him hard in retaliation for all the abuses he had inflicted. Regardless, I knew I needed to go to the police in my mother's stead.

If my mother were convicted, she would go to prison and give birth there. The baby would become a charge of the state. But I was underage, like the girl I'd read about, only sixteen. Even if I were found guilty of voluntary manslaughter, I would only be remanded to a reformatory until my eighteenth birthday. I knew that by the time I was released, my half-sibling would still be a baby. I could pick up my life again with my mother and Aunt Grace in Ithaca. We would all be together. Without the Reverend.

As the spray from the falls showered us, my mother argued and pleaded. She knew she had placed us in the hands of a monster and couldn't bear the idea of me paying such a great price for her wrongdoing. She cited stories she'd read about what girls at some reform schools endured. There were rumors of them undergoing medical experiments and sexual abuse inflicted by the matrons, not to mention being underfed and badly clothed. They were punished with harsh jobs they were forced to do outdoors in terrible weather conditions. Some young women fell ill, while others died.

Mother begged me not to tell my lie and threatened to contradict me if I went forward with my plan. But I held strong. In my young mind, I was determined to save her once and for all. I made my mother promise—made her swear to me—that she would never tell anyone the truth of our plan. Not even Aunt Grace.

In the end, my plan won out.

I sat on the edge of the bed and wept, remembering the day I had chosen to make that sacrifice and vowed never again to depend on anyone. As grateful as I was for Minx, I could feel all the old emotions rising to the surface. All the conflicting emotions I felt about my mother. My mother, who taught me to draw, how to hold a brush . . . who explained how to mix paints . . . who helped me learn to love color . . . who always complimented my efforts and made me feel that I had a special talent . . . who cared for me, fed me . . . who had loved my father, told me about his jokes and how talented he was and that she'd cried so hard when he died that she worried the baby inside of her—me—would be born marked by her tears. My sweet mother, who had been flattered by the Reverend and had fallen under his spell . . . who lost herself and allowed him to treat her like the dirt under his shoe . . . who left me before she ever got a chance to make it all up to me. When I cried, I cried for all three of us.

Minx knocked on my door. "Jenny, can I come in?"

I opened the door.

She stepped inside, holding both glasses of champagne. "You have too much pride. I know you don't want to hear me say it, and you don't believe it. But you do, Jenny. And you can't be mad at me. You just can't, because this is the chance of a lifetime. Only the best are accepted, and you are one of the best. Papa says that it's harder for you because you've been on your own and you've lost so much, that you think you have to be strong in order to take care of yourself. He says you won't allow yourself to rely on anyone to help you because those who should have been helping left you. But that we have to show you that you *can* rely on us. We have to, even if you don't want us to, because you need people to be there for you."

She took a sip of her champagne. "So please, don't be mad at me."

"You really shouldn't have done any of this without telling me. If I wanted help, I would have asked for it."

"But that's just it, Jenny. We've been living together for almost a year, and you've never once asked for help. Yet you've needed it so many times. And that's what I'm best at, helping."

"Arranging things without consulting me is an odd way of helping."

"Forgive me first, then thank me. Because we are going to Laurelton Hall, and it is going to be magical."

10

Two weeks later, we left New York from Pennsylvania Station and arrived in Cold Spring Harbor in less than an hour. As I followed Minx down the train platform, a cool breeze blew my curls into my eyes and my skirt up around my knees. I inhaled a mixture of salty air, steam, and oil fumes. I was about to spend two months at Louis Comfort Tiffany's Long Island estate, where my only obligation was to engage in my host's "quest for beauty."

The newspaper's editor hadn't been pleased but said he'd put me back in the rotation in July. I had the feeling Ben might have pulled some strings and persuaded the editor to be accommodating. I wrote and asked him as much, but he glossed over the question, replying that anyone who had seen my work knew I deserved a chance to study at Laurelton.

The breeze blew again, this time splashing me with a few raindrops. I felt a shiver of apprehension.

"Look, there's the driver," Minx said, pointing to a uniformed man who held his cap in his hand and stood beside a sleek white Auburn.

Along with the acceptance letter to the Foundation, its director, Mr. Stanley Lothrop, had sent Minx instructions and information about traveling to the colony. He gave us the train timetable, the name of Mr. Tiffany's driver, a description of the touring car that would meet us, and suggestions for what to pack: mostly casual clothes suitable for the studio and the outdoors, including swimming, hiking, and boating wear if we were so inclined. He explained that there was one formal dinner each week and at least two galas during our stay. While he encouraged us to bring our own materials, the Foundation stocked all manner of supplies for painting, drawing, sculpture, photography, ceramics, and jewelry making. And, as needed, Foundation employees could always obtain for us anything we needed from New York City.

The driver introduced himself as Smythson and helped with our baggage.

I'd been in Minx's father's car, but this was even more extravagant. Silver bud vases, each holding a red rose and a lavender iris—the two colors clashing yet somehow complementing each other—were attached like sconces to the burled wood on each side of the back seat. The scent of the flowers mixed with the scent of the leather.

We sat back and relaxed as Smythson drove, sharing information about our route and the town as we went. After ten minutes, we came to a pair of simple gates affixed with a small brass plaque bearing the name of the estate: *Laurelton Hall*.

Smythson continued on a blue gravel road for at least a mile. On either side was a profusion of rhododendrons, azaleas, and laurels. We passed a totem pole, ponds, and streams and wound through an arbor of overhanging trees and fields of more laurel, until we came to the ridge. The trees parted to reveal a cream-colored house and a Moorish tower in the distance. As we drove through a mysteriously shaded area, we lost sight of the house. Wind chimes filled the air, as another vista opened up on a blur of blue water far in the distance. Each turn offered another view, a new surprise, all creating a sense of suspense. Everywhere we looked, the landscape offered mixtures of colors—yellow day lilies, purple irises, wildflower fields, maple and red cedar trees, black and yellow birches. You couldn't cast your eye anywhere without being aware of the beauty.

"After today, you can come and go using any of the entrances you like," Smythson told us, as he drove up to a grand porte cochere. "But the first time, Mr. Tiffany likes his guests to see Laurelton the way he designed it."

And as we drove farther ahead, it came into view again: a pale mansion with an emerald-colored roof, the blue harbor beyond it.

Smythson stopped the car, came around, and

opened the doors for us. We exited into a light drizzle, the scent of rain mixed with flowers, and walked up to the loggia.

A pair of turquoise ceramic dogs—Chinese artifacts that I later found out were more than three hundred years old—welcomed us. Marble columns, the capitals decorated with red and yellow flowers, stood out against a frieze of iridescent cobalt tiles shot through with gold and amethyst and rose.

Smythson introduced us to Graves, the butler, who escorted us under the porte cochere and into another world. The vestibule suggested faraway places. Everywhere I looked were mosaics of the most beautiful peacock blues and greens and lavenders. The room resembled a Japanese temple, with a gong, a brazier, altar candles, and a tall grilled window set into the wall and illuminated from underneath. From there, we walked up a flight of steps and into the magical Fountain Court.

I couldn't do anything but stare. Fluted marble columns supported the upper stories. Dozens of globes with green, blue, and cream glass shades hung down from the vaulted ceiling. Dizzying beauty made it impossible to know where to look first. Through the windows, purple wisteria vines matched the colors of the velvets and silks on the chairs and divans.

We'd stepped into Ali Baba's cave. Into a

fairy tale. Into a theater of magic, of light, of color, of breathtaking beauty. Into a dreamer's imagination. Every inch designed by an artist to express his own personal vision.

Above our heads, the forty-foot ceiling rose to an ornate blue-and-gold shimmering dome. In the center of the room, water flowed into a blue-tiled octagonal reflecting pool surrounded by potted plants. A tall glass vase fountain transformed from purple to blue to rose before our very eyes. There were almost too many stained-glass windows. Too many jewel-toned mosaics. Too many peacock-colored tiles. Too many lush plants and rare carpets and delicate vases and design details. Beyond two twenty-foot windows lay exotic flower beds, green lawns, acres of landscaping, and, beyond all that, the blue Sound and a more distant shore.

After a few more moments of watching us gawk, Graves cleared his throat. "Shall I take you upstairs?"

We proceeded to a grand staircase. Framed watercolors of exotic lands covered the walls up to the second landing.

"The gentlemen fellows are quartered in a dormitory by the studios," he said, "while only the ladies in residence are here in the main house along with the family. You're invited to take your lunch and dinner with the other fellows in the Foundation's dining room. On Sunday evenings, you're all invited to dine here with Mr. Tiffany. And of course, the ladies are invited to have breakfast here in the main house every day if you prefer. Once you're settled in, just ring for me, and I'll tell Mr. Lothrop you are ready, and he'll take you to the studio to get you set up."

Graves opened the third door on the right. "Miss Deering, I believe you're here, in the Daffodil Room." He lifted her suitcase onto a luggage stand.

"And my paint box and supplies?"

"Smythson delivered those to the studio."

Minx's room had matching cornflower-blue and daffodil-yellow curtains and bedspread. By each side of the bed, Tiffany glass lamps in the daffodil pattern glowed. More Tiffany accessories sat on the writing table—a letter holder, inkwell, blotter, and stamp holder all in an intricate bronze spiderweb pattern over amber-colored glass.

"You both share the bathroom." Graves opened the door to a bathroom. "It opens from each of your rooms. Now, if everything is satisfactory, Miss Deering, I'll take Miss Bell to her room, right next door."

"Very satisfactory, thank you," Minx said, and winked at me.

Graves held the door. I followed him into the hall. We walked about ten feet to the next door on the right.

"Here we are, Miss Bell, the Wisteria Room."

He opened the door, and despite my determination to act sophisticated, I stepped inside and gasped. I remembered the vine of the same name on my aunt's porch in Ithaca. I wished I could tell her about this.

This room was pale lavender blue with green accent colors. Wisteria stained-glass-bordered windows overlooked the bay. Curtains of leaf-green silk interwoven with blue threads pooled on the carpet of the same blue. Both bedside lampshades dripped lavender wisteria petals over emerald leaves. The desk accessories were the same spiderweb pattern as the ones in Minx's room, but mine had green glass under the bronze overlay.

Graves placed my bag on the luggage stand and pointed to one of the two doors. "Here's your door to the bath," he said, as he opened it. I peeked into a blue-tiled space, which was as big as my bedroom in New York. The door was still open on the other side, and Minx walked through the bathroom to come and inspect my bedroom.

"If everything is all right here as well, Miss Bell, I'll let Mr. Lothrop know you're both settling in, and I'll be up in an hour's time to show you to the smoking room to begin your orientation with him."

As someone who had studied Mr. Tiffany's work since discovering that window in the Fond du Lac Mausoleum when I was fourteen, I was having a hard time quite believing I was going to be living here for eight weeks.

Graves left. Minx and I stood in the bathroom, inspecting everything from the extra-thick towels and mosaic-tiled floor to the brass faucets shaped like flowering vines.

"All this is something else, isn't it?" Minx said. "Mrs. Whitney wouldn't describe it. She said we just had to experience it ourselves without any preconceived ideas, and she was right."

"It's overwhelming . . . like walking into a dream."

"I've seen some grand mansions in Newport. Hell, I've seen palaces in France and England. This may not be as big, but it's more amazing than any of them."

We retired to our respective rooms to unpack. I put my clothes in the closet and my underthings in the armoire. Among my belongings, I'd brought some personal items to make me feel at home. A favorite book of poetry, a framed photo of my aunt and me posing together in front of her house, and the dozen letters Ben had sent me since he left for Albany. These I put in a drawer in the desk.

Ben hadn't, after all, written love letters but funny, quirky, insightful observations on the legal system, politics, and life in the state capital. Letters full of interesting behind-the-scenes stories about the investigations and the

164

people involved in the political murder case he was now covering involving a New York state assemblyman accused of killing a private eye investigating him for corruption. They read like a detective novel. Each one gave me greater insight into how Ben's mind worked and demonstrated what a fine writer he was. The more he wrote, the more I appreciated him. But although I found him attractive and had enjoyed kissing him, my feelings still weren't saturated with emotion the way I imagined they would have been if I were in love. And then there was his hungry curiosity, which extended to everything, including my past.

In one letter, he wrote that he'd run into his friend Matt Flannery, who worked for the *Times* and was also in Albany. And he'd told Matt about my being from Ithaca, too. Matt had asked where I'd lived and where I had gone to school. He wanted to know my aunt's name in case his family might know her.

I'd ignored the questions when I wrote back and filled Ben in on the trial I was sketching at the time, my classes, and Minx's escapades. But in his next letter, he asked again and joked that I was "an enigma" and that he wouldn't rest until "I've solved the mystery named Jenny Bell and then never tell another soul. I want to prove to you that you can trust me."

I shut the drawer. For now, he would just have to live with the mystery.

"Are you ready to explore the rest of this wonderland?" Minx stuck her head into my room.

I closed my empty suitcase and put it on the top shelf of the closet, while Minx rang for Graves, who reappeared within minutes. We then set off to meet Mr. Stanley Lothrop.

At the bottom of the stairs, Graves made a left, and we followed him into what he'd called the smoking room but which was also a library. A thin, pale man in his fifties rose. This was Mr. Lothrop, who shook our hands and welcomed us.

"Let's have a seat," he said.

The floor-to-ceiling windows in the octagonal room looked out onto a terrace planted with purple and blue hydrangea bushes. On the opposite wall, leather-bound volumes filled the bookshelves. The rest of the walls and the ceiling were covered with a dulled silvery paper. A painting at least fourteen feet long and six feet high hung over the leather sofa and dominated the room. It depicted a scene of debauchery. At its center, a bearded man in a robe lay on pillows, an opium pipe by his side. With a look of surprise, he stared at a threatening winged dragon. On the far right, a samurai in full armor stood in front of an elephant. A snake slithered across the floor in the foreground. Three lascivious naked women danced and preened in the background. Smoke permeated the atmosphere, muting the colors.

"The Opium Dream," Mr. Lothrop said, pointing

to the painting. "It's quite the conversation piece around here. Some guests express outrage, others interest. But no one ignores it." He didn't give us any indication of how he felt about the painting.

I wanted to glance over at Minx and see her reaction, but I wasn't supposed to know about her past problem with the drug. Instead, I focused on the most bizarre aspect of the room. Six full-size dark metal suits of Japanese armor, complete with helmets and face masks, hung on the wall by the window. Lined up the way they were, I wouldn't have been surprised if they'd sprung to life.

"Now, let's have some refreshments, and I can explain how the Foundation works and then give you the rest of the tour."

He escorted us to a grouping of chairs around a table and began to explain the schedule and expectations, only stopping when a maid appeared with a trolley that included tiny sandwiches and chocolate petit fours.

I was too nervous to eat much, but I took one of the petit fours and some tea.

"There are no rules, per se, as this isn't a school but rather a retreat and place of study to expand the boundaries of your talent. To abandon tradition, disregard the confines of your specialty, and seek fresh inspiration. Mr. Tiffany believes that artists lose much to studio methods and conditions. The one caveat here at Laurelton Hall is that no figurative drawing or painting from the model is allowed. Mr. Tiffany asks only that you immerse yourself in the beauty all around you here and use the boundless riches of the natural world as your muse." He stopped to sip his tea.

"Well, it is beautiful, no doubt about that," Minx said.

Mr. Lothrop gave us his small smile, as if his mouth were sewn tight at the corners. "That it is. I've been running the Foundation since it opened in 1918, and I am still amazed by my surroundings. Are your rooms all right?"

"Peachy," Minx said.

"Lovely." *Unlike any room I've ever imagined,* I wanted to add, but didn't for fear of labeling myself a rube.

Once we finished our tea, Mr. Lothrop started the tour. Seeing some of the rooms for the second time, I was able to take more of them in. I noticed how much of the decor favored the Far East. And how much of nature Mr. Tiffany had brought inside—in every room was a profusion of planters and vases of flowers, white lilies, pink and purple orchids, and blue and lavender hydrangeas. Bits of abalone and other opalescent shells studded the dozens and dozens of stained-glass windows and panels.

Everywhere we walked, we were accompanied by the sound of water gurgling in fountains. Each fantastic space boasted something extraordinary,

168

whether it was a Hindu-style balcony or a corner modeled after an Islamic temple. There were too many paintings and pieces of sculpture to study any one in depth.

"Mr. Tiffany believes that beauty and mystery lead to contemplation and transcendence. Great art, he says, is mystical, and artists are alchemists. Art's purpose, he likes to remind us all, is to inspire wonder and awe."

"Well, there's no doubt he's done that here," Minx offered.

Mr. Lothrop escorted us onto a loggia edged with tall fluted white marble columns, their capitals dressed with vibrant ceramic flowers— lotus, peony, poppy, and magnolia. In the center, a fountain shot sprays of water skyward. I watched as it fell back down onto the rock crystals that encircled the pool.

"He also believes that water," Mr. Lothrop continued, "is not only a vital liquid but a symbol of hope. We have seven fountains, two interior and five outside, plus four pools, several ponds and lakes, and a cataract.

"More than forty thousand gallons of water are pumped up the hill and then cascade back down to the tanks on the beach." He pointed down below, and I could see a highly decorated minaret. "That's the smokestack for the powerhouse that operates it all."

We descended a few stone steps to a terrace

covered by an arbor heavy with purple and white wisteria. I inhaled the sweet and peppery scented flowers and felt for a moment that I was back in Ithaca on my aunt's porch. In the late spring, we would often sit out there, just breathing it in.

I reached out and touched the cascade of petals as we passed by.

"Wisteria," Mr. Lothrop said, "is one of Mr. Tiffany's favorite flowers. There are vines everywhere, and it's all in bloom this time of year."

He led us down more steps to yet a third terrace with a third fountain, the water in this one also emerging from oversized rock crystals in its center. In the distance, the view of the Sound opened up even wider.

"Beyond us is the Long Island Sound, with Connecticut on the other side," he explained.

We left the terrace and took a path bordered by wildflower fields.

"There are bicycles in the garage at your disposal, and we encourage you to use them if you want to ride to town. It's only two miles away, and they have a very nice coffee shop and general store. We hope you won't want to leave for any major excursions, but if for some reason you choose to do so, just ask me or Graves to arrange for a car to the train. As I mentioned before, there are no rules, but to observe certain proprieties here and look out for your welfare, we normally have a matron who lives with the female fellows in the main building. Unfortunately, Miss Press has been called home for a family emergency. We hope that won't cause either of you any concern—"

Minx interrupted. "We live on our own in Greenwich Village, Mr. Lothrop. We're fine without a chaperone."

"That's reassuring, Miss Deering. If you do have any concerns, Miss Hanley, Mr. Tiffany's companion, is on the premises and will make sure you are taken care of."

Did he mean Mr. Tiffany's nurse, friend, lover? Secretary? Was Mr. Tiffany ill? Infirm? I'd just have to wait and see for myself. I certainly hoped he was well and there would be a chance for us to interact with him.

Mr. Lothrop continued: "If there is anything you need, please ask one of us. You are our guests, and we want to make you as comfortable as possible so you can create your finest work while in residence."

Having finished his orientation, he asked, "Now, do you have any questions?"

"Is Mr. Tiffany here?" I couldn't help but ask. I'd wanted to meet him for so long, to thank him for the masterpieces he'd created and the pleasure and solace they had given me. Now, of course, I had even more to be grateful to him for.

"Yes, he arrived yesterday. Typically, he spends

half the week in New York, the rest of his time here, and when he's in residence, he visits the studio daily to see what you are all working on. He loves being involved, so please feel free to talk to him when you see him, all right?"

"I will," I said.

By way of more landscaped gardens and pathways through laurel, oak, pine, and maple trees, we reached what Mr. Lothrop said had originally been the stables.

"Mr. Tiffany had them renovated into the men's dormitory, common living and dining rooms, and art studios."

We followed him inside.

"Here we have jewelry, sculpture, and glass-making studios, a carpentry shop, an electric forge and furnace, facilities for enameling, and a photography studio."

He led us to the threshold of a large open space with north-facing windows and skylights. "And the painting studio."

There were about ten young men outfitted in slacks and smocks, all at work.

"Each fellow has a designated area here," Mr. Lothrop continued. "You can come and go as you like, as well as use any of the other studios at will."

We both said we understood.

"Dinner is served just through there." He pointed at a door. "Every evening at seven. You might have heard, there is a competition during each session. At the end of your eight weeks here, Mr. Tiffany and I and the guest lecturers who come during your sojourn will choose one winning artist who will receive a very generous prize. In addition, he or she will be awarded a show in Mr. Tiffany's gallery in New York. Included in that event will be one piece by each of the other fellows submitted as your thesis during your time here."

The competitive spirit surged in me. I desperately wanted to win.

Mr. Lothrop stepped into the studio, and we followed. "Now," he said, "let me show you to your assigned areas and introduce you to the other fellows who started arriving yesterday. You two complete our contingent for this session."

The studio was separated into sections by virtue of the easels, drawing tables, and taborets. The walls were empty, not yet covered with the artwork that would fill them in the days ahead.

Since we'd arrived, Laurelton and its grounds had offered nothing but beauty and peace. But for the first time, in the studio, I felt anxious. Warm light streamed in through the skylights. The space was hardly dark or cramped. No unpleasant odor permeated the air—only the welcome scents of oil paint and turpentine. All the sights—canvases, palettes, painters in smocks—were familiar. This was the world I loved, yet I sensed something ominous. It hung in the air like a miasma. I glanced over to Minx, but she was happily chatting away with Mr. Lothrop.

We met Paul Cadmus and Louis Pritchard, both painters; James Miller, a photographer; and another painter named Henry Goodson, who was saying hello when Minx interrupted by waving and calling out across the room.

"Edward!" Minx left us and strode over to the farthest corner of the room, where Edward Wren stood, paintbrush in hand, in front of his easel.

He embraced Minx like an old friend, without a hint of romance, which had to be for show. Minx always had more than one beau at a time, but I knew for a fact that she'd been seeing him almost exclusively through all of April and into May, and she'd confided in me not three weeks before that they had become lovers.

Mr. Lothrop looked to me for edification, and I explained that Mr. Wren was a student at the League in some of our classes and left it at that.

Minx called over to me. "Jenny, come say hello."

I made my way to his corner.

Edward smiled brightly, but it didn't quite reach his eyes. Of all the men Minx had gone with, I understood her continued interest in him the least. Edward was charismatic but secretive. Good-looking but without soulfulness. And a bit too moody for my taste. There had been evenings at clubs where he'd sat there morosely and barely said a word, while all kinds of hilarity went on around him. Minx blamed it all on the war. Maybe she was right. I didn't have enough experience to know.

"So nice to see you here, Jenny," Edward said. "You're going to love it. The grounds are magnificent. The trees, the flowers, the views, the ponds . . ." Edward had been talking to us both, looking from one to the other. But his eyes rested on me and stayed with me as he finished his round of praise: "And there's even a waterfall on the grounds."

11

I was disturbed by Edward's somewhat menacing comment. It reminded me of what he'd said to me in Central Park, during Professor Pannell's class. I almost questioned him but instead told Minx I wanted to see more of Laurelton and took off on my own to explore. Dinner wasn't until seven, so I had several hours to kill. I stepped out the door, and as I explored the glorious grounds, my discomfort dissipated.

The estate was built on a hill that descended to the shore. I looked up at the main house, then down to the water, and decided on a different path from the one we'd taken with Mr. Lothrop.

I found myself wandering by a large glass conservatory half a city block long and filled with dozens of variations of palm trees and hothouse flowers. From there, I could see the minaret on the beach. I used the landmark to wind my way down through hanging gardens, a deep forest glade, and small twin lakes. Water was everywhere. Sparkling, shooting, cascading, reflecting, energizing, and soothing.

I reached a clearing. Below me, the slender Moorish tower shimmered in the afternoon light. As I got closer, I could make out the minaret's blue and green iridescent Tiffany-tiled surface.

Emerging from the path, I stood on a ridge. To my left were steps that led down to the beach, a dock with a rather grand-looking yacht and several smaller sailboats, and a simple cedar-shingle boathouse. At the bottom of the stairs, I walked to the edge of the shore and sat down on a wide, flat rock. Gentle waves rippled across the water. Overhead, gulls cried as they soared and dove. A modest-sized boat, sails unfurled and puffed with breeze, tacked across the bay. Mesmerized, I watched it progress into the cove and up to the dock. Its sailor expertly tied the boat up. Then, carrying a small easel and paint supplies, he disembarked. Tall and slim, he had an athlete's grace, but as he loped down the dock, I noticed he limped slightly.

The sailor was twenty yards away when he saw me. He detoured from the stairs and made his way toward me. By the time he'd covered half the distance, I started to wonder if I'd met him before. I couldn't yet make out his features, but there was something about his height and the color of his hair and his long, lean frame that tickled my memory.

"Hullo," he called out.

"Hullo," I answered.

"Are you one of the stragglers here for the Foundation's first session?" He stopped in front of me, but with the sun shining right in my eyes, I couldn't quite see his features.

177

"I am. My friend and I arrived a couple of hours ago."

He put down his supplies and held out his hand. "Glad you made it. I'm Oliver. Oliver Comfort Tiffany."

As I took his hand, a cloud moved and shielded the sun. It was the man I'd seen at Mrs. Whitney's on the night of Jock's opening. I could see his face clearly now and remembered every detail of it.

"And before you ask, yes, grandson to his excellency," he continued, a devilish smile accompanied by a single arched eyebrow.

"Oh," I said with some surprise, embarrassing myself with both my reaction and the fact that I didn't immediately withdraw my hand. But neither did he, and for an awkward few seconds, we remained there on the beach, holding each other's hand.

I let go first and imagined I saw a flicker of disappointment in his eyes.

"Welcome to Laurelton, Miss—" His voice was the blue of a smooth saxophone playing in a smoky nightclub. A hue darker than the icy blue eyes I'd noticed from across the room at Mrs. Whitney's gallery.

Oliver tilted his head a little to the left and squinted as if he were trying to place me. The wind came up and blew his jet-black hair into his face. He brushed it away, but a wave fell back onto his forehead.

The first time I'd seen him, I'd wanted to go up to him and touch him. To see if he was real. If his skin was warm. I wanted to tell him how much he resembled that Canova marble sculpture of Perseus that had kept me company on so many long afternoons. Now I'd felt his warm skin and knew he was as real as my own heartbeat. And with a shock, I knew I wanted him in a way I'd never wanted a man before.

"You haven't told me your name," he said. "And why do I think we've met? Have we?"

Nerves always overwhelmed me when someone suggested they'd met me before. The fear that I'd be recognized from one of the photographs taken during the trial almost always paralyzed me. Frequently, I had to remind myself that most of those shots had shown me from the back or had been taken from so great a distance that they didn't matter. But there was one photograph that had revealed more than half of my face as I made my way up the courtroom steps with my mother the first morning of the trial. I had just turned sixteen but looked older. I wore a dark dress almost identical to the one Mother had worn the day of the accident and had made sure to put my hair up, again as it had been then.

I remembered the sonorous tone of the bailiff calling my mother to the stand as my character witness. She did her best, crying through much of her testimony, but we both knew it was futile; killer women were all the rage at the time, what with Lizzie Borden, Lulu Johnson, Henrietta Bamburder, and others. And I didn't help my own cause. I tried to appear calm and innocent, but I was no actress, and it was difficult to pretend after witnessing my stepfather's abuse of my mother for almost three years.

No one was going to believe a clearly angry young woman over the testimony of members of a congregation who loved their minister and who saw him as a respected member of the community. Four of them were asked to speak at the trial, all praising the charismatic man of God who had stewarded them through trials and traumas.

Mrs. Marshall, a widow who we knew had her sights set on the Reverend herself before he went off and married my mother, took the stand and, when asked, told the jury how the Reverend had confided in her that I wasn't a very "good" girl. And that while I had talent, when he looked at my paintings, he sometimes feared I was an instrument of the devil.

"He complained Jenny hadn't been well disciplined—growing up as she had with an artist for a mother and no father. And how he had his hands full trying to raise her right. The Reverend, may he rest in peace, told me he prayed for her soul every morning and every night. And when he said it, he was shaking his head, as if it was a lost cause. And for all that effort, what did he get? He got killed," she said, and burst into sobs.

My fate was finally sealed when a witness to the crime was called. Lyman Templeton, thirty-three years old. Cutting through the woods on his way home from his shift at the gas station in town, he'd stopped to admire the view and had seen a man and a woman standing on the walkway above the waterfall. The roar of the rushing water had obliterated their conversation, but Templeton was close enough to read their body language. He described what he said appeared to be an argument. And how, at the end, the man took a step toward the woman, with his hands outstretched, and how she pushed him away. And how that push threw him against the railing, causing it to break and him to fall, headfirst into the cascade. And how the woman—or the girl, because he wasn't close enough to tell—stood there and watched but didn't make a move to go get help.

By the time I came back to Ithaca after reform school, I'd lost so much weight that Aunt Grace said no one would recognize me as "the girl on the bridge," especially after she'd replenished my wardrobe with clothes that fit and took me to her hairdresser, who restyled my hair.

After she died and I moved to New York, I did a more drastic makeover, chopping off my hair and getting a bob, adopting red lipstick, a little rouge, and mascara, and much sleeker, more modern clothes. I looked very much like the other Greenwich Village bohemians. When I held up that damning photo of me at my trial and looked in the mirror, I was confident that no one would connect me to the girl in the photograph taken up in Hamilton, Ontario, seven years before. Surely not worlds away at the home of Louis Comfort Tiffany and the man I now knew as his grandson.

"We've never been introduced, Mr. Tiffany, but we almost met once. This past March at a reception at Mrs. Whitney's gallery."

"What happened to prevent such an important introduction?" His eyes sparkled the way the sea did.

"A fight broke out."

"Jock Alexander?"

I nodded.

"Yes, I remember. My family and the Whitneys are old friends, and I'm a great admirer of her work. What an unfortunate night. That was a masterful piece of sculpture." He shook his head, and a lock of hair fell across his forehead and into his eyes. He pushed it back and grinned at me. "I'm sorry we didn't get to meet then, but at least you're here now."

He said it as if he'd been waiting for me, and I felt a flutter deep inside me, a sense of something being right. As if I, too, had been waiting for him.

I considered my father's message—or Aunt Grace's message—which I had committed to memory long ago: *Comfort will come but not yet. There are trials to endure, be strong.*

It had occurred to me that I had, in fact, found comfort in a window created by Louis Comfort Tiffany. But the word took on yet another aspect now . . .

"Yes, I am," I told Oliver.

"Care to take a walk? If you've just arrived, I can show you some of my secret hiding places. I've been spending summers here since Grandfather built it when I was eight years old."

He stashed his painting gear in the boathouse while I waited for him. Watching his slender form walk back to me, my fingers itched to sketch him, to draw his aesthetic lines, to get down on paper the aristocratic features, long neck, and elegant fingers.

"First you have to see our secret fort." Oliver took my arm as if it was the most natural thing in the world and led me down the beach. Where our bodies touched, I felt a heated pressure.

"My cousins and I played here for hours when we were kids. Laurelton Hall's grounds were paradise for children. And we loved it here, except when Grandfather made us dress up for his grand fetes."

"Minx's mother told me all about those. She

said they were extravaganzas. The talk of the town. That no one has seen the likes of them since."

"That's true. But I still blush at the photographs of me as a ten-year-old dressed up as a chef with a padded stomach and a long apron serving roasted pig. I'm not sure I've forgiven Grandfather for that. Or that any of us has."

I was drawn to his humor, surprised and delighted by it.

"Did all the grandchildren have to dress up?" It wasn't just that I was curious about the family and his childhood, but I so badly wanted to keep him talking, to listen to his voice.

"Yes, in quite elaborate costumes. The girls, who served the peacock, all wore pale gowns with head scarves, each carrying a torch and a basket of rose petals."

"There are a lot of you, aren't there?" I asked, recalling reading about Mr. Tiffany's family in the memoir I'd borrowed from Mr. Deering's library. I hadn't focused on any of their names then, but he must have mentioned Oliver at some point.

"Yes, my father was one of seven children, and I'm the oldest grandson."

"And you're a painter?"

"No," Oliver said quickly. "I'm a businessman like my father. He was the head of the company's finances. In fact, that's why I'm spending so much of my time here now. Father and Grandfather want me to learn how the Foundation runs from the ground up. This fall and winter, it was the jewelry studio, then the glassworks, now Laurelton Hall. Grandfather and Father expect me to take over the empire one day."

I barely knew Oliver, but I could hear gray clouding his cool blue voice.

"And you don't want to?"

We were walking through beach grass up a ways from the water. Oliver slowed his pace, turned, and examined my face as if he was searching for something specific.

"Why would you think that?"

"Well . . ." I wasn't even sure but considered it for a moment. "For one thing, you were painting on the sailboat. I saw your supplies. So it must be something that matters to you. Then, when I asked you if you were an artist, you were very quick to deny it. And just now, when you were talking about the business, your voice went flat and gray."

"Gray?"

"It's a strange habit I have. I like to assign colors to sounds and people's voices. And yours changed when you talked about being groomed."

"And not for the better?" he asked.

I shook my head. "No, not for the better."

He moved closer and spoke more quietly. "What color is my voice?"

185

"A deep blue. Almost a sapphire."

He reached out and tilted my chin up. "And it changed to gray?"

"It did," I said quietly.

"I've never heard of anything like that before. How did you come up with it?"

"I didn't. It was a game my mother made up for us to play when I was little to teach me color. And then I just kept doing it."

"You were lucky to have such a creative mother," Oliver said.

His comment struck me as odd, considering how creative his own grandfather was, but I didn't feel I knew him well enough to mention as much. As it turned out, I didn't have to, since he continued talking.

"My mother died when I was just six. Father remarried several years later, but . . ." He shrugged. "By then, I was off at boarding school most of the time. Summers I spent here."

The grassy path narrowed into a rocky incline, and walking on it took some concentration.

"When we were kids, we ran up this part; we couldn't wait to get to the fort. War was such a foreign idea to us then. Now we're the war generation."

"Did you serve?"

"Yes. My unit worked with the camoufleurs in France."

"Camoufleurs?"

"At the start of the war, the French formed a unit of soldiers who in their civilian lives had been painters, illustrators, architects, and theatrical set designers. Using their skills, they camouflaged battleships and aircraft so they were difficult to spot, shrouded gun emplacements with false buildings, and created props like fake trees that soldiers could hide in and spy on the enemy. In 1917, our government formed the Fortieth Regiment of the Corps of Engineers to aid the French. I'm not a very talented painter, despite my heritage, but I am a very precise copyist. I was just eighteen and very rebellious when I heard about the unit. Much to my family's dismay, I dropped out of college and joined up to help the war effort."

"So you were at the front till the end of the war?"

"I was." He shook his head, as if he were trying to shake off the memory. "Nothing I see will ever be as terrible. I was there for more than a year, and it was hell." He slapped his thigh. "I even got a nice souvenir for my trouble. Shrapnel in my leg. And I'm one of the lucky ones. I didn't lose it or any ability to do just about anything but sprint. Our unit was supposed to be relatively safe, but war doesn't discriminate. Soldiers are soldiers, even if they have paintbrushes in their hands." He stopped. We'd reached the summit.

I looked out at the land that stretched in front

187

of us. A ditch perched on the edge of a marsh, surrounded by a slight rise. What had it been like for him? How had he lived with the sacrifice? How had it affected his talent? How bad was his injury? I wanted to know everything about him, and at the same time nothing about him mattered except that we were standing there, together.

"See those stones, there and there?" He pointed out sections of a dilapidated wall that formed a corner, then broke, then continued on. "Those were once the walls."

We walked inside the partial perimeter. Off to one side was a large pile of shells, bleached by the sun.

"It's called a shell dump heap. Indians used shells to make beads, and we found hundreds of them in there. We also found arrowheads, bone fishhooks, and clay pipes." He reached down, grabbed a handful of shells, and put them in my hand. "If you look, you can probably still find some beads."

He scooped up another handful for himself, and we both searched through the broken pieces.

"It was our favorite place to play until Grandfather put an end to our excursions."

"What happened?"

"He heard about our discovery from one of my aunts, who found a stone knife in my cousin's pocket. Fascinated by what the site might turn up, Grandfather invited an archaeologist to investigate. There are quite a few forts like this up and down Long Island. Ours was probably built in the 1640s and used as a refuge in a time of attack and as a trading post in peacetime. Once my grandfather heard its history, he forbade us to come back here, lest we ruin it."

Oliver threw down his handful of shells and scooped up a new one. "He planned on funding an archaeological dig here. But we were kids, and rules were made to be broken. Once we learned this was an Indian fort and that Grandfather didn't want us here, we couldn't stay away. As you'll see, my grandfather has quite a collection of Native American art at Laurelton Hall. We took to borrowing headdresses, drums, baskets, and rugs, bringing them out here in the dead of night and conducting made-up rituals and ceremonies. Eventually, we got caught and severely punished."

For some reason, I felt a jolt of fear upon hearing this.

Oliver plucked something out of the mess of shells in his hand. "Here you go." He handed it to me.

The round, irregular bead had a crude hole through its middle. In the afternoon sun, it shimmered almost like a pearl but with a blue-violet tint.

"This is abalone, isn't it? I noticed some in the house."

"Yes, Grandfather uses it in some of his brass frames, inkwells, desk blotters. Even in some jewelry. I've always believed the nacre was more beautiful than pearl because there are so many colors reflected on its surface."

He held it up to the sun. "I'll put a cord through it, and you can wear it as a necklace. A memento of your first day at Laurelton Hall," he said, with another devilish grin and raised right eyebrow.

He pocketed the bead and then took my hand. "Let's go. The sun is starting to set, and it's going to get chilly soon."

I wanted to tell him it didn't matter, that his touch was warming me. But of course, I didn't. As the sky took on a lavender and pinkish tint, similar to the abalone, I glanced at Oliver. The setting sun reflected off his skin, made him look as if he were sculpted from the shell. But the feel of his fingers clutching mine, in an urgent way, as if he had to hold on, was so welcoming and familiar. I closed my eyes and tried to memorize the moment. In all its wonder and color.

12

Minx knocked on my door at six and asked if I wanted to go downstairs for a drink before we went to dinner. I said I did but needed to change. She sat on my bed while I opened the closet.

"What did you do this afternoon?" I asked, as I pulled out a dress and a sweater.

"I worked in the studio, and then Edward and I explored the estate."

"Are you falling in love with him for real?"

She shrugged. "Too soon to tell." She leaned forward. Even though no one was around, she spoke in hushed tones. "I didn't tell you this before, but when Edward isn't painting, he drives a truck for a bootlegger. He brings the stuff down from Canada." She was almost breathless. "It's all very hush-hush, but I'm not going to pretend it's not scary, too. It is. Jenny, he carries a gun."

"But you can't be with someone who—"

"Before you start sounding like my mother again, he's going to stop as soon as he gets enough paintings together for a show. That's why this session at Laurelton is so important for him. If he wins the prize, with all the attention that goes with it, he'll be able set himself up in the city with a studio and a gallery, and everything will change. He's so passionate about his art."

191

Her eyes lit up. "About everything." She bit down on her bottom lip.

"But your mother is right to be worried. She cares about you. After everything that's happened, she just wants—"

"After everything?" Minx asked. "What's 'everything'?"

I'd said something I shouldn't have. I'd alluded to the past she'd never told me about but that her mother had discussed with me. Before I could try to smooth over my faux pas, she persisted.

"After what, Jenny? Wait, wait . . . my mother told you, didn't she?"

"Only because she doesn't want anything to ever happen to you. She doesn't want you to fall in with the wrong crowd and be tempted again."

Minx walked away from me and went to the window. "And you didn't tell me?"

"I wanted to but . . . no, I didn't. I'm sorry, Minx."

She spun around. "It was almost two years ago, and it's not something that will happen again. You certainly don't have to worry about it or watch out for me. I don't need a keeper."

The invitation for drinks abandoned, Minx stomped away to her room. For the next hour, I worried that she was too angry to forgive me. But at six forty-five, she was back, asking if I was ready to walk down for dinner.

• • •

By the time we arrived at the Foundation's dining room, most of the fellows had already assembled. We'd all been thrown together for two months, and this was our inaugural meal. Fourteen artists ranging in age from twenty-two to thirty. Twelve men, two women. Nine painters. Two sculptors. Minx, who was both. One photographer and one potter. I'd wondered if Oliver would be there, since he was at Laurelton to learn the business of running the Foundation. But he was family and probably ate in the mansion with his grandfather and whoever else was in residence.

Dinner was a semiformal affair. We all sat at a long table in a rectangular room with floor-to-ceiling windows that allowed for a merging of the indoors with the outdoors. While we ate, we were treated to a view of woodlands and lawn, flowers and sky. As evening settled into darkness, the view disappeared, but tiny colored lights strung through the trees enchanted us with a different kind of magic.

Two male servants waited on us, one of whom offered us wine as soon as we sat down. Minx had told me that Tiffany was no teetotaler, but I hadn't expected us to be treated so much like guests. Everywhere I looked, even there in the Foundation's quarters, Tiffany's artistry, sense of design, and love of beautiful things was on display. Not surprisingly, the tableware was of the finest white china decorated with a cobalt-blue and gold edge and swags of green leaves. The green and blue motif continued with pastel wineglasses and water glasses—the bowls blue, the bases green. And the leaf motif continued as the decoration in the silverware.

Our three-course meal began with stuffed mushrooms, followed by a roast duck with boiled potatoes, carrots, and peas, and ending with Nesselrode pudding and butter cookies.

The conversations were tentative at first, as was often the case between strangers. But Minx wasted little time in livening things up by suggesting we all play a game to get to know one another better.

"We'll go around the table," she said. "First, say the one thing that scares you the most in the world."

Had I not been her friend and seen her do this kind of thing before, I might have felt uncomfortable about being forced to open up. But I knew she would go easy on me, at least.

After some consideration, Henry Goodson said quicksand. Paul Cadmus said poverty. Blindness and fire were other answers. I said injustice. In an instant, Edward Wren said failure.

Next, Minx asked what each of us was most proud of. Prizes and scholarships were the most common answers. Minx said hers was being Mrs. Whitney's assistant. Alan Higgins said surviving the war. I said getting to New York City on my own. Edward said his ability to survive and succeed.

She continued peppering the meal with questions. Over the years, I'd learned how to sidestep awkward topics and believed I was doing a good job, until Edward pushed me on two questions I hadn't answered at all.

"Jenny, what about you? What is your worst childhood memory?"

I took a sip of wine. "Our cat's death," I responded. I hadn't thought about the parsonage's cat for more than eight years, but this somehow seemed like the kind of meaningful yet still innocuous response that would avoid any large discussion about my past.

And then, later, when I hadn't answered Minx's question about our fathers' occupations, Edward asked, "What did your father do? I missed it."

I said he'd been an architect. I was relieved that dinner was soon over.

As Minx and I walked back up to the main house, we talked about each of the artists and our impressions of them. I was glad that we didn't talk any further about Edward. I was willing to put up with him for Minx's sake but was beginning to find him abrasive.

Later, alone in my bedroom, I sat in the window seat. Below me, the Laurelton Hall grounds glowed and twinkled with all the tiny lights strung in the trees, along the paths, across the terraces, illuminating the fountains and fanciful sculptures. Night-blooming flowers scented the air. I looked out past the estate to the Long Island Sound. The half-moon cast shimmers of light on the rippling water.

The day had been overwhelming on every level, and I wasn't at all tired. I wished I could call Aunt Grace and tell her I was there, at the Foundation, on a scholarship, with eight weeks to work without pressure, living in a home built by none other than Louis Comfort Tiffany. Just thinking his name, I shivered, remembering myself at fourteen, the very first time I ran away into the cemetery and found the Fond du Lac Mausoleum door open seemingly just for me.

Though I couldn't call Aunt Grace, I had promised Ben I'd write as soon as I got to Laurelton Hall and tell him about it. Sitting at the desk, using all of Mr. Tiffany's beautiful brass and glass writing accoutrements, I penned a letter to him. For the next fifteen minutes, I wrote and drew little sketches, telling him about our trip and the other fellows but mostly about the artistry of the estate. Finished, I blotted the letter, folded it, and addressed the envelope.

Putting my thoughts down helped me relax, and even though an hour before I hadn't believed I'd ever fall asleep, I dropped off right away.

• • •

The next morning, I woke up with the sun, thinking, as I did most days as my eyes burst open, of the place where I'd been sent after the trial. Because I was a minor, I'd been sentenced to two years at Toronto's notorious Andrew Mercer Reformatory for Women. The judge had told my mother that I'd be well taken care of there, assuring her it was a homelike place for wayward young girls.

It was anything but.

The other inmates were all also younger than eighteen. A mix of unwed mothers and unmanageables, as the matron called us, girls like me who had either committed crimes or been falsely accused of them. We were worked too hard, fed too little, and abused both verbally and physically without remorse.

Some of the girls, especially the pregnant ones, were exposed to medical experiments, and many of the babies delivered during my internment were born sickly or dead.

Because I had been sent there for manslaughter, the wardens and other girls treated me as if I were a murderer. And of a Christian minister, no less. No one befriended me. I was a leper. And I was always given the worst job, cleaning the latrines for weeks on end in the summer and shoveling snow in the winter.

I was the outsider, and, as I learned, they all

took glee in watching whoever was new suffer through the initiation into the hell I had all but volunteered for.

Pain finally woke me one morning, radiating up my back in excruciating spasms. The matron, Mrs. Clarkson, a thin woman with steel-wool-colored hair and a voice the color of mud, stood over me, holding the switch she'd just used on me.

"Get up unless you want another lashing," she spat out. "This isn't a hotel, dearie. Of all wretched women, the idle are the most wretched. Which is why, while you are here, we will impress the importance of labor upon you. Only hard work will reform you, dearie."

And just for good measure, she whipped me once more and then sent me to class.

We studied in the morning—history, geography, literature, stenography, and home economics—and worked in the afternoon either sewing, cooking, woodworking, or cleaning. Each day felt as if it lasted a week. My only relief from the boredom came at four in the afternoon, when we were given an hour and a half for physical activity. The school didn't care what we did, as long as we were moving. Regardless of the weather, I spent those precious ninety minutes drawing in the woods on the school grounds. I had no brushes or paints, no colored crayons or sketch pads. My only tools were the ordinary yellow pencils and white lined paper I used for class assignments. But it didn't matter. I still could lose myself in the quest to understand light through the way it cast objects in highlights and lowlights and shadows.

For the first two and a half months, Mother wrote often, with words of love and gratitude, of the child growing in her womb and of the time we would be together again.

When we'd said good-bye after the trial, Mother said she would be going to live with Aunt Grace in Ithaca for the duration of her pregnancy, but her letters never had Ithaca postmarks. Instead, they came from several different cities: Burlington, Amherst, Boston, then finally the Bronx.

Almost a year after she passed away, Aunt Grace forwarded me a letter she had received. She wrote that she hadn't been sure if she should show it to me, but she thought it was important for me to know what had happened to my mother.

Dear Grace,

One of your sister's last requests was that I write to you and tell you what happened. She knew you would want to know. And that hopefully understanding, you would forgive her for not coming back to you.

I met your sister when she was still married to her husband, the Reverend. I was younger than she was, an art student. At first, she was just helping me hone my craft. But then we fell in love.

She told me I was a tender relief from the abuse inflicted by the Reverend. Those were her words. A tender relief.

We never knew if her baby was mine or his. Either way, the child was part of her, and I wanted to save her—to help get her out of Hamilton and away from him for good. The original plan had been for Faith and Jenny to run away and go to Ithaca. I'd go to New York and find us a place. Then Faith would join me and Jenny would stay with you.

That was the plan, except, of course, the Reverend ruined it like everything else. Or so it seemed. Until Faith and I got a second chance when Jenny was sent to the reformatory and Faith and I left Hamilton together. We made our way to New York, stopping in different cities, claiming we were newlyweds heading back home after visiting family. We had to be careful to cover up Faith's identity, as the press would have been all over her so soon after the trial. She was paranoid, forever thinking we would get caught by someone, a reporter or a detective. I wanted to get married for real. I loved her and would have done anything for her, even work at a factory, in order to support her and the child. But she saw the artist in me and wanted me to be able to create, wanted us to get to New York as we'd planned and settle into the Village, blend in with the other artists and actors and bohemians who wouldn't blink an eye at an older, pregnant woman and a younger man.

But we never made it to Manhattan. We were staying at a rooming house in the Bronx when Faith went into premature labor. She was bleeding and in terrible pain. We both knew she needed a doctor, but she insisted that I drop her off at the hospital and then leave. She promised she'd send for me at the rooming house once the baby was born. She didn't want to risk anyone knowing that Faith Haddon—"the wife of the Reverend William Haddon, who had been murdered by her daughter Jenny Fairburn"—had arrived at the hospital with another man.

I never saw Faith again. Never held the baby who might have been my son. All I had left was the memory of her and her wish to see me become a successful artist. It became my obsession to fulfill that wish, no matter what it took. But what happened to me isn't of any interest to you. I'm writing because Faith asked me to. To tell you that she was happy those last weeks. Filled with hope. And so was I.

Signed,
A Friend

During my incarceration, Aunt Grace wrote at least twice a week. I received her long letters, rife with stories, news, and her wonderful kernels of wisdom. Many days, I believed the only thing keeping me sane were my aunt's letters. Except for the day I received that letter. I'd had no idea my mother had a lover. What else didn't I know? What else wouldn't I ever know?

Mr. Lothrop had told us breakfast began at eight, so I dressed in brown slacks and a white blouse, threw an amber cardigan around my shoulders, grabbed my sketch pad and pencils, and ventured outdoors.

All the paths looked inviting. I chose one and within minutes found myself walking through a wooded glen. I followed a stream until it emptied into a pond surrounded by lilies and irises, boxwood bushes, and weeping willows. Tall cedar trees in the background scented the air. The whole scene was a painting waiting to be committed to canvas. But it wasn't the colors that made me stop but rather the light filtered through the trees.

As I circled the pond looking for the exact place to set up, I noticed a man up ahead in a white suit, sitting on a bench, working with watercolors, painting the scene. I recognized him right away, but before I could decide what to say, he called out to me in a voice much friendlier than I'd imagined, the color of warmed bittersweet chocolate.

"Good morning," he said.

"Good morning, Mr. Tiffany."

"I take it you are one of the new fellows."

I'd reached his side and extended my hand. "I am. I'm Jenny Bell."

"Ah, Miss Light."

"Excuse me?"

"Your submission—the painting of the light coming through glass. Reflecting on stone."

I'd never given myself a moniker, but I liked it.

He extended his own hand, and as I shook it, I noticed the color of his eyes. So this was whom Oliver had inherited his eyes from. Though Mr. Tiffany's were not quite as searching, they were almost the same arctic blue.

"Let's take a walk," he said, standing. "Keep me company. I need to stretch my legs. I've been sitting without moving for almost an hour. Leave your sketchbook here with my paints. I'll tell you

203

how I feel about light. We might find we have something in common."

Along with a caramel-colored terrier that Mr. Tiffany said was named Funny, we circled the pond. Although he used a cane, his gait was sprightly, and I didn't have to slow down to match his pace.

"I started painting when I was a boy, because I was fascinated by light and color. I took photographs to try to freeze the light so I could study it later and paint it. But it wasn't until I started working with glass that I really came to feel I understood it."

For a few moments, we walked without either of us talking, accompanied by birdsong and the sounds of our footsteps crushing leaves and shifting rocks.

"I chose to paint what is most elusive, as you have, but at least my timing was right. I don't envy you the task now that the art world is walking away from impressionism."

"I'm more interested in the old masters' techniques," I said. "I want to know what they knew about light."

"Ah, chiaroscuro," he said thoughtfully.

We'd come around the other side of the pond. The sunlight filtered through the trees and cast colored reflections on the surface of the water. Mr. Tiffany pointed it out.

"Look at that magic. Light mattered to Monet,

to Cezanne, to Manet, but now Matisse is moving into almost flat color, and everyone is following. And Picasso? He doesn't care about light at all. But you can't have beauty without light, and beauty is the only worthwhile quest. Don't lose your way trying to become popular."

I didn't know what to say.

"Tell me what spot you modeled your submission on. Was that a real place?"

I missed a step but caught myself.

"Are you all right?" He reached out a steadying hand.

"Yes, fine, thank you. I was too busy looking around to look down."

"A mistake I've made myself." His eyes twinkled. We continued on. "It's hard to look away from how the light plays on this pond. It's really spectacular, isn't it? This particular spot is at its most beautiful in early morning. You'll find different areas of Laurelton Hall come to life at different times of the day. There's no time, though, day or night, when you can't find something to delight and amaze you."

"From what I've seen already, I don't doubt it."

"Thank you. Now," he continued, "back to your submission. You were painting light filtering through a stained-glass window in a mausoleum, weren't you?"

"Yes. How did you know?"

"Even without color, I could tell from the shape

and length of the shadows. Light coming through unevenly thick glass in a small narrow area. Am I right?"

"You are."

"Was the window signed?"

"Yes, it had *Tiffany Glass Co.* etched into a metal tag on the bottom."

"I'm flattered. Tell me more about the window."

I didn't want to lie, but I never spoke about Hamilton. Since I was born in Ithaca and I knew the city well, I could place my whole life before New York City there without making any mistakes.

"The window is in a mausoleum in Ithaca. One day, I found the door open, went in, and was transfixed."

"Recently?"

"No, I was fourteen."

"And what was a fourteen-year-old doing wandering through a cemetery?"

I hadn't anticipated that question, but I'd learned to always keep the lie as close to the truth as possible. There was less chance of slipping up that way.

I told him my aunt was friendly with a reverend and his wife and had taken me with her when she'd gone to visit them. I'd gotten bored and gone outside. The parsonage was on the edge of the cemetery, and I'd taken a walk. Out of curiosity, I'd tried all the mausoleum doors.

"Describe the window to me, if you would. We've placed quite a few in Upstate New York."

I realized I was holding my breath and forced myself to exhale and calm down. I wasn't talking to Ben Montgomery, whose job required him to be suspicious. This was a seventy-six-year-old man who couldn't possibly remember every window he had sold to every family in every city. Could he?

"The window depicted a peaceful scene. Flowers climbing on a gate in the foreground. A pond or a lake very much like this one, with flowers all around it in the middle section. A bay in the distance, with low hills on the opposite shore."

"What kind of flowers?"

His attention to detail made me anxious. I knew exactly the kinds of flowers depicted in the window. I'd stared at it numerous times a week for almost three years, finding peace in its landscape when I didn't have it in my life. Should I lie about the flowers? But the window had been so important to me; this man's creation had been my sanctuary. I owed him at least that one truth.

"I'm not sure I remember them all, but there were irises, yellow lilies, delphiniums, and roses on the gate."

"And was the window peach in tone overall or violet? Did it look like dawn or dusk?"

"Dusk."

He pondered what I had told him.

"Irises, yellow lilies, delphiniums, and roses on a gate. You are sure?"

"I think so. But I haven't seen it for years."

He stroked his beard, thinking and nodding his head.

I was instantly concerned. I shouldn't have given him that time frame, in case he really did remember where and when he sold each window.

"The studio makes many stock windows based on designs we use over and over. We also have custom orders that include requests for certain flowers, trees, structures, or overall colorations. Sometimes we'll create a bespoke window that turns out so well we add it to the basic designs. But a gate with climbing roses . . . we didn't use it in many windows." He stroked his beard again. "I seem to remember one like that. I think I even remember the woman who commissioned it for her father's resting place. He cultivated roses, you see. I remember it quite well, now that I think of it."

Mr. Tiffany was lost in memory for a moment. I had my hands clasped by my side, my fingers digging into the fleshy part of my palms. Hoping he wouldn't ask me anything else about where I might have seen it, because if he remembered where it was, he might remember the news stories, my "trial of the century." How a young girl named Jenny Fairburn had been found guilty in the death of the reverend associated with the cemetery where the Fond du Lac Mausoleum was kept. And if Mr. Tiffany put it all together and realized that the only difference between me and that young girl was our surname, he'd surely throw me out of Laurelton.

"The window was breathtaking. It was magic," I whispered, not sure he'd even heard me over the sound of the breeze blowing through the trees.

"I like to think about the moment people stumble on one of my windows and find themselves surprised or delighted. Now I can add the story of a little girl opening a door to a mausoleum and my window beginning her lifelong love affair with light," he said. "It's exactly why I started to create windows and lamps, so more people could share in the loveliness. See the beauty. That's what's important. The quest for beauty."

We'd circled the pond and arrived back where we'd begun. His watercolors and my sketch pad were side by side. He sat down, patting the seat next to him, inviting me to join him.

"This lily pond is lovely to paint," he said.

I was relieved he hadn't pressed me for more information about the window. Now I could relish the invitation to sit and learn from the artist who was my idol.

"At different times of the day," he continued, "it takes on very different characteristics. It's quite whimsical now but can look downright moody at dusk in shadows and—"

The dog barked and stood at attention.

"What is it, Funny?" he asked, and he petted her, keeping her back. "Probably a rabbit," he said to me. "She's a ratter by breed and if she was allowed would be off now trying to murder the poor thing."

Funny resumed her position curled up at her master's feet.

"Now that we've averted that disaster, tell me, Miss Light, what do you plan to do with your paintings?"

"I want to show, of course, and to sell."

"Hard way to make a living. Do you plan on finding a husband to support you?"

"No." The word flew out of my mouth and sounded more strident than I'd meant it to.

Mr. Tiffany looked at me askance. "The idea of marriage puts you off? Were your own parents unhappy?"

"My own parents . . . no, actually, they were very happy. Until my father died."

"What was your father's profession?"

Unlike Edward the night before, Mr. Tiffany was only being kind. It would have appeared rude if I'd held back.

"He was an architect, and my mother was an art teacher."

"How old were you when he died?"

"He died before I was born."

210

I looked away, thinking as I did too often of how different my life would have been had my father lived.

"My first wife died when my children were young." Mr. Tiffany's voice had grown distant. "Hilda was only five. And when my second wife passed, our youngest, Dorothy, was only thirteen."

He was lost in his memories for a moment, and I respected the silence.

"You've made me think quite a bit about the past, Miss Light."

"I'm sorry."

"No." He grinned ruefully. "At my age, it's sometimes easier to remember what happened years ago than what happened last week. Tell me, did your mother remarry?"

"She did."

"And how did that work out?"

"Not very well."

I hoped he wouldn't ask for more details. It wasn't just that I didn't want to tell him, it was that I didn't want to think of the Reverend in this sacred place. Mr. Tiffany's sanctuary was too beautiful to sully with remembering the man who had ruined my mother's life and changed mine forever.

"And that's the reason you aren't searching for a husband?"

"I've never looked at it that way. I've just

always viewed marriage as a job, and it's not the job I want for myself in the foreseeable future. And there are so many opportunities for women that I shouldn't have to marry to survive. That's the one thing that came out of the war—women proved how much they were capable of tackling."

"You're quite right. Twenty-five years ago, if a woman working for me got married, she had to quit her job. It's how I lost the best artist I ever had in the glassworks, Clara Driscoll. But when her marriage ended, she came back." He looked off as if he was lost in another memory and then refocused on me. "What about love, Miss Light? Don't you think a great love might change your mind about marriage?"

I said I didn't think so.

Mr. Tiffany searched my face. "Ah, that must be because you've never experienced a great love, have you?"

I shook my head.

"Look," he said, suddenly pointing toward the path.

A peacock and a peahen were sauntering toward us. Mr. Tiffany put his hand on Funny's head.

"Stay," he said, preventing her from chasing them away.

I watched, riveted by their stately progress.

"Have you ever seen a peacock fan?"

"No, but I have a watercolor of a feather. My mother painted it for me a long time ago."

212

"Maybe we'll be lucky," Mr. Tiffany said, "and he'll fan for her, in hopes she'll choose him for a mate. Did you know the pattern of the eyes on a peacock's tail is unique to each bird and how the female makes her decision?"

"No, I don't know much about them except how beautiful their colors are."

Both of us fell silent as the birds continued their journey across the grass and then disappeared into the bushes without the male showing off.

"My daughters are all married but still pursuing careers." Mr. Tiffany put his watercolors away in their case. "Shall we make our way back?"

I rose and gathered my supplies.

"How do you support yourself now?"

Mr. Tiffany used his cane to push a fallen bough off the path. The dog ran ahead, then stopped and waited for her master.

I told him that I'd been working in a tea shop but recently took a job as a courtroom sketch artist for the *Herald Tribune*.

"There's not much beauty or light in a court-room, is there? Murder and madness don't lend themselves to lovely pictures."

"They certainly don't."

"Miss Light, I'm quite good friends with many men and women who are believers in spiritualism. My interest began when I was younger and traveled extensively in North Africa. I've been influenced by the mystical meditative arts of ancient Egypt and India and have seen and heard so many things in my life that simple faith cannot explain. I sometimes sense things about people that I can't explain, and so I hope you will forgive me for intruding on your privacy, but I think you have a job to do here at Laurelton Hall, and that is to restore your soul and learn how to immerse yourself in beauty. You're wounded and need to heal. The business of living can steal away the wonder of life. One man's ugliness can blind another to the world's magic. You must promise me that if you do nothing else during your time here, you will focus on seeing without fear and opening yourself to that which is in you and makes you an artist."

I tried to hide that I was crying, but he noticed.

"I didn't mean to upset you," he said, handing me his own snowy white linen handkerchief.

I took it and wiped my cheeks. "You didn't. You stirred a memory of my mother. She taught me how to look at the world and see its beauty, but she's also the one who showed me that much of that beauty is a lie." It felt good to speak the truth out loud.

"I take it she's no longer with us?"

"No, she's not."

"First your father and then your mother. How old were you when she passed?"

"Sixteen," I said, and immediately flashed on the image of the matron at the reformatory finding me at work, washing dishes in the kitchen, and informing me in a voice that held no pity that my mother had not survived giving birth to my brother. The baby had been stillborn, she said, and then handed me a letter from Aunt Grace.

Dearest Jenny,

By now Matron has given you the terrible news. I so wanted to come and tell you in person, but the warden wouldn't allow it.

There is still much about your mother's passing I don't know, but let me tell you what happened.

Five days ago, I received a call from the Lebanon Hospital in the Bronx informing me that my sister had listed me as next of kin and that they were informing me that Faith Haddon had died giving birth to a stillborn son.

I hadn't even known your mother was in the Bronx but believed her to still be in Boston staying with friends.

I traveled as quickly as possible to the hospital and the next day collected your mother's body as well as her infant's. Today they were buried together—your mother holding the son she never saw, who never saw her—beside your grandparents at Lakeview Cemetery here at home. Many of your mother's lifelong friends still in Ithaca, along with many of my own, came to pay their respects and offer prayers—though it's late for those prayers.

I'd hoped for sunshine to ease the pain, but it rained ceaselessly. Oh, darling Jenny, what a sad day it has been, what a tragic end for my precious Faith and that poor innocent babe.

I intend to find out exactly what happened to your mother during the few weeks since I last heard from her, and I will report back to you.

In the meantime, there is so much I want to say, but I know how little comfort it will bring you. Your mother is blood of your blood. The body that gave you life. The heart that gave you soul. The eyes that taught you how to see—and how well she taught you to see.

I know how much you loved Faith and how much you gave up to protect her. And now to have those sacrifices culminate in such an end as this breaks my heart for you.

We are all we have left, you and I, and I promise you, I will be there to get you and bring you home with me the moment you're set free. All I can say is to remind you that your mother loved you with all her heart and gave you a great gift, the ability to notice beauty in this world and to create it. And as long as you continue to do both, even in that terrible place, your mother will live within you.

I remain forever and always,
Your loving Aunt Grace

"You haven't had an easy time of it in your young life, have you?" Mr. Tiffany asked now.

"There have been some challenges along the way," I said, hoping I'd kept the sarcasm out of my voice.

"Fight them with your paintings. Don't let them define you."

"I'm not sure what you mean."

"Make the unfairness and ugliness be the wind, Miss Light. Put them at your back, pushing you to search out the beauty that's not a lie. Show them that you have what it takes. That they didn't win."

We'd reached the main house without my noticing the path we'd taken.

"Now we're back, and hopefully you've worked up an appetite for breakfast."

"Thank you so much for the walk . . ." I looked down at the crumpled handkerchief. "And for this." I held it out.

"You keep it. When you don't need it, give it to the laundress. And if you want to paint the lily pond, I'm there every morning at six forty-five when I'm in residence. I'd be delighted for you to join me for the sunrise colors."

We reached the portico. I paused at the entrance, trying to escape the past.

"Open the door, and get out of that mausoleum," he said. "There are other kinds of light. Don't be afraid of them."

13

An hour later, Minx knocked on my door to say she was going to the studio to have breakfast with the rest of the fellows and asked if I wanted to come. We set off together a few minutes later.

Platters, pitchers, and chafing dishes on the sideboard offered eggs, bacon, pancakes, cheeses, cold meats, a variety of juices, grapefruit halves, fruit compote, bread, rolls, butter curls, and glistening gem-toned jams.

A buffet-style meal always reminded me of the lack of food at Andrew Mercer. The matrons stretched out supplies and fed us only the most meager portions. We were always hungry. Sometimes while working in the garden in the summer, you could sneak an apple or some berries or vegetables, but you had to eat them quickly when none of the guards was watching. If you were caught, you'd be thrown into the dark, damp basement with a battalion of rats as your only companions.

When I finally left the reformatory and came home to Aunt Grace's, the smells of her dinner table were almost too intense. I hadn't tasted butter in two years. I hadn't had salt or pepper. Or white bread. At first, I could only eat a few mouthfuls at a time. The tastes were too intense after the pallid meals I'd grown accustomed to. When I told Aunt Grace about the watery porridge, the thin slices of brown, stale bread, and the stringy bits of meat flung onto our plates, she put her head in her hands and wept. The tragedy of my sacrifice and of the deaths of her sister and nephew were nearly too much to comprehend.

But I wasn't at Andrew Mercer anymore. I took a slice of toast and a spoonful of raspberry jam and sat down. I felt shy and uncomfortable as the fellows talked about settling down for the first day of work. Although we'd all had dinner together the night before, I was still wary of the strangers around me. Sharing bits and pieces about myself unnerved me enough when I met two or three new people at a time. This was a dozen at once.

Minx, on the other hand, was in her element. She bloomed around people, and for the second time in as many days, I took advantage of her gregarious chatter to fade into the background. She continued to engage everyone over the morning meal. While they conversed, I looked around the table, assigning colors to each voice.

Edward Wren had been storm-cloud gray since I first met him at the Art Students League. Paul Cadmus was bright lemon yellow. Luigi Lucioni was ruby. Navy for Edgar Imler. Verdant green for Tom Johnson. Olive for Tristam Richards, Michael Gernand was burnt orange, Dudley Pratt burnt sienna, Peter Pierce was teal, and Henry Goodson pine green.

Edward, sitting opposite me, was looking at my plate. "Are you all right, Jenny? All this food, and you're just having toast?"

Henry, who'd heard him, glanced over.

"It's excellent toast," I countered.

"And you haven't said much, either," he continued.

"I didn't know breakfast was an audition." I tried to joke, but my skin goosebumped. And then Henry asked Luigi about the end-of-the-session prize. Edward, overhearing, commented, as did Paul and then Minx. An undercurrent of competition ran through the conversation.

Despite the rivalry, they all seemed at ease around one another. Eating, joking, talking about their work, the house, the grounds, and the food. I nibbled my toast and began to regret accepting the scholarship. I was just as ambitious as any of them, but fear was keeping me from expressing it. Edward wouldn't be the only one to try to size me up. It wasn't like this at the League. There we had been free simply to arrive, do our work, and leave without socializing if that was what we wanted. Here we were expected to share meals, the studio, and much of our free time for eight weeks.

Soon Graves arrived with the morning mail.

"I assume that some of you have given out this

address. If you haven't, feel free. A few letters have arrived already." He proceeded to sort the pile of envelopes, giving one to me.

I recognized Ben's handwriting. Of course, I'd save it for later. I couldn't open it here. But I wanted to, if only to reassure myself that he'd moved off the subject of my "mysterious past," as he called it.

Maybe I should leave Laurelton and go up to Albany and persuade Ben to . . . to what? How could I dissuade him from his instincts? Especially when they weren't wrong. Maybe if I saw him and gave him some kind of ultimatum, told him I'd break off our friendship if he couldn't find it in his heart to trust me. Maybe then he'd stop.

Suddenly, I knew I needed to leave Laurelton. Even if I didn't go to Albany. As much as I longed to spend more time with Mr. Tiffany and learn from him, I wasn't cut out to be around so many people. While Laurelton's peace should have been soothing, it seemed to be only exacerbating my sense of dread.

Yes, I'd leave and go to Albany. I glanced at Minx. Telling her would be difficult. She'd gone to a lot of trouble to get me a spot at the Foundation, but then again, she hadn't asked me if I wanted her to make the effort. She'd have to accept that I was leaving.

I stood up quickly, clutching the letter. Minx

looked over. My abrupt action must have alerted her.

"Jenny? Are you ready to go sketching?" she asked.

"Actually, I'm going to go back up to the house, I don't think—"

She frowned. "No, come sketching."

"Don't worry about me." I knew from the consternation on her face that she was worried. But as much as I treasured her as a friend, I couldn't stay. I couldn't go through this effort and discomfort all for her.

I walked down the hallway and out the door and took the first path I came to, believing it was the right way to the house. I proceeded for a few yards, until I was deep enough to be hidden by the trees if anyone was watching from the Foundation building, and then I opened the letter from Ben.

He filled me in on the trial and how well his stories were doing in the paper. He asked about Laurelton and sent a lot of good wishes that I'd settled in and was having a productive time. And then I reached the last paragraph.

> Jenny, I can tell that you don't want me to ask you questions about your childhood. But the very fact that it upsets you so much must mean something bad happened to you. Don't you see that my reasons for

asking are that I want to help you? That I care about you? I'm determined to prove to you that your secrets are safe with me. Otherwise, how will you ever trust me? How will I ever trust you? How will you ever be able to go on with your life and find happiness? I feel so strongly that you and I belong together. Pictures and words. We're a match, darling girl, don't you see? So tell me what it is that happened, and I cross my heart and hope to die if I don't just wrap my arms around you and let you rest your head on my shoulder and promise that whoever it was and whatever they did will never trouble you again.

I folded the letter and shoved it into the pocket of my trousers. Part of me did want to tell him, to tell *someone*. Now that Aunt Grace was gone, there was no one I could talk to about the past. But at the same time, I never wanted to speak of the Reverend or Andrew Mercer Reformatory again.

I knew how people gawked when they found out I had been convicted of manslaughter. I'd seen when I moved back to Ithaca how the people who knew—even friends of our family—stared at me. They couldn't help it. I tried to believe I could rebuild my life there. Aunt Grace tried to believe it, too. But there was always someone who couldn't turn away, who whispered behind a raised hand, who pointed at me in the street. There was no escaping the past.

My aunt had adjusted as well as she could. Her efforts to learn about my mother's whereabouts had not borne fruit. Other than the one anonymous letter she'd received, the last months of my mother's life remained a mystery. She even tried to raise Mother's spirit with the Ouija board but was unsuccessful. She felt she'd somehow failed her sister, and me, and nothing I could say changed her mind.

My mother had made good on her promise not to tell anyone—not even Aunt Grace—about our decision for me to turn myself in. Despite all the emotion and remorse expressed in her letters to her sister, she never did reveal the truth.

One night, I almost broke down and told my aunt what I'd done—and what I hadn't done—but in the end, I couldn't. I had to preserve my mother's memory. Aunt Grace would have viewed Mother as a monster for agreeing to the plan, no matter how insistent I was that it had been my idea.

I knew Aunt Grace always wondered about the Reverend's death. Whether it was self-defense or murder, she told me once, it didn't matter in her mind. She was only happy that he was out of our lives for good. And she loved me no matter what.

I hadn't regretted my decision to take the punishment for my mother's crime while I was first at Andrew Mercer. But after Mother died, I did begin to wonder if I had made a mistake. And once I was back in Ithaca and discovered how deeply I'd been branded, how impossible it was to leave the past behind, and saw that shadow of doubt appear even in my aunt's eyes, I became certain I shouldn't have taken the blame. I'd believed I was powerful enough to try to undo my mother's mistakes, but I was wrong.

One night, I found my aunt sitting in the darkened parlor, despondent and depressed. Her photo album was open to pictures of the two sisters when they were girls. I sat beside Aunt Grace, and she leafed through the pages. Before me, my aunt and my mother went through puberty, young adulthood, and my mother's pregnancy. Then a baby appeared in the photos, me. And then I was a toddler and then a little girl off to her first day of school, reading, making doll clothes, and painting.

My aunt reached out and caressed one of the images.

"Your mother and I often talked about how proud we were of you, Jenny. So impressed by your passion and your willingness to take risks for what you loved. No matter what life throws at you, no matter how hard it gets, don't give that up. Promise me you won't."

Despite the brave front she put on, I knew Aunt Grace never stopped believing she should have done more to save her sister and by default protected me, too, and that belief ate away at her, weakening her spirits so that when she was felled with pneumonia, she didn't have the resistance to fight it.

Without Aunt Grace to shelter me, Ithaca became even harder to bear. No matter how I tried to change my appearance in that town, I would forever be Jenny Fairburn, the girl who murdered her stepfather in one of the first "trials of the century." The words changed people.

And I didn't want to change the look in Ben's eyes. Even if he believed me when I told him I hadn't done what they said I had, he'd still wonder. There was no proof either way. The two people who knew the truth—my mother and the Reverend—were dead.

In my mind, the idea of stopping Ben's questions overlapped with the notion of leaving Laurelton. My anxiety suddenly became less focused on strangers and more on the possibility of losing one of the two stalwarts in my life.

I should go. Yes, I would mind not getting to know Mr. Tiffany, but the chance of having another early-morning walk with him wasn't enough to counter the emotional upheaval I was experiencing.

In order to leave, I'd need to ask Mr. Lothrop or Graves for a car to take me to the train. But that meant explaining. Could I just get to the station on foot? How long a walk was it?

I still hadn't come up with a plan when I realized I must have taken the wrong path and had no idea where I was. The trees were too thick for me to get any sense of what was to the right or left or ahead of me. I heard birdsong. Smelled loamy earth. Felt chilly in the shadows of the canopy of leaves that shrouded the sun. Should I double back or keep going? Ahead, the path forked. Now I was even more confused.

I remembered Mr. Lothrop telling us the estate sat on a 580-acre parcel and that Mr. Tiffany had made an effort to leave as much of the land untamed as possible. How big was 580 acres? My aunt's house was on a lot too small to even be measured in acreage. I had no reference. Could I actually be lost? Wouldn't I have to reach a clearing at some point?

I took the path to the right, and before too long, the well-placed stones became trodden-down leaves and twigs, rocks and pebbles. It felt as if the temperature was dropping. I looked up. The sliver of sky I could see through the canopy of leaves had filled with gray rain clouds. I continued on. In seconds, the first cold, mean raindrops began to fall.

I kept going through what seemed like an

endless forest, until finally, about ten minutes later, the trees thinned out enough for me to glimpse a swath of gray-blue water in the distance. At last, a landmark.

The path led me to a gate. I opened the rusted yet still ornate iron doors, and on the other side was a stone staircase leading down to the shore. As I descended, I looked to the left, then right, and recognized the dock and the boathouse. I'd clearly taken a different path but had arrived at the same strip of pale sandy shore I'd stumbled on the day before.

Even in the storm, the view was arresting. It was also familiar. As I stood there, rain dripping in my eyes, I realized *this* was the view in the stained-glass window in the Fond du Lac Mausoleum. Mr. Tiffany must have appropriated this vista. I turned, stared up at the gate. They weren't in bloom yet, but yes, rose branches wove through its iron rods, and irises were just about to bloom. I did the math. He'd built this house in 1902. The date on the mausoleum's cornerstone was 1905, so the window must have been created that same year. Why didn't Mr. Tiffany mention that earlier this morning when we were discussing the window?

The rain was letting up, but I was so wet it didn't matter. I brushed the water off one of the steps and sat down to process the sight before me. I was looking at the actual landscape that

I'd spent hours staring at in a window in a mausoleum in the Weber Falls Cemetery in Hamilton, Ontario. How could I have come so far only to find myself back again at the same stretch of water, the same shoreline?

"Jenny, you're soaking wet!"

I looked down. Oliver Tiffany stood below me, in his bathing clothes with a towel around his shoulders.

"So are you."

"I was swimming."

"In the rain?"

"Well, I started before but then got caught in it. Are you coming down?" he called. "I have more towels and a thermos of coffee in the boathouse."

I stood and descended the steep, slippery stones. I stumbled and felt my left foot twist and go out from under me. Before I could fall, Oliver's hand reached out and gripped me and held me steady.

"Are you OK? Those steps are fairly treacherous. No one uses that path here for just that reason."

"It's fine. I'm fine. I was lost and have been wandering around for . . ." I looked at my wristwatch—Aunt Grace's watch. "For almost a half hour. Where *is* the other path?"

He pointed up behind me. "I'll show you later. Let's get you dried off."

He led me into the boathouse. The main room was a combination living and dining area.

"There's a kitchen in there." He pointed to another door. "That's a studio with a sofa comfortable enough for me to use as a bed when I need to escape from the main house. In there are the changing room and facilities. Take your time. I'll get the coffee."

I found a stack of soft towels in the changing room and set to blotting the rain and drying myself as much as I could.

On the deck, under the tarp, Oliver was waiting with a thermos and mugs. As soon as I came out, he poured the coffee. When he handed me a mug, our fingers touched, and like the day before, I felt warmth where our skin met. But as soon as we were no longer touching, it was gone.

"There are several paths down here. And since you seem so drawn to the water, I'll show them to you later. Yesterday you took the most direct route."

"Blind luck." I took a sip from my mug. "This is delicious."

"Thank you. As for blind luck? No such thing. I don't believe in luck."

"Then what do you believe in?" I asked.

"Intuition."

"Yes, your grandfather mentioned the subject to me this morning."

"Grandfather is good friends with some very

smart people who believe all sorts of fascinating things. I've grown up listening to their conversations. I wouldn't go so far as Arthur Conan Doyle, who believes in communing with the dead. But I've talked to Nicola Tesla, Mark Twain, and Thomas Edison, who all believe in a form of perception we don't know very much about yet. Our brains emit energy waves. The scientists have proven that. As well as the fact that the earth itself and everything on it emits energy waves. It turns out that some of us are more adept than others at picking up on those waves, much in the way a radio picks up sound waves."

I must have shivered again.

"Are you chilled?" Oliver asked. "I can get another towel."

"No, I'm fine. But did you really go swimming this morning? It was so cold."

I pondered the fact that he was sitting there with me, wearing his swimsuit with its tank top but with bare arms and legs. It certainly wasn't scandalous for a man to be in a bathing suit, so why did it feel so strange? Goodness, in drawing class, the male models were naked. But this was nothing like sketching a model. This was a man whose eyes glittered like gems and whose smile moved something inside of me. I almost missed what he was saying and made myself concentrate.

"I do every morning, and I go sailing, too, if I

can. I practically live down here in the boathouse when I'm at Laurelton Hall. It's my hideaway."

"I'm sorry—then I've invaded your privacy twice."

"No need to apologize."

"What are you hiding from?"

"Oh, I don't know . . . the family business? Stacks of paper and lots of numbers? And if I'm totally honest, all the people here. The fellows. The visiting lecturers. My grandfather's guests. To his displeasure, I'm a bit of a loner."

"Well, I can understand that."

"Said like a fellow traveler on the same road."

"Yes, I'm finding it totally overwhelming here. In fact, I was trying to find my way back to the house because I was thinking of escaping."

"Leaving Laurelton Hall for the day?"

"No, not just for the day. I'm not sure I can cope with so many strangers or your grandfather's expectations."

"Oh, don't leave," Oliver said. He reached out and took my hand in his. "Not now that I've saved you from a broken ankle. You owe it to me to keep me company. And I need another loner to be lonely with. We're kindred spirits, you and I."

He let go of my hand. I wasn't sure what to say. Oliver said things that I thought, and I'd never met anyone who did that before. I lifted the mug to my lips and took another long sip. Oliver watched.

"Ah, but you're thinking we've only just met, and it's a little presumptuous for me to be talking about kindred spirits. Am I right?"

"Well, yes, presumptuous and outspoken."

Oliver laughed, and it sounded like the blue-green velvety underside of the leaves of a plant that grew wild in the parish cemetery.

"I wouldn't have said anything if I hadn't imagined you'd understand exactly what I was talking about."

"People don't say things like this to strangers, Mr. Tiffany."

"Please, it's Oliver. And I'm not a stranger. Not now. Would you like some more?" I nodded as he poured and continued speaking. "And I've seen your work. Yes, most of all, I've seen your work."

"You have? How?"

"My grandfather included me in the selection process for this session. He was so impressed with your depiction of light. As was I. And it's not just in your painting; it's in your eyes."

I felt my insides glow.

"So for all those reasons," he continued, "we're already very well acquainted. I predict we'll only become more so. But only if you stay."

"So you're not just intuitive but you're a psychic, too?"

"Hardly. Is it a subject that might be of interest to you?"

"I suppose so. Who isn't interested in it, really?"

I was being coy, and it felt like a betrayal to Oliver somehow, which was odd, since I'd only met him the day before.

"Then you really can't leave yet. Grandfather is going to be having one of his fetes in a few weeks, and Thomas Edison is bringing his Spirit Phone here to do a demonstration. People have been talking about it for years, but this is the first time anyone will have a chance to see it."

"What is a Spirit Phone?"

"Edison believes that while the dead might be gone from *this* world, they still exist in another dimension. And since sound waves, like light waves, can travel, he thinks the right instrument might be able to transmit the words of the dead to the living through those waves."

"I'd say it seems impossible to believe such a thing could work. But then again, I had an aunt who often reminded me that there is so much more we don't know about life and death than what we do know."

"Exactly. So you have to have an open mind to Laurelton as well. And stay in order to see Edison's demonstration, instead of being in your living room in . . . where are you from?"

"I live in New York, in Greenwich Village."

"Where else? I knew the minute I saw your painting that you weren't one of those dilettante society girls with all the right pedigrees, just dabbling in the arts."

"Do many of those wind up here at Laurelton?"

"No. Grandfather and the selection committee have eagle eyes, but a lot of them do apply."

In the distance, bells began to peal. I counted them. It was nine thirty.

"I've got to get to work," Oliver said. "Will you wait for me a minute? I'll change quickly, and we can walk up to the studio together."

I said I would, and while he was gone, I indulged my curiosity. He'd seen my painting. It was only fair that I see his.

He must have been painting or sketching before his swim, because his supplies rested on the table just beside the thermos. I opened the cover of the paper block and looked down at his watercolor.

The landscape was luminous. Done in gouache, it was suffused with a clarity of light that made it at once accessible yet a step beyond what was real. There was nothing impressionistic about Oliver's work; rather, it had geometric precision, and in that lay its beauty.

Something about it reminded me of the exquisite backgrounds in the early Renaissance paintings I'd seen in the Metropolitan Museum. Their rolling hills, cypress trees, blue skies, brooks, and mountains had the same depth and glowing hues. But Oliver's painting was utterly

236

modern. As if della Francesca or Uccello had been plopped down in the twentieth century.

"I see you found my sketches," he said, as he emerged from the dressing room wearing tan trousers, a white shirt, a tan pullover, and a tan, powder-blue, and white striped tie.

I wanted to say something meaningful about his painting. Because it deserved something more profound than just *I did,* but I was tongue-tied. I knew many artists. Some were good. A few dozen were exceptional. But rarely—I could count them easily—did I see work that truly inspired me.

Oliver looked as if he'd read my silence, heard everything I was thinking.

"I take it you like it?" he asked.

He appeared different to me now. I'd considered him attractive before, but now I saw in him what he'd seen in me, a kindred spirit.

"Yes, I do."

"I'm glad, because if you didn't, I wouldn't have as great a chance of persuading you to stay and not run away."

"And you think that me admiring your painting will do that?"

There was a pause, and when he spoke, he was smiling again. "Yes, I do."

14

That evening at dinner, the conversation flowed more freely, as the fellows had become more comfortable with one another. Oliver joined us, and even though he sat at the opposite end of the table from me, the few glances we shared helped me relax. The fluttering in my chest when our eyes met made me especially glad I'd decided to stay, despite my discomfort. I tried to convince myself that the malevolence I'd sensed in the studio was just a silly premonition born out of nerves.

After we finished a meal of lobster bisque, broiled trout almondine, and broccoli au gratin, the server came out with dessert: red velvet cake.

"I have an idea for what to do over smokes and brandy," Minx said, after everyone was finished eating. "You all get settled in the library. I have to get something in the main house, and I'll be back in a few minutes." Minx came over to me. "I wanted to—"

But Edward approached us with a frown on his face and interrupted her. "Weren't we going to take a walk?" he said to Minx in an annoyed tone.

Being the only two women in the group of men,

we were getting more than our share of attention. Especially Minx, who was flirting outrageously with everyone. I'd noticed several times during dinner that Edward appeared put out by it.

"Well, then, walk with me to the house and back, you silly goose," she said. "That's a walk, isn't it?"

"Would you like some brandy? I'm going to have some," Oliver said, as he came around to where I was sitting.

I said I would, and we walked into the library together. He settled me in a wing chair by the window, and I watched him cross the room to the bar at the far end, his long, lean elegance hardly impeded by his limp.

Was it smart of me to take his attention seriously? After all, Minx and I *were* the only two women there. If Oliver wanted female company, it was either her or me, and she appeared to be taken. Also, there was Ben to consider. While we didn't have any kind of understanding, I knew he wanted one.

Oliver came back with two snifters and sat down beside me. "Do you have any idea what Minx is up to?"

"No. She's always full of surprises. Everyone says that's part of her charm."

"Not counting you, of course, she's probably the most gifted artist here." His kept his voice low so as not to be overheard. "She'll have some competition for the prize but not much. Does she want it badly enough?"

His compliment took me by surprise and pleased me more than I could have guessed. Over the years, I had received quite a bit of praise for my paintings from my teachers, my mother, and my aunt. But since I'd started studying at the League, I'd received mostly criticism from my instructors and myself. I'd forgotten how good it felt to have my work admired.

"What do you mean? The prize itself or being an artist?"

"I meant the prize, but your question is intriguing. Do you think she lacks the passion it takes to be an artist?"

I shrugged. "It all comes easily to her. I don't know that she's ever needed to *want* anything. I'm not sure she's ever yearned to escape. She's still unaware of how mean the world really can be."

Oliver looked at me, hard, as if trying to see beyond my words. The first time he'd done that, it had unnerved me. Now it felt more like a secret way of communicating.

"How old were you when you realized how mean the world could be?"

"Fourteen."

"And what happened to you at that tender age?" He reached out and took my hand.

"That's not something—I can't—"

"I'm sorry, I didn't mean to pry. Have a sip of your brandy; it will warm you up."

"All right, everyone, gather 'round," Minx called out, as she walked into the library carrying a long rectangular cardboard box. For a moment, nothing seemed amiss, and then—no, it had to be a coincidence. Even though the box Minx held looked similar in size and shape to the one that sat on the uppermost shelf in the hall closet in our apartment on West Ninth Street—hidden, I'd believed, behind milliners' boxes containing hats Minx no longer wore—it couldn't be the same one. I hadn't brought it with me. I hadn't even opened the box since I was fourteen.

"We've got the real deal here," Minx said, as she laid the worn cardboard box on the card table by the fireplace. "And someone"—she glanced at me—"who surely knows how to use it, since it belongs to her."

The fellows, some with cigars, others with cigarettes and glasses of ale or brandy, began to gather around and watch as Minx opened the box.

I held my breath as she pulled out what looked all too familiar, even though I still held out hope that this board was similar but not mine at all. And then she unfolded it and laid it out.

No, this was not an ordinary Ouija board sold by the Kennard Novelty Company. While this one had started out that way, sure enough, it had all the telltale signs of a custom-designed

Faith Fairburn talking board. The background had been painted like a mystical midnight sky with tiny, perfect star constellations. Clusters of clouds, more stars and lightning bolts, all in shades of gray, white, and silver, filled each of the four corners. A shimmering full moon peeked out of the clouds on the left, a crescent moon on the right. In the middle of the board was a high-gloss turquoise, sapphire, and lavender evil eye, the word *Ouija* in a ribbon woven through the eyelashes. Other Egyptian symbols—a beetle, a cat, a phoenix, an ankh, and a pyramid—decorated the outer border.

I put my hand up to my mouth. How was this possible?

Minx removed an oval piece of wood and three small legs from the box and assembled the device that was meant to travel the board and pick out the letters the spirits chose. The planchette was painted in the same midnight-purple blue and also decorated with clouds and stars.

Still hoping it was a bizarre coincidence, I looked at the bottom left corner of the board. What I didn't want to see was a tiny insignia of a Hamsa hand—the mystical symbol of protection—with my mother's initials, *FGF,* in its center. But there it was.

I walked up to Minx and put my hand on her arm, turning her away from the fellows. "Why did you bring that here?" I whispered.

She looked at me as if I'd posed a bizarre question. "I thought it would be fun," she said.

"But you didn't ask me."

"Why would I ask if I could bring a board game with us? What's wrong, Jenny?"

I couldn't begin to tell her there and then. It was my fault for storing it in the closet instead of my own room. "Nothing," I said.

Minx addressed the assembled artists. "You all know how this works, don't you?"

There were assorted murmurs of assent.

"OK, I'll be the leader. We need a documenter to write down each letter the planchette points to, because it can go really fast, and there are no spaces, so it looks like gibberish until you study what's been written down." She looked into the audience. "Henry, you be the documenter. Jenny and I will be the energizers with our hands on the planchette."

"No," I blurted out.

"But didn't you say your grandfather used to work for Kennard? That you grew up surrounded by Ouija boards. Surely you—"

"I can't do it, Minx."

"Oh, come on, Jenny, the whole—"

I shook my head. I was shivering. Fighting so hard to keep at bay all the memories trying to break through. By my side, Oliver took off his jacket and put it around my shoulders. A whiff of his scent enveloped me—leather, patchouli, and vanilla.

"Pick someone else, Minx," Oliver said in a light, playful tone, deflecting the attention away from me.

Minx looked both hurt and confused, but she acquiesced. She looked at Edward.

"I'll do it with you," he said, and winked intimately.

Minx grinned back. "Edward it is. Now, listen, everyone. There are rules. We have to be serious. Some people say this is a toy, but I believe it is a portal to another realm, and I've seen that proven. Skeptics use the automatism theory to explain what happens, claiming that even though Edward and I don't realize we are moving the planchette, we are. They claim our unconscious thoughts, which Dr. Freud is so enamored of, are spelling out the words. The other theory, which I prefer, is that we actually are channeling discarnate spirits who have messages for us all."

I pulled Oliver's jacket tighter around me. The carefully constructed life I was living seemed to be colliding with my past, as Minx continued talking about how the church believed malicious forces could masquerade as positive spirits and enter our realm through the board, causing damage and even death. I could hear the Reverend's rant under Minx's calm, lovely, coppery-colored voice.

"We're going to call on the spirits," she continued, "talk to whoever shows up, and then at the end say good-bye. That's important, or else we might be leaving open a door that something negative could enter through. Let's get started."

Minx switched off the lights in the room and lit candles. She made sure Henry had enough paper and sharpened pencils. She asked everyone to get their drinks and smokes, because once she started, she didn't want to be distracted by them moving around.

"Now, anyone with a question for a loved one who has passed should concentrate on what you want to ask. What happens here tonight will be a result of how seriously you take this effort. If you think it's silly and frivolous, we'll fail."

The group stilled and quieted. Minx and Edward put their hands on the planchette.

Beside me, Oliver reached for my hand and held it in his warmer one. He leaned close to me and whispered, "You don't have to tell me what's wrong, but obviously you're upset. Do you want to leave?"

I did, but at the same time, I didn't want to draw attention to myself and be the only one of us who couldn't handle the experiment. That would make me stand out in exactly the wrong way. But there was something else, too: never before had I wanted a man to keep holding my hand so much.

I shook my head. "No, I'm OK. As Minx pointed out, there were a few of them lying about at our house growing up. I always heard they can be misused." Not a lie. Not the full truth, either. I wasn't sure there ever would be a right time or place or reason to tell him more of the truth, but this certainly wasn't it.

"Is anyone here?" Minx asked.

The planchette stayed where it was.

"Is there a spirit here?"

Still nothing. A candle on the fireplace mantel flickered.

"Is there anyone here?" Minx tried a third time.

The planchette took off, as if propelled by a strong wind, and flew up to the left corner, landing on the word *YES*.

She followed with a series of questions about the spirit's gender, which was female, and the year she had died. The planchette moved to *1-9-1-6*.

"Do you have a name?" Minx asked.

The planchette didn't move.

She asked again. Still nothing. Then she changed her question. "Do you have a message for someone here?"

The planchette sped back to the word *YES*.

"And what is it?"

The planchette zigzagged around the board far too quickly for me to string words together. Henry, who was closest to Minx and Edward, struggled to keep up. The flurry of movement continued for a few more moments, and then the planchette came to rest on *GOOD BYE* at the bottom of the board.

Minx asked several more questions, but there was no response. Then she asked if anyone had a question to put to the spirits. Paul threw out a query about who would win the Tiffany Foundation prize. Luigi asked if the spirit knew his grandfather. The planchette responded to neither.

"I think we got everything we're going to get," Minx said, getting up and stretching. She walked over to Henry. "Can you read it?"

"I can read some of it, but mostly it's a mess of letters." He pointed.

Minx looked down at the paper and screwed up her face.

Edward peered over Minx's shoulder. "I have an idea," he said. "When there are too many consecutive consonants, try to replace one with a vowel. Like here, it says *H-F-R-F*. If you put in *E* where you wrote *F,* you get the word *HERE.*"

"Good job, old boy," Henry said, as he went back to working the puzzle.

I maneuvered so I could see the piece of paper, too.

S-E-C-R-E-T-S-W-I-L-L-M-O-T-S-T-A-Y-H-I-D-D-E-N-H-F-R-F-D-A-N-G-E-R-H-F-R-F-B-E-L-E-V-E-F-A-I-T-H-G-O.

As I struggled, Henry began reading what he'd figured out: "Secrets will not stay hidden . . . here danger . . . here believe . . . faith go."

"Does it make sense to anyone?" Minx looked

out at all the shadowed faces in the candlelit room.

"I hope not," Louis Pritchard murmured. "Pretty ominous, if you ask me."

I clenched my hands, forcing my fingernails into the flesh of my palms. Gritting my teeth, I used all my strength not to go flying out of the room and into the night.

"Are you all right?" Oliver asked.

"I need . . ." What? Unsure of what I did, in fact, need, I made a helpless gesture, shrugging my shoulders and opening my hands, palms up.

Oliver grabbed my hands and inspected the deep marks. One of the crescent-shaped impressions was bloodied.

"What have you done to yourself, Jenny?" he whispered, and tenderly wiped away the blood with his handkerchief.

I had spent two years learning how to take care of myself in the reformatory, building up methods to protect myself both physically and mentally. I'd had no delinquent history before I arrived there. In my sixteen years, the worst things I'd done were fibbing about some missing homework and taking a slice of cake from the church bazaar without paying. But once I was inside Andrew Mercer, my survival depended on fighting back and never showing fear. So whenever I was scared, whenever I wanted to cry, whenever I started to shake, I dug my nails into my palms. One physical pain to distract from the others.

I hadn't relied on my old method since leaving the reformatory. Not until I saw my mother's Ouija board. Not until I heard the message that Minx and Edward coaxed out of the ether and felt the old panic return that I'd never be free of the past and its stain.

The spirit had said she was a female who died in 1916 and had cautioned someone in the room that his or her secrets would not remain hidden, to believe faith, and to leave this place.

As much as I wished I could rationalize the message, the facts were clear. My mother *had* died in 1916. I *did* have secrets that were hidden. My mother's name *was* Faith.

Since moving to New York, since coming here to Laurelton Hall, I had been so determined to escape my past. Now it seemed to be haunting me. I had been so set on never looking back. But as it turned out, that's all I had been doing.

15

Oliver put his arm around my shoulders. "Come on, let's get you out of here," he said, as he ushered me from the library, out into the warm night. I didn't ask where he was taking me. I didn't care, as long as it was away from that board.

Once we were back in from the loggia, only a few low lights burned for those returning. The stained glass and mosaics were dark. Oliver led me up the main staircase, but instead of heading right toward my quarters, he went left at the end of the corridor and guided me up another staircase. At the second landing, he opened a door into a large room. I glimpsed a curved bank of windows framing the full moon, hanging low in the night sky over the Long Island Sound.

Before I could take in any more of my surroundings, we were going through another door. Oliver flipped the light switch to reveal a large white-tiled bathroom. I smelled his cologne and soap. Big fluffy towels were piled on the sideboard. Combs, brushes, and shaving equipment rested on the sink.

"You sit here." He positioned me on the ledge of the porcelain tub. "I'm going to clean up your hand and bandage it."

After taking various items from a mirrored cabinet over the vanity, Oliver knelt by my side.

"Now, this is going to sting," he said. I heard his words, and almost in unison, under them, I heard my mother's honey-colored voice saying the exact same thing.

Oliver bent over me and, using a piece of cotton, gently swabbed at my cuts, each sting reminding me of a time when my mother had taken care of me in the same way.

After cleaning my cuts, Oliver applied a salve. As he concentrated on his task, I gazed at his luxurious black hair, at his elegant hands and long fingers.

"Last step," he said, as he reached for gauze and a scissor, then taped the bandage. Done, he held out his hand and helped me off the edge of the tub.

"Thank you," I said, and we walked out of his bathroom and into the room that I had barely seen before.

Double the size of mine, this was a combination library, bedroom, and art studio. Longer than wide, the space seemed uncluttered compared with the rest of the house, as if the person who lived here needed a respite from the busy decoration of the rooms below. Instead of stenciled wallpaper, the space that wasn't taken up with bookshelves or windows was painted a watery jade. The lamps had simple opalescent

251

white glass shades. There were no curtains. The frieze at the top of the windows was the only stained glass in the room. Thanks to the full moon, I could make out a purple-red clematis vine with dark leaves framing the sea view. Two settees with a small green lacquer table between them sat in front of it.

A shining black lacquer piano filled the last corner, its bench pulled out. Its music rack was piled with well-worn sheet music.

"Do you play?" Oliver asked me, noting my interest.

"No, but my aunt played, and I loved listening to her. I took some lessons, but I have no rhythm."

"I doubt that," he said. "You just didn't have the right teacher. If you want, while you're here, I could try to teach you a bit." He ran his hand over the gleaming lid.

"How long have you been playing?" I asked.

"Since childhood. It's one of my passions. I've even earned my keep for a while playing in a club in Paris." His voice had slipped into melancholy, and for a moment, his eyes looked off, out the window, into the blackness. Then he seemed to shake off the emotion.

"Have a seat." Oliver gestured to the settee. "I'll get us drinks." He walked over to the bookshelves. Not all were filled with books; one contained a bar setup. He reached for a crystal decanter and two glasses, which he brought over to the table. After pouring an inch of the amber liquid into each, he handed me one, left his where it was, and then walked over to the window. He cranked it open, and a briny breeze wafted in. Finally, he sat on the settee opposite me, lifted his glass to me, and took a sip. I followed suit. I was nervous and at the same time excited about being alone with him in his bedroom.

"Does your hand still sting?"

"No. Thank you for taking care of it." I glanced down at the bandage. "Very professional-looking. How did you know how to do that?"

"At the front. Even though we were a unit of artists, everyone had to know basic first aid. Sometimes more than basic." A frown creased his brow, and then he shook his head as if throwing off the memories. He'd lit one lamp, but it was the moon that shone on Oliver's face.

A sudden desire to capture how he looked at that very moment overwhelmed me. The way the shadows exaggerated his aristocratic cheekbones, how when he leaned forward toward me, his neck stretched even longer, how his mouth pursed, poised to speak. My fingers itched to draw his portrait, so that in case he disappeared, I could at least have that with me forever.

"What *did* happen to your hand?" he asked.

"An old habit of mine."

He was clearly waiting for more of an explanation, so I told him. "When I was a teenager and would get too nervous or upset, I'd ball up my hand and press my fingertips into my palm to distract myself with the pain. Sometimes I didn't realize I was pressing too hard."

"Jenny, what was going on in your life that you'd do such a thing?"

I shook my head. "I can't . . ."

Other than my aunt, I had never told anyone what it was like at Andrew Mercer. I didn't know if I had the words.

"And tonight? Why would you prefer that kind of pain to what you were feeling?" Oliver asked. "What was it about the Ouija board?"

I actually *wanted* to tell him. To let go of everything I was holding inside. To share the story. To tell him about the Reverend's abuse of my mother and the accident at the waterfall and his death and my incarceration, but it was all too terrible. I had been found guilty and convicted of a crime. Only two other people knew the truth of what happened that day, and they were both dead.

Oliver rose from his settee and sat beside me. First, he brushed the curls off my forehead with gentle fingertips. Then, with both hands, he cupped my face and pulled me toward him. Leaning forward, he kissed me on my forehead, then on each of my eyelids, and then he took my unbandaged hand and pulled me so that I was sitting against him. He put his arms around me, as if protecting me from the night and the wind and the shadows. And I felt protected. Safe. Cherished.

"Tell me, Jenny Bell," he whispered in my ear. "What is it that haunts you?"

And over the next hour or two—I never knew how long it took—I told Oliver everything. The story of my childhood. My mother. Aunt Grace. The Reverend.

"He never touched me," I reassured Oliver. "He never had a chance to."

I continued on and told him about the Reverend's death at the waterfall and the vow I forced my mother to keep. I told him about the trial and the community that renounced me. I told him about the judges and the reporters and the photographers, documenting what they concluded were the accurate details of the crime. They had a headline story on their hands, a trial of the century. They had easily fallen for the tale I had devised to save my mother and brother; sussing out the truth was not on their agenda.

I told Oliver about the hell of Andrew Mercer. I used ordinary words to form sentences I hadn't spoken out loud for six years, not since I had told my Aunt Grace. Oliver took me in his arms and stroked my hair and held me and rocked me, and I fell asleep listening to the gentle slapping waves in the bay, the leaves rustling in the trees, and Oliver's heartbeat.

• • •

When I opened my eyes, I saw ruby and amethyst and emerald shafts of light on the floor. On my hands. On the blanket that covered me. I lay on the chaise, a pillow under my head. Out the window, morning was dawning on the water. I pulled myself up into a sitting position.

"Good morning," Oliver said.

He stood at his desk, pouring coffee from a silver pot into one of two china cups.

"What time is it?"

"Almost six thirty. I just brought up the tray. I'm sorry if I woke you. Would you like some?"

"Yes, please. Did I sleep here?"

"You'd exhausted yourself talking, and I didn't want to wake you. Don't worry, though. No one knows you spent the night, and you can trust me not to besmirch your honor." He smiled a little, trying to ease my fears and lessen the awkwardness of the situation.

I wasn't really worried. The only one who would have checked on me would have been Minx, and after almost a year of living with her, I knew she never did. Her own nighttime rendezvous kept her too busy.

He walked over with two cups, handed me one, and then sat beside me.

I took a sip. And then another. As I took a third sip, I realized I must look a mess.

When I came back from the bathroom, Oliver

had refreshed my cup. I sipped at it, suddenly nervous. What had I been thinking to confide in him? Why had I said so much? Why had I trusted him? He probably hadn't believed me about my innocence. He'd tell his grandfather, and Mr. Tiffany would ask me to leave.

She was the girl who killed her stepfather.

In the days after the Reverend died, and then during the trial and even at Andrew Mercer, that was what everyone said. Branded with the crime, I endured the gossip and the jeers and the pointed fingers.

"What you gave me last night was a gift. That you trusted me with your story is something I will never forget. I will never betray you, Jenny, I swear it." And then he leaned forward and pressed his lips to mine. The kiss a period at the end of his declaration. After a few moments, the embrace changed from one of solemnity to one of passion.

Men had kissed me before—Ben, of course, had kissed me—but I'd never truly returned a kiss. I'd never opened myself up to anyone before that morning. Oliver must have sensed it, because he pulled back and held me at arm's length and looked at me. Seeing something in me he hadn't seen before. That no one had seen before.

He whispered, "Are you sure you want this?"

I nodded.

Beyond us, the rising sun poured into Oliver's

room, filtering through the stained-glass panels, radiating colors that were alive, the way the gems Mr. Tiffany used were alive. Oliver pulled me up and embraced me again.

The kisses continued, but I yearned for even more. For the first time in my life, I wanted a man with every inch of my skin. I unbuttoned my blouse and stepped out of my skirt and my underclothes while he watched. Oliver's eyes never left mine. I was proud that I could show him my truth and desire. So many days and nights of not letting myself feel, of hiding, of worrying, of thinking I'd never be able to tell someone who I really was, all dissolved in that light. Oliver took me in his arms, and I stood naked against him in his clothes, and he kissed me again. Starting at my forehead and working his way down my cheeks, my lips, neck, shoulders, belly, thighs, and then back up. I stopped him then to undress him. I'd seen many naked men in figure-drawing class but had never felt one's warm skin under my hand, had never felt the muscles on his chest, the wiry hair between his legs, or his hardness.

The whole time, the sun sent its light through the windows, clothing our naked bodies in a ruby, amethyst, and emerald pattern of leaves and petals.

16

In my room an hour later, I soaked in a hot bath and stared at my body. It looked the same as always, but everything *felt* different. My breasts were tender, my thighs tired, and when I touched myself where Oliver had touched me, I was sore.

He'd seemed surprised, but pleased, that I hadn't made love to anyone before. And, as he had been so many times before, Oliver was tender with me. When it was time to say good-bye, he'd taken my hand and kissed it over the bandage.

By eight, I'd dressed and knocked on Minx's door so we could go to the Foundation dining room for breakfast together. She didn't answer, so I walked down on my own, expecting to see her there. A few other fellows were eating but not Minx. Or Edward. I helped myself to eggs and bacon and toast. I finally had an appetite, feeling both lighter than ever and fulfilled at the same time. I was still eating when Graves brought in the morning mail.

I had another letter from Ben, which I took with me into the library after I finished eating. As I slit open the envelope, I compared Oliver's kisses with those Ben and I had shared. I didn't feel guilty, but I knew Ben wanted what I had given Oliver, and I felt a pang of sadness for my friend. I appreciated his kindness and caring. Ben might be a smarter choice. I could share my heart with him. With Oliver, I'd give it away.

I unfolded the sheet of writing paper and looked down at Ben's capable, even scrawl. The first half of the missive offered insightful and entertaining anecdotes relating to the voter-tampering trial of the governor's right-hand man. I enjoyed it until I got to the third paragraph, and the word *Ithaca* jumped out at me.

> I went to Ithaca yesterday to meet with a law professor there, hoping for some insight into a sticky point in the trial. I had a choice of two colleges where I might have gotten my information and have to admit that I chose Cornell, knowing that you'd grown up there. I wanted to see what you saw walking to school, going to church, shopping in town. I wanted to know how the air smells, how the sun sets, how the spray of their famous waterfalls feels.

Waterfalls? Had I ever mentioned them to him? Had Minx told him the story of our Central Park excursion and how I admitted to her that waterfalls scared me?

I scanned the rest of the letter quickly to see if he'd done more than just look around. Had he gone searching out the Bell family? Not that he'd find them—but then again, not finding them would also be problematic.

I believed Ben was innocently curious about my background because I was so reticent to discuss it in depth. But it still made me uncomfortable that, even for the right reasons, a *New York Herald Tribune* reporter on the crime beat was snooping around the town where I grew up.

Ben didn't mention searching for my family in the letter. But if he'd done so and failed and was now even more suspicious, would he tell me?

Or was I worried about nothing? The Ouija board incident the night before had unnerved me. Yes, Ben had said I was secretive, but he meant it as a personality trait—and that was true. He couldn't be thinking I was harboring a past as shocking as the trials he covered. Could he?

I pocketed the letter and went to the studio. Minx still wasn't around. I grabbed my supplies and went outside to sketch. I wanted to find a theme to explore while at Laurelton Hall, not just arbitrarily choose a setting and recreate it. I wanted to devote these eight weeks to a question my painting would answer. A puzzle it would solve.

I stopped a few times, observing the scenery around me. Before Andrew Mercer, I'd painted everything that appealed to me: waterfalls, woods, fields of flowers, sunsets and sunrises, the beautiful light coming through the Tiffany window reflecting on the polished stone in the Fond du Lac Mausoleum. But after? From the gouache studies in classes at the League to my finished interiors of the Fond du Lac tomb, all my work had the color drained out, somber studies in shades of gray of how light and its reflections defined space.

Laurelton was a riot of color, but even now I was attracted to the shadows. I spent the day exploring the grounds: listening to the splashing fountains, following the stream, watching Saturday boaters sailing on the Long Island Sound, discovering grottoes and pools.

In the afternoon, I found a grove of pine trees and settled on a tree stump. I drew a detailed sketch of the pattern the light filtering through the leaves made on the surface of a stone. And then one of how the shadows wrapped around a tree trunk. As time passed, the shadows became longer, and each object took on a different expression. I began to imagine a series of canvases exploring how the copse transformed as the light and shade changed throughout the day.

By four o'clock, I had packed up. On my way back to the house, I came upon a flock of Mr. Tiffany's peacocks and peahens and stopped. I'd wanted so much to see the birds' colorful tails. Everywhere at Laurelton Hall, I was surrounded by my host's interpretations of those birds. I wanted to see if the theater of the living thing would be as magical as Mr. Tiffany's versions. But it wasn't to be today. The birds wandered off, leaving me to my walk.

I got back at around four thirty and knocked on Minx's door, but she didn't answer. I examined the work I'd done that afternoon, then read for a while. About two hours later, I tried Minx once more, but she still didn't respond. I considered my options for dinner. Oliver had told me he was dining with his grandfather that night, and I wasn't that keen on going back down to the studio without Minx. So I called for the maid and asked for a tray in my room.

On Sunday morning, I found a note slipped under my door.

Dear Jenny,

I don't want to knock in case you are sleeping. But if you are awake, meet me upstairs in a half hour so we can share a nightcap. Without seeing you, the day dragged on and on. If you are sleeping, I hope your dreams are filled with magic.

Tomorrow morning there is a service in the chapel at ten o'clock. Religious or not, please come with me. Grandfather's little sanctuary is a marvel, and I very much want to be the one to show it to you. I'll wait for you at nine thirty on the terrace.

Oliver

His handwriting was like him, elegant and graceful. I touched the words with the tip of my finger and felt shivers travel up and down my arms.

I dressed and then knocked on Minx's door again.

"Hmm?" I heard her sleepy voice.

I cracked open the door. She was still in bed.

"Oh, you're not up. Apparently, the chapel is something to see, and I wondered if you'd like to come with me, but if you're still in bed . . ."

"I saw it the other day, and I'm not feeling all that well," she moaned. "I have a wicked hangover. Can you get me some aspirin powder?"

I took the brown bottle off the shelf in the bathroom and was about to spoon some out into a glass when I glanced at the label. Good thing I did, as it was sleeping powder. There was another, almost identical bottle of aspirin. I mixed up a draft of that and brought it to Minx.

"I hope you feel better. Should I bring you tea when I come back?"

"Yes, please."

Oliver and his grandfather were on the terrace finishing up breakfast. Aunt Grace would have approved of Oliver, I thought. He was classic-looking, with eyes that seemed to see so much more than what was on the surface. What kind of life did he have away from Laurelton? Was he already attached to someone? What would it be like being with him now? Would he be affectionate in public? Was I another in a string of conquests? Was he a playboy?

I was fairly torturing myself.

Noticing me, Oliver stood, met me halfway, and brought me over to Mr. Tiffany. Was Mr. Tiffany looking at me any differently from how he had before? What did he think of Oliver's arm entwined with mine?

"Jenny told me you two have met," Oliver said to his grandfather.

"We have, but I haven't seen you out sketching again, Miss Light," Mr. Tiffany said.

"I will be there again, tomorrow for sure."

"I'll expect you. I want to see you with paints, though. I didn't bring you here to stick to your graphite." He rose. "I'll see you at the chapel?" he asked Oliver. "I'm going to escort Mr. Sanderson over."

"You will," Oliver answered.

A short while later, while we walked there, Oliver told me his grandfather's firm had created the chapel interior in 1893 to exhibit at the World's Columbian Exposition in Chicago. They'd designed everything from the cleric's vestments to the windows and altar, then installed it in the Tiffany & Co. pavilion in the Manufactures and Liberal Arts Building.

"After the fair, a client of Grandfather's, Mrs. Celia Whipple Wallace, purchased it with the intention of installing it on the main floor of the new St. John the Divine Cathedral, but that never happened. Instead, it was placed inside a crypt, hidden away, and barely used. They finally shut the chapel down in 1911 in order to build a choir above it. When my grandfather heard water damage from the basement was ruining the mosaics, he paid to have it dismantled, removed, and relocated here. It took two and a half years. There are more than a million pieces of glass and mosaic. As you will learn, my grandfather is a perfectionist."

From the tone of Oliver's voice, I wondered if Mr. Tiffany put too much pressure on his grandson.

We'd reached a small stone structure sur-rounded by laurel bushes and tall pine trees. The wooden door, with a rustic cross carved into its center, stood open. Oliver stepped back to allow me to enter first.

I hesitated on the threshold. Since leaving Hamilton, I'd avoided sitting through any church service. Even when my aunt died, the memorial was held at Lakeview, the cemetery where my grandparents, mother, and half brother were buried. To me, a liturgy meant only hypocrisy, but I reminded myself that this was not the Reverend's sanctuary. This was a work of art created by Louis Comfort Tiffany.

I'd been at Laurelton Hall for less than a week and was sure I'd never get used to all the beauty, never be able to walk into a space Mr. Tiffany had designed and not catch my breath. Never turn a corner and take the view or the landscaping or the architecture for granted. There wasn't an inch of the estate that I'd seen so far that appeared arbitrarily designed or ordinary. And the chapel was no exception. The mystical space radiated ethereal light. Standing inside the door, I felt dizzy as my eyes adjusted to the dazzling interior.

I knew enough about architecture to recognize that the design was Byzantine-inspired. Every single inch—the ceilings, columns, and arches—gleamed with a warm, buttery light.

"Look up," Oliver said, as he pointed. "Grandfather calls it an electrolier." I stared in awe at the cross–shaped emerald glass chandelier. It had to be at least ten feet long.

At the head of the chapel, a marble and white glass mosaic altar glittered under the dome-shaped ceiling. The altar's reredos featured a pair of peacocks under a crown of iridescent glass, and everywhere—coming in through the windows and reflecting off the mosaics and glass—was what I now thought of as "Tiffany light." If anything on earth was holy, it was this.

Oliver ushered me to a wooden pew. "It's a blessedly short service," he told me. "Grandfather holds them mostly so everyone can experience the chapel. He'd just as soon place a rabbi or a priest or a Buddhist monk up there as a minister."

An older man, wearing a dark suit and using a cane, walked from the elevated mosaic platform down the aisle toward us. His face was suffused with a sense of peace.

"Who is that?" I asked Oliver.

"Mr. Sanderson, a concert pianist with the Philharmonic. My grandfather and he are friends, and whenever Mr. Sanderson comes to visit he graces us with his playing."

The musician continued down the aisle and then took a seat in front of the organ tucked into an alcove very close to our pew. From the instrument's decoration, I had no doubt Mr. Tiffany had designed the console case to fit. Its gold, abalone, and emerald glass matched the gleam of the chandelier. Mr. Sanderson settled himself and looked at the sheet music on the stand. Then he put his hands on the keys and began to play.

Strong, sonorous notes bellowed out from the instrument's pipes and filled the chapel. For a few blessed moments, I enjoyed the resounding tones, and then the notes started to turn into a melody.

The melody morphed into a reminder and a reckoning. The words, although unsung there in Tiffany's chapel, were loud in my mind, each one a threat.

> Lead, kindly Light, amid th'encircling
>   gloom;
> Lead thou me on!
> The night is dark, and I am far from home;
> Lead thou me on!
> Keep thou my feet; I do not ask to see
> The distant scene—one step enough for
>   me.

Such a lovely hymn to all except me. "Lead, Kindly Light" had been the Reverend's signature hymn. It had opened every service. And as time passed, I had grown to despise every one of the words and notes as much as I did the hypocrite who stood behind the pulpit preaching a kindness and compassion of which he was incapable.

> I was not ever thus, nor pray'd that thou
> Shouldst lead me on.
> I loved to choose and see my path; but
>   now,
> Lead thou me on!
> I loved the garish day, and, spite of fears,
> Pride ruled my will. Remember not past
>   years.

I couldn't sit through the rest of the song. I stood and, stepping on at least one person's feet, walked to the end of the pew. I heard Oliver say my name as if it were a question. But I couldn't stay and explain. I had to get out.

So long thy pow'r hath blest me, sure it still
Will lead me on.
O'er moor and fen, o'er crag and torrent, till
The night is gone.
And with the morn those angel faces smile,
Which I have loved long since, and lost awhile!

Those angel faces . . . My mother's face. My half brother's face, which I had never seen. Aunt Grace's face, which I missed every day. I ran down the rest of the aisle, which seemed never to end even though the chapel was not large. People turned. The last person I saw was Edward Wren, watching me with an intent expression that mystified me.

17

I walked and walked, more unaware of my surroundings than at any time since I'd arrived at Laurelton. I didn't care where I wound up, as long as I didn't have to hear the organ music.

In less than a week, there had been two strange occurrences. First the Ouija board message and now the Reverend's hymn. How could it be mere coincidence that out of every song in the hymnal, Mr. Sanderson had chosen "Lead, Kindly Light"?

Aunt Grace always said there were no coincidences, there were only messages. Like her father, she had never found religion, but she believed that life told us things.

What did I believe in?

I wasn't sure anymore.

After walking the grounds for quite some time, I made my way back to the house. I went upstairs and knocked on Minx's door. She told me to come in.

Inside, the curtains were pulled, the room shrouded in darkness. Minx was in bed, just where I'd left her an hour and a half before.

"You're still unwell?" I asked. "You must have had some night. Where were you?"

"Edward and I went into New York on Friday for a party. We stayed over, and then last night went to dinner and after to Harlem to Connie's Inn. We had too many nightcaps and drove back late."

Minx and I spent the afternoon together. Once she felt better, we went out sketching. When we returned, I found another note from Oliver asking if I was all right, worried about why I'd run out of the chapel so abruptly. He'd come after me, he said, but I hadn't been in my room. He hoped I'd be at dinner with him and his grandfather.

I hadn't forgotten that on Sunday nights, the fellows were invited to dine in the main house. The chance to have dinner with Mr. Tiffany was too great an honor. I scribbled a note back that yes, I'd be there, and asked Graves to deliver it.

For our first dinner with Mr. Tiffany, I dressed in Aunt Grace's black frock, but when Minx knocked on my door to see if I was ready to go down, she shook her head no.

"You can't wear that dress anymore. I've told you, it looks just like what it is, an older woman's dress from a decade ago. I can't believe you even brought it. Silly bunny. Come with me."

Dragging me into her room she pulled out the scarlet dress I'd worn to Mrs. Whitney's opening. "Wear this. In fact, take it. Keep it. It always looks better on you with your coloring, anyway."

Since it was our first dinner with Mr. Tiffany, he spent a good part of it telling us about the house and his hopes for us during our time at the Foundation.

The dining room was one of the more simply decorated rooms. So as not to detract from the garden views, Mr. Tiffany explained, he'd installed clear glass windows topped by stained-glass wisteria transoms to bring the outside in. The cobalt medallion carpet contrasted with white walls. The white marble mantel boasted three glass mosaic clocks, one to keep track of the time, another for the day, and the third for the month. Each design element was inspired by nature, every color chosen to complement another. As good as the food was—we started with terrapin soup—the surroundings were the sensation.

"The Fountain Court, the living hall—or the forest room, as I prefer to call it—and the dining room have been laid out not in a traditional manner but rather to take advantage of the natural beauty of this land. I'm sure you've noticed each room has been designed to offer two views, one of the harbor and the other of the landscaped hillside."

The waiters took away the soup and brought out the second course, a fillet of bass with a meunière sauce. As we ate, Mr. Tiffany continued to explain his goals for Laurelton.

I did my best to listen and managed, despite the glances Oliver and I exchanged. I'd always imagined that the descriptions of desire I'd read about in books were overblown and exaggerated. But even there at the table, surrounded by people, I longed to see Oliver's golden skin again, touch it again, feel his mouth pressing on mine, his hands on my back, my breasts, my stomach, between my legs.

From the way Oliver was looking at me, I could tell he felt the same way.

The fellows asked Mr. Tiffany questions. Paul Cadmus was the most inquisitive, but everyone except for Minx and Edward seemed entirely engaged. She was groggy, and he was restless.

Luigi asked Mr. Tiffany to describe his architectural philosophy.

"Every really great structure is simple in its lines, as in nature. Every great scheme of decoration thrusts no one note upon the eye. The charm of homes of refinement is in the artistic blending that is revealed when everything has its place and purpose." Mr. Tiffany gestured around the room. "And when every detail unites to form one perfect and complete whole."

As the next course was served—lamb with a rosemary mint sauce, brussels sprouts with chestnuts, roasted new potatoes—Mr. Tiffany talked about his hopes for our time here.

From across the table, Oliver gave me a secret smile. I forced myself to focus on what Mr. Tiffany was saying.

"I created the Foundation to be a place where students could find a stimulus in the atmosphere and surroundings . . ."

Oliver's smile widened. I was sure I blushed.

"And by the contact with other students and artists. How are you all faring so far?"

"Yes, how are you all faring?" Oliver asked, with a teasing lilt in his voice as he kept his eyes on me.

By the time dessert arrived—custard and walnut bars—the talk grew more conversational, as we all relaxed around our host.

After dinner, some of the fellows went off by themselves or went into town. A few retired to the library for cigars and brandy. Oliver and I slipped out, took a walk, and wound up down by the beach. He wanted to take me night sailing. He showed me how to help him with the mast and the rudder, and we set off for a short ride under a bright moon and a sky full of stars.

"One day, I want to paint you in moonlight like this," Oliver said. "You're so pale it gives you an almost ethereal glow."

When we were only a little ways out, we heard someone shouting out Oliver's name. Graves was standing at the top of the stone steps, his voice traveling over the water.

"Mr. Oliver! Mr. Oliver!"

He was waiting for us when we reached shore.

"Is something wrong?" Oliver asked.

"Your grandfather wants to see you," Graves said.

"Did he take ill?"

"Not that I'm aware, sir. He and Miss Hanley were only listening to music. They didn't seem in any distress."

Oliver looked at me and frowned. "I suppose we'd better go up."

The three of us climbed the stairs and walked back to the main house, where Oliver said good night to me and took off toward his grandfather's study.

Back in my room, I tried to read my novel, *The Age of Innocence* by Edith Wharton, but despite its gripping story, I couldn't pay attention. I was too busy wondering what Mr. Tiffany had wanted that was so important he'd sent Graves out to fetch Oliver.

I closed the book and contemplated going downstairs to find another. I knew a library was kept in the smoking room among the Japanese swords and armor, but that was where Oliver had gone to see his grandfather.

I still hadn't answered Ben's letter and was feeling guilty about that, so I sat at the desk and assembled pen and paper and ink, marveling again at how in Mr. Tiffany's world, even the most utilitarian objects were works of art.

I ran my finger over the stationery's embossed

insignia, flipped open the brass and green glass inkwell, and considered what to write.

I'd irrevocably changed since the previous letter I'd sent. Ben had been the last man I'd kissed before arriving at Laurelton Hall. The only man I'd agreed to date since I started at the League. He believed we were something of an item—so had I—and that when I came back from Laurelton and he returned from Albany, we'd continue seeing each other. But in one night and two days, everything had changed.

So what should I tell him? He hadn't asked me for any declarations before he left. I did care for him, but we'd made no promises. I didn't owe him an apology. On the other hand, Oliver and I hadn't spoken of what would happen next, either. And though I'd felt so certain when I was with him that I belonged beside him, there in my room, alone, staring at the notepaper, I realized I had no cause to feel certain at all.

Instead of making any unwise confessions about the state of my heart, I wrote to Ben about the house and the other fellows and the landscaping. The one thing I did confide was that I was confused by Minx's behavior and unsure of what to do. I told him about Mrs. Deering asking me to keep an eye out for Minx and her old beau Gerald in particular and mentioned that instead of working on her paintings or sculpture, she was off all the time with Edward, and I was worried about his influence on her.

At the close of the letter, I told Ben that Mr. Tiffany didn't take the *Herald Tribune*, but I'd learned it was sold in town and planned on going there in the morning and buying a copy so I could catch up on his trial and ask the newsstand man to save each day's issue for me.

And I did just that. On Monday morning, I bicycled into town and bought a copy of the *New York Herald Tribune*. Afterward, I walked across the street to Laurel Hollow's coffee shop and ordered a cup of coffee and a doughnut and sat reading Ben's most recent entry in what they were calling, of course, the trial of the century.

As I turned the page to read the continuation of Ben's article, I glanced out the window and saw a figure leaning against the wall of the grocery store. He was in shadows and wearing a hat, so I couldn't make out his face, but from his position, he seemed to be looking right at me.

I resumed reading and had almost finished when a bell chimed. I looked up as the door opened and Oliver walked in.

"Do you mind if I join you?" he asked, already pulling out a chair.

"Of course not."

"I came into town to pick up some books I ordered. I didn't expect to see anyone from the colony here, especially not you, but I'm delighted."

I pointed to the paper. "I'm afraid I'm following a trial and had to know what has happened since I've been gone."

Oliver looked at the newspaper. "The *Herald Tribune* has quite a reputation for sensationalism. I'm a *New York Times* reader myself."

"I work for the *Herald Tribune*," I told him. "As a court sketch artist."

I'd already told his grandfather and didn't want Oliver to be surprised or embarrassed when he found out.

"I'm terribly sorry. That was rude of me."

"You didn't know. You couldn't know, and I understand. I had my own reservations about working for the paper—really, for *any* paper—but a good friend convinced me otherwise."

The waitress came over then, and he ordered what I was having.

"I have a problem with the news, with reporters, with the way it all works," he said. "I think there's too much subjectivity and we're being manipulated. And that paper was always one of the worst. Though I heard they were making an effort to clean up a bit, I haven't seen any evidence."

"Oh, we are being manipulated."

"Said with a lot of conviction. Your firsthand knowledge?"

"Someone I knew," I said, then laughed ironically.

"When you spend eight years hiding the truth, it can be hard to stop."

"It is." I looked at him. How did he know that so well? "When it happened to me, the newspapers were so quick to jump to conclusions, to use the story to sell their papers, to latch on to the most salacious details."

"Yes." He sighed. "That's what they do. Damn the consequences or repercussions."

I glanced out the window again and saw the figure was still there across the street.

Just at that moment, the waitress arrived, blocking the view. After she'd deposited Oliver's order and refilled my cup, the man across the street was gone. I shivered. Something about him standing so long in the shadows unnerved me.

"Are you cold?" Oliver asked. "It's a little chilly out. Take a sip of your coffee; it will warm you up."

I did as he suggested and sipped while he took a first bite.

"Was everything all right last night with your grandfather?" I asked.

"Yes. I'm sorry about that. He wanted to . . . he wanted to talk to me."

Oliver moved his cup an inch to the right and then back to where it had been. He seemed to be contemplating what else he wanted to say.

"It's all right, you don't have to tell me," I said.

"You are really remarkable. Not like other girls, who want to know everything all the time and have a million questions and require a million reassurances."

"Sounds like you've had a lot of experience."

"I've had enough. Until I met Camille, and then I was with her, and there wasn't anyone else."

"In Paris?"

"Yes."

"And she is still there?"

He shook his head. "We were together from the last year of the war until last July, when she died of influenza."

"Oh, I'm sorry!" I said, shocked. Oliver was so young. I hadn't expected him to have lost a lover to death.

"I stayed on in Paris. I believed I'd stay forever. Then Grandfather took ill . . . and I came back."

"But he's all right?"

"Irascible. Bossy. Interfering and stubborn. But all right."

"What is he so stubborn about?"

"My grandfather was a rebel, pioneered a whole art form. He did to glass what had never been done before, but he can't accept my paintings or my jewelry designs. And the more time that passes, the more insistent he becomes that I'm just creating 'modern trash,' as he calls it. He's

281

convinced my talent—my only real talent—is as a businessman, like my father."

"That's terrible, Oliver. I haven't seen your jewelry designs, but I saw your painting, and yes, it's modern—that's what makes it so exciting. It's different and unique, and it's anything but trash. Why can't he see how good you are?"

"I take back what I said."

"What was that?"

"That you don't ask a lot of questions."

"Oh, I'm sorry."

Oliver reached out and took my hand. "Just joking. I love your questions, actually. They get right to the heart of the matter."

"I didn't mean to—"

There was a commotion outside. A truck had plowed into a car, and pedestrians were rushing about.

Oliver was up and out of the seat right away. I followed.

He pushed his way through the crowd to get to the scene of the accident.

"Is anyone hurt?" he asked the people standing beside the truck.

"No," the driver said. "The car was empty. Parked right there in the middle of the street, if you can believe it."

Oliver came back and took my arm. "I need to go pay the check. Then I'll walk you back to Laurelton Hall."

"I came by bicycle."

"So did I. Perfect. We can ride back together."

As we crossed the street, I said I was glad no one had been hurt.

"So am I. I know a good bit of emergency care, but I'm no doctor."

"But you *are* excellent at fixing cuts and bruises," I said, and held out my palm, which was healing quickly.

He picked up my hand and kissed just above the cut. A zigzag of lust cut through me. I'd never experienced anything like it. So this was what want was like. I wondered how I was going to survive it.

As Oliver paid the check, I realized that he'd skirted telling me what his grandfather had called him to his study to discuss. I only knew that it had disturbed him. *It's not my business, anyway,* I thought, as we walked out of the coffee shop. Then I saw that same man from before, but now outside the general store, where I'd bought my paper. He was hurrying inside.

"What is it?" Oliver asked.

"Just a man . . . I saw him before, too."

"But something about him is troubling you. What is it?"

"I'm not sure."

"Do you think he's following you?"

"He might be, but why would he?"

"Maybe we should go check."

Oliver took my arm. We crossed the street and went into the store.

The proprietor was helping a middle-aged woman but looked over as we walked in.

"Be right with you," he said.

Looking around, past the racks of newspapers and magazines, candy, sundries, shelves of stationery, inks, and scores of other supplies, we sought evidence of the mysterious man.

"There's no one here," Oliver said.

I was walking down the aisle of the store when I noticed light streaming from the back. "Oliver, look. There's a rear door." Approaching it, we saw it was slightly ajar.

I pushed it open and stepped into a narrow, empty alleyway. The echo of rapid footsteps grew fainter with every beat of my heart.

18

As we bicycled back to the Foundation, Oliver told me that he and his grandfather were leaving for New York before lunch.

"Aren't you staying all week?" I was trying to keep any disappointment from coloring my voice.

"I was going to. But Grandfather's changed his mind. We won't be returning until Thursday night or Friday midmorning. There's a fairly large stained-glass commission in progress, and he wants me to oversee it with him. All part of my training. Now that I've committed to learning the business, I can't very well disappear."

"No, you can't."

"Will you miss me?" he teased.

As my bike wobbled on the stony road, I did, too. How to answer? I longed to feel his hands in my hair, on my back, pulling me to him. To declare my desire was wanton. But it wasn't just being wanton that held me back. If I declared myself to Oliver, I'd be vulnerable. He'd know how I felt, which would give him power over me and distract me from my work. That's why I was here, after all—to work, not to be wooed by the handsome heir to the manor.

"My God, Jenny. I didn't ask you to write a

treatise on how you feel. A little *yes, I'll miss you* would suffice." Oliver chuckled and rode around me in a circle, cutting me off so that I had to stop.

We were on a narrow path somewhere inside the grounds of the estate. Birds sang in the trees above us. After another circle around me, Oliver got off his bike and leaned it against a tree. Then he helped me off my bike and put it next to his.

"Come this way." Oliver took my hand, leading me away from our bikes and deeper into the woods, where towering conifers sheltered us. He pulled me down beside him. The ground was thick with pine needles that made for a comfortable and fragrant carpet. Reaching out, he finger combed my hair.

"You're all windblown," he said, "and wild. I like that. But you hold back so much the rest of the time. I won't hurt you, I promise." He leaned forward and kissed my forehead.

"How did you know just what I was thinking—"

He put his finger on my lips. "I told you. We are simpatico, you and I. And become more so every time we do this." He leaned over and kissed me. Taking my bottom lip in his teeth, he pulled on it just a little, biting gently, and then let it go. Pressure, then release. Pressure, then release. My legs weakened as he pulled me closer. "Or this." His hands moved down my neck, to my shoulders, then he unbuttoned my blouse and slipped his hand inside. He murmured a pleased sound and bent to kiss the spot where my collarbones met, then lower and lower, until his lips and tongue were on my breast. He unbuttoned my slacks enough to slip his hand inside them, and soon my moans joined the birdsong. I made it out of my slacks and then brazenly went to work on his trousers so that we could be naked together in the woods at Laurelton.

Afterward, we lay there, still holding on to each other, still rocking, still reeling. My breath was ragged, and I couldn't catch hold of it to slow it down.

"Are you all right?"

"I . . . will be . . ."

"I am going to have to start carrying around protection if I can't control myself better than this for the rest of the summer."

"Minx knows a doctor in the city who sells sponges." I surprised myself that I'd shed enough inhibitions to be discussing birth control so nonchalantly.

"I don't want you to have to go back into the city and break the spell of this place. I'll take care of it. Now, enough of the mundane details of family planning. I'm going to miss you while I'm in New York, Jenny. Will you miss me?"

I took a deep breath and looked at this man, at his smooth olive skin and silky black waves, at his strong cheekbones and his sometimes

287

devilishly sweet smile that traveled up to his cool blue eyes, and I made myself answer.

"Yes."

After returning to the house, I tidied myself up and met Oliver back downstairs for a more formal good-bye. We chatted while awaiting his grandfather, who arrived shortly. I tensed up, given what had just occurred. I didn't want him to think I was anything but responsible.

"Miss Light. I hope you have a productive time while we're gone. I expect to see something bursting with color in it when we return."

Oliver looked perplexed. "Something with color?"

Mr. Tiffany gave his grandson a surprised glance. "You saw Miss Light's submission painting. Well, it turns out they are all like that. She drains the world of color to try to reach the essence of light. I'm trying to show her that she'll never find the light she's looking for unless she stops fearing color."

Oliver looked at me. "I don't think Miss Bell is frightened of anything. She just thinks she is." He gave me a secret wink that I hoped Mr. Tiffany couldn't see.

"Let's go, Oliver." His tone was cool. "The train is waiting for us." He looked back at me. "Be sure not to waste your time here, Miss Light. This place is a gift. Remember that."

I felt unsettled as I watched them walk out the door. Had Mr. Tiffany's last comment been as pointed as it sounded? Was he warning me or just being avuncular?

Taking a seat by the glass fountain, I tried to meditate as Aunt Grace had taught me. I controlled my breaths, concentrating on watching the vase and the water change color from green to blue-green to blue to purple to red to orange to yellow to green. Mr. Lothrop had told Minx and me that Mr. Tiffany not only found the sound of water soothing but believed it induced a mystical state. He often sat in contemplative silence at one of the fountains around the estate, especially this most magical one. But the music of the water flowing from the glass fountain didn't lull me. The colors didn't soothe me. Despite my efforts, I remained anxious and unsure.

19

Mr. Tiffany's parting words haunted me, so I devoted myself to finding inspiration in my surroundings. On Monday afternoon, I latched on to the idea of doing gouache studies of all the fountains. Yet I spent as much time daydreaming about Oliver as I spent painting. I wasn't used to my body. Its cravings shocked me. I'd dip my brush into the water and disappear into a flashback of a sensation or the sight of how Oliver looked leaning over me, or I would experience a scent memory of cologne on his warm skin.

The first few days of my second week at Laurelton Hall were lonely and frustrating. Oliver remained in New York with his grandfather. Minx was off with Edward, and when they showed up at meals, they always sat together.

By Wednesday at noon, I'd finished studies of four of the fountains, and I was on the lower terrace trying to capture the rock crystal font on the fifth. Each facet of the clear quartz was at least two feet high. The sun shining on the wellspring's cascade splashed rainbows onto the water's surface. I was studying the light play when I heard Minx's voice.

"So there you are. I've been looking for you

everywhere. One of the maids said she saw you out here. I'm going to have some lunch. Want to come?"

Minx waited while I put away my supplies, then linked her arm in mine, and we set off.

"You seem in a good mood," I said.

"I've been working. I'll show you after lunch."

We had something to eat and then went to the studio. On Minx's work surface were four leaves of different shapes made from red clay. They were meticulously sculpted and exquisite, with every detail intact.

"These are beautiful," I said.

"I've been working on them for a few days," she told me. "I think I've found what I'm going to concentrate on while I'm here."

I would have been more impressed if I didn't know how fast she normally worked. Four leaves in as many days seemed slow for her. But perhaps she was having as hard a time as I was at concentrating. With that thought, I looked across the room to Edward Wren's area and was surprised to see that he was watching us. Behind him was a very large canvas. Even far from finished, it was impressive. It was at least eight feet long and six feet tall. And standing in front of it, I felt as if I'd just stepped into the forest. I could practically smell the pine scent and feel the cool air on my face.

I'd seen Edward's work at the League during

the class we'd taken together. His impatience always ruined the power of his canvases. He abandoned them before they were really finished. He tried hard, but sometimes his effort showed too much. I thought he had the spark that separates the good from the great, but it was never fully realized. At the Foundation, I'd seen that spark realized in Paul Cadmus's work. And in Luigi's. And I knew Minx had it. And for the first time, I was seeing it blaze in Edward's. His painting held the promise of something great.

"I'm really impressed," I said to Edward.

"I'm not going to lose out this time," Edward said.

"This time?" I wasn't sure what he meant at all. We'd had so little interaction. And certainly never over a painting.

"Sorry," he said, shaking his head. "I was just thinking out loud about another time and place."

I glanced back at his canvas. It was such a big improvement. He'd taken a giant leap.

"Now, if the two of you lovely ladies will excuse me, I need to get to work," Edward said, interrupting my scrutiny.

"Well, that's rude," Minx scolded. "Come on, Jenny. You've seen what I'm working on and what Edward is doing. What are you up to?"

We went back to my station, and I pulled out my sketch pad. "I'm a little lost. Overwhelmed, I think."

Minx flipped through the pages, looking at my drawings and washes. I knew I should be pushing myself while I was here and stretching beyond the narrow confines of what I usually did. Stepping back and trying to see from a wider vantage point, taking in more of the scene, adding colors. But every page that Minx flipped through was filled with monochromatic light and shadow.

She lingered over a series of burnt trees that I'd discovered in a distant corner of the estate. Something about the barren branches and charcoal bark had appealed to me.

"You're so drawn to the Gothic. I love these. You've managed to make them creepy and beautiful. What if you did this . . ." Minx picked up a pencil and held it over my pad. "May I?"

"Of course."

"If you did a series of paintings of this, treating it like a triptych . . ." She drew light lines down the drawing, separating it into thirds, and then sketched in some additional branches.

Only a few lines, but she'd made such a big difference. Her instincts were so sophisticated, her eye so finely attuned to nuance, and she was so fast at seeing an opportunity in a composition. As I watched her, something occurred to me. I looked back at Edward's canvas. He wasn't working but watching us. Our eyes locked.

"I think this solves it, don't you?" Minx asked.

"I hadn't thought of doing that at all."

"Isn't this place inspiring?"

"It certainly is. I can't thank you enough."

"So I'm forgiven for taking your painting without asking?" Minx's voice reminded me of a little girl worried about her parents punishing her.

"Of course." I tried to say it as if I meant it.

"And for bringing the Ouija board?"

I hesitated. A shiver ran down my back.

"I just thought it would be fun," she said.

"It's a dangerous game, Minx. You have to promise me you won't use it again."

"You sound like my mother."

"She knows about spiritualism. You should listen to her. You don't have to believe it to respect it."

Minx pouted, suitably chastised. It was hard to stay mad at her.

"Yes, I forgive you."

She looked relieved. "Before we get back to work, let's have some tea."

We left the studio and walked to the library, where refreshments were served every afternoon from three to four.

"You were out early," she said. "I looked for you at breakfast."

"*You* were up that early?" I teased her. "I haven't seen you at breakfast all week."

"Yes, Mother. Now, where were you?"

"I rode into town to get the newspaper and catch up on Ben's trial."

We filled our cups and settled in seats by the window.

"It's been going on for so long—any end in sight?" she asked.

"They're still calling witnesses. The 'trial of the century' isn't over yet. But not to worry, Ben has assured me that once it is over, there will be a new 'trial of the century.'"

"Has Ben been writing a lot?"

"I've gotten three letters since we've been here."

"And you've written him back, right?"

"Of course."

"You sound pensive. Anything to do with Oliver?"

I took a sip from my cup.

"And don't give me that surprised expression. I saw how he looked at you on Sunday night. Are you going to tell me about what's going on with you two?"

I'd found it easy to confide in Minx about Ben, but this was different. What Oliver and I had experienced together felt sacred somehow, not the subject of girlish chatter. Though I wondered if he felt the same. Was there a friend in New York he was boasting to even now? I thought not, but I had so little experience with men that I couldn't be sure.

Minx yawned.

"Tired?"

"There's a little speakeasy in Northport." She sounded lighthearted. "A group of us went last night and had a ball. It's in a garage down an alley between an inn and an ice cream parlor."

"Who was there?" I asked, and Minx listed five of the fellows she'd gone with. Nothing about her response was out of the ordinary in any way, until she said Edward's name and I heard a hitch in her voice. "How late did you stay out?"

"Really not bad, just till midnight. You need to come next time. There's a jazz band so good you almost feel like you're in Harlem, and the bartender has invented his own version of the Hanky Panky that puts the one I had at the Savoy in London to shame."

I wanted to ask her if there was anything for sale other than drinks, but she'd already compared me to her mother twice during our conversation. I didn't want to sound condescending, though I did take Mrs. Deering's request to watch out for her daughter seriously. I realized, too, that it wasn't just the worries of a woman to whom I owed so much that I was obliging. My instincts were telling me that my dear friend might be in trouble. I had yet to see any sign of the infamous Gerald Tanner, but there seemed to be another shadow following her, one, I suspected, in the form of Edward Wren.

"Next time, I'll come," I said, not wanting to but thinking that I should. At least to make sure that no one in the crowd was tempting Minx to take up any of her old habits.

"Maybe Oliver will come, too," she said.

I raised my eyebrows. "Please, Minx."

"You know you never really answered me," Minx said.

"About what?" I asked coyly.

"About what's going on with you two."

"I like Oliver," I said. "I'm not going to pretend that I don't. But he's Mr. Tiffany's grandson, and I'm just here for a summer session."

"Don't get all upstairs-downstairs with me, Miss Bell. It's 1924! People don't care about pedigrees. Blue bloods mix with the ordinary folk these days. They even intermarry. Or hadn't you noticed?" Her voice, which had started off light and jovial, had taken a turn.

"What is it?" I asked.

"Nothing."

"Is this about me? Or you?" I asked. "Does this have something to do with Edward?"

Now it was her turn to be quiet.

"Are you worried *he's* ordinary folk? Is it that serious that you're thinking of telling your parents?"

"No." Minx picked up her cup and sipped quietly.

We went back to the studio to work for a while. Paul and Luigi were there. Neither of them was overly chatty, and the studio remained quiet. From what I'd seen, I considered Paul one of the best painters there and a leading contender for the Foundation prize. As much as I'd wanted to be in the running, I didn't think I had a chance.

After another half hour or so, Louis and Edward came in together. Louis went off to his corner. Edward came toward us, walked up to Minx, and whispered something in her ear. She giggled. I stared at his painting again. What was it about it that bothered me? I glanced back at him.

I didn't realize I was studying him until he turned and saw me watching him. A frown creased his forehead, and a frisson of alarm went through me. Maybe he was more like Gerald Tanner than I thought. Did he have his gun here with him at the Foundation? Might someone involved in smuggling liquor also smuggle opium?

Minx put down her tool and said, "I'm going to go outside and draw for a while."

"Do you want some company?" I asked.

She didn't look at me. "No, thanks. Edward is going to come."

"Be careful, Minx."

"Of Edward?"

"Yes."

"Oh, don't worry about him. He's only tough on the outside. He's had a hard time."

"I know you always say that, and I know that

you like him, Minx, but don't adopt him. You're here for your own art."

She didn't shrug off my comment the way she usually did when I warned her off helping someone too much. "This is different. He's been broken. He's seen the worst of it."

I put my hand on her arm, holding her back for a moment before she could take off. I wanted to say something that would have some impact. To tell her to go slowly and be careful. But she was so stubborn. I knew if I pushed too hard, as I'd seen her mother do, Minx would go in the opposite direction, toward the very dangers we all wanted to protect her from.

20

That night, I slept with the windows open. Maybe it was the salty breeze refreshing my dreams, but I was thankful they were all about the present and not the past. I woke up early and spent the day doing studies of two more Laurelton fountains. I avoided the other fellows. I wanted to dwell in my thoughts about Oliver. To live inside the silky cocoon of memories that we'd begun to weave with each kiss and touch and whisper.

I did eventually go down for dinner, and afterward Minx persuaded me to come along with the crowd to the Northport speakeasy. There were nine of us at a big round table. Seven fellows—Paul, Luigi, Minx, Edward, Henry, Tristam, and me. Plus Mabel Cantor, who worked at the Oyster Bay Bank as a teller, and her sister Edith, who worked in Snouder's drugstore. Both of them were in their early twenties, light and breezy and wearing dresses as skimpy and sexy as they dared, Edith's in powder blue and her sister's in cream.

Mabel told me they'd learned a thing or two about art from the fellows last summer who'd also discovered the speakeasy. Edith said that since then, she and her sister had visited the Metropolitan Museum in New York.

"We think artists are utterly fascinating," she added.

The sound of blues filled the smoky tavern, along with the scents of tobacco and marijuana. I watched Minx, but she never put anything to her lips but her drink and plain cigarettes. However, knowing there were drugs there made me worry.

I ran through the signs her mother had told me to look for. She *had* been sleeping longer. There were stretches of time when she wasn't in the studio or her room. And she'd produced so little in the almost two weeks we'd been there. Those things could be indicative of her taking opium, but she could also have simply been spending too much time with Edward.

Now she and Edward got up to dance, and I watched their bodies move in perfect sync, so sensual and suggestive it made me blush.

What did she see in him? Yes, he was charming, but he was also dangerous. I tried to view him as the exotic artist she described. A man who'd been through tough times, who carried a gun and drove a truck down darkened roads carrying illegal cargo, challenging the law and fate.

As we listened to the jazz and sipped our sloe gin fizzes and Hanky Pankys, I saw Henry's hand sneak under the table and Mabel react to it. He was doing a good job of keeping her on the edge of her seat. Tristam and Edith joined Minx and Edward on the floor, where they, too, danced as if no one was watching, draped over each other, lust oozing out of every step.

When the band took its break, everyone came back to the table. A waiter took our orders for another round of drinks. Minx opened her silver case and took out a cigarette. Edward picked up her lighter, and she held his hand while she put the tip of the cigarette in the flame. Then, before he could close the top, she blew it out and gave him a sultry look. He licked his bottom lip. She winked.

"You know about the party this weekend, don't you?" Tristam asked us all.

"A party?" Minx snapped to attention. "That's just what we need. Laurelton is beautiful, but it is a little dull, dontcha think?"

Luigi and Paul shared a glance that I guessed meant they weren't having that experience.

"Dull?" Edward asked, miffed. "Wasn't I keeping you well entertained?"

"Not that way," Minx said.

"I saw the trucks pulling up in the driveway bringing supplies this morning and did a little snooping," Tristam said. "Lothrop told me Mr. Tiffany always holds some kind of party at the start of each new season of the art colony. We're all invited, along with a mix of members of the art world, plus collectors and elites from around the city and around here. The exciting thing about this particular party is that Thomas Edison is coming."

"I heard Tiffany is friends with the inventor," I said, telling them all what Oliver had told me. "They've been friends for more than fifty years. It was Mr. Edison's electrical inventions that changed Mr. Tiffany's glassworks, giving his windows and shades new life."

"Well, Mr. Edison is bringing a new invention this weekend," Tristam said.

"Really?" Paul asked. "Do you know what it is?"

"Lothrop said he's bringing his Spirit Phone to try out."

"OK, I'll bite," Minx said. "Does anyone know what that is?"

Tristam answered before I could, and I was glad. I preferred not to talk about it. "Mr. Edison believes he's invented a telephone that calls beyond this realm to reach people who have passed."

"Well, that's easier than a Ouija board, for sure," Minx said, giving me a look.

"We have a Ouija board," Mabel said. "It's kind of strange how that little thing moves around so fast and how you'd swear you aren't pushing it, isn't it?"

Minx agreed.

"Do you believe in ghosts?" Mabel asked her.

"Isn't *everyone* interested in the spirit world?" Minx asked in a cocky tone.

It was true. Since before the war, the interest

in psychic phenomena had been high, but after the war, it reached new heights. The loss of human life that totaled in the millions led to mothers, fathers, sisters, wives, lovers, sons, and daughters all desperate to find solace. The idea that we could harness psychic energy led to the idea that we could learn other secrets heretofore impossible to access. The Industrial Revolution, with its emphasis on science, had fueled a contrary interest in what was impossible to quantify and to know.

Edith asked, "Do you really think that Mr. Edison's made a phone that can call the dead?" She gave an exaggerated shiver.

I took a long pull on my drink.

"I can't imagine he has," Henry said.

"I think it's a farce." Tristam looked at the rest of us. "Let's take bets about what's going to happen on Saturday. Who thinks Mr. Edison's phone is going to work?"

"I'm on the fence," Paul said. "I've never paid much attention to mysticism, even though I've certainly been exposed to it."

"My mother is a total believer," Minx said. "She's an expert on New York's best fortune-tellers and palm readers. I bet Mr. Edison's phone will work."

"I do, too," Edward said. "There is something so thrilling about the idea that we can communicate with souls no longer here. There are so many secrets those spirits know. So much they could share." He was speaking to us all, looking mostly at Minx, but for a second, his eyes caught mine.

There was no question about it anymore: Edward was unusually, unsettlingly focused on me. I just didn't know why.

21

On Friday morning, I explored a different path, going past the turnoff to the beach and deeper into the woods. I was no longer worried about getting lost. I'd studied a map of the property Graves had given me. Reading the legend, I discovered there were markers on the trees, hard to spot unless you knew they were there, that could help you find your way.

I'd been walking for about fifteen minutes when I reached a stone wall with an arch in the center. Looking through it, I saw more woods to the right and, to the left, an incline with a structure at its summit, gleaming in the sunlight.

I went left.

By the time I'd climbed midway, about a half mile up, the building came into focus. The octagonal white ornate gazebo was topped with a pagoda-like green tile roof. Eight columns shone with iridescent blue and violet mosaic sheathing. Wisteria vines wove through the latticework and drooped over the cornice. I smelled their peppery sweetness as I approached.

A man—whom even from the distance I recognized as Mr. Tiffany from his white suit and stature—stood off to the right, painting the folly.

If he was back at Laurelton Hall, did that mean Oliver was, too?

"Good morning, Miss Light. How nice to have company so early." He looked down at his dog. "Funny, we have a visitor. Say hello."

The dog picked up her head, looked at me, and ambled over for some attention.

Mr. Tiffany stood beside his easel, palette in hand. His painting of the pagoda, with its profusion of wisteria, was exact and impressive. Now that I was standing so close to the gazebo itself, I could see its state of disrepair. The four steps up to the interior were dismantled, and a new floor was half installed.

"I hope I didn't disturb you," I said.

"Not at all. I was just finishing up. I've been here since dawn to try to capture the sunrise colors just right. But no matter what I do, I can never quite achieve their luminosity. I do so much better with glass, but I'm compelled to keep trying with paint. I'm no different from Sisyphus, rolling his burden up to the top of the hill, only to see it roll back down again. Why do you think we do that, Miss Light? What drives us to try to re-create what we see even when we know we can never really do nature justice?"

"I've wondered about that, too. When I was"— I hesitated for just a moment—"at boarding school, they insisted I study academic subjects, not art. For those two years, I didn't have access to watercolors or oils. All I had at my disposal were regular pencils and writing paper. I felt deprived. As if part of me was missing. I tried to talk myself out of the feeling. But I couldn't."

"Is that when you became determined to solve the problem of capturing light in black and white?" he asked.

"I think so. I began a quest."

"Ah, yes, the quest. I'd venture to say some of us are born with that desire to discover or create, while others simply are not. Neither of my wives had it. And few of my children do, much to my dismay."

"Why to your dismay?" I asked.

"Because looking back at my life from this vantage point of seventy-plus years, I see that all the things that have given me the most pleasure were found on my quest for beauty." His eyes sparkled. "I'd say that's been the theme of my life. It's certainly the leitmotif for the estate and the colony. You're a beneficiary of that quest."

"Which makes me very lucky."

"But also very cursed," he said sadly.

"Why is that?"

"Because even if you capture the beauty, it's fleeting." He used his paintbrush to indicate the imagery on his canvas.

"Beauty is a kind of lie," I whispered.

Compassion filled his eyes. "You're too young to be so cynical."

"Isn't it a lie?" I asked. "Just an interpretation of what's real, a false impression created with tricks of the trade, trompe l'oeil, chiaroscuro, foreshortening . . ."

"Well, it might not be reality, but it is my truth," he said.

For a moment, neither of us spoke.

"So you have sketches in that book to show me?" He held out his hand.

I didn't feel I could refuse. I handed it to him.

He spent the next ten minutes studying my drawings and gouache sketches.

"I'm impressed but not surprised. Your drafts-manship is superior, and you have a great eye for detail. That you understand how patterns repeat all through nature and use that in your designs is sophisticated and intriguing. But these are all still blacks and whites and grays. You've been here two weeks, and still no color? You promised me at the lily pond that you were going to paint— and not your stone and glass paintings. It's time for you to paint with color. It's all around you. You can't capture light if you're afraid of its rainbow."

He paused for a moment.

"Before we accept a fellow, we get references. You know that. You had them sent to us along with your painting."

What was he saying? References? What did he know?

"Actually, I don't know anything about the application process, Mr. Tiffany. Minx Deering applied for me without telling me."

"Ah. I was aware you two were friends but not that she applied for you."

"Who wrote my references?"

"Your application came with two letters from teachers of yours at the League. Mr. Sloan and Mr. Pannell."

I felt a surge of relief. For a crazy moment I'd thought he'd communicated with my teachers from Andrew Mercer.

"Both were very complimentary, of course," he continued. "Mr. Sloan, whom I know quite well, wrote that being here might open you up to painting beyond the imagery you keep returning to over and over."

"I see."

"Miss Light"—his voice was low, and the breeze nearly drowned out his words—"why is it that you are afraid to go beyond that stone chamber you keep painting?"

I decided to be truthful. "Honestly, I don't know."

"My daughter Dorothy has been studying with the great Dr. Freud for years, and through her I've been introduced to his fascinating theories. Are you familiar with them?"

"Yes, I am." Since the war, the doctor's theories had been gaining notoriety among intellectual and artistic communities, and it seemed everyone had turned into what Minx's father called an "armchair psychiatrist."

"I can't pretend to be an expert, but I'd say the first question to answer would be when did you first paint the light coming through the window in the mausoleum?"

When I didn't answer right away, he started to pack up his paints. I still hadn't responded by the time he was done. He didn't press me but instead suggested it was time to head back to the house, so we set off, Funny leading the way.

"When I was fourteen," I finally said.

"And what was it that happened to you at fourteen?"

There were parts of the story that it could not hurt to tell.

"My mother remarried."

"Yes, you mentioned she remarried the last time we spoke. But that the marriage hadn't been a successful one for her. Was it problematic for you, too? Didn't you like your stepfather?"

"No, not at all."

"Was he cruel to you?"

"Not in the beginning. But he was to my mother. When he drank, he became mean. I think if he would have . . . I think it would have become worse."

"Would have? What happened to him?"

I began to lie. "My mother divorced him."

Mr. Tiffany turned to me and searched my face. I expected him to tell me he knew I wasn't telling him the truth, but he didn't. "Good for her. Was this all in Ithaca?"

Another lie: "Yes."

"And you said your mother has since died?"

"She did."

"When you were how old?"

"Sixteen."

Mr. Tiffany was quiet, thinking, walking. "And you first saw the mausoleum when you were fourteen?"

"Yes."

"And you painted with color then?"

"Yes."

"And you said when you were at boarding school, they didn't allow you to use your paints. Only pencils."

"That's right."

"How old were you then?"

"Sixteen. I started school five months before she died."

"When you graduated, there was nothing stopping you from resuming painting with color. So clearly, your mother's death while you were at boarding school was a defining incident for you. You need to explore that time in terms of what color represents to you, what it would require of you that you can't give it. Might you ask your aunt what she remembers about your childhood and teenage years that seemed important? She might have seen something that would help. My daughter tells me there are particular crises we endure that our unconscious can block to protect us. That the memories are so damaging that our very minds do the job of blinding us to our own reality."

"I can't ask her. My aunt died last year, just before I moved to New York."

"I'm sorry," he said. "I've dealt with a lot of death, but I've had a long life. You've dealt with a lot of it, but your life is still short. I hadn't quite gotten past my first wife's death when my second wife died as well . . . I often think death is why we paint, why we sculpt, why we write music and books. Not to leave something behind, as most people think, but to distract us from the truth of what is coming, from what is inevitable."

All around us, the woods resounded with birds chirping. It seemed almost sacrilegious to be talking of something so serious amid such joyful sounds.

"I suppose you've heard that we're having a party tomorrow evening?"

"I have," I said, unsure of the reason for the change of subject.

"And that my friend Mr. Edison is coming and will be demonstrating his Spirit Phone?"

"Yes, several of the fellows were talking about

it last night. It sounds very experimental and bizarre."

"I've always wanted to believe in life after death. In the idea that we're presented with multiple opportunities to do the right thing from life to life. I've studied mystics and Eastern religions looking for proof. I think about them all the same way I think about luck. I'd love for it to strike, but I remain a realist."

"I think I am, too."

"Mr. Edison isn't, and he thinks he's finally found a way to reach beyond our cosmos. You should volunteer tomorrow. If I'm wrong and my friend is right, maybe you can use his phone to communicate with your mother or your aunt and ask them what happened to you to drain you of color, to make you afraid."

I shivered.

"Are you all right?" he asked.

Like many artists, Mr. Tiffany was very observant, and he'd just seen something I would have preferred to conceal from him.

"I'm fine. Just a cool breeze," I said. But I feared that he, ever perceptive, didn't believe my excuse.

22

After we parted, I took out one of the bikes and rode into town. I didn't want to draw or paint. Mr. Tiffany was right—what kind of artist was I if I didn't use color? There I was, surrounded by nature, flush with late spring and all its colorful bounty, yet I continued to use my charcoal pencils and a palette of blacks, whites, and grays. I studied light but refused to paint it in all its glory.

At the bookstore, I browsed for a half hour and, since I had finished *The Age of Innocence*, settled on Edith Wharton's newest novel, *False Dawn*. I took in the other shops and then stopped at the luncheonette, ordered an egg sandwich, and opened my book.

False Dawn took place in the 1840s and was about a young man sent to Europe to buy art for his domineering father. The characters brought to mind Mr. Tiffany and Oliver, and I found myself feeling frustrated again. I'd hoped for some respite, not reminders.

After I ran out of distractions in town, I bicycled back to Laurelton. The house was a hub of activity as the staff prepared for the upcoming party. The idea of the looming festivities depressed me. I didn't want to witness another attempt to contact those no longer living. To turn what my aunt had found sacred into sheer entertainment.

I sat by the alembic glass fountain in the central court and watched the colors change and tried to listen to the soothing sounds of the running water, but there was too much activity going on around me.

Mr. Tiffany had designed Laurelton so that water from the main fountain in the central court ran through a small channel and outside, where it traveled through a series of fountains, pools, and ponds, down to the Sound. A steady stream flowed from the mouth of a vase to the mouth of a green mosaic and enamel dragon, into a crystal pond, then reemerged farther downhill in a hanging garden, where it emptied into a stone sculpted shell guarded by a statue of Venus and then spilled over into a pond surrounded by foliage.

I followed the water's path from inside the house down to the twin lakes, where I sat on a stone bench and looked out at the view. But not even the peaceful vista soothed me.

Restless, I walked down to the Foundation building, hoping that Minx or Paul or Luigi would be there, but the studio was empty. I spent the next hour laying out all the drawings and gouache studies I'd done since arriving at Laurelton. Dissatisfied with them, I kicked the sea of papers into a pile.

"Whatever it is, don't take it out on your drawings."

I turned around, smiling at the sound of Oliver's voice. A wave of relief and excitement washed over me.

"Hullo," I said.

"I've been looking for you outside everywhere. I didn't think I'd find you in here on such a lovely day," Oliver said.

"I was out earlier, but . . . Did you just get here? How was New York? I missed you," I blurted out.

"And I missed you, too." He came over, wrapped his arms around me, and kissed me.

Extricating himself a few seconds later, he said, "That's better. I have to admit, you were very much on my mind while I was gone. How did you fare?"

I cocked my head back and forth. "All right, I suppose." I gestured to the work on the floor. "No, not all right at all."

"What's wrong?"

I shrugged.

"Grab your paints. Let's go."

"Where?"

"To get you out of your funk."

Oliver waited while I gathered up my gouaches, a block of thick watercolor paper, and brushes. With one hand, he took my portable easel from me, and with the other, he took my free hand.

Thirty minutes later, we were on his boat, cosseted in a cove, anchor thrown. We both set up our paints and easels.

"I didn't bring any water," I said, realizing my mistake.

"I never bring water," he said.

Leaning over the side of the sloop, Oliver lowered a pail and brought it up, sloshing.

"Out here, nothing ever seems as bad to me." He filled two cups from the pail and handed one to me. "Paint with this, Jenny. It's magic."

"Paint with sea water?"

"Always, when I'm on the boat. Try it. I swear, it improves my work."

We prepared our palettes. I watched Oliver squeezing out cool blues, deep greens, and warm yellows and compared them with my monochromatic choices.

Small waves slapped against the side of the boat. The setting sun turned the water into gold. Above us, gulls screamed and dove into the sea, foraging for dinner. Oliver's brush danced, dipped, swept, dipped, danced . . .

I touched the tip of my brush into the water, then into the black paint. I looked at the view . . . at the sea, the distant shore, the sky, the clouds . . . at Oliver . . . at his hands, his brush, his painting, a colorful pastiche coming to life.

I felt like breaking the rules. We weren't supposed to paint from models while we were at

Laurelton Hall. But the scenery was too pretty, too peaceful, too bucolic for my mood. I began to sketch Oliver's arm, hoping I might capture both his strength and grace and the raw need I felt building inside me to touch him, to have him touch me.

I'd painted only a few indecipherable black lines, and Oliver couldn't have known I was drawing him, when he grabbed the brush out of my hand.

"No, Jenny, not black. Not gray. Look around. You're here for a reason. There's beauty everywhere you look, and it's all in color."

"Did you and your grandfather conspire to pick on me today?"

"Conspire? No, but we did talk about your work while we were on the train. We chose to give you a spot here hoping you'd expand your palette. We don't want to see you squander it."

"Why I paint in black and white is none of your business." I hated that they had been discussing me in a way that suggested there was something wrong with me. And I worried that in doing so, Oliver might have shared more about my past than I wanted him to.

Oliver stared at me as if I'd just slapped him. "No, the why isn't our business, but helping you out of your colorless prison is."

His voice was tender, trying to soothe me. But all I could think about was what he'd told his grandfather. What confidence he might have shared.

I grabbed my brush back. "Fine, then. I won't paint you. I won't paint at all. I've had it with both of you probing my psyche."

Oliver turned his gaze to my easel. "Fine, but if you're going to paint me, you have to agree to *really* paint me, Jenny. All right?"

I didn't say anything.

"Look at me, Jenny."

I turned and faced him. "I don't understand what you are asking me."

"Agree first."

How could I agree without knowing what I was agreeing to?

"Agree, Jenny," he challenged again.

I was tired of being careful. Of not inviting danger. Tired of lying and pretending. I was angry and disappointed. Determined and desirous.

"All right. I agree."

Oliver reached into my paint box of colors and rummaged through the tubes, shoving one aside and then another, until he found the tube of black paint. Holding it, he pulled his arm back and threw.

"No!" I shouted, as I rushed over to the side of the boat to try to catch it, but I was too late. With a splash, my tube of black landed in the water and quickly sank.

I turned back to see Oliver using a rag to wipe the black paint off my palette.

"What are you doing?" I yelled.

He didn't answer. Picking up a tube of cobalt blue from my set, he squeezed a curl of it onto my cleaned palette. Then came a half inch of yellow oxide. Then dioxazine purple, followed by cadmium orange . . . burnt umber . . . phthalo blue . . . cerulean blue . . . phthalo green . . . raw sienna . . . and finally, cadmium red.

He shoved the colorful palette into my hand. Gave me back my brush. Then he stood and took off his sweater, pulling the V-neck white cable-knit over his head and dropping it onto the deck. He unbuttoned his shirt and dropped that, too. Bare-chested in the cool air, he kicked off his boating moccasins, unbuckled his belt, unbuttoned and unzipped his trousers, and stepped out of them. And finally, Oliver took off his underclothes.

Standing in front of me, naked, with the sun turning his skin golden and shining on the auburn highlights glinting in his black hair, he pointed to my palette.

"You wanted to paint me? Go ahead. But paint me with the colors of the living. Not the goddamned dead."

The boat swayed, the water lapped, the birds called to one another. A breeze blew. I stared at Oliver's long limbs and smooth muscles, so like the Greek marbles in the museum that I'd sketched over and over. They had been cold white marble, but Oliver was flesh—oranges and reds and peaches and browns.

"Try," he whispered. "At least try to paint me, Jenny."

I looked at the palette and back at him. I didn't move. I couldn't. I threw down the brush.

Oliver came over and stood beside me. I felt the heat radiating off his skin. Reaching out, he picked up one of my brushes and put it in my hand, curling my fingers around it, his touch sending cascades of sensation up my own arms and down through my chest and torso and settling deep inside me.

Still holding my hand, he dipped the brush into the rich red and then into the white and then the yellow and mixed a color with me. I watched the swirls turn into a wild flesh color, not close to his in reality but the color of his skin in the setting sun. He pushed my hand so the brush ran through the color and then forced my hand over to the block of paper and stroked the brush to make the shape of a man's arm.

His touch, usually so gentle, was brutal as he painted for me, with me, not giving me a choice, as the colors took form and the form took shape. A man's shape. *His* shape.

Finally, Oliver let go of my hand, which remained poised over the paper. Without taking his eyes off mine, he stepped back.

"Paint me, Jenny." His voice was at the same

322

time a command and a promise. "Do it, take paint on the brush . . ."

I looked at the paints, at the paper, at his body. Then back at the paints.

"Choose the colors that fit how you feel. Colors to tell me what you want to do to me and with me when you finish. When we can be together. When I take off your clothes and you're naked with me here on the boat. Paint me alive, Jenny. Paint me wanting you while you're wanting me."

I stopped thinking.

I streaked yellow across the paper for an arm and then orange-red for his chest and ochre for his torso. His neck was cadmium and his thighs were deep violet and his penis magenta. I shuddered as I painted, feeling as if I were dissolving into the colors, becoming them, opening to them, letting them fill me.

The overwhelming sensations of want and effort and fear and joy all at once overwhelmed me as I painted. I added colors and then more colors, my brush dancing with them, sweeping across the page with them, as I indulged in them, exulted in them. And then, without realizing it, I was finished, as if the music had ended and the dance was done.

Oliver came over and looked at what I'd painted. Without saying a word, he took the brush out of my hand, put it down, and undressed me quickly until I was as naked as he. I expected him to take me in his arms, but instead, he picked up my palette and, with his fingers, painted circles of purple around my nipples, cobalt waves across my stomach, deep rose flower petals between my thighs.

"Love isn't black and white and all that gray, Jenny. It's turquoise." He painted a blue swirl on my shoulder. "And it's lavender . . ." Another swirl on the other shoulder. "And lemon and mauve and cobalt and viridian and orange and scarlet . . ." He kissed me while his fingers painted frescoes across my back and down my sides, and then he lifted me up with burning orange and red flame fingers, and he carried me down below. As the space between us dissolved, we rocked to a rhythm set by the boat pitching and undulating in the blue salty water and the golden warm sunset.

23

Color.

Oliver had indeed awoken me. I leaped out of bed on Saturday morning and, paint box in hand, went off in search of Mr. Tiffany to paint with him. As promised, he'd set up by the lily pond. I unfolded my easel.

"Good morning, Miss Light," he said, graciously welcoming me.

Funny rose and made her way over to me. I patted her head and rubbed behind her ears.

"You have a bit of blue paint on your neck," Mr. Tiffany said.

I'd bathed, loath as I was to wash off Oliver's artwork and his scent. Had I missed a spot? I hoped I wasn't blushing, as I reached up to where he'd pointed and rubbed at my skin.

"Is blue an indication that you've begun to embrace the inspiration of our environs?" he asked.

"It is."

"Then this is a good morning, indeed."

For the next hour, we painted in silence. Every so often, I felt a flush remembering my outing on the sailboat with Oliver. Flashes of his face, a word, a touch, a kiss, popped into my mind. *I have a lover.* A man who had run his fingers through my hair and painted on my breasts and buried his head between my thighs.

"Well, I am not surprised, but I am impressed," Mr. Tiffany said. He stood behind me over my right shoulder and examined my gouache study. "You've captured the light shining on the water just right. Clearly, you've used color before and quite well. I'm so glad you've decided to return to it and that our little chat yesterday made such an impact."

Our chat and your grandson, I imagined myself responding. But of course, I didn't. "I still feel tentative. When I dip my brush in the colors, they seem so intense they almost hurt my eyes."

"Don't let them scare you. You're in control. They're your tools."

Later, we walked back to the main house together. Almost on cue, a peacock and a peahen strolled by. Mr. Tiffany asked me if I'd seen one of them fan yet, and I said I still hadn't.

"Let's wait a moment, then. It's so spectacular, and they usually do open if I wait," he said, with a twinkle in his eye.

I would have waited as long as Mr. Tiffany was willing, but the birds weren't, and they shuffled off into the woods.

"You'll see it happen, and when you do, I promise it will make you believe in beauty the way some people believe in God," he said.

We reached the house, and before we parted, he mentioned the party later that evening and reiterated that he hoped I would volunteer to try out Mr. Edison's Spirit Phone. I not only had no intention of volunteering, but I planned to avoid the party entirely because of the gadget.

I was in my room early that evening when Minx knocked at my door, wanting to know what I'd be wearing to the party and wanting to show me her choices. I joined her in her room, where she'd laid out her outfits on her bed. She tried on three dresses and their accessories, modeling them, posing for me. We decided on a pale lemon dress shot through with gold thread, citrine earrings, a canary and green feather headdress, and gold shoes with a strap across the instep. She insisted I wear one of the runners-up, a pale silvery lavender shift made by Jean Patou and silver sandals.

"I'm not going," I told her. "I don't feel up to a whole room full of people. I stayed up too late last night and got up too early." It wasn't a lie; I did feel peaked. "Besides, all this fuss about Mr. Edison's Spirit Phone, everyone focused on trying to reach out to the departed, makes me uncomfortable. I've *told* you that."

I didn't mean for there to be an edge in my voice, but there was.

"You're still annoyed with me about the Ouija board, aren't you?" she asked, in a truly miserable voice.

"No, I'm not. Not anymore."

"Let me get you some tea with milk and sugar and some scones. That will make you feel better. Really, Jenny, you have to come. It's Thomas Alva Edison! It's a grand party at the home of Louis Comfort Tiffany! Even my father was impressed when I told him who was coming."

As promised, she delivered the tea and poured a dose of brandy into it from her silver monogrammed flask. While it helped restore my energy, it didn't change my mind about going to the party.

At seven that evening, I was in silk lounging pajamas that Minx had given me for my birthday when Oliver came to my room to escort me downstairs.

"You're not ready?" he said, when he saw what I was wearing.

"No, I'm not going."

"But why?"

"You tired me out yesterday."

"I saw Minx downstairs, and she said she'd fed you a restorative tea. Are you better?" he asked hopefully.

"You go on without me. Maybe I'll come down later."

"Aren't you restored?"

"I am, but—"

Oliver walked over to the windows. Beyond him, the sunset illuminated the stained-glass window borders and cast beams of rose, blue, and lavender onto his hands and face.

"What is it?"

"The colors . . ." I pointed.

He looked down and then, without saying a word, took my hand and pulled me with him so that the colors reflected off my skin, too. Together, we were bathed in the same ethereal light I'd fallen in love with in the mausoleum. Back then, I'd felt as if I were being embraced by the light. Immersed in it. I'd always believed that nothing bad could ever happen to me, that all that was ugly and cruel had been left outside the crypt, and that in the shade of stained glass there was only beauty.

When Oliver bent down and kissed me, my body responded instantly. Ruby and cobalt pinpricks of excitement sparked off my skin.

"You definitely have to come down to the party," he said, when he broke away from the kiss.

"And why is that?" I was out of breath and for the first time in my life understood the expression *weak in the knees.*

"Because once it's crowded, no one will notice us, and we can steal away to my room, where we won't be disturbed. And we can continue what we've started here."

My cheeks felt warm.

He tucked a curl behind my ear and took my hand.

"Oh, Jenny," he said with a little sigh. "I never want to lose you."

I knew he was remembering the pain of losing his Parisian lover to influenza.

"Even after so many years, when my mother would tell me about my father, she'd cry," I said. "I asked her how she could stand feeling that way."

"What did she say?"

"That grief is the price we pay for love. And for her, it was a small price to pay for what she'd found with him."

Oliver lifted my chin. He met my eyes. His glittered with emotion. Nodding, he said, "It's true about love and grief. But I just want to love you. I don't want to grieve over you."

He silenced my eyes with another kiss full of colors, deep orange melting into scarlet. Of course: if voices had colors, so would embraces. I'd just never considered it before.

"I can't do the things I want to do to you here," he said, as he pulled away. "This part of the house isn't nearly private enough. So please come to the party. We'll just stay for a little while, and then we can disappear." He kissed me once more, then left.

I remained where I was, on the window seat, waiting for the heat to leave my cheeks, for me to regain my equilibrium.

How could one person touching just two

inches of your skin elicit such a rich, profound reaction? Ben had kissed me, too, and while it was delightful and pleasant, it was nothing like this.

I really liked Ben. But I hadn't supposed I could tell him or anyone my secret without him wondering if I was telling the truth. I had been publicly declared a killer. Only my mother had been there and agreed to my plan. Without her, there was no one to corroborate my version. Even Aunt Grace had only known what she'd been told. When Minx had asked why I was so hesitant to date men, I always told her that I was waiting. And she'd ask what I was waiting for. I always told her that I was waiting for my career to take off. But that wasn't the truth. Something I didn't know had held me back.

I knew what I'd been waiting for. And I had found it.

24

I took a bath and dressed in the outfit Minx had chosen for me. The shift felt decadent against my skin. It shimmered in the light and, with its tiny straps and low-cut neckline, was far more revealing than anything I would have chosen for myself. I almost took it off but then thought about Oliver and left it on. I slipped into the sandals and attended to my hair, making it just so. I added lipstick, rouge, mascara, and finally dabbed drops of the Jicky perfume Aunt Grace had given me for my twenty-first birthday behind my ears and on my wrists. At the last minute, I even put a tiny bit behind my knees the way Minx did.

The living room and what Mr. Tiffany called the Daffodil Terrace beyond it were filled to overflowing with guests who had been eating and drinking for at least an hour before I arrived.

I felt as if I'd stepped inside a jewelry box. Everything shone and sparkled and glowed in gemstone shades. Mr. Tiffany's lamps and windows, lit from the outside with electrical lights, shimmered and cast reflections of cobalt, amethyst, ruby, emerald, and topaz in a hundred shades.

The men in elegant white dinner jackets or

black tuxedos set off the bejeweled women decked out in gold and platinum, diamonds, pearls, rubies, and emeralds against bare skin, set in headdresses and pinned on frocks made of silks, satins, and sequins. Exotic perfumes mixed with the scent of freshly cut flowers and smoke from cigars and cigarettes. The sound of glasses tinkling and murmurs from conversations blended in with the soft tones of a blues quartet. Waiters passed silver platters of hors d'oeuvres—chilled shrimp, oysters on the half shell, deviled eggs, smoked salmon canapés, stuffed mushrooms, artichoke and olive crostini. Other servers offered crystal coupes of champagne, or if you preferred, the bar set up in the corner offered mixed drinks.

I opted for champagne and ate a delicious briny oyster as I moved through the room searching for Minx or Oliver.

I spied Mr. Tiffany by the fountain, holding court with a group of guests, talking and gesturing with gusto. Seeing me, he motioned for me to come over.

As I approached, I saw he was holding a teal-blue leather box from his emporium.

"Miss Light, you are just in time for the showing," he said, and pushed the gold release button. Theatrically, the top sprang open, revealing a white silk interior nestling a suite of jewelry.

One of the women let out a soft moan. Another simply gasped. Everyone clustered closer.

Each piece featured the most amazing light blue lavender–colored stones I'd ever seen. The necklace was fashioned after a peacock feather, with the largest of the blue stones as its eye, ringed with more of those same blues, along with opals, amethysts, and peridots. The feather's branches formed a circlet set with more of the electric indigo stones alternating with round fire opal beads. The bracelet and earrings followed the same design, with a large single blue stone at the heart of each piece.

"May I present the Tiffany Blues," Mr. Tiffany said.

"Louis, where on earth did you find such stones?" one of the men asked.

"George D. Louderback found them in 1907 in a mine in California. He named them benitoites because he'd discovered them near the headwaters of the San Benito River. They are extremely rare. So far, we've only made this one suite. Which of you lovely ladies is going to convince your husband you can't live without them?"

There was laughter, twitters of *me* and *me*.

"I think the best way to show them off is to have one of this summer's fellows model them. Miss Light? Would you do me the honor? These stones match your eyes. Come, let me put them on you."

Shyly, I held back, but Minx, who I hadn't even realized had come up behind me, pushed me forward a bit too energetically. I bumped into one of the diamond-draped ladies, and a bit of her champagne spilled over her glass and splashed on my hand.

"I'm so sorry," I said.

"Oh, no problem. Louis has laid in enough champagne tonight for us to bathe in it."

I wasn't wearing any jewelry. The only pieces I owned were my mother's two wedding rings, my aunt's watch, and assorted costume pieces from them both that weren't my taste.

Mr. Tiffany placed the necklace around my neck and closed the clasp. Then he gently put the earrings on me, with the ease of someone who had been dressing women in jewels his whole life. Next, he asked me to hold out my hand and snapped the bracelet closed around my wrist.

I stared at the breathtaking design. All the peridots and amethysts and the large Blues were briolette cut, so that the facets faced upward, as opposed to being hidden under the piece. This allowed them to flash blue the way a peacock's feather might shimmer in the sun.

"You've outdone yourself, Tiffany," one of the men said.

Mr. Tiffany bowed from the waist.

"And how much are these little baubles?" another man asked.

"Harold, you know better than to discuss prices in public, how déclassé," his wife said.

"Don't be ridiculous, Helene. Louis is a businessman."

"All in time, Harold," Mr. Tiffany chided. "There's a party going on. The stones are rare, the designs are a delight, but we do make our jewelry to sell, so if you're interested, we can have cognac and cigars in the smoking room later and discuss it after Thomas's demonstration."

"You mean the jewels aren't the real entertainment?" a woman in the small crowd joked.

Mr. Tiffany trained his attention on me. "These stones suit you, as I guessed they would. The Tiffany Blues are almost exactly the color of your eyes. I think you should wear the suite for the rest of the evening. You're a perfect model for them. And if we sell them tonight, perhaps you'll get a commission."

"I'd be honored to wear them, but if they are priceless, maybe it wouldn't be such a good idea—"

"I don't imagine you're going to run off with them, Miss Light. Enjoy our Blues."

Oliver had come up beside me. "My grandfather is right. They are the perfect stones for you. You should never wear anything else."

"That won't be too difficult to arrange. I'm a starving artist, remember? I doubt I'll be in the market for fine jewels anytime soon."

"Come, let's get some champagne. I'd planned on stealing you away, but now that you're modeling, I think we need to make sure you're seen for a bit."

After he'd procured two glasses, we walked out onto the patio. The fountain sprayed water that sparkled in the moonlight. Strains of music wafted on the breeze.

Oliver took my elbow, and we walked down five stone steps to the next level, where another fountain dripped into a pool decorated with the blue tiles that were one of the leitmotifs of the estate. We sat on a bench facing out toward the bay, while the sounds of the water in the fountain mixed with the blues band inside the house.

"Tonight is full of magic," Oliver said, pointing up. "Even the sky has taken on the hue of my grandfather's new Blues." He took my hand and held my wrist up toward the heavens, matching the colors of stone and sky. Then he brought my hand to his lips, turned it, and kissed the slight scar on my palm.

"I submitted a design for those stones, but it was too modern for my grandfather." He shook his head. "I would have loved to see my pieces on you."

"Why don't you fight harder for your work?"

He looked at me. "I've asked myself that so many times." He shrugged. "Between the war

337

and then losing Camille, I guess I lost my fight. And Grandfather's right, there's no shortage of designers but very few people he can trust to take over the running of the company."

"But if design is where your heart is . . . no one came home from the front without scars. Body or soul or both. I've read that once you see the sheer inhumanity of what we can do to each other, what animals we are, it changes you. But that doesn't mean you can't change again. Your grandfather has devoted himself to creating beauty. How can he deny you the same chance?"

"Running a business is as noble a cause as any other," Oliver said.

"But we need beauty to breathe. If I hadn't had a place of beauty to escape to when my . . ." I trailed off, overwhelmed with emotion.

"Jenny, you know you can always talk with me about what happened. Whenever you need to. I don't doubt a word of what you said."

I sighed without meaning to.

"You and I both have our demons, but let's say we banish them for tonight." Oliver put his arm around me, pulled me close, tucked me into the curve of his chest, and then leaned down and kissed me. A breeze came off the water and enclosed us in its warm air. He was right. Why talk about the sordid past when it was so lovely there on the terrace and I was dressed like a princess and kissing a prince?

338

"I want you to promise me something," he said, when we pulled apart. "There are things I need to sort out. Will you wait for me and let me take care of them? By the middle of July, I'll have it all worked out. And we can talk about the future then."

"You're being very cryptic."

"I'm sorry. There's nothing you need to worry about. This is all that matters . . ."

And he kissed me again, as the Blues twinkled on my wrist.

"We should go back inside," Oliver finally said. "As much as I want to stay here with you, we don't want to miss Mr. Edison's demonstration. And we can be together after that. We have the rest of tonight and all of June."

"And all of June," I repeated, as a cool breeze came up off the water and made me shiver.

When Mr. Tiffany saw me reenter the living room, he came over and escorted me to a new group of guests to show off the jewels. He was still talking about the find in the mine and how rare the stones were when the butler came over to tell him that Mr. Edison had finished arranging his equipment in the dining room.

The scene had been set for maximum drama. The room was dark except for the chandelier that shone down on the inventor and the telephone beside him on a plinth like a piece of sculpture.

The black metal device was simple-looking, hardly magical in appearance. Only its position gave it gravitas.

Mr. Edison stood and patiently waited for the crowd to settle. The Wizard of Menlo Park, as everyone knew him, was in his late seventies, with white hair, heavy jowls, and a furrowed brow that gave him a serious air. But the sparkle in his gray eyes was that of a much younger man.

Finally, when people had stopped filing in and the chatter settled down to a hush, he spoke.

"I believe, rightly or wrongly, that life is indestructible. I also believe that there has always been a fixed quantity of life on this planet and that this quantity can neither be increased nor decreased. I am inclined to believe that our personality hereafter will be able to affect matter. If this reasoning is correct, if we can evolve an instrument so delicate as to be affected, or moved, or manipulated—whichever term you want to use—by our personality as it survives in the next life, such an instrument, when made available, ought to record something. I have been at work for some time building an apparatus in order to see if it is possible for personalities that have left this earth to communicate with us. If when we die we do not disappear from the universe but our spirits merely move on from this plane to another, then we should be able to contact those spirits. Contact our dead. We live in a wondrous time of investigation. Not twenty miles from here is an institute in New York City devoted to psychic phenomena. Some of our greatest minds, from Sir Arthur Conan Doyle to the dean of Harvard, believe that there is more to our world and our existence than we can understand.

"The question I've pondered is where do our souls go? And if we can tap into sound waves and project our voices through radios and telephones, then why can't we tap into the sound waves that are just outside this realm? There are numerous sightings of ghosts, spirits not ready to move on. Just recently during the war in France, a whole unit of men saw angels, spirits who came down from on high to keep them out of harm's way. Not one man having a hallucination. A whole battalion of soldiers seeing the same thing. And yet we doubt? Enough talk. I have been working on this apparatus for ten years, trying to reach beyond, and I believe I have finally succeeded."

The crowd was riveted. Everyone wanted to believe in the idea of a telephone to the dead. Even if ghosts were used as agents of fear in stories, the fact was that most everyone had lost loved ones to war and disease. Death was all around us all the time. The possibility of being able to have one more conversation, one more hour, with them was so very attractive. I turned around to say something to Oliver, but he was no longer by my side.

"And now I will demonstrate how my telephone works. Do I have a volunteer?"

As the crowd twittered, Mr. Tiffany glanced over at me. I knew what he wanted, what he expected, but I shook my head.

"A volunteer?" Mr. Edison repeated.

I saw Minx and Edward whispering, and then Edward stepped up, beating anyone else who might have been willing.

"Yes, sir. Captain Edward Wren reporting for duty, sir."

Everyone laughed, partly out of relief that someone else had volunteered.

"Very good, young man. What you are going to do is call someone using this device. Someone you cared about deeply. Someone you know has passed on. And ask them to communicate with you. Ask them for a message."

Mr. Edison held out a chair. Edward sat at the table, facing an ordinary-looking telephone. Wires connected it to a black box on the floor under the table.

"It's all set up and connected," Mr. Edison instructed. "Just hold that earpiece up, and speak into the mouthpiece like you would with any telephone."

Edward held one end up to his ear and leaned forward.

"Are you there?" He listened. Then he turned back to Mr. Edison. "I don't hear anything."

342

"Try again, son. Give it at least thirty seconds," Mr. Edison said.

"Yes, heaven is a long way off," a man from the crowd offered.

Quite a few people laughed.

"Are you there?" Edward asked, and he listened with a look of deep concentration on his face. For ten or twenty seconds, he had no reaction. Then he raised his eyebrows and looked over at Mr. Edison. He put his hand over the mouthpiece. "I can hear her!"

"Well, talk to her, boy. Ask her if she has a message."

Edward leaned even lower to the phone, almost kissing the mouthpiece. "Do you have a message for me? I would give anything if you did."

I heard his voice quavering and was surprised by this atypical sign of emotion from him.

Edward waited. Then he began to speak slowly, haltingly. "Someone here . . . someone here is keeping a secret, hiding her past . . . Faith warns . . . Faith warns . . . this person shouldn't remain here . . . it could be dangerous."

There were oohs and ahs in the audience. People turned to look at one another, seemingly believing that Edward was, in fact, getting this message through the receiver.

I didn't turn to my right or left. I didn't allow the expression on my face to change. There could be a dozen people in the room who fit the

343

description Edward's spirit gave. A woman with a secret? How many women at the party *didn't* have one? Aunt Grace had taught me all about mind reading. It wasn't psychic energy at all. It wasn't communicating with spirits. Some people could just pick up on others' thoughts. And as Oliver had explained, the brain emitted energy waves. Some people were like radios, picking up on those waves. Edward could be one of those radios who'd picked up on someone else's thoughts. But if that was true, who had been thinking that message? Why did someone want to frighten me away from Laurelton? Or was a voice from beyond the grave really using Mr. Edison's Spirit Phone to send me a warning?

Frozen, unable to move, I stood by and watched the crowd surge around Mr. Edison, converging on him to discuss his psychic contraption. Even the usually serene Miss Hanley, in her yellow silk gown, was at the head of the line, gushing over his achievement. I wanted to escape, but I couldn't. Not before I had my turn to talk to the inventor. I needed to understand more about his machine. To find out how easily it could have been manipulated.

A waiter passed by with champagne, and I greedily accepted a crystal coupe. I surveyed the vast room, looking at all the partygoers, friends of Mr. Tiffany and fellows at the colony, both from that season and from previous ones. There had to be close to a hundred people present.

Another waiter passed, and I gave him my empty glass.

First the Ouija board, then the hymn, the shadowy figure in town, and now the telephone. I needed to find a logical explanation for each. Otherwise, I'd have to accept that my mother was sending me messages. Oh, how I wished my aunt was still alive. She was both pragmatic and open to the impossible. She'd tell me if real danger lurked or if I was taking a series of coincidences too seriously. After all, *faith* was a noun, not just my mother's name. Millions had died in 1916. And "Lead, Kindly Light" wasn't an obscure hymn.

"You looked dazed," Minx said, as she approached, holding two glasses of champagne. Thrusting one into my hand, she said, "Take a sip."

Minx's eyes appeared sleepy again. This had to be the third or fourth time I'd seen her like this since we'd arrived here. Her mother had warned me what signs to watch for.

As a bootlegger, Edward surely had access to opium. As much as I hadn't wanted to talk to him, I'd have to. I needed to let him know that Minx was susceptible and had had problems in the past. That he shouldn't tempt her. But I couldn't do it at the party. Not when I was upset and possibly jumping to conclusions.

Minx motioned to Edward, who was stuck in a crowd of people. "Let's go save him from all those people."

I'd been waiting for Mr. Edison to be free, but, glancing over, I saw that, like Edward, he was still surrounded by a throng.

Minx pulled Edward away, and the three of us escaped into the shadows on the terrace.

We sat at a table decorated with flowers and candles that flickered in the breeze. The cool air felt good on my skin. I took another sip of the pale yellow liquid and felt the bubbles go straight to my head. I hadn't eaten much all day and was already on my second—or was it my third?—glass of champagne.

"Edward, you were amazing. Wasn't he, Jenny?" Minx asked me.

"Yes."

Leaning forward and whispering so no other guests could hear, she asked, "Edward, it's just us. What was it like hearing the voice? Was she old? Young? Did she sound human?"

"I don't understand what happened. I think I'm still in shock." He raised his glass and emptied it in two gulps. When he lowered it to the table, he jostled my arm. My glass fell to the floor, breaking and spilling its contents.

"Oh, no, it's all over your gold shoes," I said to Minx.

"Don't worry, you silly bunny," she reassured me.

"Let me get you another," Edward said, pushing the shards away with his foot. "I want another myself, anyway. Minx, are you ready for a refill?"

Minx said she was, and Edward went in search of more champagne. She watched him walk away until he'd disappeared inside the house and then turned to me.

"He's working so hard on his painting. I've never seen anyone want anything so much as he wants that prize."

"Yes, but the style . . . have you noticed how much it's like yours?"

"What are you saying?" Minx bristled.

Seeing her reaction, I knew I'd made a mistake mentioning it then and there.

"You're looking for reasons not to like him, aren't you?" she asked.

"Of course not. I like him fine. I'm just concerned that he's taking advantage of you, and—"

Before I could say more, Edward returned with champagne. Minx turned away from me and picked up her glass.

"A toast!" she said. "To the ghost in the phone!"

I shuddered.

"Aren't you going to drink?" Minx asked me, an edge in her voice.

I raised my glass to my lips and drank.

"Everything OK here?" Edward asked, sensing the tension between us.

"Of course," Minx answered.

I took another sip of the champagne.

Changing the subject, Minx pointed to the Tiffany Blues bracelet I was still wearing. "I've been wanting to get a good look at it all night," she said, as she reached out and turned my wrist this way and that. "Isn't it the most glorious color, Eddie?" she asked, holding out my arm for him to take a closer look.

Edward inspected the bracelet, and as he turned it to position it in the candlelight, his fingers touched my skin. They were icy cold. It must have been from the champagne glass, I thought.

As we talked about the combination of colors and the design, I felt a headache building. I shouldn't have been surprised, with all I'd had to drink. I stood up to leave, to go to my room.

"Are you all right, Jenny?" Minx asked, reaching for me as I stumbled.

"The champagne's given me a wicked headache. I want to go upstairs . . ." I held on to Minx, unsteady on my feet.

"We'd better help you," Edward said, as he took my other arm. "Let's go in around the back so we don't ruin the party."

"Yes, the back," I mumbled. "Wouldn't want to disturb Mr. Tiffany's gala."

We walked off the terrace, around the path to the kitchen, in through that door, and then up the servants' staircase.

Edward opened my door, and Minx helped me to my bed, where I lay down, relieved to be away from the noise and any chance of embarrassing myself with the guests.

"My head is pounding, and my eyes hurt so much."

"Minx, do you have aspirin powder? I think that's what Jenny needs," Edward said.

"Yes, aspirin would be an excellent idea," she said.

I closed my eyes. I felt soft, gentle hands slipping Minx's shoes off my feet and the coverlet being laid on top of me. I was too tired to open my eyes and thank Minx for taking care of me. Or was it Minx? I detected a citrusy scent mixed with tobacco. Edward's scent.

I must have fallen asleep, because the next thing I remembered was Minx putting her arm around my back and pulling me into a sitting position.

"Here you go," she said, as she supported me and held the glass up to my lips so I could drink. I drained its contents, and Minx lowered me down.

I woke up to bright morning light coming in through the windows. I felt awful. Parched and groggy. At first, I couldn't even remember what had happened, and then it came back, slowly, out of sequence. Gingerly, I pushed the coverlet off and sat up, noticing that except for shoes, I was still fully dressed.

I stripped off all my clothes, spreading Minx's lovely evening gown on the bed, and walked naked into the bathroom. I turned on the tub's spigots, added a large dose of rose-scented salts, and while the bath filled, I went over to the sink to brush my teeth. My mouth felt as if it was filled with cotton.

I caught sight of myself in the mirror. Dark mascara smudges were under my eyes. Red lipstick was smeared around my mouth. My skin was sickly pale. My hair was pressed down on one side and sticking up on the other. I was still wearing Mr. Tiffany's beautiful earrings, which highlighted even more what a mess I looked. Reaching up, I unhooked the first and then the second and laid them on the marble countertop.

Next, I looked at my neck. Then at my wrist. Both were bare. I wasn't wearing either the necklace or the bracelet. Minx must have removed them the night before, I thought. I'd put the earrings with them after the bath.

I washed my hair and soaked in the hot water, hoping the heat and the minerals would restore me. After almost fifteen minutes, I stepped out of the tub and toweled off. I wasn't myself yet, but I definitely felt better.

I took the earrings back into my bedroom to place them with the other jewels, but I didn't see them on the desk. Or on the bureau. Or the bedside table. Or the fireplace mantel. There were no other surfaces where they could possibly be.

Then I considered that Minx must not have wanted to leave them out. I opened the armoire and looked in each drawer. Not there. Maybe Minx hadn't removed them at all, but they'd somehow slipped off when I slept. Pulling back the covers, I stripped the bed. Panic started to build deep in my stomach. Had I lost them? And then, with relief, I realized what must have happened. Minx must have taken them off to protect them and given them back to Mr. Tiffany right away but had just forgotten about the earrings.

Once I was dressed, I placed the earrings in one of the thick, creamy envelopes from the full complement of stationery in the desk.

I left my room and knocked on Minx's door. When there was no response, I went down to breakfast.

Minx, Mr. Tiffany, and several of the guests who had stayed over were already seated and eating. After greetings were exchanged, I went up to Minx and whispered in her ear, asking if she'd given Mr. Tiffany the bracelet and the necklace.

She turned in her seat to face me. "No, I didn't, Jenny. I only took off your shoes. I didn't touch the jewelry."

"You must have. You just don't remember. You had a lot of champagne, too."

"Not that much. I remember taking off your shoes and pulling up the cover and seeing the bracelet on your wrist. I thought about taking it off, but you'd fallen asleep."

"Then Edward did."

"He'd left already. Are you sure the pieces aren't in your bed?"

"Not there. Not anywhere. I took the room apart."

I glanced toward the end of the table at Mr. Tiffany. Somehow I was going to have to tell him that I'd lost his precious jewels. That other than the earrings, the Tiffany Blues suite was missing.

Before I had a chance to even begin to figure out what I was going to say, he'd gotten up and out of his seat and was coming toward me. I suddenly felt more ill than I had the night before.

"Are you all right, Miss Light? Miss Deering said you went to bed feeling unwell. I hope it wasn't anything you ate?"

"I think it was just one glass of champagne too many. But I do need to talk to you . . . I . . ."

"Yes?"

"Not here."

"Why don't you have some breakfast first? I'm not finished with mine. And whatever it is, I'm sure it can wait."

I had no choice. I took a seat a few places down from Minx beside a New York socialite and her husband who had been at the party. While I

352

waited for Mr. Tiffany, I drank two cups of black coffee and tore little bits off a piece of toast, but I couldn't eat any of it.

Finally finished, Mr. Tiffany rose and came around to me.

"I have a few minutes now," he said, and gestured toward the smoking room.

The octagonal room, with its large painting of the opium smoker's den and the Japanese armor at attention, was empty. Mr. Tiffany shut the door and turned to me.

"Let's have a seat. Why, what is it, Miss Light? You're shaking."

I held out the envelope. "The Tiffany Blues earrings are here . . ."

He took them from me.

"But the rest of the jewelry . . ." I choked back a sob. "The necklace and the bracelet are gone."

Mr. Tiffany remained calm. "I'm sure you simply misplaced them. Let's sit down and figure this out."

He asked me multiple questions, and I explained about not having eaten and drinking too much champagne. About the headache and my eyes hurting and feeling dizzy. About falling asleep dressed and not waking up until morning and still not feeling quite right.

Mr. Tiffany reassured me again and told me not to worry. He quietly arranged for Graves to have a few members of the staff do a full search of the rooms where the party had gathered, the terraces where we'd sat, the hallways and stairways.

Then Mr. Tiffany and Graves escorted me to my room to have "a look around," as they put it.

I sat by the window, feeling ill and frightened, watching as they examined everywhere. They searched under and around every surface, moving the bed and the desk away from the wall. They even rolled up the carpet.

Before he left to continue the hunt, Mr. Tiffany assured me the jewels would turn up, but he didn't seem as certain as he had been before.

Minutes after they left, Oliver knocked on my door.

"I looked for you last night after the experiment and couldn't find you, and then I found Edward, and he said that you'd felt ill and had gone to sleep and—" He smoothed down my hair. "You've been crying. What's wrong?"

We sat on the window seat, and I told him. For the first time, I noticed it was a stormy day, and there were small whitecaps in the Sound. Without any sunlight, the stained-glass windows didn't cast any reflections at all.

After I'd explained, Oliver took me in his arms and tried to reassure me. Failing to soothe me, he ordered up some tea and scones and tried to make me eat, but I couldn't.

"You have to calm down, Jenny. You'll make yourself sick. Yes, the stones have some value, but even if something has happened to them, it's not going to be a hardship to Grandfather or the store."

"But what will he think of me? He'll throw me out of the Foundation. He trusted me, Oliver. What will *you* think of me?"

Despite any reassurance he offered, I remained distraught.

Oliver was still sitting with me when, later that morning, there was another knock on the door. He opened it to find Graves, who told him the police were downstairs and Mr. Tiffany was requesting that I speak to them.

Oliver accompanied me back to the octagonal smoking room. Two men in dark suits were seated under *The Opium Dream*.

Mr. Tiffany introduced me to Detective Logan and Detective Marsh. He then took my hand and spoke to me patiently and kindly.

"I've relayed everything you told me to the detectives. What happened, how you felt, how you took ill. In reviewing the situation, they think that perhaps someone drugged you last night in order to take the jewelry. We've all heard of similar situations, so if that is what happened, I don't want you to feel you are to blame. You are the injured party as much as I am. You're not under any suspicion. But the detectives would like to talk to you and go over it all again. Would that be all right?"

I held back my emotions and said that yes, of course it was fine. But my insides were churning. The last time I had been questioned by a detective was in Hamilton, eight years ago, on the evening of the day the Reverend fell to his death off the bridge. Despite what Mr. Tiffany said, what if these men were suspicious and started digging into my background? What if Oliver hadn't believed my story? What if he'd told his grandfather and Mr. Tiffany had already told the police? What if they discovered my real name? Found out that I'd pled guilty to manslaughter and was sent to a reformatory? Would they assume the worst? Once a criminal, always a criminal?

I clasped my hands together to stop them from shaking as the interrogation began.

Detective Marsh asked most of the questions. Over the next hour, I explained—sometimes twice, sometimes three times—every moment of the evening from the time Mr. Tiffany put the jewels on me to when I woke up and realized the necklace and the bracelet were missing.

I answered every question truthfully, but when they asked what had happened once I'd reached my bedroom, my memory became foggy.

"That's when I felt the most ill," I said. "My head was pounding, I was dizzy, and I couldn't keep my eyes open. I know that Minx took care of me, but everything else is a blur."

After another fifteen minutes, Detective Logan asked Mr. Tiffany if he could talk to Miss Deering. Minx must have been summoned earlier, because Graves arrived with her only moments later.

She gave me a brave look and sat down with a typical flourish. Unlike me, she didn't seem the slightest bit nervous. If anything, she seemed almost excited. When Mr. Tiffany introduced her to the detectives, she said she was pleased to meet them, as if she was.

"Were you with Miss Bell after Mr. Edison's demonstration ended?"

"I was."

"And on the terrace, drinking champagne?"

"Yes."

"And you helped her upstairs once she felt ill?"

"I did."

"And were you alone?"

"No, Edward Wren helped me take Jenny upstairs."

"And did Mr. Wren go inside Jenny's room with you?"

"Only as far as helping me get her onto the bed, and then he left."

"And was she wearing the jewelry when he left?"

Minx nodded. "Yes."

"She was still wearing the jewelry after Edward left?"

"Yes. He only stayed a minute or two—it wouldn't do to have a man in our rooms."

If I hadn't been so anxious, I might have laughed at Minx's sudden sense of propriety.

"Had you had champagne, too?" Detective Marsh asked her.

"I had."

"How many glasses?"

"Just one."

Minx had never had just one glass of champagne in her life, but I wasn't going to rat on her. I knew she couldn't have taken the jewels and just wanted this interview to be over with.

"And so you would have noticed if the jewels were missing?"

"Well, I was concerned about Jenny not feeling well, as opposed to what she was wearing, but yes, when I covered her, I saw them. They were hard to miss."

"You had seen the jewels earlier in the evening and know they were the same ones?" Detective Marsh asked.

"Yes."

"Can you describe them?"

Minx did.

He asked her to go over her actions once again from the time we went upstairs until I drank the headache powder.

"And after Miss Bell drank the aspirin, how long did it take her to fall asleep?"

"She was asleep off and on from the minute we

put her on the bed. I had to wake her up to take the powder."

"And how long did it take her to fall asleep then?"

"I'd say it was almost immediately."

"And what did you do then, Miss Deering?"

"I undressed and went to bed."

"And did you hear anything during the night?"

"I did not."

"Do you think you would have?"

"The bathroom is between us. Though I imagine if she were screaming, I would hear it."

"Do you have sleeping powder in the bathroom along with the aspirin?"

"Yes, I do."

Detective Logan turned to Mr. Tiffany. "Can we go upstairs and inspect the bathroom?"

"Of course, if, that is . . . Ladies"—Mr. Tiffany addressed us—"is that all right with you both?"

"Yes, but why?" Minx asked, more curious than concerned.

The detective didn't answer.

"Do you really think someone went into her room during the night and took off the jewels?" Mr. Tiffany asked the detective.

Again, he didn't answer.

"Well, all right, let's go up," Mr. Tiffany said.

Together with the detectives, Minx, Oliver, Mr. Tiffany, and I all climbed the stairs. I stood by the window looking out, while Minx showed the police her potions and powders.

"How could I have let this happen?" I asked Oliver.

"I'm quite sure you didn't let this happen at all, but someone took advantage of you and gave you something to make you sleep," he answered.

I was afraid to talk to the police. To be questioned. To be involved in any way with a crime. I imagined I might start screaming. I had done nothing. Again. And this time, I wouldn't take the blame.

Minx was in the bathroom with the detectives. I heard her voice, so calm and helpful. She'd lied to the detectives so easily about the champagne . . .

Mr. Tiffany had been watching the detectives from the bathroom door, but he turned and came over to us by the window. He looked at me kindly. "I know you are upset. As am I. But none of us believes this was your fault."

"I think I should leave Laurelton. I've caused too much trouble."

"Absolutely not. I haven't gotten you to paint our lily pond yet," he said reassuringly. "Miss Light, someone has taken advantage of you. And we will find out who and why. One way or another, we *will* get to the bottom of this."

"Why are you being so kind to me?"

He was silent for a moment, then answered even more kindly, "Because I know that others haven't been."

25

I didn't sleep well Sunday night, which hardly surprised me. And on Monday, I didn't work well. I'd taken my supplies down to the beach to try to do some sea studies. The day was warm and sunny, but my sketches were dark. I was just about ready to quit, when Oliver came down the steps. I felt a flicker of excitement seeing him, but given my worries, it went as dark as my paintings.

"I missed you at breakfast," he said.

"I wasn't hungry."

"Wasn't hungry or wanted to avoid everyone?"

"I just don't understand what happened. How could I have not realized that someone was taking a bracelet off my wrist or a necklace off my neck?"

"Easy if you were drugged." He took my hand. "I'm sorry to be the bearer of bad news, Jenny, but Grandfather asked me to find you. The detectives are on their way, and they want to talk to you again."

I cringed. Each time I had to talk to the police meant yet another time I might inadvertently reveal a clue about my past that they could use against me.

"I know how hard, impossibly hard, this must

be for you," he said, as he took my hand and led me over to a large flat rock.

He hopped up onto the rock with me. We sat, facing the calm sea, watching the seagulls soar and dip, the clouds roll by. Oliver put his arm around me, pulled me toward him, and stroked my hair.

"What are you thinking?" he asked.

"I've managed to keep the past buried for so long without anyone finding out. If it comes out now, it will ruin everything."

"People will understand. I understand."

I shook my head. "You're different."

"Are you suggesting I'm prejudiced just because I think you're the most marvelous girl in the world?" He kissed my forehead.

His words would have melted my heart under any other circumstances, but I was frozen with fear.

"My grandfather thinks you're terrific, too."

"Only because he doesn't know . . . He *doesn't,* does he? You didn't tell him? I imagined he might know from how he was talking to me yesterday."

"No, I promised you."

"I would leave if I didn't think it would cast even more suspicion on me."

"Grandfather doesn't suspect you. I don't."

Oliver was quiet for a moment. As if weighing what he was going to say.

"Jenny, I don't want you to be upset by what

I'm going to tell you, but I do want you to be prepared."

I sucked in my breath. The expression on Oliver's face made me even more afraid. I clasped my hands together and dug my fingers into my palms.

"What is it?"

"The reason the police are back is that they received a note." He stopped.

"A note?" My voice was expressionless.

"Accusing you of stealing the jewelry, with information about where the missing jewelry is."

I started to tremble, and Oliver held me closer.

"C'mon, we need to go back to the house."

Together, we gathered my things and started up the stone steps. Halfway, Oliver stopped me.

"Jenny, no matter what they find, I want you to know that I believe you had nothing to do with this."

"What do you think is going to happen?"

He shook his head. "I don't have any idea. But if the note does lead them to the jewelry, then it's obvious someone is trying to set you up."

"But why would anyone do that?"

"I just don't know."

We continued walking, trying to figure it out.

"Is there anyone you've met here whom you slighted in any way?"

I shook my head. "Not that I can think of, no."

"Is there anyone you still are in contact with

from Canada who would want you to get into trouble?"

"No. I lost contact with all of them once I was sent to Andrew Mercer. Even my friends Martha and Sarah. I couldn't really blame them. I was a convicted criminal. I suppose there are members of the Reverend's congregation who still despise me, but it's been six years since I left Hamilton. How would any of them know I was here? I haven't been Jenny Fairburn since 1918."

Oliver pulled me close to him and whispered, "If you think of anything, promise you'll tell me. I want to help you. And you can trust me."

I can't trust anyone! I wanted to shout. My life had only proven that. But I didn't say anything. I just let him hold me and for the moment pretended that we were a normal couple on an outing by the shore on a lovely June day.

"Don't be afraid. I'll be here with you."

"Thank you," I whispered.

As we approached the lawn, I saw a peacock stroll across the path. Each time I'd seen one before, I'd stopped to watch and wait. But so far, none had fanned for me. That morning was different. After we passed him and walked on another ten yards or so, I turned and saw him in the distance, in the shade of the trees, opening his tail. But of course, he wasn't close enough for me to see any of his resplendent color. The bird was just a silhouette in the shadows.

Detectives Logan and Marsh were once again seated in the smoking room with Mr. Tiffany. Clouds shifted outside, casting shadows on the six full-size suits of Japanese armor standing side by side like a jury awaiting evidence.

There were fewer pleasantries today. Detective Marsh got right to the point. "Miss Bell, I'd like to ask you one more time if you have any knowledge of where the missing jewels might be. Things will go much better for you if you tell us instead of us finding them without your assistance."

I couldn't help myself. I dug my fingernails into my palms. The pain seemed to be the only thing keeping me sane. "No, I told you. I never took them off. I went to sleep wearing them on Saturday night and woke up without them."

"We have received information that requires we search your room again. I take it that would be all right with you?"

I wanted to refuse to let them in. I knew about policemen and detectives. Like for reporters, it was their job to solve their cases. To be efficient. Nuance didn't interest them if it interfered with them shutting a file and seeing someone go to jail.

"Yes, of course," I said.

We all left the smoking room and trooped up the stairs—Mr. Tiffany, Oliver, Detectives Logan and Marsh, and myself. We stopped in front of my room.

"Do you typically lock your door, Miss Bell?" Detective Marsh asked.

"No. I don't have anything of any value."

I opened the door, and everyone followed me inside.

"And this is the closet?" he asked, pointing.

"Yes."

He opened it. My minuscule wardrobe hung from the hangers, taking up about a quarter of the space. Two pairs of shoes and my slippers were lined up in an even row on the floor. Marsh pushed the hangers aside and felt along the back wall. Then he looked above to the shelf.

"I take it this is your suitcase?" he asked, pointing.

I told him it was.

"Can we look inside?"

"Of course."

Marsh lifted the suitcase off the shelf and put it on the floor. He and Logan squatted and inspected every corner and pocket but came up empty.

Detective Logan turned to me. "Do you have another suitcase?"

"No, that's my only one."

He took a notebook out of his back pocket. No bigger than the palm of his hand, it had a cracked black leather cover. Flipping it open, he went through a few pages of notes.

"Do you have something else that might be referred to as a 'case'?"

I thought about the word for a moment. "My paint box?"

"Perhaps. Where is that?" Detective Logan asked.

"In the studio."

Logan looked at Mr. Tiffany. "I assume it's all right for us to go there?"

"Yes, as I told you earlier. Anything you need to do to find the jewelry and clear up this mess."

We made our way out of the house and walked down to the studio. I stumbled twice, and each time Oliver reached out and helped me. The second time, I noticed Mr. Tiffany watching us, a slight frown on his face.

Eight of the fellows were working—painting or sculpting—inside the studio. Minx wasn't there. But Paul Cadmus was. I also noticed Edward.

Detective Marsh spoke to them. "I'm sorry to disturb you all, but could we have a few moments here?"

"Is something more amiss?" Edward asked with a tone of annoyance.

"Sir?" Detective Marsh asked.

"I'm in the middle of painting and—"

"It will just be a few minutes."

As Edward reluctantly stepped away, I caught a glimpse of his painting. Closer to being finished, it was even more striking and powerful than it had been two days before. And the style seemed even more familiar, but I couldn't figure out why. What did it remind me of?

"Can you show us where the case is, Miss Bell?" Logan asked.

At my station, I pulled out the battered wooden paint box that my aunt had given me for my nineteenth birthday. My hand shook as I gave it to Detective Marsh.

He took it from me, laid it on top of the desk, and opened it. Inside was a jumble of paints.

One by one, Logan removed each tube and laid it on the table. To the right, he lined up sixteen tubes, all wrapped in the same "Sam Flax New York" labels. To the left, he placed two other tubes. These wore "Windsor Newton" labels, a more expensive brand. Windsor Newton paints were imported from England. Windsor Newton was Minx's brand.

Logan gave his partner a look I couldn't read. Marsh picked up the Windsor Newton tube of iris green and inspected it closely. Then he checked the Prussian blue. Then he looked at me.

"Those aren't mine," I blurted out. "You can see that's not my brand."

"Then you won't mind if we examine them?"

I shook my head.

Marsh pulled the paper wrapper off one of the first tubes, exposing the foil underneath. Down the center, a clean cut exposed the tube's innards. Like a gaping wound. He stuck his pencil inside, moved it around, and extracted a dark green mess, like a sinewy part of a plant, about eight inches long.

"What on earth?" Oliver said.

"Does anyone have a rag?" Marsh asked.

Without thinking, I reached for one of the rags I used to clean my brushes and handed it to him.

Logan wiped the paint off the mysterious object. It was the bracelet that I had been wearing on Saturday night.

"But how—" I swallowed the rest of what I was going to ask.

Logan continued wiping away the paint, and now it was obvious that the bracelet was no longer intact.

"The setting is incomplete," Mr. Tiffany said in a somber voice. "The pavé stones are intact, but the Tiffany Blue has been removed."

"I don't understand," I blurted out. "Why would anyone take it apart?"

"The value is in the major center stones," Oliver answered.

I sank down to the floor. The bracelet had been found in a tube of paint in my own paint box. I didn't need to watch Logan inspect the tube of Prussian blue. We all knew what he was going to find. To no one's surprise, he extracted the necklace, also without its center Tiffany Blue stone.

Oliver leaned over and offered me his hand to help me up.

"Jenny, it's too obvious. No one is going to believe you had anything to do with it."

When I didn't take his hand, he sat beside me.

"No one would do this and leave the evidence in their own paint case. At least, no intelligent person. And you *are* an intelligent person. I don't have any doubt that you have been set up. And neither will anyone else."

I looked at his face. Into his eyes, so I could know for sure that he believed what he was saying. That this discovery hadn't changed how he felt about me. His eyes were as clear as aquamarines, and the expression in them gave me a glimmer of hope.

I let Oliver help me up from the floor.

"What my grandson said is true, Miss Light. No one is going to believe you would do this and leave the evidence in such a very obvious place."

Even Detective Logan looked at me sympathetically. "Is there anyone here who might have it out for you?" he asked.

I shook my head. "I don't know." The full weight of the past forty-eight hours overwhelmed me. The Spirit Phone and the hymn and the Ouija board and the robbery. Everything pointed to one person. But why would she have it out for me? Why would Minx want me to leave the Foundation, when she was the one who had applied on my behalf to come here?

26

What if . . . No, it wasn't possible . . . But there were no other explanations. What if I was right and Minx was taking drugs again? What if she was worried I'd go to her mother and tell her and ruin her summer of fun? What if Minx was working on Edward's painting, helping him in exchange for supplying her with opium? How far would she go to get rid of me? Maybe she'd manipulated the Ouija board to scare me away. Then planted the hymn. When neither plan worked, she'd told Edward what to claim he heard on Edison's Spirit Phone. I'd seen them whispering just before he volunteered. And then, to get me out of the way for good, she stole the jewels, planted them in my paint box, and alerted the detectives.

But it was all so preposterous. Minx didn't know enough about my life to concoct such an intricate plot against me. I had never talked about my mother or the year she died, and Minx certainly didn't know anything about the Reverend, much less his favorite hymn. And I trusted that Oliver hadn't told her anything. Besides, both the Ouija board incident and the hymn happened before I confessed everything to him.

No, I knew it wouldn't do for me to continue with this line of thought or even to whisper my suspicions to anyone. If I was wrong, I'd be getting Minx into terrible trouble and would make myself look like a fool.

Then again, Minx had teased me a few times about my reluctance to "spill" about my past. She had always tried to coax my secrets out of me. I couldn't forget the message from the Ouija board our first night at Laurelton: "Secrets will not stay hidden . . . here danger . . . here believe . . . faith . . . go." Or "Believe Faith . . . go."

The detectives stayed for several hours. I found out later that they asked to see each student's paints. Minx was the only one who used Windsor Newton.

We sat in her room later that afternoon, drinking tea she'd spiked with brandy from her silver flask and smoking cigarettes, and I listened to her recount everything about her "interrogation," as she called it.

"It lasted almost an hour," Minx told me. "I was, in fact, missing those two tubes, iris green and Prussian blue. But you know I haven't been painting here. I've only been sculpting. I told them I hadn't opened my paint box at all since arriving."

At least part of that was true. She hadn't been painting, as far as I knew.

"And I told them that it was ridiculous to think I would have taken the jewelry and destroyed it and planted the remnants of the pieces in my best friend's effects. They asked me if I had any reason to want you to leave Laurelton. I do believe I smirked at Detective Logan for that one. Why in the world would I want you to leave Laurelton? I'm the one who went through hell and high water to get you here."

I loved Minx. I'd never seen her exhibit anything but compassion and generosity toward me. And yet . . . and yet . . . I couldn't help but wonder. She had changed since she'd come to Laurelton. She was less focused on her work and more distant and dreamy when I talked to her. I'd blamed her developing relationship with Edward. Since I'd never seen her forgo her bevy of admirers for just one man before, I'd assumed she was falling for him hard. Or, I feared, falling for what he could give her.

Oliver and Mr. Tiffany returned to New York early that evening, and Minx went off to find Edward. Left on my own, I stayed in my room and tried to come up with a plan.

The next morning, Graves gave me a letter at breakfast. Ben wrote that he expected to be back in New York in July and was anxious to see me and pick up where we had left off. That the longer we were apart, the more he realized how much I meant to him.

He also mentioned that he'd read about the theft at the Tiffany mansion and was worried about me. He asked me to write immediately and tell him that I was all right. And then he ended the letter with a paragraph that added to all the other anxiety I was feeling.

I know that you have had a hard time in the past and are afraid of sharing your troubles with me. I think I understand why now, and I want you to know that when you are ready to tell me your truth, I will believe it without doubt. I have seen how selfish people can be, how ruthless, how frightened, how cruel, and how sometimes even the best people make the worst decisions. Jenny, I want to help you come out of the shadows and stand by your side in the light.

I read it over and over. What had Ben discovered? Was he referring to my real past, or was his overactive imagination filling in blanks? Had he found out about Hamilton? Had *he* been the one to tell Minx? If he had and she now knew my mother's name and the date of her death and information about the Reverend, it would explain everything. All she would have had to do was manipulate the planchette for the first effort, place the hymn on the organ for the second, and tell Edward what to say on the Spirit Phone for the third.

But how was I going to find out? I couldn't just write back to Ben and ask for an explanation without admitting secrets he might not have actually discovered.

Oliver called me on Thursday to assure me that his grandfather had pretty much convinced the police I was as much a victim as he was.

"Until they find the stones or another clue, they aren't going to rest, but I don't want you worrying that they are going to show up and arrest you. All right?"

"I'll try. But until they do find out who did it, it's still an open case, and I'm still a suspect."

He tried to reassure me. And I pretended that it was working.

"Listen, I'm going to be playing at a jazz club in Harlem on Saturday. It's just the diversion you need. I'll drive out that afternoon to pick you up and bring you into the city with me. Why don't you tell all the other fellows? I'm sure everyone could use a break."

By Saturday, the police hadn't gotten any further in solving the Tiffany Blues theft. I worried that Oliver would have changed his mind and started to suspect me, too. But when he arrived at Laurelton to pick me up, he was so concerned and caring that I decided I was overreacting.

At eight thirty, the caravan took off. Oliver and me in his two-seater. Minx, Edward, Paul, and

Luigi in Luigi's jalopy. And Henry in his Ford, with a last group including Mabel and Edith.

As we drove over the bridge toward the city, which was as tarnished in places as it was shining in others, sadness overtook me. In three weeks, I was going to have to vacate the Foundation for good. I'd been at the colony for almost a month, and other than going into town a couple of times, this was the first time I'd left. If it hadn't been Oliver asking, I wouldn't have gone at all. Despite the events at Laurelton Hall, I didn't want to return to traffic and strangers, ugly buildings, and bums. I wanted to be buffered from the world, cocooned by beauty at Mr. Tiffany's estate.

"You're pensive," Oliver said, taking my hand.

"I was just thinking about how sad I am that my time at Laurelton is almost over."

"My grandfather seems very invested in you. I could ask him if you could stay for another session."

"I couldn't afford to. I have to get back to work. And while Mr. Tiffany might have felt that way before the robbery, I doubt he wants anything to do with me anymore."

"I'm so sorry that the detectives haven't found the culprit. I know how disturbing this must be for you. We're both sure that they will find out who did it and you'll be completely cleared."

"Do they think Minx is a suspect?" I asked.

"No, do you?"

"No. I can't imagine that she could do anything like that to me . . ."

"I hear a 'but' in your voice."

"It can't be her." All my suspicions were going around and around in my head. I sighed. "Oliver, let's not talk about all that anymore tonight. Talk about your music. You said you had done it full-time in Paris?"

"Yes, that's how I paid the bills. Painting during the day and playing piano at night. For almost four years."

"Would you have eventually minded giving up Tiffany and Company if you'd stayed?"

"If my grandfather believed in my design ability, I might have. But now I'm the one being morose . . ."

"Which dream was harder to walk away from? Tiffany or France?"

He concentrated on the road ahead of us. "Have you ever given up a dream?"

"No. I've given up reality. My dreams are all that have kept me alive. I took the scariest job I could imagine so I could have more time to paint and save money to go and study in Paris."

"It must have been very difficult to walk into a courtroom in New York the first time."

"It was. The lawyers, the judge, the jury . . . listening to the testimony, watching the accuser's face . . . remembering . . . remembering . . . and then, during one of my first trials, there was a shooting in the courtroom." I told him about what had happened and how I'd taken the victim's daughter home.

"I read about it," Oliver said. "The papers called it a crime of passion."

"Yes, passion," I said, the word tasting terrible in my mouth.

"You're thinking of the Reverend?"

A wave of nausea coursed through me. It had been years since I'd heard that name spoken out loud. Aunt Grace and I had made a pact never to utter it.

"Don't . . . don't refer to him. Ever. Please, promise me."

Oliver took my hand. "I'm sorry."

"Promise me," I pleaded.

"I promise," Oliver said solemnly. "Jenny, I want to keep seeing you when you're back in New York. But I'm going to have to go to Newport in July."

"I don't expect you to see me every day. I have work and school . . ."

"I just don't want you to think I'm not serious."

I laughed. "Impossible. You are one of the most serious people I've ever met."

"Is that a bad thing?"

"I guess it can be if it makes you worry too much."

Now he laughed. "Oh, it does that."

"You shouldn't worry so much."

"Pot, meet kettle."

"I know. I also know how too much worry keeps you from being happy. Aunt Grace taught me an exercise that really helps. She said that every morning, I should give myself just fifteen minutes to worry. To cram all my fears and concerns into that one period, so that for the rest of the day, whenever I feel the worry creeping up on me again, I can stop it, knowing I can attend to it during the next morning's session. It's amazing how much anxiety gets diffused that way."

"So you do that?"

"Every day."

"And it works?"

"Most of the time, yes. Not this week so much."

We were off the bridge now and came to a stoplight. Oliver leaned over, brushed my hair off my face, and then leaned in and planted a soft, sweet kiss on my lips. The touch made me thrill.

"If I could, I would take all the worry in your world and roll it up in a ball and throw it as far as I could out to sea," he said.

"I bet you would. And I would take yours and do the exact same thing."

"OK. Tonight you won't worry, and I won't worry."

"Perfect."

"Now," he said, "I have a present for you."

"You do?"

"Something I made."

"Really? When can I have it?"

"It's in my pocket. Reach in."

As I put my hand into Oliver's jacket pocket, I realized I'd never before received a present from a man.

I recognized the box immediately. For a moment, the anxiety returned—Mr. Tiffany had presented the Blues in just such a teal-blue leather and gilt box.

As if he knew what I was thinking, Oliver repeated the evening's mantra: "Tonight we won't worry. Remember?"

"Yes, all right."

He pulled the car to a stop on 131st Street and Seventh Avenue in front of Connie's Inn, a speakeasy where Minx had taken me a few times to hear her favorites—who soon became mine—Louis Armstrong, Fats Waller, and Fletcher Henderson.

A pool of yellow light from the streetlamp shone into the car.

"Now," Oliver said, "open your present."

I lifted the box's lid. Inside, on a bed of white satin, lay a simple platinum chain with square modern links and a charm of two platinum hearts, one inside the other. The design was very modern. Something for the future, not from the past. Nothing like any of the Tiffany jewelry I'd seen in the shop or at Laurelton Hall.

The outside heart was paved with diamonds, the inside one with lavender-blue stones, the same stones as in the bracelet that had been taken off my wrist. I turned the charm over and read the words engraved on the edge.

To Jenny from Oliver—joined hearts & souls 6/16/24

I held it up into the light. The hearts dangled and danced.

"Do you like it?"

"Oh, yes."

"I wanted to give you that abalone shell we found at the fort the first day we met, but it shattered when I tried to put a bezel around its hole. I hope this makes up for it."

I fumbled with the clasp.

"Let me put it on you."

I handed it to him and asked, "You said you made it?"

"I designed the links and had one of the jewelers in the shop fashion them while I made the mold for the hearts, matched the stones, set them, and engraved it myself."

He draped the bracelet over my wrist and closed it.

"I'm never taking it off."

He bent down and kissed the back of my hand where the clasp lay against my skin.

I knew even as it happened that the moment would stand out of time for me forever. For those few seconds, everything was possible. Nothing could hold us back.

A few minutes later, we walked into Connie's Inn, where a blues band filled the place with music. The air was smoky and tinted pale blue from the cigarette smoke. Women in glittering dresses and bejeweled cigarette holders sat with men in formal dinner wear and slicked-back hair at black mirrored tables. We made our way around waiters balancing trays and customers on the dance floor and reached a group of three tables near the front which were reserved for Oliver.

Minx, Edward, and the rest of our party arrived just after we did. Oliver ordered champagne, oysters, and caviar. One of the owners, Conrad Immerman, came over, welcoming Oliver and then Minx, whom he also knew.

The champagne flowed, and the band played. Mostly, we danced.

"Tonight one of our favorite musicians is here." The bandleader interrupted the set and spoke into the microphone. "And we'd like to ask him to come up and play with us. Oliver T."

"Oliver T?" I asked him.

"I don't use my last name. Too many family associations," he said, as he got up.

Oliver walked over to the piano and sat down. The spotlights shone down on his black dinner jacket and ebony hair. He positioned his long, elegant fingers over the keys.

Oliver had played for me at Laurelton that first time I was in his room, and he had both impressed and moved me. But with the crowd and the backup musicians and the champagne, he wasn't the Oliver who had thrown my black paint away. Who'd kissed me on the sailboat. Who'd held my hand when we walked through woods and made love to me in his bed. His voice was an even deeper blue velvet, and it was mesmerizing everyone in the club, especially me, with a melancholy love song.

> If you were the only girl in the world
> And I were the only boy
> Nothing else would matter in the world
>   today
> We could go on loving in the same old
>   way

I hung on every note, every word. I wanted to close my eyes and float on his voice, except I didn't want to stop watching him, with his eyes half shut and his thick hair falling over his forehead and his fingers making love to the keyboard. Every note, every word, sent thrills up my arms and down my back, and deep inside me I throbbed to the beat of his song.

How could he have given up both his art and

383

his music to run Tiffany's? I understood that Oliver's father had never been interested in the artistic side of the family business. But Oliver was. At the same time, he loved his grandfather and wanted to do the right thing for him and his legacy. But Oliver really was an artist. He needed to create. It would destroy him to bottle up his soul because his grandfather didn't want any competition. Because that was what it had to be, wasn't it? Mr. Tiffany had been the rebel and the renegade. He wanted to keep that designation. Not cede it to his younger, modern grandson.

Oliver played several songs, often looking over to me. And then, in the middle of a fairly jovial line, I saw his face grow grave. While he kept playing on with one hand, with the other he motioned to me to come over. I felt awkward and unsure, but his expression was insistent. Beside me, Minx and Edward were twisted into an embrace and weren't paying any attention. I couldn't ask Minx what she thought Oliver meant. So I did what he wanted. I got up and sat beside him on the piano bench.

"Sing along with me," he whispered.

"But I can't sing," I whispered back.

"Just do it, Jenny," he said impatiently. "Sing."

So I did. I sang softly, following his lead and watching his fingers fly over the keyboard.

"Run!" The shout came from the audience.

I looked at Oliver. He was peering out, focused

on the back of the room. I followed his gaze to where at least six, maybe eight, men in dark, bulky suits were making their way through the crowd.

"It's the police!" another voice shouted. "It's a raid!"

I turned back to Oliver in panic.

He kept playing but stopped singing and whispered, "Don't worry. Just keep singing. It is a raid, but if you just sit here with me and sing, everything will be fine."

People shouted and screamed as they tried to evade the police, but it didn't look like anyone was getting away. Two policemen were blocking the front door. Another two were blocking the stage exit. In the melee, I lost sight of Minx and Edward and the other fellows.

"What's going to happen to us?" I whispered.

"They'll probably question us, but they won't arrest us," Oliver answered.

"They are going to take us away." I clutched his arm.

"Jenny, listen to me. They will not take us away. Remember, tonight's not for worry. They never arrest the band. Usually the owners, sometimes the guests."

"Minx?" My voice trembled.

"We can't do anything yet. I promise you're OK, and they will be, too."

I remained by Oliver's side while he played on.

When the room had cleared of everyone but us and the jazz trio, one of the policemen approached.

"Any of you drinking?"

"No, sir," Oliver said. "We're just the entertainment."

"Well, you can all go home. The show's obviously over."

Oliver took my arm, helped me up from the piano bench, and started to lead me toward the exit.

"My bag," I said, stopping, looking back at the table where we'd been sitting. "I have to get my bag."

"No, you don't. If you walk over there now, the cop will know you were a patron and not part of us. Just forget about the bag, I'll get you another one."

"My aunt gave it to me. I can't lose it."

But Oliver kept a tight hold on my arm as he walked me through the club's kitchen and out into the crisp evening. Down the block, we stood under a dark, moonless sky, watching the commotion on the sidewalk as the patrons were hustled into the waiting paddy wagons.

"We have to find Minx," I said. "Her parents will send her away if she gets into any more trouble."

"No. We have to get to the car. Right now, we have to take care of ourselves. There's nothing we can do for Minx until she's been booked. Then I promise we'll get her out."

Oliver held tightly on to my arm until we reached the car and I was safely inside. Then he joined me. He took off his jacket and put it around my shoulders.

"You're trembling," he said.

I watched the last of the police cars disappear down the street.

"Jenny?"

I continued to shake.

"Talk to me, Jenny. I know the broad strokes of the incident in Hamilton but not the details. Did the police come for you? What happened between the time they arrested you and when you went on trial? Did they hurt you? It might make it easier to tell me instead of holding it all inside."

Why was he pushing me to tell him more? What else did he want?

I opened the car door and took off running, to get away from the questions, from the night, from the scene, from the chaos, from him.

Oliver ran after me, shouting, but I didn't stop, couldn't stop. One block, then another. I didn't know what he was calling out; I couldn't hear him over my labored breathing. I just kept moving. I had no idea where I was or where I was going except that I needed to get away.

27

My shoe heel caught in a crack in the sidewalk, and I tripped. As I fell, I heard my dress rip. Then I felt a sharp pain in my shoulder. My knee began to throb.

"Are you crazy?" Oliver said, as he reached me. "It's two o'clock in the morning. It's damned dangerous around here for anyone, no less a woman alone wearing silk and platinum and diamonds."

"I'm not wearing platinum—" I started to say, then stopped. I'd forgotten about the bracelet, the first serious piece of jewelry I'd ever owned.

"You most certainly are!" I'd never seen him angry. A vein throbbed in his forehead. His eyes were narrowed to slits, and his mouth was pursed.

He helped me up. Noting my missing shoe, he looked around, spotted it, pulled it out of the crack, and helped me put it on.

"Can you walk?" he asked.

"I'm not sure," I said, as I tentatively put some weight on my foot. It hurt but not more than I could bear. "I'm fine."

With Oliver half holding me, half pulling me, and neither of us saying a word, we walked the ten blocks back to the car.

"You're sure you aren't hurt?" he asked once

we were inside his roadster and he started the engine. "You were limping."

"I'm fine."

He pulled away from the curb.

"Where are we going?"

"To the station house. To bail everyone out."

"Will Minx be arrested? Have a record?"

"No. Raids like this are just the police putting on a show for the newspapers, to make it look like they're not on the take."

Neither of us spoke again until Oliver turned right onto 125th Street. "It's only a few blocks now."

"I can't go inside. Not even for Minx," I said.

What if they'd asked her whom she'd been with and she'd given them my name? What if they recognized me from the club? What if they wanted to question me? What if they had talked to the detectives on Long Island?

"Can you let me out a block before the station house?"

"Why? Where are you going?"

"I'll get a taxi and go to our apartment in the Village—" I stopped. "No, I can't. I don't have my keys. They are at Laurelton. And the landlady is mostly deaf. She never wakes up in the middle of the night, no matter how loud the racket."

Oliver took my hand, kindly this time, and held it as he drove with the other hand.

"How about you just stay in the car, Jenny. You'll be fine."

Oliver parked in front of the station house. Only five minutes later, he returned.

"We have an hour before they are processed," he said. "Let's go find a place to get something to eat. Then I'll come back and bail them out."

Two blocks away, we found an all-night diner. We sat in a booth with cracked leather seats, and a waitress with a stained apron gave us menus. We ordered eggs with toast and bacon, but when the food came, I only pushed it around on the plate.

"I'm sorry," Oliver said. "Your first encounter with a raid can be terrifying."

I took a sip of the strong sugared tea Oliver had insisted I order. The heavy white mug had a chip on the handle. The whole last week had been terrifying. My fingers crept to the bracelet he'd placed on my wrist, and I played with the heart charm.

I felt the need to explain more about my past. It seemed inevitable now that I must tell Oliver everything.

"The police didn't hurt me. No one ever laid a hand on me, until Andrew Mercer. After I turned myself in, I was arrested and put in the county jail and stayed there alone for two days and two nights until Aunt Grace arrived from Ithaca. She hired a lawyer, who got me released on bail. I stayed with her in a boardinghouse until the trial, while my mother remained in the parsonage, according to our plan. Aunt Grace begged me to tell her the truth, and for a fleeting second, I thought I might. I came so close to telling her everything so that I could go on and live a normal life just like any other girl." Tears filled my eyes.

"But there was no going back. My mother had been in such a desperate state there at the waterfall, and I was the stubborn and determined daughter ready to finally save her.

"When they put me on the stand and I looked out at my mother sitting in the audience, her arms crossed over her belly, crying, I knew no matter what the cost, I couldn't sentence her to prison for an accident. I couldn't deprive my half brother or sister of a mother. Though our family was small, it was very tight. I had watched my mother and Aunt Grace live together and raise me when I was small. I was willing to do anything for them, including keeping a secret that would have ruined their relationship.

"So I pled guilty and sat and watched a case against me unfold and was sentenced to hell.

"For four months after I was sent to Andrew Mercer, I received letters from my mother. Brief communications about her health, her love for me, and our future together. Sweet and simple promises to serve me stacks of cinnamon toast for breakfast every day and to take me on picnics and to the emporium to purchase whatever fabric I fancied for a new dress. But they were all postmarked from different places: Burlington, Amherst, Boston, New York. Which is where she and the baby died. At that point, everything I'd done was rendered useless. It was too late to save myself. I had no proof. And it was obviously too late to save her."

I stopped and glanced at our reflection in the grimy diner window.

"You can't torture yourself thinking about what you might have done."

"I know. But . . ."

"There's something else, though, isn't there? Some other doubt?" he asked.

When my words came, they were hesitant and hard won. "Sometimes I can't help but wonder about the value of my sacrifice. After all, my mother and brother didn't live, and eight years later, I'm still haunted by a crime I didn't commit and am still so scared that I'm running away from the police."

I took a breath. There was more, but I wasn't sure I could even explain it.

"It will help if you talk about it, Jenny. Holding it in will only keep it festering."

I told him about the anonymous letter Aunt Grace had received and the unknown man my mother had run away with.

"It's just that now, especially with Aunt Grace

having passed away, all I'm left with is this enormous sense of betrayal that I can't quite put my finger on, because my mother meant so much to me. She was my world, and she gave me so much. She wanted me to have a rich and full life. But how was she able to watch me—watch her daughter throw her life into ruin for some man? Especially after everything that had happened? How could she love me but abandon me? That's the mystery I'm still grappling with. That's what I'm so desperate to know."

Oliver reached out and brushed a curl off my forehead. "She must have been scared and distraught, not thinking. I honestly can't imagine. And I can't begin to imagine how you felt. What you did was so brave, Jenny." He reached out and touched the charm on my bracelet. "You have such a beautiful heart. I'm sure she loved you. It was her love that inspired you to do what you did for her. If there are secrets we need to confess, if there are plans we need to change, we will. Now that we've found each other, everything will be all right."

I believed him. I felt for the first time since Aunt Grace's passing that there was someone who was going to stand by me and help me unravel all the tangled threads of my past. With everyone gone and no hearts to protect, I had started to wonder if there might be a way I could prove my innocence. I hadn't the slightest idea where to begin, but maybe Oliver could help me figure out how to accomplish it, to finally be at ease with myself and my place in the world.

Back at the station house, I waited by the car as Oliver paid the five-dollar fine for each of the fellows who had been with us at the club, and they all filed out.

Minx ran over. "What a crazy night. A first for me. I've finally made it to jail!" She sounded excited, as if it had been a real adventure. I cringed.

She turned to Oliver. "Thank you. I appreciate you coming to our rescue."

Edward followed behind her, not at all pleased. He frowned, as if it bothered him that she thanked Oliver.

"No thanks necessary," Oliver said. "It could have been me in there if they'd raided the place fifteen minutes earlier."

I felt my stomach clench. Fifteen minutes was all that separated me from having been brought to a police station and booked. Even though they had no intention of prosecuting the patrons, I would have had to endure the ritual of being imprisoned for the second time in my life. Even with Oliver by my side, I wasn't sure I could have withstood it.

28

We returned to Laurelton just as dawn was breaking and all retired to our rooms to get some sleep before the day started. Three hours later, I knocked on Minx's door to take her down to breakfast with me. When she didn't answer, I opened it and saw that not only wasn't she there, but her bed clearly hadn't been slept in.

But I'd gone up with her the night before. Why hadn't she stayed in her room? Where had she gone?

I went to breakfast by myself and found Mr. Tiffany, who must have arrived the evening before, dining with two guests. They were having a spirited conversation about a play that had opened on Broadway, *She Stoops to Conquer.* Not having seen it and being tired still, I was quiet as I ate my toast.

Mr. Tiffany noticed. "How was your week, Miss Light? Did you get some good work done?"

"I tried." I gave him a half smile.

He examined my face. "You don't seem yourself at all. You're not still upset about the jewelry, are you? I don't want you to be."

"Thank you. I can't help but still be upset." *About that and so many other things,* I almost said.

"I'm sure Oliver told you, neither of us thinks you would have been so foolish as to hide the jewelry in your own supplies."

"I so appreciate your faith in me," I said.

"For the rest of the month, I want you to focus on your work and nothing else. I'm counting on you in the competition for the prize." He softly added, "But that has to be our secret."

"Thank you."

"Will you paint with me tomorrow morning?"

"Yes," I said, brightening. "I'd like that."

Talking to Mr. Tiffany had reminded me that no matter what else happened, it *would* be a crime for me to squander the opportunity being afforded me at Laurelton Hall. I went down to the studio with a little less heaviness than I'd had before breakfast.

I was the first one there. Given the late night, I assumed everyone else was sleeping in. It was Sunday, after all, and Mr. Tiffany encouraged us all to take Sundays off to explore and experience things that would help our painting. The service in the chapel would be starting in a half hour, but I didn't want to attend. I didn't want to walk in the woods or down by the shore or ride into town. I wanted to paint. I needed to paint.

Before I settled in at my station, I walked past Edward's. His was always messy, with supplies left out, tubes of paint with tops off,

396

brushes still dirty, canvases stacked against one another before they'd had a chance to dry. But I didn't care about his mess. I wanted to study his canvas. I had to be sure. I examined the landscape, the view through a cluster of trees at a storm breaking over Oyster Bay. The painting was exceptional. I could feel the wind, the chilly air, and the encroaching rain. The scene was elevated from merely a decoration to a meaningful message about nature.

I leaned forward on my elbows to study it. No doubt about it, this was far better than his work at the Art Students League. It possessed finesse, subtlety, and raw beauty.

"Do you have a problem with my painting?"

I started. "Not at all." I turned. "I was just admiring it. It's so good, Edward."

He grunted. "You seem surprised."

"I didn't mean—"

"You have a problem with me, don't you, Jenny Bell?" he asked, spitting out my last name.

"Not at all."

"Liar."

I was shocked by the nasty edge in his voice and how fast he had turned on me.

"You don't think I'm as good a painter as you are," he continued. "You think I got here on some kind of fluke. You're worried I'm a bad influence on Minx. Everything you think is wrong. And you and your friend coming to save our souls last night, all high and mighty in his fancy car, and you with your shiny new bracelet."

"Edward, Oliver wanted to help."

"He wanted to show off. Like you're trying to show off for Mr. Tiffany. But you're not doing that great a job, are you? You're so timid with color. Why is that?" He gestured to my corner. "Why all the drawings, Jenny? Why all the black and white and gray? We're in paradise, and you keep painting like you're the one in prison and having a hard time breaking out." His lips curled in a smug expression.

I felt sure his comment referred to the night before. He couldn't know about my past. But the look in his eyes made me wonder. If Minx had found out, had she told him?

"What's the matter, Jenny? Cat got your tongue? Everyone wonders about your strange sketches and sycophantic behavior, cozying up to Mr. Tiffany and his grandson. Everyone's wondering what kind of game you are playing."

"Edward, are you teasing her?" Minx walked in. She clearly hadn't heard everything he'd said, only the tail end. She looked relaxed and rested as she came up to us and linked her arm in his. "We're going to drive to the ocean today for a little fun. Please come. Don't spend Sunday in the studio."

"Last night was enough fun to last me a while. I need to work."

Minx put her hand on my arm. "Jenny, you won't tell my mother what happened last night, will you?"

"Of course not."

She leaned forward and kissed my cheek, whispering in my ear at the same time, "Or about what Edward does for a living?"

I shook my head. "No, I won't."

She let go and stepped back. "Are you sure you won't come?"

"I'm sure."

"Okay, then. Edward, let's go."

Once they left, I was alone in the studio again, still standing in front of Edward's painting. Now I was sure I knew what was wrong with it. The canvas possessed all the sculptural magnificence of Minx's work. Her renderings. Her spontaneity. Better than his alone because of her stunning color sense. Better than hers alone because of his seriousness and raw power.

But why would Minx have done this? Even if she was crazy about him—which she obviously was—what reason would she have to cheat for him? We were all in competition here. The Tiffany Foundation prize would mean a great deal to whoever won it. Even to Minx, who, for all her wealth and connections, had a desire to excel.

I couldn't figure it out. Back at my own station, I settled down to work on my triptych but got nowhere. I still wasn't used to the color and yearned to return to my blacks, whites, and grays. Mr. Tiffany was right. I couldn't allow all the things that were happening to distract me and ruin this opportunity. Not the sublime connection I'd forged with Oliver, not the nightmare with the necklace and bracelet or any bizarre occurrences with the Ouija board or the Spirit Phone or the hymn, not Minx's behavior or Edward's canvas.

I picked up my palette and opened my box of paints. Oliver had thrown out the black gouache but not the black oil. I reached for it automatically. Squeezed out a curl. Then an equally big one of white. I could have stopped there; it would have been so much easier. And I wanted to, but instead, I took a deep breath and forged on, building my palette.

I squeezed out swirls of cadmium blue and cerulean, royal purple, verdant green, ochre, sepia . . . all the colors of the water and the woods.

Tentatively, I picked up my brush. It had been difficult when Oliver stood by my side, but now it was worse. Why was it so hard?

"Something in you broke a long time ago, didn't it?"

I spun around.

Mr. Tiffany stood in the shadows, watching me. Funny was by his side.

"I'm worried about you. If I hadn't put those

jewels on you, none of this would have happened at all." He took a step closer to inspect my work, then looked at me.

"I don't need to know what happened to you, child, but you need to put it on your canvas. Otherwise, you won't ever get past it and reach your potential. We're all broken in one way or another, but it's through the cracks in our souls that the light comes through. And the light, Jenny, that's our art. Now, paint. Paint as if your life depends on it."

He turned and left, his words echoing in the large studio.

Paint as if your life depends on it.

29

"Do you like this one?" Minx asked later that day. We were in her room, and she was trying on frocks for our Sunday-night dinner with Mr. Tiffany.

"I do."

She took off an orange silk chemise and tried on a peach-colored one and posed in the mirror. "What do you think? Is this better?"

"I think the orange," I said. "You got some color today at the beach."

She opened her dresser drawer and pulled out two different necklaces, holding up first one, then the other.

"And my amber beads or coral?"

"The coral," I said.

She left the coral on top of the dresser and proceeded to look for the earrings that matched it.

"Why did you keep that Ouija board if you never wanted to use it?"

"For sentimental reasons. Even your mother understands. It's not a game, Minx."

"I don't think it's a game. Edward and I believe it's a true direct pathway to a spiritual realm of the dead. We want to try it again. Since the experience with the Spirit Phone, we're both really curious who else is out there. What they have to say."

"Do you have a nail file?" I asked her, holding up my index finger and showing her a ragged edge. I hardly cared, but I needed to do something to distract myself from my anxiety.

She opened another drawer, fished around, and handed me an emery board.

"I never even heard you mention spiritualism before we came here. Why now?"

"You also never saw me in a sailboat or swimming before we came here," she retorted.

"And I never saw you drugged."

She put her hands on her hips and turned to me. "What are you suggesting?"

"I'm not suggesting anything. You're not yourself. You're tired all the time. You're never in your room. Edward is a bootlegger who carries a gun. I'm sure he's in contact with people who deal drugs. I'm watching it all happen, and I don't know what to do to stop it, Minx. I'm worried."

She pulled the peach dress over her head, dropped it on the floor, and changed back into the pants and blouse she'd been wearing before the fashion show.

"There's nothing to worry about," she said. "You're wrong." She shook her head sadly. "Edward said you'd be like this, but I didn't want to believe it."

"Like what?"

"He warned me that you'd be jealous of our relationship and would try to get between us. He told me that you practically propositioned him once in New York and were upset that he'd chosen me over you. That I had to watch out."

I took her by the arms. "Minx, that's crazy. Do you really think I'd ever do that?"

"Well, Edward is the most exciting man, and—"

"Is that why you set me up with the Ouija board, the hymn, Mr. Edison's phone? To get me to leave because you believed I was after Edward?"

She looked at me with a totally confounded expression.

"What does this have to do with the Ouija board or the phone? What hymn?"

I almost believed she was truly confused, but I wasn't going to let her trick me into questioning my own sanity and perceptions.

"Did Edward put you up to it to get me to leave so I couldn't figure out what was going on between you two?"

"Jenny, what are you even talking about?"

"I'm not interested in Edward. I never was. He's just telling you all those things."

"Why would he do that?"

"To get between us."

"But *why* would he do that, Jenny?"

It took me only a second. He was doing all

this for the painting competition. He needed her because of her wealth, connections, and talent and had seduced her with his air of danger and access to her drug of choice. He had obviously won her over. She was crazy about him, and there was nothing I could say to convince her of his duplicity. Should I call Mrs. Deering? Did I have any choice? Except I hadn't actually seen Minx paint Edward's canvas. I hadn't witnessed her taking any drugs. I wasn't sure. And I had to be sure before I told Minx's mother, or she'd never forgive me. I'd never forgive myself.

"I swear to you, I never propositioned Edward. He must have misinterpreted something, though I can't imagine what. I'd never been alone in a room with him before coming to Laurelton. Even if I wanted to seduce him, which I don't, I've never had the opportunity. Minx, you are my closest friend. Cross my heart, I would never try to do that to you."

She shook her head. "No, I never really imagined you would. I'm just so nuts about him, I get crazy sometimes." She hugged me, and I hugged her back. She had lost weight since she'd been here. I could feel her spine through the thin fabric of her dress, and it worried me. Wasn't weight loss another symptom of drug use?

"Now, what are *you* going to wear tonight?" she asked, more like her old self.

• • •

After dinner that night, Oliver and I took a walk, and I told him about my suspicions. He and his grandfather were leaving the next morning, and he made me promise not to do anything until he returned to Laurelton Hall on Thursday.

"Just paint, Jenny. That's what you are here to do. Stay as far away from Edward as possible and paint. All right?"

I agreed, and for the rest of the evening, we didn't talk about the robbery or Minx or Edward or the speakeasy raid. We went up to Oliver's room, where we kissed until our lips were sore and made love until the first rays of dawn's light warned me to get back to my room.

Despite what Oliver told me to do, for the next four days and three nights, I became the Laurelton ghost. I hadn't spied on anyone since those days in Hamilton when I'd skulked around the parsonage, worrying about my mother and when the Reverend might take his rage out on her again. Now I did the same with Minx, trying to follow her wherever she went, needing to know for sure if she was out to get me or was in trouble herself or if nothing at all was going on.

I watched her and Edward at meals and in the studio. I remained with all the fellows after dinner every night instead of going back to my room. When Minx bade me good night at our doors,

I stayed up listening for any sign that she was leaving her room to go meet Edward. That proved to be the most difficult part of the surveillance. She was so quiet when she slipped out that I often lost out on my chance of following her.

On Thursday afternoon, we were all in the studio. I noticed Edward stepping out. And then, about ten minutes later, Minx left, too. I put down my brush and palette, and, trying to be unobtrusive, I also left. I hesitated in the doorway to put enough distance between us so she wouldn't sense me following her.

Minx led me on a long hike through the woods to the chapel. I remembered Oliver telling me the sanctuary remained open during the week for the fellows or staff to use for meditation or prayer. But Minx wasn't religious. Her parents went to church, she'd told me once, but only because it was a social obligation. And I'd never even seen her in meditative silence. A spinning top, she moved from one activity to the next.

From behind a cedar tree, I watched Minx open the chapel door and disappear inside. I hung back for ten, maybe fifteen minutes, thinking of what to do next. All the sanctuary's windows were stained glass, so there was no way I could gaze in. But if there was a lock on the door, I could peek through the keyhole. Or even try to open the door a crack.

As quietly as I could, I approached the building, treading carefully on the uneven river rock. I sidled up to the door. There was no lock to peek through, but the door itself was slightly ajar. Minx mustn't have closed it behind her. I put my ear up against it and listened.

I heard murmuring—Minx's voice and a man's—Edward's, I was sure.

I was afraid to push the door open any wider for fear it might creak and alert them that someone was there. But I had to know what was going on, and there was no other way to find out. With my forefinger, I widened the crack. No creak. Widened it a bit more. Still no creaking. I'd created enough of a space to step inside. Quickly, I closed the door behind me, lest any daylight come through.

The interior of the chapel glowed with gold and emerald. A curious scent filled the sanctuary. Not the incense you'd expect at a place of worship. No, the atmosphere in Mr. Tiffany's chapel was tainted with the stink and smoke of another substance altogether.

I could hear Minx's and Edward's whispers, but I couldn't see them. I crept deeper into the chapel, moving carefully along the west wall, past the arches, up to the chancel.

They were supine on a blanket behind the altar, passing a lit opium pipe between them. Minx's blouse was open, her breast exposed. Magenta and orange, lemon and green, ruby and lavender and cobalt reflections bathed Minx and Edward in light.

Reaching out, Edward stroked Minx's breast languidly. She threw her head back, luxuriating in the petting.

Edward's hand stopped. His fingers lay cupping her breast. The two of them appeared to be asleep. I took a small step closer and inspected the paraphernalia at his feet. Matches, the pipe, an aluminum tin, other objects I didn't recognize. But I knew the smell, as would anyone who went to nightclubs in New York.

I backed out of the chapel, closing the door behind me. As I headed back to the house, I couldn't get the picture of Edward's hand stroking her breast out of my mind. I'd seen him move his hand like that the night of Jock's showing at Mrs. Whitney's studio.

Suddenly, I remembered why it seemed familiar.

It was the last year we lived in Hamilton. My mother and I were coming home from town. She'd stopped to chat with a neighbor, but I had gone on ahead. A young man—I was fifteen, and he must have been twenty or so—sat on our steps, stroking the parsonage's cat. I didn't really see his face, but I was riveted by his hand moving back and forth on her fur in a mesmerizing rhythm.

When he saw me, he asked after my mother. I said she was on her way and went inside, but a few minutes later, I heard shouts and looked out. My mother was on the porch. The young man was standing on the path away from the house, as if he'd started to walk away and then stopped. He yelled something and stormed off.

My mother came inside, flustered. When I asked her what had happened, she said he was the brother of one of her students at the volunteer center and that he was upset because she'd been critical of his sister's artwork.

But I couldn't dwell on a long-forgotten and meaningless memory when I had an important puzzle to figure out.

What was going on? I was confused. There were so many pieces not fitting together. Did having proof of Minx's drug use explain why she'd been tricking me to scare me into leaving Laurelton Hall? Because certainly, the messages weren't from the "other side." It was all too coincidental. She had to be manipulating reality to make it look as if my mother was sending me warnings—so that I'd leave and not discover exactly what I had discovered.

Minx was smoking opium again. And she was helping Edward cheat by painting his submission for him. If I left, she'd be able to win him the Tiffany Foundation prize and all its rewards. But what was I going to do? If Mr. Tiffany found out what was going on, he'd go straight to her mother, and the Deerings would send Minx away again. Then Minx really would hate me. Forever.

30

I slept badly and still hadn't figured out what to do by Friday morning. When I knocked on Minx's door to see if she wanted to go down to breakfast with me, she called out that she'd slept late and I should start without her.

The dining room was empty, but the sideboard was stocked. I took some eggs and bacon and sat down to eat by myself. When Graves emerged to inquire if I had everything I needed—which I said I did—I asked him if Mr. Tiffany had returned from New York yet. He informed me that he hadn't but was expected before evening.

Graves also handed me a letter from Ben. I started to open it and then stopped. His last letter had hinted that he'd figured out something about my past. If he really had dug deep enough and found a thread to follow, I didn't want to read about it in the dining room, in case Minx walked in.

She didn't. I took the letter to my room and opened it, relieved that Ben had written about the trial he was covering and an idea he had for his novel that he was excited about and nothing about my past.

I didn't see Minx at lunch. Or at all that afternoon. At five, I went up to my room, first knocking on her door, to no avail. Where was she? Back in the chapel with Edward?

I needed to talk to Oliver but didn't know if he had returned. Should I dare go to his room to look for him? What if I bumped into Mr. Tiffany in the hallway? Though he had to have noticed a bond forming between Oliver and me, it would have been improper for me to be seen sneaking into his bedroom. I couldn't risk going up on my own.

At six o'clock, when I knocked on Minx's door again, she finally answered it. She said that she'd been napping but that if I waited, she'd splash some water on her face, and we could go down to dinner together. She acted as if nothing at all had happened between us. And perhaps as far as she was concerned, it hadn't. Eventually, we walked down to the Foundation building together.

The conversation at dinner was all about our upcoming competition. There was talk of previous winners and an effort to figure out if the judges typically chose a painter or went out of their way to choose another discipline. From the way Edward was talking, he believed his painting—*his and Minx's painting*—was going to win. I thought so, too. The canvas stood out from the others. And why wouldn't it? It was the only painting that had the benefit of two masters.

Minx seemed uninterested in the topic. As if she'd never been interested. But I knew she had been. The first week we'd been there, she'd been as ambitious as any of us. Now I noticed she barely ate, just seemed to float above the conversation. Of course, she was high again. I could see it in her eyes, hear it in her voice.

"Jenny, I think you have a real shot at winning," Paul said.

Beside him, Luigi agreed.

"We've all noticed your recent incorporation of color," Tristam added. "It's like you've woken up."

Paul looked pleased for me.

This wasn't the attitude Edward had suggested they had toward me. I turned to glance at him, to see how he might be responding, but he and Minx were deep in conversation, and neither seemed aware of the rest of us.

A few of the fellows had plans to go into town that evening for a concert in the band shell and asked us if we wanted to come. Both Minx and I begged off. I hoped to find Oliver and talk to him. Edward said he was going to stay behind and work on his painting. He took a good amount of ribbing from the others, who said he was trying too hard, but I could tell he was giving them all pause.

Everyone cleared out, leaving Edward and Minx and me at the table. Rather than remaining with them in an awkward trio, I announced I was going up to the house.

Oliver and his grandfather had indeed returned from New York and were entertaining guests out on the terrace. When Oliver saw me walk through the central court, he invited me to join the party.

"I'm not dressed, and I'm tired."

"Are you all right?"

"Yes. Just working hard. Maybe too hard. I need to talk to you about something, though."

"I missed you this week." He picked up my hand and played with the bracelet he'd given me. As the tip of one finger touched my skin, I felt as if I'd imploded. Shivers ran up my arm and down my back. I was certain my cheeks flushed.

"I feel the same way," he whispered. "Once everyone retires, I'll come up and get you, and we'll take a walk and talk, and then afterward . . . afterward we won't talk. All right?"

"Yes, more than all right."

He leaned down to kiss me. I worried that the guests might see and pulled away from his embrace.

"I don't care who sees us, Jenny. I'm crazy about you. Don't you know? I'm in love with you."

I sucked in my breath. I wanted to swallow each word. To keep it inside me forever. I tried to say the words back to him, but I didn't know how. Not yet. Not with all the people around. I whispered, "I feel the same way. I do."

In my room, I opened the window and watched the half-moon shimmering on the bay and shining down on Mr. Tiffany's guests. Candles winked, and diamonds glittered. I listened to the music wafting up, heard champagne corks popping, smelled the women's perfume in the air.

I waited for Oliver, barely moving, not wanting to disturb the slow burn inside me. I'd never felt this kind of exquisite pain. Knowing what was coming, anticipating its pleasure. I wanted to stand perfectly still, like a statue, until he came and got me. Until he touched me again—even if it was just the tip of one finger pressed against the inside of my wrist.

The party ended around midnight, and shortly after, I heard a knock on my door. I opened it to find Oliver with two glasses of champagne.

We went downstairs and out onto the terrace, where the moon played with the spray in the fountain and the scent of the roses was strongest.

"Do you want to tell me what's wrong?" he asked.

"Yes, but not while we are still so close to the house. Let's walk a bit more."

We climbed down a flight of stone steps toward the next level. Heavy foliage on either side of the stairs hid the view of the lower terrace below us. We could hear only the gurgling of the water from the fountain.

"What's upsetting you?" Oliver asked.

"It's about Minx," I said, as we took the final step. "I'm worried about her."

"There is absolutely no need to be worried about Minx." A disembodied voice had come from the darkness below us.

Oliver and I both started as we took the last step and looked at the scene on the terrace.

Minx sat on the stone bench in front of the rock-crystal fountain. A bottle of champagne in a silver bucket and two crystal glasses were beside her. Edward was standing, waiting for us, a deep frown creasing his forehead, the muscles in his neck tense.

I sniffed and smelled the sickly sweet opium mixed in with the scent of boxwood hedges.

Even if I hadn't caught the odor, Minx's dreamy expression would have given her away. Had they been brazen enough to smoke the drug right under Mr. Tiffany's windows?

"You should be minding your own business, Miss Bell," Edward said, putting a forceful inflection on my last name again.

"Minx *is* most certainly my business." I started to step forward, but Oliver held tightly to my arm, holding me back. I wrested free.

"Jenny, don't," Oliver said.

Ignoring him, I walked up to Edward, who stepped away from me, closer to the fountain. The backs of his legs must have been touching the ledge.

"And she's not all right. You know she's not. She's all doped up. You have to stop giving her opium."

Edward's eyes widened in shock. "I'm not giving her anything. Where would you get such an idea?"

I moved closer to him, whispering the next part, not wanting Minx or Oliver to hear me. "I won't say anything about the painting, but you have to stop giving Minx drugs."

"You're mistaken," he said with feigned innocence.

"You can't fool me. I know Minx. I live with her."

"Well, you are wrong."

Oliver came and stood beside me. "Jenny—"

I turned to him. "I need to do this." I looked back at Edward. "I am not wrong. I saw both of you in the chapel. I watched."

"Jenny, have you been spying on me?" Minx's voice was soft and so hurt it made me want to weep.

"I care about you, Minx, and he's . . . he's taking advantage of you. Don't you see that he's using the drugs, your addiction, to get you to paint his—"

"That's enough," Edward interrupted. "What Minx and I are doing is none of your business."

"I'm her friend!" I cried. "Her only friend here. You're just using her."

Minx rose from the bench and walked toward us but slipped on the stone tiles wet from the fountain spray. Edward bent to assist her, but I moved between them.

"*I'll* help her," I said, and reached out for my friend.

"No, get away from her." Edward's words came out like a growl.

Oliver stepped in and bent over Minx. "Are you hurt?"

"My foot . . ."

"Take my arm," he said.

As soon as she put pressure on her left foot, she gave a moan. Oliver held her up, and she limped with him back to the stone bench.

"See what you did?" Edward said to me.

"You have to leave her alone," I pleaded.

"Or what?" he taunted.

I didn't care if Minx or Oliver heard me now. "Or I will go to Mr. Tiffany and tell him who painted your entry."

"Fine." He was stroking his left arm with his right hand, in almost the same hypnotic way he'd been stroking Minx's breast in the chapel when I'd spied on them. "If you do, I'll tell him what your real last name is and who your mother was and that you spent two years in a reform school for killing your own stepfather."

The words hit me like a blow.

"How do you know—" I managed.

"I've known who you were for more than a year, since you first started at the League. I almost didn't recognize you. The name change helped, and you're all grown up. But you're not so different-looking, not to someone who watched you every day at the trial. And . . ." He hesitated. "And because you look like your mother now." Edward almost whispered the last few words, as if they pained him.

"Who are you? Why would you have been at my trial? I don't understand."

"I was there," Edward said now. "I was there for all of it. I knew everything about the Reverend and everything about you." He was still stroking his left arm. "You went to the parochial school, and I went to the public school, where your mother was my art teacher. I had nothing; no one gave a damn about me except Faith. She believed I was special and was helping me. Nothing had ever mattered to me as much as those art classes. Your mother was opening up my eyes, opening up my world."

I forgot my fear for a moment, caught up in how that boy must have felt to have someone like my mother in his life.

"For three years, she taught me, showing me what I *could* do instead of what I *had* to do. And then she married the Reverend and quit teaching.

"I didn't see her again for a year or two, until she volunteered with the factory workers' kids.

My sister was one of her students. I went to pick her up one day and ran into Faith again. When she reached out to shake my hand and say hello, her sleeve pulled up, and I saw the black and blue marks on her arm. I'd been around. I knew what they were. She'd always been so kind to me when I was her student, so I had to ask if she was OK. Later, she told me no one ever asked. Everyone turned the other cheek. Your mother was so frightened. So lost. She broke my heart that day.

"After that, we were together. She worked with me on my paintings. I listened to her talk about her problems. And we fell in love. What a dream for a kid like me, to be tutored in art and lovemaking by a beautiful and artistic woman. And for her? She told me it was a tender relief from the abuse inflicted by the Reverend."

That phrase—*tender relief*—I remembered it from the anonymous letter Aunt Grace had received shortly after my mother's death.

Edward saw the recognition in my eyes.

"You wrote that letter to my aunt?" I had to know for sure.

He smirked. "Yes, that was me. You even saw your mother and me together one day. I came by the house. She was angry at me for tempting fate. Worried what would happen if the Reverend saw us. I told her just to say I was the brother of one of her students. But we quarreled. I saw you watching from the window. Always watching. Always around.

"Faith wanted me to become a successful artist. She talked about it all the time. After she died, it became my obsession to fulfill her wish, no matter what it took. First, I enlisted, and after the war ended, I drove a delivery truck for Coca-Cola, until I eventually found myself transporting more than just soda pop." He shrugged and snickered.

"But that gave me the money I needed to settle in New York and go to the Art Students League, where I met my little Minx, who I knew would finally get me where I needed to be. When you showed up at the League last year, I couldn't believe it. Here I was, about to finally turn my life around after losing the first woman—the only woman—I'd really loved, after losing the one person who believed in me. Here I was, about to finally find the success I deserved, even if it was with some spoiled little society girl hopped up on drugs, and in walks Jenny Fairburn—oh, excuse me, Jenny *Bell*—with that same fire in her eyes that Faith had. Sad just like Faith, too."

As he continued speaking, a look of sadness filled Edward's eyes, too.

"I couldn't risk you finding out who I was. I needed you out of my life so that I could move on. But there you were, becoming Minx's best friend, moving in with Minx, being in our classes, then being accepted here into the Foundation, of all things."

I looked over and saw Minx. She was staring at Edward, a tragic expression transforming her face. Despite the drugs, she understood at least some of what she was hearing.

"You were intruding on my life." Edward continued talking, not to me but at me. "Complicating it in ways you could never know. But that wasn't my problem. My problem was just getting you out of it."

At some point in Edward's tale, Oliver had come up beside me and put his arm around me. "Are you all right?" he asked.

"I don't know."

I was so confused. Edward Wren was my mother's lover? He was the man she'd planned to abandon me for? My mother was a passionate woman, an inspiring presence. She had always wanted to be loved. But in the arms of this man? Why? What did she see in him?

I would never know. For both me and Edward, the proof of our tragic stories was lost forever, in the grave where my mother was buried.

"I thought I was all done with you," Edward was repeating. "And then you showed up here. And in no time, you were Mr. Tiffany's favorite, vying for *my* prize. And don't think you can go to Mr. Tiffany to tell him about my painting. I'll be right behind you telling him my side of the story. How do you think that will go over? Who do you think he'll believe? Me or the convicted murderess?"

"It wasn't Minx at all," I said, the realizations truly dawning on me. "*You* manipulated the planchette on the Ouija board. *You* knew my mother's name was Faith and the year she died. *You* knew the Reverend's favorite hymn. *You* made all that up on Edison's phone. You wanted to scare me away from here so I wouldn't catch on."

"Of course, it was me, hoping to get rid of you. But you just wouldn't stay out of things."

Minx stood, wincing. "You did all those things? To Jenny? And the Tiffany Blues? Did you take them too?"

He didn't answer her.

"Did you?" Limping, she took one step and then another toward Edward, but before she reached him, she tripped and fell.

Oliver stepped away from me to help her up and then hold her back, but she shook her head and waved him off. Heading for Edward, her fists clenched at her sides, either in pain or in fury. And then, just as she was about to reach him, she slid and fell yet again, this time crying out.

I watched Edward reach out toward her.

"Stay away from her," I said, and stepped in front of him to assist Minx myself.

Edward tried to push in front of me. I jerked

away. Edward slipped. Fighting to keep his balance, he reached out and grabbed the only support available—my arm.

I twisted out of his grip, causing Edward to finally lose his footing and fall backward.

The sound of his head hitting the rock-crystal fountain somehow seemed louder to me than the water splashing, louder than Minx's cry as she got up onto her knees at the edge of the pool. Oliver rushed forward and climbed up onto the ledge and into the pool where Edward lay. Putting a hand under each of his shoulders, he lifted Edward up. Water splashed everywhere as he dragged Edward's unmoving form over the fountain's rim and laid him on the stones. Leaning over him, Oliver put his ear to Edward's chest.

Blood pooled under Edward's head. The stain grew. Dark red-black in the moonlight. A beautiful color, I thought irrationally. The same shade as the roses on the trellis that scented my room every night.

Minx still kneeled by the fountain, sobbing. I went to her and crouched beside her, putting my arm around her, holding her and stroking her hair. Over her shoulder, I watched as Oliver stood and backed away from Edward's body.

No, it wasn't possible that it was happening all over again. What was it Mr. Tiffany had said about patterns repeating? That it was part of nature? But it wasn't the same this time, not really. It was worse. This time, my mother wasn't the one whose actions caused the accident. This time, the blame really was mine. What was going to happen to me now?

31

For what seemed like a long time, none of us did anything. We just sat in the dark on the terrace, Edward's body stretched out on the stones. As Minx's opium-induced high wore off, she leaned against me, still sobbing.

Rubbing her back, I whispered calming words, but they had little effect.

"I thought he cared about me," she finally said. "Why was I such a fool?"

"You weren't. He was so diabolical, Minx, he fooled everyone."

She glanced over at him. "He looks like he's just sleeping, doesn't he?"

"He does." I held her tighter.

"We should go back to the house. We have to call the police," Oliver said.

"No." Minx shook her head. "We can't. We can't tell anyone about this."

"I don't expect either of you to lie to protect me," I said.

She stared at me, confused. "Protect you? Why? What did you do?"

That's right, I realized. Minx didn't know about the accident with the Reverend except for the oblique comments Edward had made in his rambling speech. But then, if she didn't know . . .

"Minx, why don't you want Oliver to call the police?" I asked.

"If we tell them, it will come out about the drugs, and I can't let that happen. My parents will send me to that horrible sanitarium again."

Then I understood. "But what else can we do?"

"Maybe . . . maybe we can just bury him here," she said.

"We can't do that," Oliver said. "His family will miss him and then worry about him. The police will be called in regardless, and then we'd be in even more trouble."

"His parents are dead and so is his only sibling. We *can* just bury him," Minx retorted.

I stared at her, surprised that she was capable of being so pragmatic in the face of this tragedy. I'd either overestimated her feelings for Edward or underestimated her survival instincts.

"There must be someone who'd notice he was missing," Oliver insisted.

"He had no one else. No real friends," Minx said. "He's a bootlegger; anyone who knew him will assume he got into trouble at work and—" She pulled back and looked at me. "Jenny, what was Edward talking about? What was he threatening you with? What was he going to tell Mr. Tiffany?"

I gave Minx a brief version of what had happened eight years before. It was time for the truth. I was tired of the lies. I knew we loved each other like sisters and that I could trust her. She'd no more betray me than I would betray her.

"But how could your mother let you take the blame?" she asked when I was finished.

"If she'd gone to prison and had the baby there, they would have taken him away from her. I was sixteen. She knew the worst that would happen to me was two years of reform school."

"But couldn't she just explain that it was self-defense?"

"Minx, he was a minister. My mother couldn't take the chance that the jury would ever believe the Reverend was an ogre. He was a man of God. Beloved by his flock. A husband trying to subdue his artistic, passionate wife, exercising his legal right." I sighed. "My mother was just a woman, after all. Who would have believed her?"

"And so you took her place and were convicted?"

It was still so difficult to talk about. Would it always be? "And then my mother died during childbirth. My mother and my baby brother. And my mother was the only one besides me who knew the truth. Everyone else only heard my lie. I was the one who confessed to fighting with him. I was the one who confessed to pushing him. Me. I confessed to it all. And now"—I turned to include Oliver in my glance—"if you call the police in and they question us . . . I've already been convicted of manslaughter once."

"But Minx and I will swear to what we saw," Oliver insisted.

"After they find out who I am—and they will—they won't believe you. My gentleman friend and my best friend? You're hardly two impartial witnesses without ulterior motives."

"And then it will come out about the drugs," Minx said, her voice frantic. "Oliver, we have to hide his body."

"Yes, we have to." I sounded as hysterical as Minx.

"It's wrong. We can't," Oliver said.

"We don't owe Edward anything," I pleaded. "He was despicable to get Minx hooked on opium again and use it as bait so she'd paint his entry for him. He was cruel to try to trick me into thinking my mother was reaching out to me from the beyond and warning me to leave Laurelton. And when that didn't work, he risked my life, giving Minx sleeping powder instead of aspirin for me so he could come back to my room later and steal the Tiffany Blues and set me up to take the fall. So that I'd be thrown out of the Foundation."

A minute passed. Then another. Oliver rose and wearily walked away from us, to the edge of the terrace. Standing alone, he looked up at the sky, bright with stars.

Only the sounds of cicadas and a single owl's hoot broke the silence. Finally, after several minutes, Oliver turned back. "It's wrong. The only thing to do is contact the authorities. We all know you didn't push him, Jenny. He fell. It was an accident. I'll make sure the police believe you."

I shook my head. "You can't make that promise. You can't be sure."

"Oliver, have you considered your grandfather?" Minx asked, her question so cunning I almost felt bad for Oliver, who, I knew, wouldn't be able to argue this point. "He's seventy-six years old," she continued. "Laurelton is his sanctuary. Now it will be the center of crime and scandal. What will this do to him?"

"Minx is right," I said. "Could he bear the stress? Can you risk that?"

It wasn't fair of us to use Mr. Tiffany to sway Oliver, but neither of us was thinking about fairness. We were two scared young women focused on our futures and our pasts.

After Oliver agreed, our nightmare intensified. The next hour was the most gruesome I'd ever experienced. Neither Minx nor I could bear to touch the body, but Oliver couldn't move it off the terrace himself. Twice we tried. First, Minx couldn't go through with it. And then I couldn't. Finally, on the third effort, the two of us managed to overcome our dread and assist Oliver. We tried hard not to let any part of the body touch the ground, but we'd only taken a few steps when Edward's right arm dropped down and his fingers trailed in the dirt.

We laid the body down. Oliver rearranged Edward's limbs, and with renewed intention, we lifted him up and trudged down the path toward the unfinished gazebo.

The new floor installation was complete, but Oliver knew about construction from the war. He showed us how to pry up the wooden slats, and we went to work. Once that was done, we dug in the dirt.

After two hours, it was time to lower the body into its grave. Oliver didn't even ask us to help. Minx and I held on to each other and watched him gently roll Edward into the shallow resting place. Edward's body landed facedown in the dirt, and we left him that way.

Oliver and I covered the body with soil while Minx looked away.

By the time the night sky gave way to mauve, we were done putting the floor back in place. Our clothes were filthy, the flesh on our fingers ripped, our nails torn, but Edward was no more. Or was he? I wondered if what my aunt believed was really true. That those who go over to the side of death are never truly gone.

We walked back toward the mansion, Oliver leading the way. Minx was limping, and I was rubbing my wrist, still throbbing from Edward's grasp. We were halfway there when I realized my bracelet was missing.

We raced back to the terrace and, while the sun began its climb, searched every inch of the stone patio and inside the fountain, but my bracelet was gone.

"I'll make you another," Oliver promised.

"But what if it was in his hand? What if we buried him with it?"

We retraced our steps from the terrace down to the gazebo and up again, hoping it had fallen off. But finally, Oliver called off the search. We needed to return to our rooms and clean ourselves up before anyone awoke and saw us. Oliver said he'd drain the bloody water from the fountain and refill it. Then he'd go to Edward's room, pack up his suitcase, and get his things off the premises so it would look like he'd picked up and left.

I bathed and dressed and then sat by my window, not knowing what to do next. Again, more resilient than I had expected, Minx took over. I assumed because of how she'd felt about Edward that of the two of us she'd be the more distraught. But no. She went downstairs, got us breakfast, brought it up on a tray, and forced me to eat toast with marmalade and drink tea she laced with sugar.

Afterward, I tried to apologize. "I'm so sorry. I know you loved him and—"

She shook her head, then spoke, haltingly at first but with more assuredness as she went on. "He was wild and different and dangerous, and that excited me. But it scared me, too, sometimes . . ." Her eyes filled. "I'm not sure I loved him." She whispered the last few words so softly I almost couldn't hear her. "Certainly not the way you love Oliver. And he loves you. After what he did for you tonight, there's no doubt about that."

Oliver came for us at around ten o'clock and took us for a sailboat ride. He made it sound like a fun excursion to anyone who might have seen or heard us on our way there or back, but the whole point was to get us away from the mansion and the studio to prepare what we'd say if anyone asked us if we'd seen Edward.

By noon, Minx was unwell. She'd been through withdrawal before, she told us, and didn't think it would be as bad this time, because she'd only been smoking once or twice a day and only for a little more than a month.

Oliver turned the boat around but not before I held her while she got sick over the side. Back in her room, the sweats, stomach cramps, and nausea were worse. I brought her cold towels and water and held her head when she was sick again.

At around six, Oliver came upstairs to check on how she was. She was still in bad shape, so he went to the kitchen and made plates for us all. He and I picked at our food. Minx was too ill to eat at all.

I slept in her room that night, and by morning, she seemed much better. We bathed and dressed in preparation to go to breakfast together.

"How are we going to go downstairs and act like we're all right? I'm so nervous," I said, a ridiculous understatement considering that I might be accused of manslaughter if Edward's death was discovered.

"It was an accident, Jenny," Minx said, as she sprayed perfume on. "We have to pretend everything is normal. You have me, and I have you." She applied lipstick with a shaking hand and then handed me the tube. "You look even worse than I do; put some on."

Before we left her room, there was a knock on the door. She opened it to find Graves. Mr. Tiffany was requesting our presence downstairs.

Our host was in the smoking room, sitting on the divan under the large painting of the opium dreamer. The painting lent a surreal note to the meeting. I couldn't help but glance up at it, the decadent subject matter more disturbing that day than it had ever been before.

Mr. Tiffany offered us seats, thanked Graves, and waited until the butler had shut the door behind him. When he finally spoke, his voice was cool and unemotional, and he didn't meet my glance.

"Given the tragedy of what occurred here two nights ago, I think it best for us all and the reputation of the Foundation for the two of you to leave this morning," he said. "All the arrangements have been made. You'll both be sailing to France tomorrow on the *Queen Mary*. When you arrive in Paris, you"—he focused on Minx—"will be seeing a doctor who specializes in addictions. If necessary, you'll go to his clinic for as long as it takes. If not, you'll be joining Miss Li—" He stopped himself from calling me by his nickname for me, cleared his throat, and continued. "You'll be joining Miss Bell at the Académie Julian." Still looking at Minx, he said, "Since your cousin is using her apartment, your mother and I have arranged for another flat for you both." He turned his head slightly toward me but looked just above me. "And a stipend for you, Miss Bell. If you'd remained for the rest of this session, I feel sure you would have won the Foundation's prize. This is that payment."

He returned his gaze to Minx. "Your mother is here. In the central court. I've had tea set up. You can talk there. I only shared that we had trouble with one of our fellows here and that he lured you back into your habit. When I suggested the idea of Paris for you both, she agreed with the plan. I haven't mentioned Mr. Wren's name or that he's disappeared." Mr. Tiffany cleared his throat. "I think, Miss Deering, you'll find that she's very thankful for my interference and very sympathetic to your plight. You are extremely talented. The real crime would be for you to waste your ability. Use Paris, study hard. I expect to see great things from you."

Having been dismissed, Minx stood and, favoring her right leg, took a few steps, then looked back at me. Mr. Tiffany waved her off. "You need to see your mother alone first. Miss Bell will be there shortly."

Once the door closed behind Minx, Mr. Tiffany reached over to the occasional table on his right and picked up a wooden cylinder. He held it in his hands and twisted its top around and around as he spoke.

"My grandson has been engaged to a lovely young woman for the last six months," he said, still looking down at the wooden object.

I didn't hear whatever he said right after that. How could Oliver be engaged? I didn't understand.

Mr. Tiffany was still talking. ". . . and the wedding is set for this winter, after which he will take over as the head of Tiffany and Company. As much as I have admired you, Miss Light, as much as I have come to care about you . . ." His voice sounded gruff. "All that matters is that my grandson has done a very brave and stupid thing to protect you. And now I have to protect him. I've known for quite some time about your history—"

"My history?"

Finally, he looked into my eyes. "Yes, in Hamilton, Ontario. And at Andrew Mercer."

I was practically speechless. "But how?"

"The first time we spoke, you told me about the stained-glass window that inspired you. I remembered exactly which window you described and where it was. What I didn't understand was why you'd lie about it. I know a private investigator who has done work for me before. Once I told him where it was and the little bit you'd told me about your family, it wasn't difficult for him to get the full story."

"But you never said anything."

"What was there to say?" Mr. Tiffany looked back down at the cylinder in his hands. "You've had a hard time of it. A cruel twist of fate threw you off course. But while you were here, I watched you continue to right your sails. You began to evolve into the painter I know you will be. I wish I could continue to mentor you, but for Oliver's sake, you have to go. I can't allow you to disrupt his future any more than it's already been disrupted. He had his heart broken once after the war, and once was enough. If anyone were to find out about what happened on Friday night . . ."

"Do you know—"

He knew what I was asking. "I saw enough from my window to ask Oliver what had happened. And too much for him to lie. If anyone were to put the pieces together, his reputation would be seriously compromised. I trust you are innocent, but how would it look? With your history, what would happen to you? What would happen to my grandson, who would be viewed as an accomplice?"

I wanted to put my hands up to my ears and stop listening. I didn't want to leave Laurelton. Leave Mr. Tiffany. Oh, God, I didn't want to leave Oliver, not after I'd found him.

"If you care about him as much as I believe you do, you'll agree with me. After all, you and I both want the same thing for him, Jenny. We want the best for him, don't we?"

"No," I said, in a voice twisted with sadness and anger and disappointment. "You think he should be a businessman. That's not what's best for him. He's such a talented designer . . ." I put my hand around my wrist, where the bracelet had lain. "He shouldn't be running numbers and watching over production. It will stifle his soul."

Mr. Tiffany stared at me, aghast. I wasn't sure if it was that no one ever talked back to him or if he was simply stunned by my accusation.

"I will make a deal with you," I said. "I'll go along with your plan. I'll step out of your grandson's life on the condition that you encourage him to be what he was born to be, *your* grandson, taking over *your* job as the creative director, designing jewelry. Because he has *your* talent, Mr. Tiffany. Let him be the artist he is meant to be. That's all he wants. He's going along with your plans because he wants to please you, but it's wrong for him. You're going to wring all the joy out of him if you put him behind a desk instead of a drawing board."

For a moment, the only sound in the room was the infernal splashing of the fountain coming through the open window. Mr. Tiffany got up, walked over to it, stood with his back to me, and looked out. We remained quiet for a full minute.

When he faced me again, he still held the wooden cylinder, and as he spoke, he continued rotating the top.

"I'd been designing windows for quite a while when my young wife died. I was broken. As despondent a man as you can imagine. Soon after, I received a grand commission, one that had the potential of catapulting my reputation to its next level. I didn't think I could create anything beautiful anymore. I considered turning it down. Even closing the glass studio and abandoning my quest for beauty. But without it, what was there? I forced myself to work on the window and soon discovered I could channel my grieving and despair into my art. I spent months on the design and then oversaw the glass manufacturing and every aspect of the assemblage. The finished window was as spectacular as any I'd ever made. Finally, it was ready to ship to the client. I insisted on helping my workmen pack it, because it had become something of a talisman to me. The window had showed me I could survive the worst grief I'd ever known, not only survive but create despite it.

"We were almost done packing when there was an accident. There might have been a fault in the frame or in the leading. I never learned what happened, but as a result, the window crashed. The glass shattered at my feet.

"I threw everyone out of the room and sat there, alone with my broken window. It was as if my wife had died all over again. I couldn't bear that all my hard work was ruined. I just sat and stared at the glass for hours. I was still sitting there when the cleaning woman arrived at the end of the day, as she always did.

"Using her broom, she swept up the glass, pieces tinkling as they joined one another. When she was done, she looked down at the pile, put her hands on her hips, and said, 'Well, look at that. I can make a pretty glass painting, too.'

"I rose and walked over to where she stood. The way the setting sun illuminated the workroom and reflected off the mirror in the corner, the glass seemed lit from below. And was, in fact, terribly beautiful.

"I filled a dustpan with that broken glass, and I made this with it." Mr. Tiffany handed me the wooden cylinder. "Hold it up to the light."

I did, and inside the kaleidoscope I beheld a beautiful design incorporating all of Laurelton's colors. The peacock blues and greens and purples and lavenders. I twisted it and watched the pattern break apart and shift into another equally magical but different one.

"I made it so I would never forget there is beauty even in broken things. That through the cracks, light still shines."

I revolved the kaleidoscope once more and watched the glass rearrange itself and blur as my tears fell and made the colors even more brilliant.

"I know that what happened to you broke you. I know this will make those cracks open again. But I want you to have this. Take it with you, and when you feel like you are losing hope, hold it up to the light, and remember me telling you that there is beauty, Miss Light, even in broken things."

Epilogue

March 13, 1957
Laurelton Hall, Laurel Hollow
Oyster Bay, New York

My charm bracelet caught on a branch of a burned bush, and I stopped to untangle it, so I was looking down when he reached me. I saw his feet planted on the charred ground. I saw his hands reach up to help me. I heard his voice say my name so softly that it might have been my imagination, but it wasn't.

"Jenny," he whispered.

And then he cupped my face in his hands and looked at me.

Thirty-three years showed on his face, as I knew it did on mine. I was fifty-seven years old, with lines in my forehead and softer muscles and a thicker waist. He was sixty, with silver hair that still fell in waves over a now-furrowed forehead. But when I looked into Oliver's eyes, I saw they were still the same aquamarine blue.

He touched the bracelet. "You wear it?"

"I've worn it every day since it first arrived in the mail."

I'd looked at the package that arrived on my twenty-eighth birthday and started to cry

442

just seeing the sender's name. I cried harder recognizing the narrow leather jewelry box. And then I cried still harder as I took out the bracelet and put it on, remembering the night Oliver had put the first bracelet on me four years before. And then, with gratitude, I shed the last tears, realizing that Mr. Tiffany had acquiesced and that Oliver had become the designer he was meant to be.

Ben had noticed the bracelet, of course, and asked me about it. At our wedding, once we'd said our vows out loud to the judge, I'd made a vow to myself that I'd never lie to my husband. And in the first five years we were married, I'd upheld that vow. Until one day, I told Ben I'd bought the bracelet for myself. One last lie after a lifetime of lies. But Oliver was something separate and apart from my marriage to Ben. Something precious that I couldn't give up even if I could only keep him in memory and dreams.

Oliver touched one of the charms.

"I never took the bracelet off except when I gave it to a jeweler to add the new charms you sent," I said.

He tapped each one and set them all swaying, glinting in the sunshine.

Oliver had sent five charms over the next twenty-nine years. Never with a letter. The ornaments said all they had to, every one a clear memory of our time together. A musical G clef, a crescent moon, an artist's palette with each dab of color a different gemstone, a sailboat, and a bouquet of amethyst citrine and ruby flowers like the ones that grew all over the estate.

"All the flowers," I said now, gesturing to the blackened woods, the burned-out site. "All the trees. Beautiful Laurelton." I sighed. "All gone."

"It hadn't been beautiful for a long time." He sounded so sad. "There was very little left anymore. Just a shell waiting to be torn down."

"Do they know what happened?"

He shook his head. "No, they don't. Someone said they saw some boys, teenagers, running away from the entrance the night the fire started."

"So it was an accident? Were they smoking?"

"The boys had nothing to do with it."

"How do you know?"

"Let's walk. The path to the Sound is clear enough. I've been living down there in the beach house since the night of the fire."

"Is that how you knew I was here?"

He pointed to the ridge. "I saw you standing there and recognized you right off. I wondered if you'd heard. I didn't think you'd come."

"I had to. I wanted to."

Oliver took my arm—his touch stirring me despite myself—and led me down the steps of one ruined terrace and on to the next. I expected to see the rock-crystal fountain, but it was gone.

Where it had stood was just an empty, ruined pool covered in ash. I shivered.

We reached the next landing. A few yards ahead of us, a peacock stood in the sun, and as I watched in disbelief, he opened his fan and displayed all the wonder of his magical feathers. Every beautiful shade of blue, from cobalt to turquoise, and of green, from emerald to pine, and luscious lavender and violets—all the shining colors and tones and hues that Mr. Tiffany had spent a lifetime capturing in mosaics and glass and jewelry. All the resplendent magnificence that had inspired one man to create a mansion and an empire and to present a vision to the world that had remained unequaled.

Neither Oliver nor I spoke as the bird preened, strutting, showing off his plumage. I held my breath and waited, while memories of the time I'd spent at Laurelton, surrounded by beauty almost as grand, opened like a fan in my mind.

After a few moments, the bird closed his tail. We remained where we were as he walked off and into the woods. And then he was gone. Like the summer. Like the house and the gardens and the gazebo and the chapel and everything at Laurelton. Like Mr. Tiffany, who had died twenty-four years before.

I suddenly had a very real feeling, a sense of knowingness that settled over me that finally, after all this time, the dead were at peace. My father, my mother, Aunt Grace, even Edward and the Reverend—that the ghosts of the past were finally behind me.

Oliver left my side and loped over to where the bird had been. Bending, he picked something up and returned to me, holding out the single feather the bird had left behind.

"A last gift from Laurelton Hall," he said.

I looked down at the feather's eye, remembering the jewelry with which Mr. Tiffany had adorned me the night of the party, when Edward had pretended to make contact with my mother on the Spirit Phone. As magnificent as that suite of jewels had been, it hadn't truly captured this glory, I thought.

"All the time I was here, I always wanted to see a peacock fan. Your grandfather said when I finally did, it would make me believe in beauty."

"And has it?"

I wanted to tell Oliver that *he'd* made me believe in beauty, but it hardly seemed appropriate after all this time. But it was true. Oliver had given me color and caring and passion with his beautiful thoughts and jewels and sensitivity. He and this amazing place had made me see that not all beauty was a lie, that there was, as Keats had said, truth in beauty, too.

We reached the beach, where the scent of the fire was much less noticeable, and sat at the same table we'd sat at the very first morning we met.

"I'm sorry about your husband," Oliver said.

"Thank you. He was a good man and a wonderful writer."

"I read his work. He deserved the accolades."

Ben had followed Minx and me to Paris after that fateful summer of 1924 and went to work for one of his family's papers, the *International Herald Tribune*. He'd been a godsend and helped me heal. Eventually, he finished his first novel, the first of six, one of which won a Pulitzer Prize and catapulted him to fame among the literary set. We never had children, but we had our careers. And if I never loved Ben the same way I'd loved Oliver, we had a strong marriage. We were each other's best friend until he died in 1955 of a cerebral hemorrhage.

Minx had also remained in Paris and became as well known for her bronze sculptures as for marrying and divorcing five times. She managed to avoid opium for good, and during the Second World War, she became very involved with the Resistance and created a network to smuggle information out through artwork. Ben and I both worked with her during those dangerous times.

"I've followed your career," Oliver said. "I was so pleased to see you become a successful artist, ironically quite famous for your use of color." He grinned, and for a moment, I saw a younger Oliver, out on his boat, forcing a palette of colors into my hand.

It had taken me some time to get over what happened at Laurelton. I was haunted for years by Edward's confession, his death, and Oliver's betrayal. I'd held a grudge, angry that he'd never told me about his engagement, and then, when the bracelet arrived, I remembered Aunt Grace once telling me to paint the anger out of me. And I had done that. I had painted every emotion out of me, and it had worked.

"I came to one of your openings. In Paris, in forty-eight," Oliver said.

I was astonished. "I didn't see you."

"You had a whole circle of admirers around you. Ben was there, and Minx, and I thought it would be best just to slip away. I did buy a painting, though."

"You did?"

He nodded. "A beautiful gardenscape. I've had it hanging in my office all this time."

I was stunned and fell silent. I needed to change the subject for fear I was going to become too emotional. "And you . . . you became a world-famous designer," I said. "I used to go into the Tiffany store in Paris sometimes to look at your work and felt so proud. I was going to write to tell you, and to thank you for the charms, but I just never felt right about it."

"My career has gone well. Very well. But I can't say the same for my marriage. I'm on my own now, too," Oliver said. "Divorced five years ago."

"Now it's my turn to say I'm sorry."

He shook his head. "No need. We have three wonderful children, but we were never well suited to each other. My children's mother is happily remarried."

"And you?" I asked him.

"I never did meet anyone else," Oliver said pointedly.

After so long, I didn't know what to say. I didn't want us to keep chatting about our respective lives. This meeting, after so long, was too momentous for small talk. I wanted to tell him how much his charms had meant to me. How, throughout all these years, I had never forgotten the passion we'd shared. But I was suddenly shy, suddenly that twenty-four-year-old girl again, unsure how to begin a conversation.

"Did you ever find the Tiffany Blues?" I asked. Back to a much safer topic. "Minx and I always wondered."

"I did. They were in Edward's room. Hidden in his pillow, of all places. Grandfather placed them in the vault. They're still there. I take them out every so often and think about resetting them, but I never have had the heart. I might now, though."

His words stirred so many feelings in me that I wasn't sure how to respond. So I asked him what I hoped was a safer question. "You were going to tell me about the fire?"

"Yes, the fire. The couple who bought the

estate was originally going to leave everything pretty much intact and restore what was here. But they waited so long the house fell into an impossible state of disrepair. Last month, I discovered through an architect friend that not only were they going to tear everything down, but they were going to subdivide the land and build two other houses on the property. I was always sorry I hadn't stopped the estate from selling Grandfather's house in the first place, but my ex-wife wanted to be in Newport, and I . . ." He shrugged. "That doesn't matter now. What does matter is that I couldn't stop thinking about what the owners might find if they razed the land. Would they discover him? And what if your bracelet was with him? I couldn't take any chances. If there was any evidence, it was time to destroy it once and for all. I had my agent offer the couple several times what they'd invested, and now the land and the house—what's left of it—belong to me."

"Oliver, are you saying you bought it back so you could burn it down?"

He simply lowered his head, as if it would be too much to speak the answer out loud.

I stood, turned, and looked up, to where the house had stood, where now there was nothing but the burned-out skeletons of times past, of memories, of who we had been and what we had dreamed of together.

I was still looking up at the ghost of the house, thinking about our summer together so long ago, when Oliver came to me and wrapped his arms around me and held me.

"I didn't follow you to Paris, and I should have. I stayed away and let you go. I broke us. I didn't mean to, Jenny, but I did."

He spun me around so I was looking at him now. At the same beautiful man I'd met on this beach so long ago, who'd kept me in his heart for so many years, whose heart I had worn on my sleeve since the first time he'd spoken to me.

Behind him, the blue water sparkled with the pinks and purples of the setting sun, and the clouds glowed with a peach and rose hue—as if Mr. Tiffany had designed the scene himself.

"I believed at first that your grandfather broke us." And for a minute, I hated Mr. Tiffany all over again. Hated how manipulative he'd been. Hated what he'd stolen from me and from Oliver. And then I looked down at the feather I'd put on the table and back at Oliver, into his eyes. "But I came to understand that he didn't. Your grandfather was making the only decision he could. He was right on all counts. Plus, he gave me and Minx an opportunity to begin again, to fulfill our dream of Paris and careers. No, it wasn't Mr. Tiffany who broke you and me. And it wasn't you. It was my own fear of my past. It was my unwillingness to trust and to believe in love. I had found it in you, just as I know my mother had it with my father, and maybe even in some way with Edward. She'd suffered so much. I knew it then, but I *understand* it now that years have passed. I have no lingering doubts any longer that my mother loved me or about the anguish she must have felt throughout the ordeal with the Reverend, the trial, and its aftermath. She was just a woman, after all. Full of flaws. But also passionate, vulnerable, and full of love."

I stared out across the Sound at the opposite shore. Remembering my very first day at Laurelton. Remembering meeting Mr. Tiffany.

"Your grandfather taught me something the day he sent me away that started the healing process within me, and it has stayed with me always."

"What is that?"

"That there is beauty even in broken things."

Oliver bowed his head as if he'd just heard a benediction. He leaned forward to kiss me, but just before he touched my lips with his, he said, "And he was right, Jenny, wasn't he? He knew the truth. The beauty . . . the light . . . it always finds its way through the cracks."

As it turned out, more than dreams survived the scorching of Laurelton Hall. Something precious endured. And in the ashes, under the slivers of colored glass, amid the burned-out, blackened woods, it came to pass that I found my heart again.

Acknowledgments

Writers are solitary creatures, but even if we write alone so many people go into making our manuscripts into something a reader can hold in her hands.

First, to my editor, Rakesh Satyal, whose idea it was that I move a bit out of my comfort zone. I am grateful to him for that and his careful editing—this book shines so much more for all his effort.

To my wonderful publisher whom I am so lucky to also call a friend, Judith Curr, who I appreciate more than words.

To Lisa Sciambra, Ann Pryor, Suzanne Donahue, Loan Le, Milena Brown, and everyone who works behind the scenes at Atria Books—your hard work and creative thinking is greatly appreciated.

To Alan Dingman, for covers that get better with each book and are all I could ever ask for and more.

To Dan Conaway, my amazing agent and knight in shining armor! Also to Taylor Templeton, for her hard work and kindness, and everyone at Writers House whose help is invaluable.

Special appreciation to the Thomas Watson

453

Library at the Metropolitan Museum of Art and the New York Society Library.

I also want to thank Lauren Willig, fellow novelist and dear friend, who was so generous in helping me get this idea off the ground. Also friends, sounding board, and general A+ think tank: Liz and Steve Berry, Doug Clegg, Alyson Richman, Randy Susan Meyers, Sarah Branham, and C.W. Gortner.

And to Natalie White, who keeps me sane by running AuthorBuzz so very, very well!

To every single bookseller and librarian, without whom the world would be a sadder place.

I very much want to thank my readers who make all the work worthwhile. Please visit MJRose.com for a signed bookplate and sign up for my newsletter at MJEmail.me.

And lastly and as always, I'm very grateful to my family and most of all, Doug.

About the Author

New York Times bestselling author M. J. Rose grew up in New York City exploring the labyrinthine galleries of the Metropolitan Museum and the dark tunnels and lush gardens of Central Park. She is the author of more than a dozen novels, a founding board member of International Thriller Writers, and the founder of the first marketing company for authors, AuthorBuzz.com. She lives in Connecticut. Visit her online at MJRose.com.

Center Point Large Print
600 Brooks Road / PO Box 1
Thorndike, ME 04986-0001 USA

(207) 568-3717

US & Canada:
1 800 929-9108
www.centerpointlargeprint.com